A Place
Far Away

a novel

⌇⌇⌇⌇

Vahan Zanoyan

⌇⌇⌇⌇

This book is a work of fiction. All names, persons, organizations, places and events are the product of the author's imagination. Any resemblance to actual persons, events and places is entirely coincidental.

ISBN: 1481033573
ISBN 13: 9781481033572

Library of Congress Control Number: 2012922364
CreateSpace Independent Publishing Platform
North Charleston, South Carolina

Cast of Characters (In Alphabetic Order)

Abkar	One of Ayvazian's bodyguards
Abo	Same as Apo, but Eastern Armenian pronunciation
Agassi	Caretaker of Edward Laurian's estate
Ahmed Al Barmaka	Billionaire VIP from Dubai who buys Lara's contract
Ali (the enforcer)	Disciplinarian of insubordinate prostitutes in Dubai
Alisia Galian	One of Lara's sisters
Anastasia	Ukrainian prostitute in Moscow who mentors Lara
Ano	Pimp working for the Ayvazians in Dubai
Apo Arslan	Trafficker based in Istanbul (Western Armenian spelling and pronunciation)
Aram Galian	Lara's youngest brother
Arpi Galian	One of Lara's sisters
Artiom	Head of post office in Aparan
Avo (Avetis) Galian	Lara's younger brother and closest sibling to her
Dr. Hakobian	Medical doctor in Ashtarak
Edgard	One of Ayvazian's bodyguards
Edward Laurian	Swiss/Armenian investigative reporter
Farah	One of Al Barmaka's concubines
Ferda	Turkish name of Farah
Gagik Grigorian	Old revolutionary and friend of Laurian
Gago, Khev Gago	Nicknames of Gagik Grigorian
Hakob	Restaurant owner in Yerevan
Hamo	One of Ayvazian's bodyguards
Hayk	Agassi's fifteen year old grandson
Lara Galian	Youngest daughter of the Galians who gets abducted
Leila	Arabic name given to Lara while in Al Barmaka's palace
Manoj	Al Barmaka's business manager

Martha Galian	Lara's oldest sister
Melikov	Medical doctor in Moscow caring for Ayvazian's prostitutes
Nadia	Arabic name given to Natalia, Russian concubine of Al Barmaka
Natalia (Nadia)	One of Al Barmaka's concubines
Nerses	Roadside restaurant owner in Vayots Dzor
Ruben	Martha's husband
Sago	Hayk's cousin
Sago Galian	One of Lara's brothers
Samvel Galian	Lara's father
Saro	Mayor of Vardahovit village
Serge	One of Ayvazian's bodyguards
Sergei Ayvazian	Oligarch and human trafficker
Sevak	Minister of Agriculture of Armenia
Silva Galian	Lara's mother
Sirarpi	Laurian's sister who was abducted and killed by human traffickers
Sona Galian	One of Lara's sisters
Sumaya	Manager of Al Barmaka's concubines in Dubai
Susannah	Prostitute in Dubai
Timur	Apo's business associate and assistant in Istanbul
Vartiter	Agassi's wife
Varujan	Agassi's son (Hayk's father)
Viktor Ayvazian	Sergei Ayvazian's nephew and business associate

Glossary of Foreign Words

(Armenian)

Aghpar	Colloquial: brother. A reference to those Armenians from the Diaspora who returned to Armenia in the 1940s
Aper	Colloquial: brother.
Apres	Bravo
Arayi Ler	Ara's Mountain
Ari	Come
Aziz	Dear--Arabic root
Balés	My child, my dear--an endearing way of addressing one's child
Barev	Hello
Bari Akhorjak	Bon Apetit
Drsetsi	Literally outsider, meaning foreigner
Dsdesutyun	Until we meet again
Du	you
Du es?	Is that you?
Duk ek?	Is that you?--plural
Eghav	Done, it is done
Gampr	Armenian sheep dog
Garmrakhayd	A type of trout with red dots on the skin
Ha	Colloquial--yes
Hairenadarts	Someone who has returned to the fatherland
Inch aretsir?	What did you do?
Jan	Dear--common suffix used after first names
Ke neres	Forgive me
Khev	Crazy
Khorovadz	Armenian grilled meats and vegetables
Khung	Incense
Kurig	Sister (dimunitive)
Kyank	Literally life, also used as a word of endearment while addressing someone
Lav	Good
Merelots	Memorial Day
Mi ban asa	Say something

Mi gna	Don't go
Oghi	Vodka, Arak, most fermented fruit liquors
Oriort	Miss
Ov e?	Who is it?
Paron	Mister
Tikin	Madame
Tuff	A volcanic stone
Vonts es?	How are you?
Yayla	Summer grazing meadows where villager take their herd and live with them for the season
Yes em	It's me

(Arabic)

Abaya	Ladies' long dress
Akh ya ana	Oh me…
Allahu Akbar	God is great (part of the Muslim prayer)
Azan	Call to prayer
Habibty	My dear (when addressing a female)
Iqal	The circular band worn by men over their heads that holds their headdress
La Ilaha Illa Allah	There is no God but God (part of the Muslim prayer)
Ma fi mushkele	There is no problem
Ma'a al salame	Go in peace
Muazzin	The clergy that chants the call for prayer
Ya Habibty	Oh my dear

(Turkish)

Agha	Male title of rank and respect
Effendi	Male title of rank and respect
Khanum	Female title of rank and respect

A Place Far Away

The asphalt road ended at the foot of the mountain. One of the cars turned left and headed toward the dense rock formations that spread up the mountainside like a thick forest of rugged, vertical boulders. The second turned right for about one hundred meters, then took a sharp left onto a narrow dirt road, leaving a cloud of dust in its tracks. The boss was driving because a special visitor he had invited to spend the day with him as his guest was sitting in the passenger seat. His driver-bodyguard, a big, muscular man with a shaved head, was in the back.

The boss knew his way up the narrow, curvy road, and drove confidently, but the visitor was not sure where they were headed. Parts of the road were so steep that he felt his weight shift to the backrest, as in an airplane during takeoff, and he could see only the sky from the windshield. The boss had to lean way over the steering wheel and look down toward the hood of the car in order to see the road they were driving on. Neither the steepness of the road nor its sharp turns and narrow sections seemed to bother the boss and the bodyguard, but they made the visitor very nervous.

The boss, who until that point had been talkative and lively, had fallen silent. The visitor hoped this was due to his need to concentrate on the dangerous road, but it nonetheless accentuated the eerie feeling created by the desolate and treacherous slope. He looked out the side window after they had made a sharp turn and saw through the dust the narrow trail over which they had just driven, curving some fifty meters down the slope. He deeply regretted agreeing to this visit.

They finally reached a plateau, five-hundred meters above the foot of the mountain where the first car had stopped. It was an open oval field covered with thick grass and weeds up to mid calf, but with jagged, rocky edges. The car scraped against the overgrown wild berry shrubs as it ascended onto the field. The boss stopped the car a few meters into the field, and as they stepped out and started to walk, a flock of startled chucker partridges flew from under their feet and disappeared into the valley. The visitor was startled too, but he couldn't help thinking of his family. He had counted nine birds, and the loud, rapid flapping of their wings was still ringing in his ears.

The men stood there for a few minutes surveying the field.

"This is what I have in mind," said the boss. "It is not large, a little over five hectares, but everything grows very fast here. No need for water either; the thick mist every morning brings in enough humidity." He lifted his right foot to show the wet cuffs of his pants and his soaked shoes as evidence. But his guest noticed that the enthusiasm had disappeared from his speech. He sounded almost bored, as if he wanted to get the trip over with.

"I want you two to walk over there," said the boss, pointing to the other end of the field and looking at the bodyguard. Then he turned to his guest and said, "You can picture the area much better from that angle."

Before he could say anything, the bodyguard put his arm on the visitor's shoulder and led him toward where the boss had pointed. The boss remained by the car and watched them walk awkwardly through the grass.

The flock of partridges was still in the visitor's mind when he thought of saying a prayer. He could recite the Lord's Prayer and even some of the Psalms, but that was quite different from praying, and he was not in the habit of praying. Nevertheless, he couldn't help thinking that God had sent the flock of nine birds as a sign that his family would be safe. He looked in the distance at the steep peaks of black rock, at the misty clouds that were beginning to gather like a halo around the sharp summit, and saw it as another sign of where he was headed. "Watch over my hearth," he said to the clouds, "protect my family." That was the closest he could come to a prayer.

The boss stood very still, watching. It took over ten minutes for the two figures to get to the edge of the field. The last stretch was rocky and dry, with virtually no grass. When they reached the edge, they turned and faced the boss. The edge of the ravine was immediately behind them, and the visitor had a glimpse of the void before turning around. The bodyguard waved his hand horizontally as if to outline the entire area of the field for the visitor. The boss waved his hand too, as if to say hello. Then the bodyguard brought his arching arm back and swung it straight at the visitor's chest. The visitor lost his balance and toppled over the edge.

The two men who were in the first car watched from the foot of the mountain as the visitor came flying down and landed with a loud thud in the forest of boulders. By the time the boss and the bodyguard had descended from the plateau, the two men had retrieved the broken body and were rushing it to a hospital.

I

Lara Galian is too young to dwell on questions of life and fate. She has even stopped asking how she got to where she is at any given time. She is where she is. Asking how and why gives her only headaches, not answers. Things happen to her in ways and for reasons that are not clear to her. Most often it is someone else that causes a change in her situation. She has just turned seventeen and cannot think of any major decision that she herself has made about her life. She has lived a series of reactions to circumstances created by others. Perhaps because of that, she has become very aware of time.

Not that time matters to her as such; she is too young for that too. But she has developed a fear of missing out on the *passing* of time. She wants to be aware, aware as time passes. Fast or slow does not matter; it is not a concern with wasting time either. But since she cannot control events, she feels the need to not lose track of the time in which they happen. She dreads the thought of suddenly realizing that a whole month has passed and she has not even felt it. And it has occurred to her that if she could tie events and sometimes places to a block of time, she would have a concrete feel of time itself. That is why she started recording things. First only in her mind, and when she realized that she was losing memories, she started writing short, cryptic notes: *August 27, the Australian, crazy moustache, Sheraton Moscow, $800, borderline tolerable.*

Throughout her life everyone has said how beautiful she is. Miracle eyes that leave a mark on someone's soul... Heavenly skin that seems to glow like pale onyx... But she is not sure what that really means. In the mirror she sees a face like any other, give or take. A long time ago her looks seemed to have meant something to her mother, who would tell her how she took after some great-aunt that she had never met. "You're the spitting image of your Araxi Dadik," she would say. That did not mean much to her either. She later found out that her mother had not met her great-aunt. The claimed resemblance was based on stories passed down from generation to generation. Both her mother and her mother's stories about her are now vivid memories to which she clings; the more distant the memories the stronger she tends to hang on to them. Clinging to memories seems to be the only defensive instinct left in her. Lara is very much aware of this, but is not dwelling on it at the moment. It is an awareness stored in the back of her mind for future reflection, assuming that that type of future opportunity ever presents itself.

Now her looks have come to mean a great deal to all the men, too many of them, considering her age, and perhaps at any age. Each one different, and yet in many ways the same. There are those who want to love and reward her beauty, and those who want to abuse it and strip her of all dignity. Either way, she has come to realize that they merely seek ways of possessing it; it seems to her that is all men ever want when it comes to her looks.

But sitting here in this crowded jail in Dubai, she does not feel beautiful. She does not feel anything other than the uneasy uncertainty of what might happen to her next; obviously, that too is beyond her control. It is mid-March and Dubai is hot already, with temperatures hovering around thirty degrees centigrade. The air-conditioning unit in the jail cell works, but it is very old, noisy and full of accumulated mold. There is a stale smell of sweat and urine in the air that spreads a uniform mood of malaise over everyone in the room.

There are a dozen women in the large cell, where they gather during the day. At night, they sleep in smaller quarters, two to three prisoners per room. They are of different ages and colors, all there for the crime of prostitution.

৵ ৵ ৵

Lara is the fifth of eight children, with four older sisters and three younger brothers. There is only a little over a year between the siblings. As a child, she was closer to her younger brothers than to her sisters, especially to the next youngest sibling, Avo, who is only thirteen months younger than her. Lara could outrun the boys in the fields, climb any tree, and would even go with the boys to catch frogs in the irrigation canals in the fields around their village.

She was the first of the siblings to explore the forests on the mountainsides beyond the fields past the border of their garden. For her younger brothers, that was where the world ended. Going past their garden was one thing, but crossing the vast fields and reaching the slope of the mountain and then actually entering the forest was something they could not even contemplate. Even Avo, who did everything with her, had tried to talk her out of it instead of agreeing to join her, as she had hoped.

So she went alone, without telling anyone. Soviet forestation programs had created the forests when they planted patches of thick pine and spruce trees on otherwise barren mountainsides. From a distance, they looked like the map of a cluster of green islands, scattered in a grey sea. That was one of the many remaining legacies of seventy years of Soviet rule. It was late afternoon and already lights and shadows were playing in the forest. She could see the fascinating lights before she even walked past the first tree, but what surprised her at first was the total quiet. She had expected some sounds, the rustling of some beast over the pine needles, maybe even a scary howling of a wolf. But the forest was empty and the silence seemed scarier to her than any wild beast's cry.

She felt the trees were staring down at her, as an unwelcome intruder in their dominion. As she walked deeper into the forest it became darker, but she was sure that the trees could see in the dark. She stopped a few times to listen, but then was drawn further in. She wandered in the forest for a long time, not realizing that she was actually lost, before finding her way back home. It was already nighttime when she reached home, earning the wrath of her mother; but to her surprise her father just held her and, with no anger in his voice, asked what had she discovered in the forest. Lara was quiet for a while. Unlike her usual perky self, she stood there, with her father's strong arms around her, clinging to him. He looked at her wide-open eyes and felt her rapid pulse.

"What did you discover in the forest, my girl?" he asked again.

"Nothing," whispered Lara. "There was absolutely nothing there other than trees."

But her father sensed her fear mixed with a wild excitement, and realized that Lara had discovered a part of herself in that forest. She is too young to understand that now, he thought, but he was sure the experience would stay with her for many years to come. And in fact, the forest's impact was already evident. From that day on, Lara had no patience for either the indoors or for the indoor chores that girls are expected to do. This worried and exasperated her mother, even though with four older daughters in the house doing chores, she felt she could let Lara have her way. But she remained worried about Lara and her unconventional ways.

"She's too different from her sisters," she'd tell her husband. "At her age, her sisters had already started taking an interest in their looks. They spent time in front of the mirror; they *wanted* to be pretty, to be noticed. Lara has no sense of it at all. All she wants to do is go out and roll in the mud…"

Her father would try to calm her down. "It will all come to her too, Silva. Don't worry so much. She'll get there, maybe a bit later than the others, but she'll get there."

"The others would kill to have her looks," the mother would go on. "And yet she doesn't have a clue! She should have been a boy; she's our first son, not Avo…"

Each in their own way had established a special bond with Lara. Her mother, because she worried more about her than any of her other children. However, in spite of her anxieties, she harbored a bit of relief that Lara's unconventional ways might in fact someday have a liberating effect on her. Good looks were not always a good omen; they could lead to misery as easily as to happiness. But maybe a strong personality would help even out the odds; at least that's what Silva Galian hoped. Her father's bond was different. He saw in her a part of himself and his murky past; given his troubled and disjointed family history, that link mattered. Of course Lara was not aware of any of it at the time. All would later be revealed to her gradually through remembrances.

Her father died when she was sixteen, just one month before her saga started. He fell off a cliff in the highlands, some say while cutting wood, others say while checking out a forestation project—the story is not clear.

But his death was so sudden and unexpected that it devastated Lara. Her prolonged, happy childhood ended as abruptly as her father's life.

♫ ♫ ♫

She has heard that there are many other girls from her country, over a hundred by some accounts, in jails in Dubai for the same offense, but there is only one in her cell, Susannah, whom she met the first day she landed. She is older, maybe in her thirties; it is hard to tell. There are signs of fatigue in her eyes, and the first lines of narrow wrinkles have started to appear around the corners of her eyes and mouth. When they first met, Lara remembers thinking that Susannah looked Persian. She too has large, dark eyes, and when she looked closely at her face she thought that each part taken alone looked very Armenian, but the face as a whole looked Persian. It surprised Lara that she noticed these things. None of it really mattered, and before she left her village she would not even have noticed such similarities, let alone analyzed them. But since then she has become more observant. They are not close friends, but have helped each other a few times, even though their first interaction was not easy.

"So how did you end up here?" Susannah had asked, looking her over from head to toe, amazed at her youth and beauty.

"They forced me," Lara had answered.

"You mean you did not want to come?"

"Of course not."

"Where else would you rather be, girl?"

Lara had hesitated at first, not knowing where such conversations could lead to, nor seeing much point in them in the first place. But then she had said, "Home. Our village."

Susannah had laughed out loud.

"So, you miss home, eh? What did you have at home in your village? Your doting mama? Is that what you miss, you sweet little girl?"

Lara did not understand how Susannah could show such disdain toward a mother's love or memory, but kept quiet. She did not know Susannah's story, and did not necessarily want to know. So she just withdrew into herself.

"Listen, girl," Susannah had said, "let me tell you something. I *applied* for this job! I *wanted* to come. I worked hard for six months in the godforsaken backstreets of Antalya just so they would bring me to Dubai. Do you understand that? The sooner you get it through your head that this is who we are, this is what we do, the better for you!" And when Susannah had seen the stubborn hesitation in Lara's eyes, she'd snapped at her—"Well, have you done anything else? Have you *been* anything else, in your long, illustrious life, Ms. beauty queen?"

Eventually Lara had begun to like Susannah. *She means well*, she had thought, *even in her apparent hostility*. They had gone out with groups of clients a few times together, and learned to watch out for each other.

Now they live in the same apartment complex near the St. George hotel in Dubai. Most of the time they go to their clients' hotels or apartments, but once in a while they bring them to their place. Usually it is a single client, spending anywhere from fifteen minutes to an hour with them, and sometimes overnight. Occasionally, a group of two or three go to parties, sometimes with ten or more men. That is when things can get tough, because the men are inevitably drunk, and they try to outdo each other. Their typical clients are Pakistani, Iranian and Arab men, but rarely locals. Europeans and Americans appear on the scene also, though not as frequently. They are warned to steer clear of local men, because there is no recourse against them. That does not limit their client base very much since most of the population of Dubai is expatriates anyway.

Everyone knows that Lara does not fit in. The others in the group are all in their late twenties and thirties and none of them stands out physically. Lara clearly has not been brought to Dubai to do fifteen minutes with a Pakistani for twenty-five dollars. The plan is to have her become dedicated to one of the local princes. Someone has to notice her and ask for her exclusive contract; almost like a marriage, albeit a temporary one. They can get a lot more for her if she gets noticed and is sought after, and Ayvazian is aiming high. He wants two hundred and fifty thousand dollars for her contract for three years. Pretty steep, but then again Lara is unique. And he knows they'll negotiate the price down, regardless of where he starts. He has quietly put out the word, and two "recruiters" are already in discussions with him.

The other women in the cell are a mixed bunch. There are a few Russians, with whom Lara can communicate if she chooses to, but, aside from a rudimentary knowledge of the Russian language, she has nothing in common with them, so she keeps her distance. The Russians stand out, as they have fairer skin than the rest, blonde hair, and are very thin. There are two black women from Somalia, who pretty much keep to themselves. They are the most conservatively dressed in the bunch with blouses and pants that do not reveal much, and they apply relatively modest makeup. There's a young Moroccan girl, possibly Lara's age, beautiful, but, in contrast to Lara, is jovial, talking to anyone who will listen and giggling non-stop at her own crude sexual jokes. The top several buttons of her white shirt are unbuttoned, revealing a skimpy red bra that can barely hold her breasts. There are others from Morocco, who keep to themselves and try to ignore their flamboyant compatriot. They are somewhat older and have been down this road before. There is nothing to celebrate in this cell. They will either be worth the efforts of a resourceful and willing sponsor, who will rescue them at the cost of gaining rights to their bodies and souls, or they will stay here until they're deported back to Morocco.

Lara sits at the far corner of the cell on a foam cushion on the floor, staring at the wings of a dead, dried up wasp stuck to the dirty wall. It looks like it has been there for years, which doesn't say much for how well the cell is cleaned. She has her hand in the pocket of her jacket, holding a small ring. It is a thin, simple gold band, which her thumb is rubbing in a slow circular motion. She has her hair in a ponytail, has buttoned up her white blouse, and has thrown her large, square headscarf over her lap, to cover herself a bit more than what her black miniskirt can manage. There is no breeze in the cell, but the delicate wings seem to be moving, vibrating. Is it the breath of the twelve women? Is it her breath? Can she still cause movement somewhere, even in a dead insect? The dead wasp's shivering wings seem to be signaling, almost waving to her. They are so thin, delicate and transparent that it's hard to believe that they once gave the wasp flight. These are organs of flight. Lara remembers the wasps in her village, how alive and active they used to be, especially in late fall, when they would buzz, rush, dash around non-stop. She remembers how her younger brothers once had to destroy a wasp nest under the overhang of the roof of their village house. They wrapped an old rag in a lump at the end of a long stick, doused it in kerosene, lit it, and pushed it against the nest. Lara even remembers how impatiently they had to wait until mid afternoon for the winds to subside, otherwise it would be impossible to direct the flame precisely to the target. The nest caught fire in an instant, burnt violently for a minute, then crumbled. Most of the wasps perished. Some caught fire as they tried to fly away from the nest and went ablaze like sparks jumping out of a fire, glowing for a few seconds, and then dying. The wings ignited first. Light, flammable organs of flight. And Lara remembers how mad the few that survived had become, and how one brother was stung so badly that his face remained swollen for days. Lara, barely twelve at the time, remembers feeling happy for the survivors and their revenge. So now she feels the wings of the dead wasp are talking to her in this cell. There is an old bond here that no one else can possibly understand.

But her village and the old wasp's nest are far from where she is now. *Saralandj*, she utters aloud, and almost instantly regrets the slip. *Saralandj*. Her village, way out in the outskirts of Aparan, a historic town in Armenia where an ancient battle had once been fought, and won. A village so primitive that life means only hardship for the adults, and only children can remember it fondly. Lara remembers it fondly. Children do not dwell on the ordinary harshness of life, even as they suffer through it. Saralandj. That is where her grandparents and father returned after their senseless exile to Siberia ended, after Joseph Stalin finally died. They were "forgiven," like so many others who managed to survive the ordeal. But that is the story of another long ordeal, which, as the elders tell, her great-aunt Araxi Dadik did not survive.

Allllaaaaaahu Akbar, Allaaaahu Akbar, Allahu Akbar… The call to prayer snaps her out of her reverie. It comes suddenly, five times a day, and is very loud especially here in jail. There must be a mosque somewhere on the premises. The high pitched, spirited voice of the *Muazzin* fills the air. Lara remembers how shocked she was when she first heard it; it almost sounded like the wail of sirens, but then she heard the melodic nuances of different calls, and started enjoying the *azan*. *…La Ilaaaaha Illa Allaaaah…* The voice grows louder and more animated as the *azan* progresses. Some of the girls make faces and cover their ears. But Lara finds the chant soothing, almost like a lullaby.

Neither Lara nor any of her cellmates know what to expect next. They sit in the cell, accept their meals at precise intervals, and wait. They're served rice, beans, sometimes a piece of meat or chicken, on old, discolored aluminum plates, heavily dented from years of use. All the guards are women, in police uniforms with headscarves topped by police caps, and all look alike. Chubby, covered from head to toe except for their faces, even though they are not in the company of men. They are tough and kind at the same time. It is hard to tell the difference sometimes. Lara thinks it would be impossible for them to adopt one style that fit all the inmates. She sees a disguised compassion hidden behind their stern and firm manners, or maybe she just wants to see it, she is not always sure. But at least they are women. That is a consolation for her, regardless of how they act. Men have not treated her kindly.

Four days have passed since the arrest, which had not been a classic raid as one sees in the movies. Nor had it involved being caught in the act, either soliciting or being solicited, with evidence and witnesses. Her "agent," a portly Armenian woman named Ano, had gathered a group of them one afternoon, some of whom she had not met before, and told them that their protection was no longer active, and that they had to go to jail for a while. That was all. Ano had done her best not to make too much of it, even though her face was more somber than usual, and her thick black eyebrows seemed more stern and unyielding.

Most of them had been either too dumbfounded or too accustomed to the scene to react. "Do not be concerned," Ano had said. "We'll get you out eventually. We always do. And you won't be in any danger while in jail."

"Maybe this is how things are done in Dubai," Susannah had told her later, "but I can tell you this is unusual. Many things get arranged in our business, but I have never seen a bust being arranged like this, almost in a civilized, orderly way. At times like this, anywhere else, usually the 'agent' just disappears and leaves us at the mercy of the police. Here, she left us at the mercy of the police herself, without disappearing. Maybe her big bosses did not pay the police enough, or maybe someone higher up complained. Maybe one of your own customers was the son of some royalty here, who got angry with us for the naughty things his kid was being exposed to. Who knows?"

It has been four days and there is no news from Madame Ano, except to tell the girls to hang in there a while longer while she tries to work something out. They have taken their names and fingerprinted them. Their passports have been provided to the police by Madame Ano herself. After almost three months in Dubai, with an average of fifteen client visitors a day, Lara and the other girls had started taking their "protection" for granted. And now they sit here very conscious of the fact that each idle day in jail is costing them dearly.

Five prayers. Three meals. Not much else. Fourth day. Lara writes in her tiny spiral-bound green notebook. Then her hand goes back into her pocket in search of the ring.

II

Although Lara landed in Dubai only several months ago, her saga started much earlier than that. Even she does not yet know all the details. It is only later, much later, that she finally puts all the pieces together and solves the puzzle, to the extent that such puzzles can ever be fully solved. But the simple fact that triggers everything else is that her beauty did not go unnoticed, not only among friends and relatives, but also through the eyes of organized crime. Sergey Ayvazian is a name that she will get to know a lot better in time, because that is where it all begins.

Ayvazian's men notice her playing in the streets of Aparan, the closest town to Saralandj, where she is visiting her aunt. She is wearing rags, barefoot, hair unkempt, and barely sixteen. Although she is taller than normal for her age, she is full of childish enthusiasm in everything she does. It is very clear to the men that she is a potential gem in their trade.

Ayvazian at first refuses to consider her. Her case is too complicated. She lives at home with both parents and has relatives in Saralandj and Aparan. This is not the profile he favors. He likes the girls in orphanages and boarding schools; handling them is much simpler, with no strings attached. And the orphanages of Armenia are full these days, with many war casualties, refugees from Azerbaijan, and homes broken due to severe poverty. Fathers leave for Russia looking for employment and never return. The economic conditions in the villages and small towns of Armenia are catastrophic, creating perfect hunting conditions for the traffickers. So why bother with this girl, with all the complications?

Then they show him a few pictures. Close-ups of her face, taken with a powerful telephoto lens, reveal such a captivating youthful beauty that even a hardened oligarch like Ayvazian is moved. There is one masterful photograph where she is jumping rope, her skirt flying up in the air, her hair scattered, her laughter roaring and bursting out of the photograph, where she looks like a nascent goddess ascending toward heaven. Ayvazian takes that picture from the file and keeps it in his wallet. He is keenly aware that his business needs a major boost; all recruits in the past year have been low-earning mediocrities in terms of age and beauty.

They check out the Galian family. Eight children. The father is a postal employee in Aparan, earning around $25 per month. They have some live-stock in the village of Saralandj, although they have sold most of their stock in the past decade in order to survive. From around one hundred head of sheep and fifteen cows in the early nineties, they are down to five sheep and one cow. They cannot possibly feed eight children with what they have. In the spring and summer they gather wild greens from the meadows and mountainsides, which they either dry or pickle for winter consumption. They do the same with summer vegetables from their garden—tomatoes, eggplant, green beans, turnips, cabbage, peppers, cucumbers, cracked wheat and corn. They pickle and preserve whatever they can. They also stock up cheese made from sheep's milk. But they cannot feed eight children year round; there is no doubt that there are hungry nights in the Galian household, especially toward the end of winter.

Ayvazian notes with some interest that the Galians are not local to Aparan. They settled here after their return from Siberia because his aunt was married here; besides, as recent immigrants, they had no place else to settle. Galian has a reputation as a hard working, honest man. But he also is different from the rest of the villagers; regardless of whether the differences are good or bad, that tends to create a distance between him and his neighbors. The villagers say that he reads to his children, something that mothers and older sisters may do from time to time in Saralandj, but not fathers.

But Galian is known to gather his children on holidays, especially religious holidays, and definitely on Memorial days—*Merelots*, which usually fall on the Monday following a religious holiday—and read to them. Even more unusual is that he reads to them not only the classics of Armenian literature, like Toumanian, but also the Bible.

"The Bible?" asks Ayvazian's man of the villager telling the story.

"I've seen it myself," says the villager. "It is an old, torn book. Leather covers. Certainly not published here. It is not even in our Armenian. It is the book of an *Aghpar*"—which is the slang word literally meaning "brother," referring to the thousands of Armenian survivors of the Turkish genocide who returned to Armenia in the mid-forties. The *"agh-pars"* like to refer to themselves as *"Hairenadarts,"* literally meaning "one who returned to the fatherland." Either way, it was a word with heavy connotations among the locals, who resented the inflow of immigrants from abroad with whom they had to share scarce food supplies during the Stalin years.

The Bible has been in the Galian family for generations, and has traveled with them through exiles from Eastern Turkey, to Egypt, to Lebanon, then Armenia, then Siberia and then back to Armenia. If the family ever owned any other valuables, they are long since lost during these forced marches and exiles, but the Bible has somehow been kept and protected over some seventy-five years.

"Is he religious?" asks Ayvazian's interrogator.

"If he is, he keeps it to himself. He has never set foot in a church, even after Independence. He never talks religion to anyone. He just reads the Bible to his children."

The Galians' *Aghpar* status is an extenuating circumstance to the girl's otherwise inconvenient profile. It simply means that the villagers would not be as protective of the family as they would be to one of their own.

So Ayvazian decides to approach the family directly. It was not unheard of in those difficult years that families would give up their young children for some cash up front and the promise of a better future for the child than they could provide. In fact, in the villages and small towns of Armenia this had become relatively common in the most difficult years right after Independence. "We can make an attractive offer to the parents," Ayvazian figures. "Lara deserves a better future than she can expect to have in the streets of Saralandj."

Ayvazian sends his top recruiter and operator, who happens to be his nephew, to do the job. And so Viktor Ayvazian, accompanied by two of his bodyguards, finds himself in his shiny black Mercedes SUV in the muddy main street of Saralandj on a Saturday afternoon. It is a narrow unpaved road, more like an obstacle course of mounds, holes and rocks, not meant to handle any automobile, let alone a large one. The villagers stare at them from windows and the roadside, keeping their eyes on the car for a very long time, staring in trancelike bafflement. Even though the four-wheel drive vehicle can manage most mountain roads in Armenia, they have to stop the car around twenty meters from the Galian house and walk the remaining distance. The road has too many deep potholes full of muddy water to take a chance with the car.

Lara's mother notices them first from the kitchen window. It is not a sight one sees every day in the streets of Saralandj. Three men in fancy clothes and Italian loafers struggling up the road to get to their house. It would be comical, if only she had been in the mood to laugh. The two bodyguards have clean-shaven heads and muscular arms, but cannot hide protruding bellies that simply do not fit with the overall image. Under their coats there are bulges, which indicate weapons at their waists. The third man, Viktor, looks different; he has thick black hair combed straight back, and is dressed in grey; grey shirt, darker grey jacket with black stripes, lighter grey trousers, and darker grey, almost black loafers.

Galian is in the back garden. He has watered the vegetable patch and dug around the six fruit trees in preparation to water them. He inspects the grafts, content with his handiwork and satisfied with the way the grafts have stuck and sprouted. He examines again the three plum grafts on one of the apricot trees, and the two peach grafts on the second. The shoots are already around fifteen centimeters long, and look healthy. The kids will have a lot of fun picking plums and peaches from the apricot trees, he thinks.

Mrs. Galian sends one of her older daughters to the back garden to call her father. "Tell him to drop everything and rush inside," she tells her, almost in a panic. Viktor, flanked by his two bodyguards, has finally managed to get to the house.

And then things begin to get really awkward. The Galian house is basically two rooms. One serves as the bedroom for the eight children. The second serves as kitchen and dining room in one corner and bedroom for the parents in the other. The toilet is a shack outside at the far end of the garden with a deep hole dug into it. On bathing days, they bathe in the kitchen corner of the parents' bedroom, sitting on a small wooden stool on the floor. So the "guests" are invited into the kitchen side. They are offered chairs from the dining table, and the Galians sit on their bed. There is a strong smell of manure in the room, because that is what they burn in the small stove in the corner of the kitchen—cow manure mixed with hay and dried in the sun in the shape of round, loaf-sized cakes. That is also the main source of heat in the winter, with the stovepipe passing through the other bedroom before going out, and thus heating both rooms. The second source of heat used to be the hundred or so sheep cuddled in the low underground hall under the main house, with the warmth from their bodies rising into the house. But now, with just a few sheep, that source of warmth is not as effective.

The conversation with the Galians does not go as Viktor had expected. He starts by explaining to the parents that their daughter Lara has a very special gift, that he and his uncle are willing to help her reach her true potential, that she could become a very successful model of international fame. They offer to take upon themselves all the initial costs of training and schooling her for a percentage of her future earnings. Their offer also includes an immediate advance payment of $300 to the parents for the rights to become their daughter's agents.

Although Viktor is confident in the strength of his offer, he feels as if he is in unfamiliar territory. The surroundings are totally alien to him; and he is uncomfortably aware that some of the children are eavesdropping from behind the door. He has always felt uncomfortable not knowing who is listening to his words, even if they are children. The lack of control over this environment is so troublesome to him that he regrets holding the meeting here instead of inviting the father to one of their offices or coffee shops.

"But she's only sixteen," says Lara's mother. "How can she start something like that now?"

Silva Galian is a tall, thin, pale woman. Viktor cannot gauge her age. He reckons she could be anywhere between forty-five, if one focused on her eyes and lips, to almost seventy, if one were to consider her pale color and the state of her wrinkled hands.

"That's the right age to start in this business," replies Viktor. "In fact, some of the most famous European models have started much younger, some when they were only ten."

As he speaks, Viktor becomes unusually aware of his voice. How does he sound? Firm? Friendly? Sure or unsure of himself?

The father is quiet and just stares at the visitors. He has run in from the garden, dirty, his hands and hair covered with mud and twigs, and is trying to fathom the visit, the visitors and their offer. He wipes his hands on his trousers and listens. He openly stares at Viktor's face as he speaks, checking his slick hair, dark eyes, handsome and well groomed face with clean, silky skin. There is no doubt in his mind that the offer has to be categorically rejected. That is not what he is thinking about. He is wondering how much trouble he should expect from these thugs once he tells them no. He knows of Viktor's uncle. Sergey Ayvazian, although a relatively secretive man, is known to him by reputation and hearsay, and there probably is more mystique and mystery surrounding him than any of the other rich oligarchs in the country. These people normally do not accept no for an answer.

Viktor feels uncomfortable under the father's quiet stare. He wishes the father would speak instead of the mother. But he does note that the man is quite handsome, even though time has caused a lot more wear and tear on his face and hands than his age would normally cause. He has the old, aristocratic nose of ancient Armenian nobility, wide forehead, thick curly hair, which has turned grey around his temples, and very bright and penetrating eyes. He reminds Viktor of the mythological characters that he learned about in school; he had always imagined the mythical god Vahagn to look something like Galian, except maybe with longer and crazier hair and a long curly beard. The man clearly looks out of place in so much poverty, an unfamiliar feeling for Viktor. He has never given a second thought to poor people before. They looked like they belonged where they were. But somehow he does not feel that poverty is becoming to Galian, and realizes with some discomfort that a man can come down in the world as well as move up.

"But how can she go to Europe at such a young age?" the mother asks. "She has not even been outside Aparan, except just once when we had to go to Yerevan a few years back to greet her uncle at the airport. She is still in school. She knows nothing."

The mother is aware that $300 is the entire annual salary of her husband. Even if all the promises they are making about future income do not materialize, the $300 is a major factor for her. But she knows that her questions are basically to give her husband time to think and weigh the options. He will have the last say.

"We will take care of everything," says Viktor, answering her but looking at him. "She will first meet my uncle, and then we will get her papers in order--a passport, some other certificates--you do not have to worry about a thing. Then she will start an apprenticeship in a beauty salon in Athens, Greece, which my uncle knows. Greece is a very safe place, and we have many friends and contacts there."

Viktor gestures to one of the bodyguards who produces a small booklet from his coat pocket. It is a flyer of a beauty salon, portraying attractive ladies in beautiful clothes and perfect make up, looking successful, proud and happy.

"This beauty salon is where most models in Greece are recruited from," says Viktor as he hands her the leaflet. "While doing her apprenticeship, she will be paid a modest amount, but more than enough for her to live on. She'll probably even have something left over to send home. By the time she is seventeen she will have her first full modeling job and an opportunity to win over the whole world!"

The mother starts leafing through the booklet, more as a courtesy than anything else, and turns toward her husband to see if he wants to look at it; he gently shakes his head. So she stops leafing through it and hands it back to the bodyguard.

Of course it does not matter that the story does not make much sense and that a beauty salon has nothing to do with modeling. Viktor knows that these peasants wouldn't know any better. The important thing is the promise, the bait, the hope.

"I don't know," says the mother. "I just don't know. My Lara is still a child..."

Samvel Galian finally stands up. "Thank you very much, Mr. Viktor," he says. "And please thank your respectable uncle on my behalf. Your offer is indeed very kind and generous, but we simply cannot accept. As my wife said, Lara is still a child. She could not possibly face such a challenge. We do not *want* her to face these challenges. Thanks again for your visit and your generous offer."

Having said his only and final words standing up, it is obvious from his body language that he has ended the meeting and asked Viktor and his men to leave. There is an intensity in Galian's soft and polite manners that disarms Viktor. The confident, I-always-get-my-way thug attitude melts away in this poor peasant home, where he feels as out of place as he actually is. There is no point in further talk. "As you wish," he says, and stands up. The bodyguards stand up also.

As Viktor and his bodyguards leave the house, Lara comes rushing in with two of her younger brothers in close pursuit, her laughter cascading and filling the whole front yard. She has a carved wooden object in her hand, apparently snatched from one of her brothers, who are chasing her into the house to retrieve it. She is bursting with life. A light summer blouse, dirty with mud and stains, some of which look like manure, does not hide her maturing body underneath and will not contain her young breasts much longer. Her feet are bare and muddy, her hair dirty, curly and all tangled up in hay and grass. But when she looks up in shock at the visitors and her charcoal-black eyes meet Viktor's, his heart misses a beat. The late afternoon sunlight falls on her face, highlighting the black birthmark on her slender neck. To his surprise, he feels an overpowering urge to have her. This girl is not just beautiful. She is also *desirable* in a wild, uncontrollable way that mere physical beauty does not always inspire. As he walks back the last twenty meters to his car, there is no doubt in Viktor's mind that they must have Lara Galian join their operation.

Sergey Ayvazian was not surprised by the report, but he was not amused either. His first instinct was to blame his nephew for messing up the operation, but the more he thought about the story the more he became convinced that there was little Viktor could have done against a determined and principled father. The girl's profile was wrong, as he had known from the start. But sometimes the best candidates came with the worst profiles, and he realized it was up to him to fix things.

There were only two possible courses of action for Ayvazian. To drop the whole thing, which was what his conservative instincts were telling him, or to remove the impediments and capture the prize, which was what his basic impulses of the trade were telling him. He did not take too long to decide.

ℒ ℒ ℒ

The invitation for Lara's father to visit Martashen, one of the larger villages in Armenia and the hometown of Ayvazian, came only a week after Viktor's visit. It was from Sergey Ayvazian and was very cordial, but it was also clear that this was not something that could be turned down. It was delivered in person by two messengers, one of whom was one of the bodyguards with Viktor on the first visit. In the eyes of the villagers, they all looked alike. Foreign—clean and well pressed shirts, trousers with creases, shiny loafers, sunglasses. None of them belonged in Saralandj.

"Mr. Ayvazian appreciates your decision," the spokesman told Lara's father. "In fact, he agrees with you, even though that may seem somewhat paradoxical given that he made the proposal to you in the first place. But in reality it is not. He is a father and has a daughter himself. So part of him clearly sees your point of view, while another part of him sees the incredible professional potential of Lara, which he feels should not go unrealized."

The spokesman waited for some reaction from Galian, but got nothing more than a gentle, barely noticeable nod. "At any rate," he continued, "as you know, Mr. Ayvazian is in many different businesses, and would like to discuss with you an entirely different business proposition, having to do with animal husbandry, for which Aparan and especially Saralandj are ideally suited. Mr. Ayvazian has a plan to import cattle from Holland and Switzerland and develop a whole new breed of dairy cows in Armenia. These cows give 25-30 liters of milk a day, compared with the 5-7 liters that the local cows give. It is not only an incredible business opportunity but also will revolutionize the dairy business in the entire country. The ideal location for such a farm is Saralandj. He is impressed with your principled stand as a father and believes you would make an ideal business partner."

Galian listened silently and carefully, as he had done with Viktor. He tried to size up his visitors. There was no doubt in his mind that he could never do business with these people. They were from a different world. He wished to be left alone, to live quietly in his own village. As he sat there listening, he could not help recalling the words of his late father, who had told him that the ultimate human dignity was in living within one's means. "The minute you try to go beyond your own means," he had said, "you compromise not only your freedom, but with it also your dignity. It is better to live dignified and free in poverty, than to pretend to be something that you are not." Words to live by thought Galian, listening to the fantastic stories about Dutch cows in Saralandj.

But turning down two offers from Ayvazian in one week would have been too dangerous, especially when the second one did not involve his daughter. This was carefully planned by Ayvazian; this was a personal invitation for cooperation and friendship with an open and vague agenda. No reasonable rejection could possibly be explained as an objection to the proposed agenda, but could only be understood as a personal slight. That could put his whole family in danger of retribution. Martashen is in the Vayots Dzor region, around an hour-and-a-half from Yerevan. Ayvazian owned a ranch there in addition to his mansion in Yerevan. Galian would have preferred to visit him in Yerevan, which was only a forty-five minute drive from Aparan, but he did not feel he could request such conditions, especially when his visitors were providing transportation to Martashen and back.

Galian had an eerie feeling that Sunday morning when he got into the black Mercedes SUV. He had bathed and shaved, but had the same rags on as always. Very few in Saralandj had special clothes for Sundays. He was going just for the day, so there was no call for long goodbyes. But he bid farewell to his family anyway, and gave the boys instructions on what needed to be done in the garden. He kissed his daughters, and lingered a bit longer with Lara, giving her a second kiss on the forehead.

ℒ ℒ ℒ

That was the last time Galian saw his family. The news of the accident reached Saralandj late that evening. His body arrived the next evening. The details were very sketchy. They had gone to a small village in Vayots Dzor called Sevajayr, famous for its sharp peaks and ravines. Ayvazian knew the area well, because he went there often to hunt mountain goats. There is one steep meadow in particular where the goats gather almost year round. It is well protected because the place is virtually inaccessible by car or on foot. But Ayvazian would land at the top of the peak with a helicopter, and shoot the grazing goats around two to three hundred meters down into the meadow. The goats he slaughtered rolled down the steep meadow into the valley below, where his men collected them.

The story was that the conversation turned from animal husbandry to the medicinal value of the wild plants and herbs growing all over the mountainsides in Armenia, and finally to wood. Wood is rare in Armenia. Almost all construction is done in stone, which is much more abundant. *Tuff*, a type of volcanic rock is by far the most abundant, and comes in many different colors—from light pink to black and many shades of red and yellow in between. Almost all of Yerevan, the capital city, is built of tuff.

But wood was beginning to become popular in new buildings and villas, for flooring, paneling and for kitchens and patios. Imported wood was very expensive, and generally of inferior quality because it was rarely dried and processed properly. So Ayvazian was looking into investing in a wood processing plant in Dilijan, a town in Northern Armenia famous for its rich forests. And, as it turns out, Galian had worked one summer in Dilijan as a lumberjack, and knew a thing or two about cutting and treating wood. Upon hearing this Ayvazian said he was delighted; he claimed that now they had found another potential area of cooperation, and invited Galian for a drive to Sevajayr to look at some his properties where he was planning to plant trees. "One cannot build an industry on the existing forests," he declared. "Our forests are our national wealth. But we can plant the trees we want to cultivate into wood."

The story became sketchier past this point. Up on the slopes, Galian tripped on a fallen branch and plunged into the valley below. A terrible accident, the eyewitnesses said. Of course, there was absolutely nothing that Ayvazian and his men could do. It was early evening by the time they recovered the body from the valley and brought it to a hospital in Yeghegnadzor, the largest city in the region and the capital of Vayots Dzor. He was declared dead on arrival. A quick autopsy showed death from the fall, with several broken bones and severe head injuries. A police report was written the next day confirming the accidental death. The case was closed, and the body released to be returned to his family.

III

Ayvazian's men did not wait the customary forty days of mourning before appearing at the Galian home again; they returned four weeks after Galian's death. This time Lara was inside helping her mother in the kitchen. The place was dark, and smelled of sheep manure. It was the most depressing place the men had ever seen. It felt as if even the old cracked walls were mourning; they could almost hear a wailing in the air, coming from no one in particular.

This time the men had come with gifts. New clothes for Lara, a wool shawl for the mother, a crate of fresh fruit, coffee and canned meats, all compliments of Mr. Ayvazian, they said.

Once again they expressed their deep regret for the accident and asked about how the other children were doing. The main topic about Lara's future as a model followed very quickly. This time they offered $500 as advance payment for the right to be her managers. The mother hesitated but then agreed, as they knew she would. It was all arranged very quickly. They would return the next day for Lara. The first stop would be Yerevan, then Moscow to finalize paperwork, then off to Greece. Lara would be able to stay in touch with her mother. They gave the mother a cell phone and told her that they would pay for it. They promised that soon Lara would have her own phone too, and they would be able to call each other anytime.

That night, Lara and her brothers and sisters stayed up very late talking. There were five beds, a chest of drawers and a long and narrow closet crammed in their bedroom. Two of the beds were narrower than a twin, crafted a long time ago by their grandfather from wood and plywood; Martha and Avo each occupied one. The other three beds, also homemade, were a bit wider, and four sisters shared two and the two youngest brothers shared the other. Lara and Alisia shared a bed. There was hardly any walking space between the beds. They all sat on their beds that night in their homemade pajamas, all of which were sewn over the years by Silva Galian and handed down to the next sibling as each outgrew it. Their conversation centered around their efforts to understand what was happening to Lara. This type of thing didn't happen in Saralandj. The best that a girl could hope for was to marry someone from the village and start her own family, living pretty much the same life as her parents.

The girls didn't know what to make of Lara's new life. There was a cautious excitement, mixed with a hint of jealousy in the air. Alisia was the least reserved; she was combing Lara's hair and telling her how beautiful she looked and how she'd have such an exciting life traveling around the world. A visit to Yerevan alone would have been an adventure for them. Martha was more quiet and reserved, absorbed within her own thoughts.

But Avo was by far the most somber and sad.

"*Kurig, mi gna*," he said. "Sister, don't go."

That broke Lara's heart. She jumped down from her bed, wistfully walked to him and gave him a hug. This normally would have made Avo uncomfortable, but at that moment he found it acceptable and comforting.

"Avo," she said warmly, "don't worry, it will be fine. I'll return soon. We'll all be fine."

"*Mi gna*," repeated Avo, this time whispering so quietly that only Lara heard him. She held him tighter and rocked him for a few minutes. "Don't worry," she repeated. "Everything will work out."

Lara tried to change the mood. She started asking what each one of them wanted her to bring from Greece. They had no idea what to ask for, but the topic was exciting nonetheless. After a month of living in an oppressively mournful house, they all felt the need for something happy, something hopeful. Lara started teasing Alisia. "I know why you're happy to see me go," she said laughing. "You want to have our bed all to yourself." Alisia chuckled and the traces of a smile appeared even on Martha's face.

Lara went from bed to bed, giving her sisters and brothers hugs and stroking their hair. She stayed a while with Martha, the oldest, who was engaged, but the wedding had to be postponed because of Galian's death, and because the family now was far too poor to provide the most basic dowry. Lara held her for a long time, almost as if she was the older sister. "You'll get married very soon," she whispered in her ear. She then went to her youngest two brothers, held each under one arm and kissed each on the cheek. "So what would you like me to bring you from Greece?" she asked.

"Do they have good sling shots there?" asked Aram, the youngest.

"I guess so," laughed Lara. "I'll look for the best one in Greece!" At the end, Lara went back to Avo and just sat with him for a while, without speaking. He had not smiled or laughed all night. He had not said anything except his two pleas for her not to go. After a while, Lara gave him a kiss and left the room. She went and got in bed with her mother and stayed the night with her.

Silva Galian was far too drained to be emotional the next morning as she saw her daughter off in the black Mercedes SUV, the same one her husband had boarded only a month earlier. She was dressed in black, with a black scarf covering her hair that accentuated her paleness. Her face looked like that of a ghost. Heavy bags had formed under her bloodshot eyes that were totally void of any expression or human emotion. A month of crying had exhausted her. She had already said her goodbyes the night before, when she explained to Lara as best as she could what was happening, how she was to get the rarest chance of a lifetime to make something of her life, how she should always keep herself well, treat her new sponsors with respect, never get too spoiled or demanding, and endure whatever hardship came her way.

"Never forget where you are from and who you really are," she said.

Lara listened carefully, and understood most of what her mother was trying to say. But the last instruction was not easy. *Where I am from is easy, Saralandj, of course,* she thought. *But who I really am? What does that mean?* She realized, even at her tender age, that she would probably struggle with that question for a long time.

Lara's mother had prepared a bag for her. It was a blue, old and over-used shopping bag from a department store in Moscow, which one of the relatives had brought years ago. The colors and some of the lettering along the sides had long faded, but the bag was still sturdy enough to carry the few items that she packed for her daughter—a pair of socks, underwear, a blouse, a pair of pants, and an old dress, which she had washed and ironed the night before.

There was one more item, which she took out and showed Lara, before putting it back carefully at the bottom of the bag and making sure that the clothes covered it thoroughly. Wrapped in an old, embroidered hand-kerchief was a small, thin gold ring, a plain wedding band that had once belonged to Araxi Dadik. "Your father wanted you to have this," she said without much emotion. "He loved you very much, Lara. He loved all his children. But you are his youngest daughter, and with you he felt a tie to his past."

Lara had lost much of her own vitality in the past month. She had never thought about how much her father had meant to her until he was gone. His death was far too sudden and unexpected, and she missed him terribly. What she missed the most was his reading. She was not afraid that she might forget his face one day, which Avo had told her was what he was wor-ried about. Lara was too old for that, and besides, she thought his face was too impressive to forget. But she did worry that she might forget his voice, his reading voice, and the way he read all those stories. Toumanian's stories in rhyme, *"One Drop of Honey," "The Dog and the Cat,"* and especially *"David of Sassoun,"* which could captivate anyone from three years old to eighty-three, her father would say. Why eighty-three? No one knew or asked. That was Galian's way of talking.

Lara loved the Bible stories too. Her father took many liberties with the Bible reading. He would read them the first verse of Genesis, immediately followed by John 1.1, moving from the Old Testament to the new in the same paragraph. *In the beginning, God created the heavens and the earth. The earth was without form and void, and darkness was in the face of the deep. In the beginning was the word, and the word was with God, and the word was God. And the spirit of God was hovering on the face of the waters....*

Although Armenia had many lakes, Lara had never seen a large body of water. But she had seen the fog descend from the mountain peaks down to the forests in Saralandj, thick, slow and overwhelming, covering and owning everything in its path. She thought maybe that too was the spirit of God, and that's how it must have been back then, except it hovered over the face of the waters instead of the forests of Saralandj. Lara loved all the Jesus stories, especially the miracles, but there never was any real religious context to any of the readings. They read the Bible just like they would read Toumanian. It was literature and stories that captured the children's imagination and uplifted them from the daily realities of Saralandj. Galian's grandfather had given that gift to his father in the freezing and dark nights in Siberia. His father had read to him too, in this same house in Saralandj.

Most of all, the children and Lara loved *Merelots* days. There were at least five in the Armenian calendar, four falling on Mondays, and the fifth being the big one, held on January 7, the day after Armenian Christmas. No one worked on those days. They first went to the cemetery to pay their respects. The dead are revered in Armenia, often more so than the living. Even though this is supposed to be a sad day—an opportunity to re-mourn the already mourned dead—the Galians did it differently by turning it into a family outing, which, on nice days sometimes turned into a picnic. The cemetery of Saralandj is on top of a steep hill. The kids would start with their traditional race from the bottom of the hill to the top, and Lara would normally win. Up there, they would burn *Khung*, incense, and say prayers for the dead. For Galian, what mattered was keeping the memory of his parents alive. Sometimes he would borrow a tape player from the village and play old duduk music. Their family had a fenced section in the cemetery where Galian's parents and few aunts and uncles were buried. There were stones and crosses for his grandfather and aunt Araxi who had died in Siberia, but no graves. Their remains were lost in Siberia.

The addition of Galian's grave had changed the meaning of *Merelots* forever for his children, who, until his death, had not personally known anyone buried in their family cemetery.

She cried with her mother, often moved as much by her mother's grief as by her own. The sudden disappearance of her father had brought Lara closer to her mother. Her sisters and brothers had also fallen silent. They all had more work to do; the happy playful times of village life had abruptly ended for them all. Everything had happened far too suddenly for Lara to be able to sort through the avalanche of different emotions passing through her. She desperately tried to push aside the feelings of fear and anxiety as she left her whole life behind and climbed into the car. That too was a relatively new experience. She had ridden in a car a few times before, but only in her uncle's old and dilapidated Russian Niva, nothing like the shiny, clean SUV that she was climbing into now. She kept telling herself that this was another chore she had to do, probably not much more difficult than milking the sheep or cleaning the barn. The drive away from the village had not been a drastic life-changing experience.

But as they entered Yerevan, that sense began to give way to the fear and anxiety that she had managed to suppress at first. Almost nothing seemed familiar. The traffic, the street noise and smell, the tall buildings and the general clutter suddenly heralded not only a new world but also the loss of the world she had left behind.

♌ ♌ ♌

Except for two female servants inside and two bodyguards outside, Ayvazian was alone when they dropped off Lara that day. His mansion was impressive, with marble pillars marking the entrance and two statues of lions at each side of the main gate. Inside, more white marble and more pillars.

"Now remember, this man is your new lord and master. You belong to him. You obey him in everything," one of the female servants instructed her sternly as she brought her to him. She was a middle aged, portly woman, better dressed than anyone Lara knew in Saralandj, with short wavy hair that already displayed some gray around the temples. Her eyes seemed warm and stern at the same time, the latter a reflection of a dismissive 'I've seen it all before' attitude exuding impatience.

Lara could not help feeling hopelessly in awe of the opulence surrounding her. How could such places actually exist? Was this one of the palaces of kings that her father used to read to her about?

Ayvazian was seated in the living room in a huge armchair, smoking, and reading the paper. He was in his early fifties, with a bald head, round face and a substantial belly, which seemed in a struggle to break free of the buttons of his tight black shirt.

"*Paron* Ayvazian," the female servant said, "*Oriort* Lara Galian. Mr. Ayvazian. Miss Lara Galian." Then she left the room.

Ayvazian looked at his new possession for a long moment. Meanwhile, Lara observed the maroon velvet sofas, heavy overstuffed chairs, a cupboard full of crystal glasses and bottles, thick drapes at the windows and a white marble table between two of the chairs. And now a heavy man was staring at her.

"*Barev*," he said. Hello.

What a heavy room, thought Lara, and to her surprise, was actually amused for having had that thought. "*Barev*!" she chirped, a bit too enthusiastically, which could easily have been a sign of her nervousness. But despite her nervousness, there was no fear in her voice or posture. She looked and sounded confident, young, innocent. Until her father's death, Lara had not experienced anything bad in life, except their poverty, which, to her, was not bad or good, just normal. Her father's death, traumatic as it was, was not an ongoing "threat" to her. It was a catastrophe that had happened and changed her life forever, but it had ended. She stood there like those species of animals that have never faced a natural predator, and therefore do not have the instinct of defensive measures.

"Sit down," said Ayvazian pointing at a chair near him. "How was your trip?"

"It was fine, sir."

"Are you tired?"

"No sir."

"Are you hungry?

"No sir."

"You must be hungry," said Ayvazian. "Anoush will fix you something."

Anoush must be the servant, thought Lara. "Thank you, sir."

"You know you're starting on an incredible journey, don't you?" said Ayvazian, aware of the fact that he had to break this girl and her innocence. "Are you prepared for it?"

"Yes sir."

But all that Lara could think at that point was how unusual the man looked. His black eyebrows stuck out on his broad forehead above his clean-shaven face, but seemed unusually still even when he spoke. He had a deep voice and spoke in slow, deliberate sentences, with minimal intonation. It was a formal, impersonal style of speech that belied the expressive face and eyes. Unlike his voice, which sounded detached and bored, Ayvazian himself was very much interested in everything, and seemed to observe all.

"I have some work to do now, but I will talk to you again later. Tomorrow you have to go to Moscow. But tonight you will stay here. In a few hours you can call your mother, if you wish."

"Thank you, Paron Ayvazian." Lara decided to try saying his name out loud; that somehow helped her understand the individual better. The man did not look like an 'Ayvazian' to her. Perhaps more like a 'Papazian' given his size and deep voice. But Ayvazian seemed pleased by the sweet mention of his name.

He pushed a button on the side table next to him, and Anoush appeared again at the door. She walked Lara outside, and returned for instructions. After a minute she came out again, and asked Lara to follow her.

Their first stop was a small bedroom with a queen-size bed. There was a small suitcase on the bed, open, with some clothes in it.

"This is your room for tonight," said Anoush, still in a stern, almost military voice. "This is your suitcase. There are pants and shirts, some underwear, and a nightgown for you in there. I think they will fit, at least well enough for now. You can do more shopping in Moscow tomorrow. There are shoes beside the bed that you should try on later. One or two pairs of them should fit you. Now come with me."

Lara had no chance to answer, as Anoush was already leading her out of the room. She had never had a suitcase before. She remembers seeing an old, very large suitcase in their house, all torn and the locks broken, which her mother used as storage. But she did not know what it was or was normally used for. It was just beginning to sink in that things were truly changing for her. She'll have to learn a lot very quickly if she is to survive what's coming her way.

The next stop was a bathroom, adjacent to the bedroom. Anoush led her in, closed the door, and proceeded to draw a bath.

"Take your clothes off," she ordered. "You have to take a bath now."

Lara hesitated. Undressing in front of this stranger was not something she wanted to do. Besides, they bathed once every two weeks or so in Saralandj. There were lighter washings, every day for the girls and every few days for the boys, but taking a full bath was a complicated ceremony. They had to boil water in the large pot over the cow-manure burning stove in their "kitchen". Then they had to mix the hot water in batches with cold water in another, smaller pot until they got the right warmth. They would bathe quickly, sitting on a small wooden stool on the floor, being careful that the water would not run towards their parents' bed at the other end of the room. After shampooing their hair, they would rinse and dry quickly before they caught a cold, and go straight to bed. You could not be out and about after a bath if you did not want to catch a cold. For the girls, washing their hair was the big issue. It took a very long time to wash and rinse, and even longer to dry. The girls needed twice as long to bathe as the boys, and their bath consumed twice as much cow manure for heating the water as the boys'. But here the water was pouring already hot into the bathtub. There was no sign of any fire anywhere, none of that pleasant smell of burning cow manure, or of the even more pleasant crackling sounds of the fire while one bathed. This bath was almost clinical, unceremonious, and astonishing in how far removed it was from her reality. Suddenly, nothing was familiar.

"Take your clothes off!" ordered Anoush again. "We do not have all day."

"I don't need a bath," said Lara, but her voice had already started sounding unsure and hesitant.

"Go on, girl," said Anoush. "I am no different from your mother. Do not be shy. You have to bathe now. Take your clothes off."

The bathtub was filling quickly, and the rising steam was filling the bathroom. Anoush checked the temperature of the water, was satisfied, and turned back to Lara.

"C'mon, c'mon, I said we don't have all day," she snapped, and this time approached Lara to help her undress.

Lara was finally undressed and stepped into the bathtub. The hot water actually felt wonderful. She began to relax a little. Anoush poured water on her head with a small bowl, and started shampooing her hair. Lara first tried to do it herself, but eventually gave in. Anoush then soaped her body, asked her to stand up in the tub and soaped her thighs and buttocks with a loofah, often too fast and rough, turning her skin pink. She had no hesitation going over her private parts, as routinely as she would do her shoulders and back.

But then Anoush stood there watching her as she was drying off. "You are a very attractive young woman," she said, deliberately looking at her. The tone of her voice changed somewhat. "Have you had any boyfriends?"

"Of course not," snapped Lara.

"Have you ever been naughty?" Anoush persisted with a smirk, staring straight at Lara's crotch. "You can tell me, you know, as I said I am just like your mother."

"Of course not!" Lara repeated, now blushing heavily.

"Fine, fine," said Anoush, trying to give a soothing tone to her voice. "Nothing abnormal about any of that stuff, you know." Then, turning her voice a bit more motherly, added. "But tell me, when was your last period?"

"Around ten days ago," said Lara quickly, covering herself with the towel. "Where are my clothes?"

"Here," said Anoush. "Put these on. You have no use for your old clothes any longer." She handed her underwear, a pair of pants and a blouse.

Wanting this whole experience to be over, Lara quickly got dressed without objecting. Anoush handed her a comb. "Comb your hair," she ordered. "Your supper will be ready soon. I'll be back in a little bit."

Finally alone, Lara took a long look in the mirror. How could things be so different only an hour away from home? In the past few hours she had seen so many things that she had never seen before in her life. She now was in a world so far away, so different from where she was only a few hours ago, that it was difficult to feel any connection, any continuity between where she came from and where she was now. It suddenly struck her that perhaps the hint of fear that she was feeling had nothing to do with the awe of the extravagance surrounding her, but was coming from a sense of not knowing her way around this place. The foreignness itself was troubling and scary. Until this moment, Lara had had almost full knowledge of her surroundings; her house, garden, every sheep and every plant in their garden, every utensil in their kitchen. And now, she knew nothing. *How did I get here?* she wondered. Is this what her mother had meant when she had said, 'Remember where you're from'?

Supper was superb. Roasted chicken, grilled potatoes, salads. Lara had never eaten like this at home, even during celebrations, like at her cousin's wedding. Anoush was still somewhat stern during supper, but in a strange way Lara started to like her. She was now the stern mother figure, rather than the stern stranger ordering her around. She sat with her and watched while she ate, tending to her, offering to help with the fork and knife. She acted concerned for Lara's well being. She even asked her about her family, her sisters and brothers, but did not dwell much on her parents. Lara found herself opening up to her, telling stories about her village and the adventures she had there with her brothers.

Back in her room, bathed and fed, Lara was feeling hopeful and excited, even though the anxiety of unfamiliar surroundings lingered. She lay on her bed in her new clothes, and her mind kept jumping back and forth between Saralandj and the present. Suddenly she felt a sharp sting of guilt about the meal she had just enjoyed; she was so taken by her new surroundings that she had not thought of her family. She took out Araxi Dadik's wedding ring, held it and rubbed her thumb around it slowly. She was deeply moved by what her mother had said about her father wanting her to have it and about her being his strongest link to his past. Now the ring had become her strongest link to *her* past, to her lost father and to the legendary Araxi Dadik. It was one thing to hear stories about someone she had never seen, and another altogether to hold in her hands something very personal that belonged to her.

Then Anoush appeared at her door with a phone. "Your mother is on the line," she said with a smile.

"Mama, Mama jan," screamed Lara. "*Barev*. This place is incredible! How is everything at home?"

"All is well, my girl," came her mother's somber voice. "Are you okay? Is everything fine with you?"

"Mama, yes! Please do not worry. All is well here. I think everything will work out fine, for all of us. Mama jan, please do not worry about me. I am serious. Did you have enough to eat this evening?"

Her mother was surprised by the last question, but she ignored it. "Okay, child," she said to Lara's pleas asking her not to worry, but there was a nagging doubt in her voice. What would a sixteen-year-old know, especially so soon after leaving home? "Remember everything that I told you, Lara. Don't ever forget what I told you last night."

"No, Mama jan, I'll never forget. I thought about your words many times today. You are very wise, Mama jan. Very wise. I love you."

"Lara, listen, whatever happens, always keep your head together, no matter what. You will feel confused sometimes, and you will be overwhelmed with new experiences, but never lose your head, child. Remember what I am telling you, never, ever, lose your head...that's all you have!" *At least that is all that will ever be on your side,* she thought, but did not say out loud.

"Yes, Mama jan, yes. I promise, I won't lose my head. I also promise to remember where I came from and who I am!"

That last sentence brought tears to her mother's eyes. Her little girl remembered. She has been listening. She is not only beautiful, but also smart. *Oh, Lara,* she thought, *would you have been better off if you did not have the looks of your Araxi Dadik, who was miserable her whole life? Are good looks a curse in our family? I hope not, Lara my child, I really hope not…*

Lara's mother wiped the tears flowing down her cheek, and Lara could hear the anguish in her voice.

"Please don't cry, Mama, please don't cry…" she pleaded. "All will be well, I promise."

Anoush had been listening outside the bedroom door. That should put the mother's mind at ease for a while, she thought. They could not have her asking questions about her daughter's whereabouts, or go talking to the police. They would not have Lara call for a while, at least until she was wise enough not to tell her mother what was really going on. Anoush walked back into Lara's room and said it was time to end the call. "You have to go to bed now," she said. "You have to travel tomorrow. Viktor will be here in the morning to take you to the airport. Now put on the nightgown I gave you and go to bed. I'll come and wake you up in the morning. Good night."

The connection with home ended as abruptly as it had started. She changed into the white cotton nightgown that Anoush had given her and went to bed. She was happy. Happy that she had a chance to tell her mother that all was fine, that she was okay. She felt entranced with her surroundings and settled even with Anoush. She would have to learn to trust her. That was her world now. Paron Ayvazian, Anoush and Viktor, whom she remembered from the brief encounter as he was leaving their house in Saralandj. This was her new world. Don't worry, Mama jan, she thought while she lay in bed staring at the ceiling, still rubbing the ring. I'll be fine. And I'll never forget…

Anoush's report to Ayvazian was short and to the point. "She is clueless," she said, "and be careful, she could be fertile." That was all—the ultimate executive summary.

Lara was still lying in bed and staring at the ceiling when Ayvazian barged in. She saw him standing up for the first time. He was a big man, with a huge belly protruding from his torso almost as if it did not belong there. Before she could even figure out what was happening, he had shut the door behind him and was on her bed. The stench of cigarettes on his breath was overpowering. He grabbed her hair, brought her face to his, and kissed her roughly on the mouth. Then his hands were all over her, on her breasts, and down her buttocks to her crotch. Lara was almost paralyzed by shock. When she recovered her senses a bit she fought him with all her might, but could not fend off the overwhelming physical power of her attacker. The first time she tried to scream brought such a vicious slap on her face that she thought she was going to faint. She forgot about screaming. Ayvazian pushed her hands behind her head, and ordered her to keep them there.

"Do not move your hands!" he ordered. Then he yanked the nightgown up to her neck and attacked her breasts. "Do not move!" Lara froze. Off came her panties, and Ayvazian leaned back for a moment to savor the moment. Lara's hands were sliding down to cover her sex, but he roared again, "I said don't move!" and his powerful hands again forced her hands to the back of her head. "Do not move or I'll tie you up!" he barked again as he ran his fingers down her thighs, then back up to her crotch, feeling her.

He then left the bed to undress. He took his time, not letting his eyes off Lara for a moment, who lay there shaking, her eyes shut tight, her hands firmly placed under the back of her head and grabbing a lock of her hair for dear life, her right leg thrown over the left in a desperate attempt to hide her nudity.

He took off his pants and underwear and approached her slowly. Her fear, her tightly closed eyes and trembling body aroused him. "Today is the first day of the rest of your life," he said jerking her legs apart, as if these were the most original words of wisdom he could impart to the young girl. "And I will show you what the rest of your life will be like!" He then penetrated her with such force that Lara thought this was it—this was how the end would come. The pain was like nothing she had ever experienced in her life.

Anoush walked into her room around ten minutes after Ayvazian had left. Lara was bundled up under the sheets, sobbing. She pulled the sheets away, but Lara did not move. The sheets were bloody and there was blood smeared on the inside of her thighs. Anoush tried to comfort her; they could not have her so traumatized that she totally withdrew into herself.

"Sooner or later you had to go through that," she said. "That is how men are. The pain will pass. And soon you'll even learn to enjoy all that, I promise you," Anoush said.

But Lara would not speak. She had stopped crying. Her face was so blank and expressionless that it gave Anoush a chill. This was not the first time Anoush had to clean up after Ayvazian, but she had not seen this reaction before. The girls usually *wanted* a shoulder to cry on. They clung to her, seeking a measure of comfort, an explanation. But Lara had withdrawn into herself and would not come out.

"C'mon, child," said Anoush finally. "We have to get you cleaned up. You cannot sleep like this. I'll let you bathe alone this time while I change these sheets. You still have to rest, and you still have to travel to Moscow in the morning. Nothing has changed."

All Lara felt was an overwhelming desire to be back home in Saralandj; to leave all of this here and go back to her village. What had happened here was so foreign to her that it didn't fit anywhere in her conscious world. This was an entirely unrelated digression, an entirely uncalled for departure from her life, and therefore not part of it yet; it was as if the actors in a play had made a major error mixing up different scripts, and she just had to return to her own original play. Yet, she found herself going through the motions as instructed, but first fetched the ring from within the crumpled sheets before allowing herself to be led to the bathroom. The ice-cold expression stayed. The silence continued. But she did what she was told. This time, it was extremely painful to sit in the bathtub. It felt like her insides were on fire. But she washed, dried, and put on a new set of pajamas provided by Anoush. She then went to bed.

The next morning Viktor came with two bodyguards, and they drove to the airport. Anoush gave one of the bodyguards Lara's suitcase. Lara had combed her hair back and tied it into a ponytail. She was visibly in pain while she walked, but her face was like a rock, and she did not speak.

IV

The apartment in Moscow was much smaller than the mansion in Yerevan. It had three small bedrooms, a small living room, a kitchen, and two full baths. The furniture was far more modest and unpretentious also— old dirty sofas and chairs in the living room with worn out armrests and dirty and faded brown wall to wall carpets, darker around the edges by the walls than in the middle section, which looked like it had been walked on for decades.

They put Lara in one of the bedrooms. This place had a housekeeper also, about Anoush's age, with the same no-nonsense temperament. She took charge of Lara and showed her around. Under no circumstances was Lara to leave the apartment without one of the men. She was not to open any windows or curtains. She could eat whenever she was hungry, but had to clean up the kitchen. If she needed anything she was to tell Nono, the housekeeper. She was not to touch the telephone, even if it rang.

Having finished the instructions, Nono left Lara alone. She sat on her bed, her chin resting on her folded knees, still stunned by what had happened the night before. Was it really all because of her looks? Did all the girls who were considered good looking have to go through such pain? There was a small round mirror on the wall, with an ornate but cheap plastic yellow frame. She left the bed and stood in front of the mirror for a long time, staring at her face. She could not find the answer there, the answer to why this was happening to her, the answer to what Ayvazian had done, to her being here, to her captivity.

That night she ate for the first time in twenty-four hours. She had refused breakfast and lunch, but when the apartment was empty for about an hour that evening, she went into the kitchen and had a piece of bread with some cheese and slices of sausage.

It was around midnight when Viktor walked into her room.

"I will not beat around the bush," he said. "We need you to grow up and grow up real fast. This is what you will do for the rest of your life. You will please men sexually. That is all. You do not have to like it or enjoy it, but you will do it and you will do it as if you like it. You will make the men feel welcome. You will pretend to enjoy it. You will not act miserable while pleasing a man. Do you understand?"

Lara stared at him for a moment, but kept quiet. She had been lying on top of the bed covers in her clothes when Viktor walked in, but was now sitting up at the edge of the bed, with Viktor standing very close to her. It was awkward for Lara; she did not want to look up at his face, but when she lowered her eyes her face was two inches from his waist, which she did not want either. She tried to move away from him and stand up, but Viktor put his hands on her shoulders and pinned her down.

"Fine," he said. "If you don't want to talk, you don't have to. But you *will* open your mouth when I tell you to. Tonight you will learn about the finer pleasures of oral sex."

Viktor appeared to Lara as a surreal being, with no connection to the reality of that moment. Her defenses had somehow isolated the voice from the man. She did not see his lips move as he spoke; his voice seemed to be coming from his face, as if from a radio. Then the source of the voice moved toward her, and grabbed her hair, and she turned everything off.

Lara endured the most horrifying indignities that night. She was forced into oral sex and raped twice, once by Viktor and once by one of the bodyguards. When they finally were done with her, Nono took charge of her to make sure that she did not do anything desperate. A bath, some water, and to bed.

But Lara's attitude had started to worry Viktor. She had not resisted, but had remained totally and absolutely passive. The only reaction that appeared on her face while they were abusing her was caused by the sharp pain in her sore genitals. Otherwise, she let them do everything they wanted with a totally blank expression. This would not go well in the trade. She could not act the role by remaining passive. She had to learn to play the role of seductress. She had to learn to enjoy being *naughty*—that was a huge turn-on for men. But Lara seemed like she had no notion of how to *be* naughty, let alone act as if she enjoyed it. There was no way for them to force that on her. She had to buy into it on her own. They decided to leave her alone for a day. Nono would monitor her carefully.

The third day in Moscow they brought another young woman to the apartment and introduced her as Anastasia. Anastasia was from the Ukraine, in her mid-twenties, and had been working as a prostitute in Moscow for the Ayvazians for around four years. She had short blond hair, with bangs reaching her eyebrows, an attractive body that was thin and small, but with slightly pronounced chest and behind, and seductive, fashionable clothes. She too had entered the profession under false pretenses. But she had been older and took to her new environment much more easily. In a few weeks, prostitution felt so natural to her that she did not even remember what she had been like before.

Anastasia was brought in to help Lara accept her new life. So the men left Lara alone another day and night. She needed to recuperate, both physically and emotionally, and, in doing so, she had to accept her new life. Anastasia took her out and talked almost non-stop. Lara's silence did not seem to bother her. She took her first to her own apartment, a small studio in one of the poorer sections of Moscow, and explained that place was entirely hers. She paid the rent herself.

She worked on her own, but for Viktor. She still had debts to Viktor, she explained, which she was paying off every day. Once the debts were covered, she said, she would be entirely on her own, and would have young girls working for her. "Yes," she said, "don't look so surprised. We can do what these men do better than them. We can run our own business and be bosses just like them, even better than them. How can they know our business better than we do?"

They were talking mostly in Russian, with some Armenian thrown in here and there. Having worked with the Ayvazians for several years,

Anastasia had learned a few rudimentary Armenian words and phrases, about as much Russian as Lara knew. They talked about birth control and Anastasia was amazed to hear that Lara was not on the pill.

"Did they use any protection?" she asked.

Lara was not sure.

"Did they use condoms?" she asked, hoping that Lara would understand what she was asking. But Lara did not. Anastasia then opened her purse and took out a condom, tore open the package and rolled it out.

"You see this?" she asked, losing her patience. "Did you see them use this? Did you see them put this on themselves before entering you?"

Lara hesitated again. "I think Viktor's bodyguard did. But I'm not sure about Viktor. I have no idea about Ayvazian." Lara was feeling guilty that the whole thing might have been her fault.

So Anastasia started from the beginning, patiently giving her a lecture, almost like a mother would do. Seeing Lara's worried looks, she decided to turn the situation into more fun, and taught Lara how to use make up, how to approach men, what men were really all about, and how to make the most of a sexual situation and take care for her own body.

"Look," she said, "they will fuck you and abuse you everyday anyway, whether you like it or not. You might as well get paid for it, no? It is not going to stop, I assure you. In fact, unless you learn to cope with it now, it will only get worse for you. Much worse. There will be new men every day. Some terrible, some nicer, but still bad. Let me tell you that some will smell so bad you'll hold your breath longer than you ever thought possible. Some will force you to do things that you never could even imagine. There will be indignities. It is not you who decides these things. They will just happen. So what do you want to do? Just let it happen and act sore, or let it happen and benefit?"

"But why should we let it happen at all?" asked Lara. "Why *should* it happen in the first place?"

"Because we are women and they are men, and they need sex, and thank God for that! We can give them something they need. Very simple. There is no deep philosophy here, Lara, so stop being so serious. You are young, beautiful, and extremely desirable. If you do not mess this up you can be big, very big, and you can own an empire! I am not kidding."

"I'll write off a third of your debt if you bring her around in two days," Viktor had told Anastasia. That was incentive enough for her, even though she actually believed what she was telling Lara.

Then they had gone shopping, and Anastasia had introduced Lara to the special wardrobe of her new profession. She showed Lara heels, miniskirts, low-cut shirts, lingerie, all with an unending energy and enthusiasm, and non-stop chatter and laughter. "You know," she told Lara as she was trying on a new blouse in one of the discount stores, "you remind me of my baby sister. To tell the truth, she's the only one in my family that I liked, and the only one that I miss."

That may have been the right time for Lara to open up a bit also, but she found herself resisting getting close to Anastasia. Anastasia could be contagious; her laughter, her smile, her apparent happiness, the lightness with which she seemed to accept her reality, all were potentially tempting. But at the same time, they disturbed Lara deeply. She missed home so much that it caused her physical pain. She longed to be held by her father, to hug her mother, to be in their kitchen and feel the warmth and smell the familiar scents. She did not want to be tempted into adopting Anastasia's attitude, no matter how comfortable it looked. This was Lara's inner struggle. *I want the happiness I left behind, not yours*, she thought as she stared past Anastasia's radiant face.

Anastasia was developing a liking for Lara. She loved her looks, her innocence, her gradual, cautious but stubborn struggle against her new circumstances. Anastasia had not made any real friends in the profession, and she needed one, one that depended on her and that she could nurture. Lara was perfect. In the early years working in Moscow under Viktor she was so scared of him that she sometimes froze in his presence. He had slapped her around a few times, until she understood how to handle him. Now she practically managed herself, with no interference from Viktor as long as she made regular payments to him. She called Viktor and told him that he should leave Lara with her that night. "Just leave her with me," she said. "We will soon reach a turning point."

❧ ❧ ❧

Ayvazian arrived in Moscow the next evening and met with his team. They had their business apartment in Moscow a few blocks from the building where Lara had been dropped off.

"What's the play on the Galian girl?" he asked.

"I think once we get all her papers in order we should send her to Dubai," said Viktor. "Ano can run her there. Or maybe we can sell her contract to Ano up front."

Ano was one of the pimps who worked for them in Dubai. She managed about twenty-five prostitutes there, who were mostly from Armenia but included a few Russians and Ukrainians.

"Ano cannot afford her contract, even for a year, and we can't get her full value in Dubai," said Ayvazian. "She's a cut above Dubai for sure."

"But she is only sixteen," said Viktor. "Dubai would be a great initiation for her. We'll bring her to the higher market in Moscow in a year or two. She is not ready for Moscow."

"What is she going to make in Dubai?" asked Ayvazian, a bit annoyed at his nephew. "$400 a night? $600 tops? Don't you think that would be a waste of this sixteen-year-old beauty?"

"Of course, uncle, of course. But only a few days ago she was milking sheep in Saralandj! We cannot take a chance by bringing her into the high street Moscow scene right now; she just doesn't have the style. She needs to develop and get into it properly. Anastasia is a great initiator, but she needs firsthand experience."

"Why not Turkey?" asked Ayvazian.

"I think Turkey would be too rough on her. Let her go experience the Dubai scene first, you know, the Iranians, Pakistanis and Arabs for a year. Let her turn seventeen, and then we'll do the big cash out. "

"Unless of course we can sell her contract now in Moscow for a fortune, as an un-initiated virgin prize," said Ayvazian.

"If we can, great," said Viktor. "But this is not the right market for it. Even that type of sale is more likely with an Arab Shaikh than here in Moscow. I agree that Ano cannot afford her, but some local big shot could."

And, of course, Lara was no longer a virgin, but Viktor did not want to bring that up and upset his uncle. Someone like Lara, while still a virgin, would command the highest price of all. But Ayvazian had insisted on having that prize himself.

"How long before the papers can be finalized?" asked Ayvazian, giving the first clear indication that he was beginning to concede to his nephew. He was sitting in his usual large armchair by the window and as he lit a new cigarette, he sensed a slight hesitation in Viktor.

"Here's the problem," said Viktor, becoming aware of his voice quality again, wanting it to come out as measured and convincing. "There is no way we can make it believable that she is thirty-one. The UAE government will no longer issue visas to any woman under thirty-one unless she is accompanied by a husband or a father. And even they cannot turn a blind eye when they see Lara holding a passport showing she's thirty-one. No way."

"So what's the solution?"

"I'll have to marry her."

Ayvazian burst out laughing, his faith in his nephew somewhat restored.

"Marry her?" he roared amid bursts of laughter. "Marry her? Aren't you already married? And who will believe that you married a sixteen-year-old?"

"First," replied Viktor, "remember that Viktor *Ayvazian* is married, but Viktor *Arakelyan* is not. Second, we will get Lara a passport that shows she is twenty-one. That we can sell; she's tall enough, and with the right clothing and makeup, we can make her pass for that age. But thirty-one, we cannot."

A year earlier Viktor had been deported from Dubai. His legal violations were far too many, but in the end that was not the real problem. The problem was that he had violated the ultimate unwritten law, namely, offending the system itself by his carelessness and reckless behavior. He had flouted his girls publically far too often, argued with their key protectors in Dubai and once even refused to make payments to them on time. His deportation orders had come suddenly and were executed even more hurriedly. He was physically forced to leave Dubai within an hour of the order. He had left everything behind, in the able hands of Madame Ano, and vowed to return.

Ayvazian had been furious. How could this young reckless adventurer be allowed to jeopardize everything that he had painstakingly built in Dubai over the past several years? He disciplined his nephew very harshly. He made him pay all that was due to the bosses in Dubai from his own pocket, plus he penalized him heftily for the indiscretion, by taking the Moscow portfolio from his control. That was a heavy blow indeed, but Viktor accepted it and vowed to regain it within the year.

In two months Viktor had a new passport with a new last name. He made his first trip with the new passport to Dubai soon thereafter. He zoomed through the airport passport control and customs without any problems, but once in Dubai, it became known to all that Viktor was back. The authorities turned a blind eye, considering that the young man had already paid his dues before arriving. It is always easier to forgive indiscretions if the debts are paid—at least for the men in the system. With women, it was different, as always.

In the end Ayvazian agreed to the plan. Lara would go to Dubai for a year and be handed over for Ano to manage, while they looked for a good opportunity to sell her to a local dignitary for a year or two. After that, Lara would have to return and join the big leagues in Moscow. One year in Dubai would generate between sixty and seventy thousand dollars. Someone of Lara's caliber could average that much in two or three months in Moscow, if she was ready. *"If she is ready,"* repeated Ayvazian, putting the entire burden on Viktor.

ℒ ℒ ℒ

It took two weeks to get her a fake passport, according to which she was Lara Galianova, a Russian citizen, born in 1983, twenty-one years old. In another week they had secured the marriage certificate. They did not tell Lara that she would be officially married to Viktor, until the papers arrived.

"Congratulations," Viktor said to her. "You are now officially Mrs. Viktor Arakelyan," even though they had not changed her last name in her documents.

Given everything else that had happened, Viktor's announcement of her new marital status did not shock Lara. Nor was she surprised by her total lack of emotion regarding the news. Back in her village, marriage would be the single most significant event in a girl's life. Birth, marriage and death—those are the key milestones of the cycle of life. Even children, which change the whole rhythm of life drastically, were considered a consequence, not a main event. And here was Lara staring at a piece of paper showing that she was married, as if it was an old document with no relevance to her whatsoever.

Lara spent most of the time in those weeks with Anastasia. She rarely went back to the Ayvazian's apartment in Moscow, preferring to spend the nights in Anastasia's tiny apartment. Viktor's men were never absent and made sure that both girls were constantly aware that they were being watched. In the first few days Lara had thought of escape several times. She thought of getting her hands on a cell phone and calling home. But she had no idea of how to go about any of this. She had no number to call, even if she could steal or borrow Anastasia's phone. And then the scariest thought of all occurred to her: even if she managed to get in touch with her family, what would she tell them? What would she tell her mother? What would she tell Avo? How could she possibly tell them what had happened to her?

With Anastasia's help and encouragement, she eventually got into the nightly scene of the prostitutes, and had her very first paying customer. Viktor was following all this from a distance, but let Anastasia handle her. The customer was an American businessman. Anastasia negotiated $200 for an hour with Lara. That was more than the going rate for the older prostitutes, but Lara was clearly different. The American was taken by her youthful beauty and freshness. She had provocative clothes, but very light and understated make-up. It was not obvious from her appearance that she was a professional; she looked more like a loose teenager out for mischief. She was quiet, unrushed, and almost passive in her calm, and the middle-aged American found that attractive. They went to his hotel, Anastasia in tow like a protective mother taking her daughter to school for the first time, and waited downstairs in the lobby. "See you in an hour, dear," she said in Armenian. "And remember to take the money first."

Lara surveyed the room quickly, and waited for the American to make the first move. The room was impressive and imposing. It had a king-size bed that looked enormous to Lara. There were six pillows, lined up in two rows of three against the headboard, and two smaller cushions in front of them; she wondered what they were for. There were also cushions on the couch and two more on the chairs in the other corner of the room. That's over a dozen pillows, she thought, more than they had in their house in Saralandj where ten people used to sleep. She remembered how her mother would fold old jackets and rags to use as a pillow one winter when they had to sell the wool stuffed in some of their pillows.

The American approached her and gave her a gentle kiss on the forehead. He then produced two green bills from his wallet and handed them to Lara. Anastasia had shown Lara various currencies and explained the value of each; dollars, Russian rubles, even Japanese yen, so she would know the amount was right. She put the money in a small purse, which contained Araxi Dadik's ring. She rubbed the ring with her thumb for a second before the American took her hand and led her towards the bed.

Until then, Lara's only sexual experiences had been rapes. But now she was here voluntarily, if one could call it that considering how she had ended up in this situation in the first place. But still, at that moment, no one had physically forced her to be in that room and to undress for that man. She was doing it herself, mechanically, calmly. That thought both scared and pleased Lara. I am actually doing this, she thought. Have I let them win, then? Or have I done the only logical thing? Will I still win in the end? Forgive me, Mama jan, she thought, as she got into bed with nothing on except the skimpy underwear that Anastasia had bought for her. For Lara, none of the rapes of the past few days were as dramatic as this moment. The total inevitability of the moment was lost to her. Short of committing suicide and ending it all, she really had little choice about being here and acting the way she was acting. She was simply too entangled in the moment to understand that.

But in a strange and paradoxical way, she began to feel that she would have to take control of this side of her life from now on. "This is going to happen regardless," Anoush, Nono and Anastasia had constantly told her. This was like a force of nature and, back home, she had learned very early in life that one did not fight nature. Neither fear nor anger had any useful purpose in Saralandj, where one went along with nature in order to survive. Even morality and honor, which were very big in Saralandj and even bigger in her home, had no useful purpose in nature. Nature was amoral. When a calf was stillborn or the wolves slaughtered a few sheep, there was no point in blaming and even less in judging. You controlled as much as you could, such as feeding your livestock in the spring and summer, preserving as much food for winter as you could, planting as much as possible and harvesting in the fall. But when winter came, you withdrew indoors and survived with what you had. You *managed* nature. You *never* fought it, and you could never judge it either.

And now, Lara thought, I face another force of nature that I need to manage; that really is all there is to it. *In the beginning was neither the word nor action, nor darkness nor light, nor spirits floating over waters,* she thought. *In the beginning was innocence. Then someone said let there be reality. And there was reality.* For Lara, there was nothing in between.

The American was incredibly nice, or so it seemed to Lara. He was gentle to such an extent that Lara thought nothing was going to happen. But it did happen. And it happened gently. She was surprised. Sex was not pure violence, after all. There was no pain. Granted, not much pleasure either, but at least there was no pain. And there were no insults, no forced indignities. The American put on a condom, just like the one Anastasia had shown her. She watched him with detached curiosity as he discarded it afterwards. She found herself doing everything as if it was meant to be, almost as if she wanted to. But she did not know what she wanted, except that she had to manage this new force of nature.

She did not realize that an hour had passed, until Anastasia called. The American answered and handed the phone to Lara. "What is going on?" she asked Lara in Armenian. "Are you okay, dear?"

Anastasia was anxious to take Lara and leave. She had been sitting in the hotel lobby the whole time, and had to turn down a couple of solicitors, not to mention the unpleasant argument that she had with the concierge, who told her she could not sit in the main lobby and had to go to the lobby bar, and even at the bar they would not let her sit at one of the sofas nor at a table, but made her take the corner barstool.

"Anastasia, I'm fine," said Lara. "But he is talking to me in English and I don't understand what he wants."

Anastasia was happy that there was no stress in her voice. "Give the phone back to him," she said. She had had several American and British clients in the past few years and knew enough English to get by.

"I love this girl," said the American on the phone. "I want her to spend the night with me."

Anastasia was on full alert. Could she turn this into something much bigger with Viktor? Could she negotiate away half, not just a third, of her debt?

"All night with her very expensive," she said slowly. "How much you pay?"

The maximum that Anastasia herself had ever charged for a whole night was $750. But she was prepared to sell Lara for more than double that amount.

"Name your price," said the American.

"Two thousand," said Anastasia without hesitation. "Cash. Now."

"Okay," said the American. "Come up and collect."

He had already counted the money when Anastasia knocked on the door. Twenty one-hundred dollar bills. He did not seem to be bothered by the fact that he had already paid two-hundred dollars.

"Two thousand," he said, handing her the wad of cash. "But do not bother us until noon tomorrow. Now, please leave."

"Fine, I leave," said Anastasia in hesitant, broken English, "but I talk to her first."

"Make it quick," said the American, and disappeared into the bathroom.

"Lara, *aziz jan, vonts es?* Lara, dear, how are you?" asked Anastasia. "Is everything okay?" Anastasia's Armenian accent, especially when she used colloquial phrases, amused Lara.

"*Ha, normal.* Yes, all is normal." Lara's voice and tone were bland but matter-of-fact and in control.

It was almost scary, but also comforting for Anastasia. It did not seem that she needed to worry about the young girl tonight. "He wants you to stay here all night," said Anastasia. "I agreed. It is a lot of money. Are you okay with that?"

"Stay here all night?" asked Lara.

"Yes. Just stay with him, hold him and go to sleep. He'll probably do it one more time in the morning. That's all. I'll come pick you up around noon.

"Okay," said Lara. She had the same unfamiliar feeling of empowerment that she had felt at the beginning of the evening.

Anastasia decided against disclosing to Viktor the full price that she got for Lara, which was extremely risky. She had never lied to the Ayvazians about money before, but this was a special case. Aside from wanting to keep a part of the money for her and Lara, she did not want this experience to cause exaggerated expectations. That prospect scared her the most. She knew she would always have to live up to this performance, but what if this was just a fluke, the result of a stupid infatuation on the part of the American? She told Viktor she got $1,200 for Lara for one night, and gave him the money. That was still a very good price for an all-nighter. She kept $500 for herself, and gave Lara $300 in addition to the $200 that she had received from the American, but told her she would keep Lara's share with her, because for sure someone would go through her purse in the coming days. They could never explain that type of money. This was a fortune for all involved.

Anastasia thus got her first taste of running a girl rather than working herself. She found it incredible and highly addictive. She imagined having twenty or thirty girls who would work for her, like Ano, the famous pimp in Dubai, was rumored to have. The income could be thousands and thousands every day. By the pure coincidence of a lucky first trick, Anastasia had stumbled into the world of pimps and managers. But it was not that simple. She would first have to buy the girls from the traffickers or other bosses. If Lara could turn two thousand dollars in one night, what would her contract be worth? Even if she averaged just a thousand a night—that's over three hundred grand a year, even allowing for off days—what would her contract be worth? If she had the money, would she pay fifty thousand for the contract and hope to more than quadruple it within the year? Anastasia thought, yes, she certainly would.

♌ ♌ ♌

Already over two months had passed since Lara was brought to Moscow. All paperwork was complete—passport, marriage certificate, and visa. It was time to organize the move to Dubai, but Lara was already performing very well in Moscow. With Anastasia's help, she was averaging close to a thousand dollars a day. Viktor was taking everything they declared in those days, and paying Lara a $300 a month salary. He sometimes had suspicions that Anastasia was not giving him all the earnings, but was happy with the overall take and decided not to dig deeper for the time being. Besides, in spite of Lara's success in Moscow, the plan to take her to Dubai was still very much in effect and Anastasia would no longer be able to interfere in her business. She had been instrumental in bringing Lara around, but her usefulness would diminish over time. But there still were a few more details to sort out before Lara could leave. Inoculations and a routine medical checkup were at the top of the list, and Viktor was not rushing. It was the end of August, and Dubai would be smoldering in fifty degrees centigrade heat. The most lucrative client base of expatriates would not arrive for at least another month. So he took his time and enjoyed the money while they waited.

Meanwhile, Viktor had arranged for Lara to start sending some of her money to her mother. They had to keep the mother content, and they had not allowed Lara to talk to her again. They were still not sure how she would behave on the phone. The first phone conversation and the regular money flow would have to be enough to keep the mother at bay. "Never send more than Viktor gives you," warned Anastasia. "They will find out and ask where you got the money from! You cannot be too careful with them."

Anastasia had been insisting that they take Lara for a medical checkup. Viktor did not seem to be concerned about that and had dismissed the requests as a waste of time. They had taken her to see their regular doctor, Dr. Melikov, who took care of all their girls in Moscow, around ten days after they brought her to Moscow. He had done a quick routine exam, and dismissed her. That was good enough for Viktor until there was a real complaint, and Lara had none. But Anastasia kept insisting.

"Take her to Melikov for a full checkup," she kept saying almost every time she saw Viktor. "What do you have to lose? He only did a superficial examination last time. Let him do a thorough checkup and run some tests. She's been with too many men already. And she *really* should be on the pill; he should at least prescribe that!"

Viktor finally agreed. One of the bodyguards drove her to Melikov's office. He deliberately did not tell Anastasia, who was with a client at the time and would not have been able to go with her anyway. Lara had seen Melikov over two months earlier and knew the routine, even though being examined by a male gynecologist had shocked her at first. This time, after the same routine exams, Melikov drew some blood and asked Lara for a urine sample. Then he left her. She waited in the examination room for what seemed a long time. When he returned, he was smiling gently.

"We need to run some more tests just to make sure all is okay." He said with a grin. "We'll have to move you to a different room. Keep the hospital gown on; don't worry about your clothes. The nurse will bring them to you soon."

"Is there a problem?" asked Lara.

"No problem at all. Just another check."

"Where do we have to go?" Lara was not comfortable leaving the examination room in the hospital gown.

"Just a few doors down the hall, on this same floor. The nurse will accompany you. You can walk or go in the wheelchair if you want."

Lara was not comfortable walking in the hallway in the gown, so she opted for the wheelchair.

"Don't let her suspect a thing," Viktor had told Melikov when he called to tell him that Lara was two-and-a-half months pregnant. "Put her under and abort."

"Right now?"

"Right now. Do you have a problem with that?"

"No, no problem," said Melikov. "But she will find out when she wakes up, and she will have some pain."

"I don't care what she finds out once it's all over," said Viktor. "I just don't want her to freak out now. When will she be able to return to work?"

"Normally two weeks, otherwise you run the risk of infections."

"Can't you do anything to shorten that to a few days?"

"I'm not sure about a few days. But if she has any bleeding I'll stuff her with a special sponge. That way she can start in five to six days. But she needs to come see me regularly. It is risky."

"Five days," said Viktor. "Do what you have to do to get her back to work in five days."

"I'll try," said Melikov hesitantly, "as long as there are no complications during the procedure."

"Good. Make sure there aren't any complications."

Settled in another examination bed in the new room, Lara was beginning to get a bit restless as one nurse placed her feet in the stirrups, and another approached her with a hypodermic needle. Before she could ask a lot of questions, the nurse told her that she had to administer some intravenous antibiotic medicine, because they had detected a slight infection. They did not want to take the time to set up an IV. They would give her a shot of morphine directly.

"You're very lucky we caught it now," she said. "This could get pretty nasty if not treated early."

The nurse moved fast, found her vein, and shot the injection. Lara stared at the brown liquid in the syringe as it was emptied into her vein, and then the lights went out.

ᘏ ᘏ ᘏ

She woke up gradually. First, she could detect a faint light in the room, but no sound and no feeling in her body. Then slowly the light became brighter, and she felt nauseated. The large, rectangular light fixture on the ceiling was blinding her and she had to shut her eyes. Then came a pain, in stages, just like the light; it started in her abdomen as a sharp pinch and quickly grew sharper and stronger. A headache spread from the center of her brain to her forehead and she felt a strong buzzing sound in her ears. When she tried to sit up, the abdominal pain forced her right back to a horizontal position. She then let out a scream, which surprised her more than anyone else.

A few hours later they released her. They assured her that all was well, and she'd feel perfectly normal in a few days. The nurses were much less attentive now, almost rude. They insisted that she leave. As she was wheeled out to the lobby of the clinic, she saw Anastasia waiting. That was when she burst out crying.

Viktor had called Anastasia and asked her to take Lara to her place for the night. He had also told her about the abortion, and that Anastasia had to explain to her what had happened. He hung up before Anastasia could get one word in.

They took a taxi back to Anastasia's place. Anastasia just held her. They did not speak in the car. Lara was clearly in pain, but her ice-cold mask of a face had returned, the face that Anastasia had encountered when she first met her.

"I could have dreamt of anything," said Lara later, wrapped in a blanket and sitting in Anastasia's old sofa, legs uncomfortably folded under her. "Anything. My village, my mother, my father, my sisters and brothers. I could even have dreamt of that horrible first night with Ayvazian. I could have dreamt of our sheep and the Saralandj forest. But I didn't; instead, I dreamt of blood. I saw blood in that room. It was terrible, and very strange. It was blood in a small bucket. But not totally liquid. It looked lumpy, as if it was clotted.

Anastasia did not have the heart to tell her that what she had seen was not a dream; that in a semi-awake moment she had actually seen the physical result of her abortion. But she had been too groggy to realize, and had probably gone right back to sleep. In some Moscow clinics they kept the bloody evidence in the room and even showed it to the patient, to make them understand what their actions entailed. But in this case they had not done that. The evidence had been removed by the time Lara came about.

Later that night Anastasia told Lara what had actually happened in Melikov's clinic. This was another opportunity for some long-overdue lessons to be delivered. Anastasia explained that she now had to take a pill every day.

Lara listened with the same ice-cold expression, and after a long silence asked, "Why didn't they tell me that I was pregnant?"

"Viktor's orders," answered Anastasia.

"It was Viktor who told them to abort?"

"Who else?"

"And they lied to me, just like that. They said I had an infection. They took me in, put me under, and lied to me."

"Look, Lara, I won't say that what they did was right, but frankly, what else would you have done if you had known the truth? Could you have a child now?"

"That's not the point," said Lara, and withdrew back into her silence.

Anastasia decided to remain quiet for a while. Lara seemed to be sorting things out in her mind.

After another very long silence, Lara asked, "How can you work with people who abuse you so much?"

It seemed to Anastasia that Lara might finally be ready to open up to her. At least she sensed her need to talk, which she regarded as another milestone.

"Lara, listen, there is always something worse in life. True, these people have beaten me, raped me, and have been exploiting me financially for years. But they also liberated me from a worse fate."

"Liberated you? From what?" Lara looked unconvinced and very angry.

"Yes, liberated me. If they had not taken me out of Turkey I would have been dead by now. As I said there is always something worse. Let me tell you a story. When I was nineteen, my uncle took me to Turkey. 'There is a great job as a salesgirl in a large department store,' he said. We went by boat. When we arrived, he took me to a place called Aksaray. It was a very busy place; there were a lot of Russians. We met a Turk in a coffee shop. He was a skinny man with a thick mustache. I didn't like him from the start. He had beady little eyes and looked at me as if I was a new toy. My uncle said that he was the owner of the store where I was going to work. Right there, in the open, while they were drinking Turkish coffee and smoking cigarettes, they negotiated and my uncle sold me. They were talking Turkish so I did not know what was going on. But I saw my uncle take money from the Turk. He counted the money, and then he stood up and told me to go with the man. 'He'll show you where you are going to live and start you on your new job,' he said. This was my own uncle, Lara, do you understand?"

Lara was listening with the same stone cold expression, but her eyes were wet again.

"Anyway," continued Anastasia, "I was very scared but my uncle had already left, so I got in the man's car and he took me to a small dirty apartment and started talking Turkish to me. I did not understand a word. Then he said a few words in English, but in those days my English was not any good either. He just walked over to me and started ripping my clothes off. I had no idea what was going on. He smelled terrible. I started fighting him and he beat me so hard I thought I was going to die right there. Then he raped me. I still did not know what was going to happen or what was expected of me. I kept fighting him and demanding in Russian to see my uncle. Then others walked into the room. Two other men. One of them spoke a little Russian. There was only a dirty mattress on the bed, nothing to cover myself with. He asked me to get dressed, and I quickly put my ripped clothes back on. They took me to another apartment in the same building. There were four other women there, and two men. The Russian-speaking Turk told us that we had to work as prostitutes. He said they had bought each one of us for a lot of money, and that we had to work to repay what we 'owed' them. They had paid someone else money for us, but now we owed them! I was so mad, and I remember I was on the verge of screaming at them when one of the girls beat me to it and started to yell and complain. I could not tell where she was from, because her Russian was very broken. Then the Russian-speaking Turk said, 'Now we will show everyone what happens to the girls who don't cooperate.' And they held the girl, in front of all of us, ripped her clothes off and beat her so hard that I can still hear the sound of the blows falling all over her body; she was almost unconscious at that point, and her mouth and nose were bleeding. We could see huge red bruises on her buttocks and sides, and they were still slapping and kicking her. Then they raped her repeatedly and sodomized her with a rubber stick. They were forcing us to watch all this, laughing the whole time. I can still hear their laughter. At this point she was unconscious and face down on the bed, barely breathing. We were all petrified, I most of all, because if that girl had not started her ranting when she did, I would have been the one lying there on the bed. No one stirred. Then one of the Turks approached the girl and urinated in her hair. 'This is just half of what will happen to any of you if you do not cooperate,' said the Russian-speaking Turk. The others laughed. 'If this is not enough to make you fall in line, we will slowly kill you.' They looked at us as if we were cattle or dogs. 'Clean that bitch up,' the Russian-speaker said, and they left, leaving just one guy to guard us. That is how I started in this business, Lara. So now tell me again, how bad was Ayvazian?"

Lara had stopped holding back her tears. She just stared at Anastasia, the happy, energetic prostitute, and for the first time truly wondered what she was made of.

After a long silence, Anastasia added, "Do you know what my uncle sold me for? One thousand dollars. One thousand dollars! You made more than double that in one night."

"How did the Ayvazians liberate you?" asked Lara, her voice barely audible.

"Well, they bought me from the Turk. They have business in Turkey too, you know. They sell girls there and the mustached Turk who had bought me sold me to them. I pleaded with them to take me out of Turkey. So they brought me to Moscow and we made a deal. I will work for them until I repay ten times what they paid for me, and then I will be free. *Ten* times. I had already made the Turk much more than he paid my uncle, and now I had started a whole new cycle of debt and bondage. But it was worth it to get out of there."

This had been by far the most exhausting day for Lara, both physically and emotionally. She was still bleeding and was in pain; she was expected to see Melikov again in a few days. But now she had to close her eyes. Close her mind. Close her body and her entire being. Everything in her had to shut down into silence before it exploded. She thanked Anastasia for being there for her, for all the comforting words and explanations, and then went to bed.

It was early the next morning that she jumped out of bed and wrote her first cryptic note, which began her daily habit of record keeping.

Today I lost a child I did not know was growing inside of me. I did not know they had decided to kill it, did not know what they were doing when they were killing it. Now it's dead; now I know. My friend Anastasia wants me to believe that I'm lucky.

V

Edward Laurian is always shocked by the contrast between the beauty of the mountains and the miserable state of the infrastructure surrounding them. Having lived in Switzerland for the past eight years, and accustomed to the seamless way in which a road and a mountainside fuse in the Swiss highlands, the country roads in this small Caucasian country, that was recently freed from the former Soviet Union, represent a rude violation of his sense of aesthetics. Man should not leave his mark on nature when it does so much harm, he thinks every time he drives on this road.

But the crude sense of pure functionality, void not only of aesthetics but often of any environmental concerns that had driven public projects during the Soviet Union, still survives here. During Soviet times, meeting production quotas was more important than any other consideration and Laurian understood that. But today, it is not even a concrete target such as a production quota that drives the process. There are no quotas. There is very little production, for that matter. What prevails is a passive, dismissive indifference, as the population, caught by surprise between the end of one regime and the chaotic wait for the birth of another, tries to scrape out a living.

The drive from the village of Shatin to his estate near Vardahovit is only twenty kilometers, but it can take over an hour given the condition of the road and would be considered a hard trek by any measure. That short stretch has been the stage for a fascinating part of the medieval history of Armenia. It is also home to old forts, monasteries, tombs of princes, grave-yards of various ethnic groups and ruins of ancient cities, which persist quietly and stubbornly, oblivious to the utter insignificance of the life of the villagers around them.

The natural beauty of the region is another attraction that captured Laurian early on. Mountainous and rugged, with steep cliffs and valleys, rivers and streams gushing through almost every ravine, the region can simultaneously inspire both awe and total peace. Even for someone accustomed to the Swiss mountains, this is a clear step up. But for Laurian, it is much deeper than that. He can *feel* this place in a way that he cannot feel any other place on earth. He can feel the history. He can visualize King Smbat in his fortress, built in the fifth century, directly above the road he is driving on, on top of an impregnable mountain chain. He can visualize how the fortress eventually fell six centuries later to Seljuk Turks, who used thirsty horses to sniff out the underground clay pipes that supplied water to the castle, and proceeded to cut off the water source and take the fortress. He can see the scene rolling in front of his eyes like a movie. He can go beyond and imagine an old civilization, which in part belongs to him; or maybe it is the other way round, he cannot be sure. At least the history belongs to him. Or at least that is how he feels.

As he enters Yeghegis, another ancient city that was destroyed and rebuilt several times between the fifth and eleventh centuries until an earthquake demolished it for good, the road seems somewhat less damaged than the thoroughly destroyed section of Shatin, but even here he has to maneuver through segments with potholes big enough to swallow up the better part of his Toyota Prado. The climb up the narrow curvy road can be dangerous, especially if one is not familiar with the area and does not know what to expect at the end of the next turn. The old, rusty pipe carrying irri-gation water to the villages has burst again, letting loose a gush of water, which probably is the main cause of all the damage. Built in the 1940s, it has not been repaired since. It was built well, with solid stone foundations, but the harsh winters and constant water damage of over sixty years have taken their toll.

He has to cross three villages to get to his house. Most of the villagers either know him or know of him. Some refer to him by name; others simply call him the "American." Before moving to Switzerland, Laurian had lived in the US for several years. To those who know him well he is "Edik," the Armenian short version of Edward. To those who know him less well, he is "Paron Edik," Mr. Edik. He always greets the villagers as he drives past them, and he always gives a lift to any hitchhiker that he passes on this stretch of the road, which he considers his turf.

It is late afternoon, in late September. Most village men are sitting in the village square in front of backgammon sets and chessboards or just doing nothing. Schoolchildren have already returned home, unloaded their heavy backpacks, and are out in the streets playing. The village cowherds are bringing the cattle back home from grazing in the fields about that time, which is always a distraction for most drivers and even an annoyance to some. But Laurian enjoys watching the cattle move on the street in lazy, deliberate steps, totally oblivious to car traffic, looking content after a day of grazing in the mountain meadows, regurgitating their meals as they walk and gazing beyond the car with dreamy eyes. This is what belongs on this road, he thinks, not my Prado.

After completing one of the more dangerous turns on the road into the village, he calls Agassi, the caretaker of his estate. Agassi is both guard and gardener, and lives in the guardhouse year round with his wife, Vartiter. He is in his fifties and has lived in the region all his life. Laurian hired him soon after he had bought the lands, even before the construction of the homestead was completed.

"Should be there in about 30 minutes," he says. "Is everything in order?"

"Ha, Edik jan, all is normal," says Agassi. "We're waiting for you. Varujan caught some *garmrakhayd* for you this morning. It is in the fridge. I've turned on the water and gas in the main house already. Do you want me to turn on the heat in your bedroom?"

"How cold has it been at nighttime?"

"Not too bad, but toward morning it can get chilly."

"No need for heat, then," says Laurian. "I'll be there soon."

Varujan is Agassi's middle son. He is one of four children who have given him fifteen grandchildren. All live in the neighborhood villages of Shatin and Vardahovit. Varujan is a master hunter and fisherman, and is the only one in the entire region who never comes back empty-handed when he goes to the rivers in the area to catch *garmrakhayd*—meaning red-dotted in Armenian—a wonderful fresh water trout known for the red dots on its skin.

Although it is approaching seven in the evening, it is still light outside when Agassi opens the huge gates to the estate. The guardhouse is right inside the gates, and the main house some hundred-and-twenty meters into the property, past the old apple orchard and sheltered from view by a grouping of tall poplars. Agassi says no one has planted the poplars, and they have never been watered, but they have grown so tall and healthy that he is convinced there is a natural water source under them somewhere. "We really should drill here, Edik jan," he says every chance he gets. "Imagine having our own water source right here on the property."

Not that there is any shortage of water. Drinking water is abundant and free, and is generally used to water all the plants and trees around the house as well. Most of the forty hectare plateau, at around two-thousand meters altitude, used to be agricultural land divided into one to two hectare plots that the villagers cultivated during Soviet times. The main crop was wheat, but some years they grew barley and corn. After the collapse of the Soviet Union these lands were privatized, and most villagers decided to sell their parcels. It did not make sense to cultivate small areas and take the full responsibility of marketing their crops on their own in a system that went overnight from state run socialism to pure capitalism.

Laurian had bought the entire area from twelve different villagers. The place had some twenty-five mature apple trees, and over twenty walnut trees. It was also full of wild pear, apple and plum trees, which Agassi says can easily be grafted to better stock. Instead, Laurian has focused on adding a few hundred evergreens and poplars, and about a dozen weeping willows. Poplars and weeping willows are by far his favorite trees.

It has been almost six weeks since Laurian's last visit. The whole place is a lush green with the new trees, and Vartiter's flower garden is bursting with color. A row of pine trees and poplars adorns each side of the path leading to the main house. He takes a quick walk around the property before darkness falls and looks approvingly at the changes since his last stay in early August.

Laurian has asked the Mayor of Vardahovit village, Saro, to join him for dinner that night. Saro is a soft-spoken, kind and intelligent man in his early forties. He has lived in the region all his life, though not always in the village of Vardahovit. After each absence, Laurian likes to sit with Saro and hear him talk about the new developments in the region, the problems the village is facing, and especially news of newcomers into the area. Vartiter has prepared the red-dotted trout, some chicken soup, and set the table outside on the front terrace, which has the most spectacular view of the mountains and of sunsets. Miracle sunsets, Laurian calls them.

Laurian fills their wine glasses and makes the first welcome toast before Saro starts his report.

"We've had some excitement here since your last visit," he says, "and I'm afraid most of it is not good news. Ayvazian has been buying deserted homes in Sevajayr and has bought one in Vardahovit as well."

"What does he need houses here for?" asks Laurian. "Does he need a place to keep all the mountain goats that he murders every year?"

Laurian is a hunter himself but hates the hunting style of Ayvazian and his friends. Sevajayr is very close, only a twenty-minute drive from his house. He is opposed to hunting the mountain goats and the bears that are native to the region, and has helped the governor of Vayots Dzor pass several laws regulating and even restricting hunting these animals. But people like Ayvazian act above the law, and not even the Governor can always prosecute them.

"No one knows exactly," says Saro. "They usually come in the night, in cars with darkened windows. They have guards and bodyguards whom we see. But we do not know who else is staying there, if anyone. But," chuckles Saro, "as you can imagine, everyone in the village has an opinion."

"Do we know any of the bodyguards?"

"Some look familiar because they have been in these parts before. They have accompanied Ayvazian a few times on his hunting trips. At least once his nephew Viktor has been seen as well. One of our villagers swears he recognized one of the bodyguards from that incident around eight months ago, when the man from Saralandj fell off the cliff. But, to be honest with you, these guys all look alike to me. You know, the shaved heads, body building in their youth, which is turning flabby around the edges, always in dark sunglasses, regardless of the time of day or weather. I swear I sometimes think it is a disguise."

"Any names?" asks Laurian, smiling at Saro's description of the bodyguards, yet concerned about their presence in the area.

"Not yet. But we'll find out sooner or later."

"Do you think Ayvazian had anything to do with the incident?"

"I don't know. That happened more than eight months ago and has long been forgotten. We have not heard anything more about the Saralandj man. All we know is that his family still lives there. Rumor has it that Ayvazian has actually helped them by sending food and money to the widow."

"And you believe that?"

"One never knows, Edik jan. Even men like Ayvazian sometimes have a conscience. You never know what motivates them."

"I don't believe it for a minute," says Laurian, staring into the mountains. "I bet he has not given the Saralandj man a second thought since the accident."

$$ \text{\textit{Ω} \quad \textit{Ω} \quad \textit{Ω}} $$

Darkness had fallen on the mountains and the fields. There was only one thin sliver of bright red where the sun had set behind the western mountain chain. Saro had made one last toast, emptied his glass, and bid farewell. Agassi's wife Vartiter had gathered the dishes, asked if Edik needed anything else, and then left for the guardhouse. She is an incredible woman, thought Laurian. The hint of a faint smile permanently imprinted on her face, hair always combed back in a bun, intelligent eyes on a face one could tell had been very beautiful in her youth. In spite of the harshness of aging in these mountains, she had retained her elegance. Her energy seemed inexhaustible as she approached every chore, from the needs of the extended family to the cows to the garden. In many ways, Vartiter was the matriarch of the family. Sons, daughter, in-laws, fifteen grandchildren and even Agassi were in awe of her; she was the central pillar on which everything and everyone in the family depended.

Laurian opened a second bottle of wine, lit a cigar, and sat on his favorite terrace, thinking. Albinoni's Adagio was playing softly on his iPod inside, mixed with the typical evening sounds from neighboring villages, which would fill the air a while longer before total peace descended on this remote mountaintop. Dogs barking, cowherds calling their long, musical calls in attempts to convince the last stubborn cows to enter the barn for the night, night birds chirping in the poplar trees, and the first bats of the evening emerging from their lairs to start their frantic nighttime flights, all filled the air with the magical, condensed burst of life that Laurian loved. He then heard the snorting sound of wild boar from the far end of the field in front of his house. That got his attention for a minute, for that was one animal he did not mind hunting, but he soon changed his mind and sat back in his chair. He would do no hunting tonight.

"What are you up to, Ayvazian?" he thought, staring at the sky. "This time you've come too close to home to ignore…"

The western sky was totally dark now, but he could see traces of light in the east at the other side of the house. He stood up and walked around, and sure enough the half moon was peeking out from behind the eastern mountains. By daybreak, before the sun would make its comeback, the moon would set where the sun had disappeared. The temperature had dropped significantly in the past thirty minutes. He put out his cigar and walked inside.

The house was a spacious single story stone construction of tuff, travertine, granite and basalt. It consisted of one large common room, four en suite bedrooms and a kitchen. It also had a large basement, used largely for storage of garden machines and tools, which doubled as a garage in the winter. Arches, arched windows, columns, every detail designed by Laurian himself, was handed over to an architect to produce the necessary drawings for construction. In the common room he had his library, a gun cabinet and leather sofas and armchairs. He went to his library and browsed through the various English and Armenian books. He was in no mood for prose; this was a night for poetry. His library was practically complete with all of the Armenian poets that he liked—Charents, Isahakian, Sevag, Sahian, Varoujan, Siamanto, Turian and Medzarents. He scanned the shelves quickly, but had already decided on Medzarents. He picked the volume of his complete works and sank into a leather armchair. The poet had died at the age of twenty-two, leaving behind a small volume of poems that Laurian considered the most sensitive and lyrical poems ever written. Every sunset, every flower, every green field, every mountain road and every night sky in Vardahovit reminded him of a Medzarents verse. Laurian often wondered what invaluable treasures he would have created had he lived to be twenty-five, thirty, forty-five, sixty-five.

But as he sat there reading, his mind wouldn't let go of the latest news. He had heard of the incident eight months ago. Saro had recounted to him all the details that he could gather at the time, but they did not amount to much. A poor man had come to visit Ayvazian in Martashen. They had driven to look at his tree farm plan near Sevajayr, and he had fallen off a cliff and died. It was an accident. The police investigation had been closed in twenty-four hours. But what business did this poor man have visiting someone like Ayvazian? No one questioned it, because so many people visited Ayvazian. But Laurian was an investigative reporter and simply could not accept the story as told. Not much was really as 'normal' as it seemed.

Laurian knew in his heart, but did not yet want to fully admit to himself, that he was struggling with something bigger and deeper than just the news of an oligarch buying deserted homes in his neighborhood. This one man, Sergey Ayvazian, represented so much evil that Laurian could easily be blinded by his own rage and be driven to tackle problems bigger than his means would allow.

What made matters worse was the fact that the specific dirt on Ayvazian touched a very personal nerve in him. This was not just another story of corruption on a grand scale. Ayvazian's disregard of village life and of the villagers, his inhumane hunting habits, his total disregard of the welfare of the country that he exploited every day, were issues that Laurian could easily turn into a personal cause and crusade. But perhaps the deepest and darkest issue of all, which Laurian fought hard to keep covered even from his own thoughts, was Ayvazian's rumored involvement in human trafficking—an issue so personal and painful for Laurian that he could not maintain his objectivity as an investigative reporter when dealing with it.

He read a verse that touched him most deeply:
> *to have the hope of disappearing into the night*
> *and to surrender to the whims of a narrow trail*
> *to cast aside like a scab all boredom and gluttony*
> *and to wrap the sick soul in peaceful harmony...*

To have the hope of disappearing into the night...He thought what that might have meant to the romantic young poet, and wondered what it could have meant to some of Ayvazian's victims. There were many rumors of Ayvazian's enemies disappearing into the night, none of which were proven. Medzarents, who died from a severe infection caused by dagger wounds inflicted on him by Turkish hooligans in Istanbul, had not written a single bitter or angry poem. He saw nothing but beauty in the world. He celebrated life and nature most of all. Disappearing into the night meant liberation for him, not captivity. But are people disappearing into the night here in these deserted homes of Sevajayr and Vardahovit?

"Ayvazian, what are you up to in my region?" Laurian asked into the moonlit night.

𝔏 𝔏 𝔏

The next morning Laurian woke up earlier than usual and, although he had not had a very restful night, felt full of energy. As he washed and shaved, he took a long look in the mirror, as if challenging what he felt he needed to do. That morning, the bags under his dark brown eyes appeared to him as signs of wisdom, not fatigue, and the graying hair on his temples reinforced that sense. The rest of his hair had very little grey, but was thinning. Laurian generally did not care about such in-mirror inspections, but sometimes he liked to stare into his own eyes when he was trying to confirm something to himself.

He took his customary walk around the southern part of his property. The land was a long strip of flat farmland surrounded on three sides by four-hundred-meter cliffs. It was a fortress of sorts, with rivers flowing in the valleys on both sides. He loved to walk by one side of the property and return from the other. At the tip, one could see the two rivers merge. A truly spectacular feast for the eyes, of valleys, mountains, rivers and meadows that would take one's breath away, especially in certain months of spring when they were colored by brilliant wild flowers.

Laurian has adopted the village Vardahovit, and cares deeply about what happens in these parts. He helps the villagers whenever he can; fixing torn tin roofs, arranging funding for an irrigation project, campaigning hard to get the roads repaired, and helping them complete the construction of a simple community hall in the village square. He likes Mayor Saro. Saro was instrumental in gathering and combining the parcels from the twelve villagers and providing him with one piece of land.

After returning from his walk, he called Saro again. "Let's go drive around a bit," he said.

Saro arrived with gifts for Laurian's two young nieces who live in the United States. He knew how much Laurian doted on the girls, the children of his only living sister. He removed the gifts from a bag and showed them to Laurian.

"This was woven by my daughter," he explained, handing him a colorful wool purse with a long shoulder strap. It had beautiful colors, mostly apricot and blue, with thin stripes of dark red.

"And this," he said proudly, "was made by my nephew. Look at it carefully," he told Laurian, handing him a carved wooden duck. Laurian inspected it. He barely noticed a very thin line, almost like a crack in the wood, on the side. Then he realized that there was a smaller duck inside, nestled so seamlessly within the outer one that it was almost impossible to notice.

"Thank you so much, Saro," he said, truly impressed by the handiwork of both gifts. "The girls will love these."

"I know you like sending them gifts from Armenia," said Saro happily. "So I assumed you'd be even happier to send them gifts from Vardahovit."

"You're right. I'll ship these as soon as I get down to Yerevan. Thanks again. I know the girls will love them."

Laurian then asked Saro to drive by the houses that Ayvazian had bought. Vardahovit village was only two kilometers from his house, and that stretch of the road, although very old, was in relatively good condition. The deserted house was at the far end of the village, past the new community center, right at the edge of a cliff overlooking a sharp drop of around eight-hundred meters into the river below. They circled halfway around it and turned back; they could not check the back of the house by car, as there was no room to drive between it and the cliff. There was nothing suspicious from the outside. The windows were closed and curtains drawn. The door seemed to be locked. There were no cars outside, probably suggesting that none of the bodyguards were present, but they could have been dropped off there. At Saro's insistence, they did not get out of the car, nor knock on the door. Laurian wanted to at first, but Saro convinced him that it would alert them prematurely, and that it was better to let them think that no one was concerned with their presence until they learned a bit more.

Then they drove to Sevajayr. That was a much harder ride, as there was more severe damage to the old stone road. The surface was entirely worn away, and only the stone foundation remained, which was in disrepair as well. Sevajayr is a tiny village, with just a handful of families, and it has many more deserted homes than Vardahovit. Saro thought that Ayvazian had bought at least two, and they drove by them. There was a SUV parked in front of one of the houses. Like the house in Vardahovit, the windows and doors were closed, and they had no way to see inside. They watched from a distance for a while, but no one came out or went in.

♌ ♌ ♌

Back at Laurian's house, Saro started to worry. He sensed that Laurian was not going to let go of Ayvazian's presence in Sevajayr. Laurian was not a citizen of Armenia. He came and went. He could easily start something that he wouldn't be able to finish, something that Saro would have to sort out later. The thugs would not go after Laurian, given the complications of harming a foreign citizen, but they could easily go after Saro.

It was past noon and they sat on the back terrace this time, because the sun was too strong in the front. Vartiter brought coffee. Laurian was serious and deep in thought.

"Saro jan," he said more deliberately than he normally talked, "this is our village, right?"

Saro did not like either the question or the tone, but went along with it. "Right, Edik jan, of course it is our village."

Laurian always had high regard for the Mayor. He had come to know him to be honest, hard-working, and devoted to the interests of the village. This was unusual in the post-Soviet social structures, and needed to be appreciated and supported, in Laurian's opinion. Saro had had many opportunities to ask for personal favors from Laurian, but never did. The only issues that he brought to him concerned the welfare of the villagers—an irrigation system for the village, torn roofs, roads in desperate need of repair. In a country where almost everyone Laurian's age was born and educated in the Soviet Union and had to adapt to a total collapse of practically everything they knew, and almost everyone younger had known nothing but transition (depending on his mood, he'd sometimes call it chaos or rationalized chaos), one was often at a loss how to even define a reliable person, let alone actually find one. So when one did find one, it would not be right to put him at risk in his own fluid, unsettled system, or so Laurian believed.

"Look, Saro, I know it is more dangerous for you to be involved in this than me, but believe me, it is also far more dangerous for you and your family if we let this go on without knowing what they are up to."

Saro was quiet. Laurian understood his concern and decided to come straight to the point.

"Saro, listen. I realize I don't live here permanently, and you and your family are here year round. I know you have a lot more at stake than I do and you may be a much more direct target of Ayvazian's actions than I'll ever be. But think about this: If what he is doing here, right in the middle of our village, is something bad, something illegal, something criminal even, and we know nothing about it, does that make you feel any safer than trying to find out?"

Saro thought about it for a minute. The natural inclination in the post-Soviet system was to leave those in authority alone. It was a culture left over from seventy years of Soviet rule. The individual had no value, everyone was dispensable for the general good, and authority figures could never be challenged without serious and often fatal consequences. One could only accept reality, especially when supported by power, and no matter how unjust, could not fight it. The Western, activist approach of not adapting to a difficult situation had virtually no place in this psyche.

"No, it does not make me feel safer," he said finally. "More than you I want all this removed from the village. But what can we hope to do? What exactly are you proposing?"

"Well, we cannot develop any plan of action without knowing what they are doing. And I agree with you that we need to be very careful. I will follow your advice just as I did earlier in the car. We will not go knocking on doors and asking questions. We will let them think this place has nothing but a bunch of scared and ignorant peasants. That is what they believe anyway; otherwise they would not have come here. Fine so far?"

"So far, yes," said Saro, noticeably relieved that he was not facing a reckless reform-minded foreigner who would come in with guns blazing and leave the locals to clean up his mess. And Laurian could easily be like that. He had seen him in his more indignant moments, when he was so fed up with the corruption in the country that he would go on a rampage about everyone in authority. That always was a source of concern, even though Saro agreed with every word he said.

"We need to organize a stakeout. A constant twenty-four hour watch. Monitor every movement in those houses. I am sure eventually we'll get a clue. They will slip up at some point."

Such a plan seemed borderline harmless to Saro, on the condition it was done with utmost care.

Vartiter approached from the guardhouse with a trayful of grilled chicken, cheese, sausages, cut-up tomatoes and cucumbers, scallions, pickles and bread.

"Can we take Agassi into our confidence?" whispered Laurian while Vartiter was still out of earshot.

"I think we can. He and his family can help with this."

Vartiter approached them with a broad smile, and Laurian stood up and took the tray from her. He knew that that was a "foreign move," as local men would never consider helping a woman with something that is deemed to be her job. But Laurian did not care.

"Thanks so much, Vartiter," he said—another sign of him being an outsider, as one never thanks someone for something that is expected of them anyway, especially a woman serving lunch. "Where is Agassi?"

"Down in the lower orchard watering the new fruit trees," she said. "He should be almost done by now. He's been at it since this morning."

"Vart-jan, ask him to join us."

Vartiter stepped inside to bring another plate for her husband. "Bring the *oghi* too," said Laurian. Agassi not only understood things better but also remembered them much better with a glass or two of vodka in him.

"Okay," laughed Vartiter, "but you know you won't get much work out of him for the rest of the day if he starts on your *oghi* now."

Vartiter set the table and left.

"We need to form a reliable group," said Laurian to Saro, who was becoming both excited and afraid of what they were about to do. "Like a committee." The old Soviet mentality understood committees better than anyone. "We need twenty-four hour surveillance without raising any suspicion."

"That's key," said Saro. "No suspicion. Otherwise the whole village will pay dearly, I assure you. Every move should be seen as normal and routine."

"Absolutely," Laurian agreed.

"And, Edik jan, you have to stay behind the scenes. Involvement by you would raise the most suspicion of all. You play the role of the foreigner, who comes to enjoy his dacha here once in a while, and has no idea how the locals live…" Saro noticed the sharp look in Laurian's eyes. "Sorry," he said, "a thousand pardons, Edik jan, but you know what I am saying, right?"

"I know," smiled Laurian. "I'll play the dumb foreigner role. Do not worry about that."

They spent over two hours with Agassi planning the operation. Vartiter popped in a few times to refresh the table. If she was curious about what the men were talking about, she did not show it. She'd hear it all from Agassi later. They identified six individuals who would monitor the three homes, with the one in Sevajayr that had the car in front getting the full twenty-four hour treatment, and the others would be watched on a lighter schedule. Agassi's family would be heavily involved. His two sons, one of whom lived in Vardahovit, and the other, who worked at the small hydroelectric power plant near Sevajayr, were well positioned. Three children were added to the list. Children would be very good for the task, as the bodyguards rarely took them seriously, and they could naturally be anywhere and everywhere playing in the villages. There was another reliable man from Shatin, which was far from the surveillance targets, but Saro and Laurian would arrange for him to get a temporary job in Sevajayr working the beehives. The villager closest to one of the houses in Sevajayr had over seventy-five beehives, and surely would need some help gathering the honey.

Rules and instructions were drafted. How to watch without being seen, make everything look natural, do not get too close, always keep the lights off. Laurian had two pairs of binoculars, which he donated to the operation. But he was much more uncomfortable donating his camera; a Nikon D-90, with 18X zoom and a special nighttime photography feature; it would be very useful. But, if detected, it would look totally out of place in the hands of any of the villagers in Sevajayr.

"My grandson Hayk is the best photographer in the whole area," said Agassi proudly. He can hide in the beekeeper's barn in the upper loft and try to take pictures from the tiny window. No one will notice a thing."

"Isn't Hayk in school?" asked Laurian. "This may take a few days, maybe longer. Can he skip classes for that long?"

"We'll get permission, don't worry. Hayk is very smart. He'll make up for the missed classes in no time."

"He has to stay way inside," said Laurian, allowing his concern to show on his face. Hayk is only fifteen. He is a smart kid, very alert and always very respectful when talking to Laurian, but fifteen nonetheless. "This is a delicate task," he said. "There is a light on the camera that will show even from a distance. He cannot hold it out the window, or even at the window. He has to do the best he can by staying at least a meter inside. And he needs to learn some basic features of the camera. Are you sure he can handle this?"

"You show him everything, Edik jan, and he'll follow your instructions to the letter. I know my Hayk well."

After the details were worked out, they planned various meetings with each of the recruits, and Agassi left them. Saro also stood up to leave, but Laurian signaled him to sit down.

"I have some business to tend to in Ashtarak," he said. "That is just thirty minutes from Aparan and Saralandj. I want to go visit the family of the Saralandj man."

"Edik jan, that was more than eight months ago. What connection could it have with this?"

"It happened here, and it happened with Ayvazian. What more connection do we need?" asked Laurian. "We should talk to the family. It can do no harm. Will you come with me?"

Saro was reluctant, but accepted. If nothing else he could make sure Laurian did not do anything rash.

"Okay, then. We'll leave in the morning around nine and we'll be back by evening," said Laurian, and Saro left.

♌ ♌ ♌

It was late afternoon. There were still a few hours before sunset, but the sun was already low and not uncomfortable. Laurian moved to the front terrace, where the scenery was the most spectacular in early evening. He sank in one of the teak lounge chairs, put his feet up on the coffee table, and fired up a Romeo & Julietta Churchill cigar. He could make it last for about two hours, time that he would need to think through everything that had happened since his arrival twenty-four hours earlier.

The evening was unfolding in spectacular fashion on the horizon. There were more shades of colors in the sky and on the mountainsides than one would have thought existed. A thousand shades of green, a thousand shades of red and orange, a thousand shades of white, he thought in awe. The sun itself seemed so touched by the sky in which it was sailing, that it appeared to be acting bashfully, unwilling to shine too brightly so as not to disturb the symphony of colors. *Nature is paying its eternal tribute to Medzarents*, thought Laurian. He must have been looking at a sky like this when he wrote:

> *Joyful are the apricot lights of the sweetly escaping night*
> *Golden strings wrapped around the velvety fog of incense*
> *Blue ribbons, rainbows, floating sounds, mystique rose*
> *Candles that calmly melt into their own teardrops of light …*

Yes, he must have seen just this… And now nature is giving it all back, in honor of his memory. Years ago, he had tried to translate Medzarents to a British colleague, but eventually given up.

"The most difficult thing in the world to translate is poetry," he had declared, "especially when one understands it."

Vartiter appeared again from the guardhouse.

"*Mi ban sarkem utes, ha?* May I fix something for you to eat?"

"*Ha Vart-jan. Apres.* Yes, Vart, bravo. *En karmir ginin el ber.* And bring the red wine also."

Tchaikovsky's piano concerto #1 was playing in the house and became momentarily louder as Vartiter opened the front door to go in. Laurian preferred the music to reach him through the closed door, more as a distant background than center stage; the centre stage performance was different, unfolding in front of his eyes. The sun had perched on top of the mountain behind which it would soon disappear, as if unwilling to take its leave from the magical sky, its last few movements deliberately slow and reluctant. He watched as it finally slipped behind the flanks of the mountains, as if coaxed, or perhaps nudged, by one of the movements of Tchaikovsky's concerto.

The commitment was made. He would not back down now, although he was keenly aware that he was powerless against the local oligarch. No matter how much he likes to think this is his region, it actually is not. In practical ways it is much more theirs than his. The likes of Ayvazian laid their claim a long time ago and it was not easy to unseat them. But he would not turn his back on this one, regardless of the consequences. He would organize and mobilize the villagers. He would give them the means to learn and, if necessary, fight back. After fourteen years of independence, it was time to give a push back to the vested interests. Granted, most of what he knew about Ayvazian was hearsay. The worst that was attributed to him could not be proven. The only thing that he had seen himself was his hunting of the mountain goats, and the cruelty of that totally revolted him. Because of that, he tended to believe most of the other rumors, provable or not.

He gazed at the mountains for a long time. The background music playing inside was now Khachaturian's *Masquerade*. The mountains were silent, attentive, majestic, and were staring back at him as if they were the real lords who kept watch over this space. It is neither you nor them, they were telling him. *It is us. We've been here before the beginning. We'll be here past the end.* Khachaturian fully agreed.

He then had the urge to finish a poem he had started writing on his last visit. Sitting here, in front of his house, he had experienced such total peace that he could not resist putting it down on paper. He went inside to fetch his notebook and the portable table light, and sat back down at the table. His unfinished poem was waiting:

Midnight. Infinite calm
On this remote mountaintop
　　　　Not a whisper, not a movement
In this deafening silence
　　　　Only being and inspiration

In front of me, the poplar trees
Dissolved within their own shadow
Silently float into the night
　　　　Not even a chill in their leaves
　　　　Not a shiver in their tender branches

The mountains keep watch from afar
Under the over-bejeweled sky
> *Awesome and majestic*
> *They are the lords of this fiefdom*
Masters of this moment, of this night

This is the poem that he had to finish tonight. He did not think long. He wrote:

And I try to fathom
That which the night keeps handing out
> *The life that bursts out of these peaks*
> *The unbridled invisible torrents that abound*
> *The rhythmic heartthrob of the earth*

And here it seems that the mountains
Have decided to accept me
And they're talking to me right now
> *"A part of you was always ours*
> *Now a part of us is yours..."*

He turned off the table lamp and sank into the night. The last verse practically wrote itself, as if descending upon him like a revelation. He belonged here now. That was his answer to Ayvazian. Welcome back, Laurian, the mountains called. He smiled in the dark and filled his glass for a last toast.

VI

The drive to Ashtarak was long but uneventful. Saro offered to drive, and Laurian accepted. There was likely to be some drinking in Ashtarak, and he did not want the responsibility of being behind the wheel. Saro's Chevy Niva could manage most terrains in the countryside, even where there were no roads, which was an added plus. They arrived around noon to meet one of Laurian's old friends for lunch. He knew the area well, as he had been the deputy Governor of this region a few years back. Laurian trusted him, although Saro was anxious as usual.

Laurian was anxious too, but in an entirely different way. He wanted to get to the bottom of things as quickly as possible. Once he zeroed in on a mystery, this impatience was trademark Laurian. In his mid-forties, he had been an investigative reporter for almost twenty years, working for Swiss, British and American news agencies, and covering everything from wars in the Middle East to regulatory violations in oil trading to financial scandals of the rich and famous.

Writing was a passion for him, whether he was working on one of his documentaries or his poetry. Intense and uncompromising when focused, he was the antithesis of the dismissive mentality of the general public in most post-Soviet societies, including Armenia, which, in situations like the one he and Saro were in at the moment, could be a liability and a handicap. But he and Saro knew that his tendencies were closer to the rebellious Armenian character.

"I am you without seventy years of Soviet rule," he'd say. Then he'd look them straight in the eye and add, "You are me, *with* seventy years of Soviet rule."

And Saro and many others actually believed him. They remembered stories about their own past, their ancestors, their unyielding character, their moral fiber. Laurian fit better with their crazy old stories than they themselves did. But still, they didn't see the point.

We are who we are, Saro and other villagers thought. *And he is who he is. No amount of analysis and soul searching will change a thing.*

Laurian first set foot in Armenia in the late eighties to cover a story. It was the eve of the collapse of the Soviet Union, which, according to Laurian, was the single most important historical event for those who had lived through the cold war and had become accustomed to seeing the world largely in that context. In that bipolar world divided between the USSR and the USA, Asia had not yet woken up, either economically or politically. And when one pole of a bipolar world starts to crumble, it is news of a lifetime.

The British news agency sent him on a mission to document the changes in some of the smaller republics. Russia, and more specifically Moscow, was being covered every day, but little attention was being paid to the periphery, to the fifteen Soviet Republics. Laurian campaigned for and was given the assignment to cover the Caucasus as his main area of focus. That meant three republics—Azerbaijan, Armenia, and Georgia. In December 1989, all were still part of the Soviet Union, which although formally still intact had already started to unravel. The old system was dying so fast that no one was quite sure which way things would go or what would replace the old structures. For the first time in over seventy years, independence did not seem to be a crazy romantic dream for these republics. However, as the old Soviet economic support structures were being dismantled either deliberately or out of neglect, the charm and shine of independence was beginning to come under doubt. Those were exactly like the Dickensian best and worst of times, and Laurian documented that dilemma thoroughly in those days.

He spent the last week of a two-week assignment in Armenia. Although ethnically Armenian, he had been estranged from the Soviet Republic like most Armenians living in the Diaspora. The deliberate policy of the Soviet Union during the Stalin years to isolate their republics from the outside world had an immense impact on separating the Armenian communities around the world from their homeland. Another major dividing force was that most of the Diaspora communities did not originate from Soviet Armenia, but from Western Armenia, which was now part of Turkey.

Laurian's ancestors hailed from Nakhijevan, a small enclave sandwiched between Armenia and Turkey, which in the twenties Joseph Stalin put under the administrative control of Azerbaijan, even though it had no shared borders with Azerbaijan. That is how the map of the Southern Caucasus started looking like one big jigsaw puzzle.

Laurian's father had migrated to Switzerland as a teenager and apprenticed with a jewelry designer in Geneva; eight years later, he had his own jewelry shop and had become a successful businessman. He had then gone back and married the young girl that he had fallen in love with before leaving Nakhijevan. Laurian and his two sisters, Arpi and Sirarpi, were born in Geneva. Laurian had lost track of his relatives in Nakhijevan. His parents didn't like to reminisce and claimed that they did not have any worthwhile memories to share. His youngest sister, Sirarpi, died when she was twelve. Laurian's only family now was Arpi, who, after marrying a Swiss banker, had moved to New York when her husband was transferred there. It was her two daughters, Houri and Lorig, who had become the focal point of Laurian's affections.

"I first met Gago in December 1989," Laurian explained to Saro in the car. "That was my first visit to Armenia. December 1989. I'm sure you remember how it was back then. The first anniversary of the big earthquake in Gyumri, the boiling over of the Karabagh war, the Empire had already fallen to its knees. Gago was a crazy revolutionary in those days, with a thick black beard, skinny like a skeleton, but with the wildest fiery eyes imaginable on what would otherwise pass for a corpse!"

"What's his full name?"

"Gagik Grigorian. *Khev Gago*, back then. Crazy Gago."

"He must have fought in the Karabagh war."

"Yes, he did. But he had no patience for the politicians. He saw no downside to a total revolution, and no upside to caution. I have to admit, I was young then too, and I liked him!"

"And now?" asked Saro, hopeful that both had settled down a bit with age.

"Oh don't worry. The beard is gone, the skeleton has some flesh on it, the crazy eyes have mellowed a bit too. But make no mistake, the old flame is still there under the ashes."

"Long live the ashes, then," said Saro. "Listen, Edik jan, I beg you, what we're up against in Sevajayr and Vardahovit is not for crazy revolutionaries. Those days are gone. We need to be very careful. And wise. *Shat khelok, Edik jan*. Very wise."

"I know, I know. Don't worry so much. I'm telling you, you can trust Gago, *khev* or not. He is a wealth of information about this region, as you'll soon see. But he is discreet, honest and loyal. I will not tell him everything, just to put your mind at ease, but I can tell you now that I would not have any hesitation to tell him the whole story of why we're here. I won't though, because of you, not because I don't trust him."

"*Ha*, Edik *jan, ha,*" repeated Saro a few times as Laurian was assuring him. "And that's exactly how it should be, at least until we figure this out."

When they pulled into the parking lot of the hotel-restaurant, Saro was not prepared for what he saw. Gagik's passionate embrace of Laurian was so intense, so powerful, that they both almost fell to the ground.

This guy is crazy, thought Saro, watching the old revolutionary run toward them in his military fatigues and grab Laurian with such force that it was not clear whether he was embracing him or wrestling with him.

"*Edeeeeeek, aper jan!*" he kept yelling. "Edik, my brother! It's been far too long! How are you? How *are* you?"

"Fine, fine, Gago. Listen, this is my friend Saro, the honorable Mayor of Vardahovit."

"Vardahovit?" asked Gagik. "Where in the hell is that?"

"What do you mean where is that, Gago?" said Laurian. "You know exactly where it is. In Vayots Dzor. It is my village."

"You mean good old *Guli Duz?*"

"Now you owe our honorable Mayor five-thousand drams," said Laurian. "Don't you know that's the old name of the village, the one the Azeri Turks used to call it? The Armenian name is Vardahovit. There is a five-thousand dram penalty for anyone who uses the old name. Please pay up."

Gagik's laughter was so powerful that it infected them all. Even Saro couldn't hold back. They all laughed uncontrollably, almost in tears, as Gagik pulled out a 5,000 dram bill from his pocket and handed it to Saro.

"My sincere apologies, Mr. Mayor jan, Saro jan, *aper, ke neres*… Saro, my brother, forgive me."

Still laughing, Saro was not sure what to do, and looked at Laurian.

"Gago," said Laurian, doing his best to sound serious, "since this is your first offence, and since you are not from our region and did not know the law until now, we'll forgive you. Put your money in your pocket. Let's go eat."

"No way!" Gagik insisted. "I like your new law, so I'll abide by it. But if you ever come up with stupid new laws that I don't like, watch out!"

Saro felt awkward and uncomfortable, as if being forced to take the money. "I'll send you a receipt," he said sheepishly. "This is going to the municipality."

Another roar of laughter burst from Gagik as they walked into the restaurant.

𝒳 𝒳 𝒳

Gagik had preordered and the table was already set. They filled their glasses and started a boisterous conversation.

"Have you been to Saralandj lately?" asked Laurian, once the first couple of nostalgic toasts were out of the way.

"Saralandj?" Gagik asked in surprise. "How do you even know about that village?"

"Now, now, Gago," said Laurian, "we're from Vardahovit, remember? We're two hours farther away from Yerevan than Saralandj! Why wouldn't we know about it?"

"Did you know that Saralandj was off limits to tourists during Soviet times? I remember back in the eighties there was this visitor from the United States, a kind, old lady, who had a long-lost relative whom she had managed to locate in Saralandj. But the village was not on the Intourist map of allowed places for foreigners to visit. Do you remember Intourist,

Saro jan? Edik, that may have been before your time in Armenia. At any rate, we had to secretly smuggle the old lady into the village so she could see her relative."

"Why was it off limits?" asked Laurian, even though he was anxious to get back to the main topic.

"Far too backwards, that's why," said Gagik. "We were not supposed to show the outside world a village that miserable! Think what they would then say about the mighty Soviet Union." Gagik was now on the verge of totally getting off track.

"Okay, fine," interrupted Laurian. "Have you been there lately?"

"No, not recently," said Gagik. "But tell me, what do you want to know?"

"I'm interested in the Galians," said Laurian without hesitation.

"The Galians, eh? The farthest house of the farthest village of Aparan. You really like faraway places, don't you, dear old faraway friend. "

"I love faraway places," said Laurian seriously, leaning over the table and looking straight into Gagik's eyes, indicating that the joking around was over and they were on to the main topic.

"Well, poor Samvel Galian died in an accident in your neck of the woods some eight or nine months ago. What took you so long to show up?"

Saro was not sure whether he should feel new respect for the guy or be even more concerned than he already was.

"What's their story?" asked Laurian, ignoring the question.

"Their *story*," said Gagik, putting deliberate emphasis on the word 'story,' "is not simple to understand. The Galians are arguably the poorest family in the whole region. The father dies mysteriously in some remote, no, wait, in some *faraway* place in your backyard. The family is devastated, but then, a few months later, starts to recover."

"Recover?"

"Recover. They've bought ten new sheep in the last six months. The oldest daughter is married with a dowry. The youngest son, by far the most promising in school, is back to school and is excelling. They have paid all their debts. What else do you want to know?"

"How?" asked Laurian.

"Well, as you can imagine, we were curious too. The mother says her daughter is sending money from Greece. She is a famous model or something like that. But we checked. The transfers are not from Greece. They are from Moscow. I have no idea why she has Greece set in her head."

"They have a daughter in Moscow?" asked Laurian. "How did she end up in Moscow?"

"Well, Edik jan, here is where things get fuzzy. We do not know for sure. We don't even know if she is still in Moscow. That was a few months ago. The mother won't say much because I don't think she knows much. If she knew, she would have said something by now. By the way, she is very sick. She has been to the hospital here in Ashtarak a few times. But she is very quiet about her daughter's whereabouts. All she says is that her youngest daughter has a modeling job in Greece, and is very successful and she is sending money. When they tell her that the post office in Aparan says that the money is being transferred from Moscow, not Greece, she yells at them. 'You idiots know nothing,' she says. 'My Lara is in Greece, and she is a first class model.'"

"How old is this youngest daughter?" asked Laurian.

"Around sixteen, maybe seventeen. I'm not sure exactly."

"How would her sixteen or seventeen-year-old daughter get a modeling job in Greece?"

"Yes, how indeed. She says Ayvazian found her the job."

The name fell on Laurian and Saro like a ton of bricks.

"Sergey Ayvazian? From Martashen?"

"None other. His men were seen in Saralandj a few times back when poor Samvel Galian died, but not since. Maybe you know more about that side of the story than I do. He is from your region after all." The sarcasm in Gagik's voice could not be missed.

"What do you know about this girl? Did you say her name is Lara?" Laurian was very much aware that Saro was getting uncomfortable with the whole conversation.

"Yes, her name is Lara. And I don't know much. She is a kid. Only one thing is sure—she is no longer in Saralandj, and she is supposedly sending all that money to her mother. Imagine that. A sixteen-year-old saving her orphaned family. Oh, also, I have not seen her since she was a baby, but those who have say she is beautiful physically, apparently very beautiful."

Although Laurian was very much aware of Saro's nervousness, he couldn't let this go yet.

"Tell me more about the father," he said. "Samvel, right?"

"Yes, Samvel Galian. Would you believe he was born in Siberia? I liked him. We got drunk a few times together. Quiet guy. Maybe one of the few in Saralandj who actually liked to read. I went to their house once many years ago and he was sitting there with a bunch of his children and reading to them. Who does that in Saralandj? No one! But go figure: Both parents are from Musa Dagh, and he was born in Siberia!"

Saro, who had been quiet this whole time, showed the first sign of curiosity. "How did Siberia come into the picture?" he asked.

Laurian was somewhat relieved, thinking that Saro's nervousness was waning a bit. But he misread the question. Saro was even more nervous, because those who were exiled to Siberia during the Stalin years always had baggage.

"How much time do you have?" asked Gagik, eager to start the story. But before Laurian could finish the phrase "not a lot," he had already started.

"It's 1915," said Gagik in an animated voice. "Armenians are being slaughtered like sheep everywhere in the old country. Most of them are citizens of Turkey. The men are rounded up and killed first, mostly by their own 'brothers in arms' in the Turkish army, where they are serving. At that time, the villages in the region were helpless. Mass deportations start, mostly to the Syrian deserts. Anyway, these folks in Musa Dagh are crazy, see? Crazy like me, right, Edik jan?" At this point Gagik could barely control his laughter.

"Gago, please, let's get to Galian. Siberia, remember?"

"I'm getting there," said Gagik, and continued, "When they get the deportation orders, they say fuck this, we're not going. So they gather all their women and children and sheep and goats and donkeys and everything they have and climb up to the top of their mountain and set up camp. This is no fairy tale, Saro jan," he told the Mayor. "This really happened! Now the Turkish soldiers come to the villages of Musa to deport them, and find no one! Only deserted homes! The Armenian peasants have already deported themselves!" The *Crazy Gago* laughter returned for a moment. "But not to some god forsaken Syrian desert to be slaughtered, but right there, on their own mountain, thumbing their noses at the Turkish army! Saro jan, I swear I'm not making any of this up," he told Saro, who was more baffled by his passion in telling the story than by the story itself.

"Gago, please," said Laurian, who knew the Musa Dagh story well and was mindful of the time. "We do not have much time. We still have to return to Vardahovit today. What about Galian? It's him we're interested in."

"I'm coming to that, I swear. Listen, these peasants fight the organized Turkish army for forty days—well, actually Galian told me the battle went on longer than that, more than fifty days, but some Austrian novelist writes a novel about this and calls it the *Forty Days of Musa Dagh*, see, so now everyone thinks it was a forty-day battle. Anyway, they capture a lot of weapons and ammunition from the Turks, but, towards the end, their food supplies run out. There are a few thousand people on that mountain fighting for their lives. They know they won't be able to keep up the fight without supplies and with winter coming. At this critical moment, a French warship appears on the Mediterranean Sea. So they send an urgent message saying, 'We are a stranded population of Christians fighting annihilation by the Turks. Please rescue us!' The French come through and rescue the entire population; they just take everyone on the ship and bring them to Egypt, to a seafront town called Port Said. They erect tents and dump the entire population of the seven villages of Musa Dagh on the beaches of Port Said."

"Gago, please tell us about Galian," said Laurian, a bit too impatiently.

"Okay, fine, what's happened to you anyway?" snapped Gagik. It was his turn to sound impatient and bothered. "You've gotten more impatient instead of patient in your old age. You won't let an old friend just enjoy telling a great story anymore? This is a great story that you just can't rush through like I'm doing. But fine, here it is: Samvel Galian's grandparents meet and get married in the tents at Port Said! Now isn't that some story? Now listen to this. In 1919, the First World War ends. Musa Dagh is in a province of Syria called Iskenderoon. So after somehow living in these tents for four years, the French gather up everybody and return them to Musa Dagh. Samvel Galian's grandmother is in the heavy months of her pregnancy with his father, Gregor Galian, during the journey back. Gregor is born the day they arrive, five minutes after they enter his father's old ancestral house! Five minutes! Five minutes into the house and the kid is born! They say he is the first birth after the homecoming. Big celebrations. You can imagine, right?"

Both Laurian and Saro had to admit that the story actually was getting interesting. Gagik was encouraged.

"So good old Gregor," he continued, "our Samvel's father, grows up in his village in Musa Dagh. If I am not mistaken, his father is from the village of Bitias, but do not hold me to that. We were a bit drunk when I heard that part. But at any rate he spends most of his summers in the mountain, not in any village, with his maternal uncles, who had about a thousand head of sheep and goats, a huge fortune, and lived way up in the mountain, grazing the livestock, and hunting wild boar, and did not come down to their home in the village until early winter. The exact same system of *yayla* that we have here, you know, Saro jan."

"Gago," interrupted Laurian again, "I have to admit that the story is getting interesting, but are we going to get to Siberia and Saralandj anytime soon?"

"Siberia and Saralandj are coming right up!" said Gagik. "Just bear with me a few minutes longer. In 1939, when Gregor is barely twenty and having a grand old time hunting boar in Musa Dagh, the whole region of Iskenderoon becomes Turkey. Don't ask me how, but Turkey just annexes it and no one objects. Edik may know a lot more about this than I do. But one day it is Syria, and the next day it is Turkey. Something like that. Of course those villagers cannot go back and live under Turkish rule. They just waged a war against the damn Turkish army. So the entire population is mobilized once again and exiled, this time to Lebanon, to another remote village on the Syrian border called Ainjar. That is where Gregor finds himself in 1939. A faraway place, desolate, swampy, with mosquitoes and malaria. The French actually sponsor them again and build one room per family, and leave. Many die the first few years. Sorry," he says, noticing the impatient looks from both Saro and Laurian, "but that is important. It is important because when our very own Soviet agents appear in the village of Ainjar in 1946 and 1947, they are talking to a tired, sick, half dead population and trying to convince them to go back to Soviet Armenia, where they say everything is so abundant people do not know what to do with the surplus! Samvel used to say that the elders told stories of how the recruiters would say the hens lay eggs in the streets and no one collects them, because everyone has so much!

"So anyway, the Galians decide to come to the Motherland. Gregor, his parents, and two sisters, Arax and Mary, all board a ship from Beirut. Gregor is around twenty-seven and, according to Samvel, he is not very enthusiastic about leaving Lebanon. But his father insists. 'Look,' he says, 'I am an old man, and I have seen nothing but exile my entire life. I am not going to Armenia at my age to build a future. I am going so I can die on

Armenian soil instead of some obscure corner in these foreign lands. I am tired of wandering in foreign lands all my life.' So they get here. Imagine Yerevan in 1947. We're talking famine conditions. Gregor's father is very sick and cannot work. Gregor finds a job as a mason. But here is an incredible twist of fate. In 1949 they get exiled to Siberia. One morning the troops come to their home and say the entire family is being deported for nationalistic feelings unbecoming of a model Soviet citizen. You get that, Saro jan? Nationalistic feelings unbecoming a Soviet citizen! Remember those days, my brother? Anyway, Gregor's father, who has returned to Armenia for no other reason than to die in the Fatherland, dies in Siberia! The man who was afraid of dying in some obscure corner in foreign lands, dies in Siberia! Now that is hard to take."

There were tears in Gagik's eyes, and his voice was calmer, more somber. Neither Laurian nor Saro dared interrupt him now, no matter how late it was getting.

"Look," said Gagik, this time trying to control his tears rather than his usual *Crazy Gago* laughter, "now I am really going to cut it short. Gregor's sister, Araxi, is supposed to be this incredible beauty. Before they get exiled, in Yerevan, she falls in love with this guy, also a recent immigrant but I'm not sure from where. He is totally madly in love with her too. They are supposed to get engaged in a week. He comes in the morning to see her as usual, and sees they are all gone. When he hears about the exile to Siberia, he is devastated. He wants to go to Siberia himself to find her. He goes to the authorities and pleads with them to send him to Siberia. But they say no, they won't accept him! He stands in the street and starts cursing Stalin. Can you imagine that? In 1949, standing in the City Square, openly cursing the great leader for the privilege of being exiled to Siberia. The act is so preposterous that even the most tight-assed Stalinist apparatchiks do not take him seriously. The story is that the guy dies of grief, but no one really knows what happens to him. The Soviets in those days were not about to send anyone to Siberia because they *asked* to go! No sir! Siberia was reserved only to punish people, not to reward them! Now, Edik jan, my dear journalist friend, tell me that is not a great story in itself!"

"It *is* a great story, Gago," conceded Laurian, no longer trying to rush anything. This story was worth listening to regardless of how much relevance it had to their main inquiry.

"Anyway," continued Gagik, "Araxi ends up marrying someone else in Siberia. So do Gregor and Mary, his other sister. And here we finally come to Samvel Galian, who is born to Gregor and Martha Galian, in Siberia, in April of 1955. Martha is also originally from Musa Dagh, but a different village than Gregor. That part is over my head, Saro jan. I can never keep the names of the seven villages straight in my head. At any rate, Stalin has died by then, and almost all the political exiles are pardoned, and the Galians are released to return to Armenia. Now, why Saralandj? You may ask. Why indeed. A godforsaken place that probably looked like paradise to the Galians when they finally arrived there. There is no reason other than the family of Martha's sister's husband is from Saralandj. The Galians are recent emigrants and have no clear "home" to go to. So they come with Martha's sister and her husband and settle in Saralandj, with Samvel a one-year-old baby. His beautiful aunt Araxi never makes it. She contracts tuberculosis in Siberia and dies before Samvel is born. Samvel has never seen her, but everyone in the village talks about her legendary beauty."

There was a long silence when Gagik was done. Each was carried away in his own thoughts.

"How do you know all this?" asked Laurian, finally releasing the burning question of the investigative reporter within him.

"Some of it comes from Samvel himself," said Gagik. "As I said, we used to get drunk together once in a while. But the details come from his file. You know how detailed the files that they used to keep in those days were, especially on families who were exiled for nationalism. Samvel asked me once if I could get him the file on the Galians. Up to the year you got here, Edik jan, I tried but no one would listen to me. But after your visit, I do not know what happened, or maybe it was the times, not you, but all locked doors and safes seemed to be opening up. No one cared anymore. Things were crumbling right and left. No one gave a shit about Soviet secrets. I got his family file. I read it, and then gave it to him. It should still be in their house somewhere. But I've told you everything that matters already."

In part because he sensed Saro's impatience and in part because he himself had to absorb all the new information, Laurian decides to end the meeting. Even though it was already late, they would be in Saralandj soon enough. At that point, Saro tried to convince Laurian to skip the visit to Saralandj.

"We already know everything," he said. "We won't learn anything new there, I assure you. What if we are spotted nosing around the Galian house, and word gets to Ayvazian? It will blow our entire operation."

"Saro, I just want to see them. No harm in that. The stupid foreigner, on a tourist's impulse, reaches Saralandj, formerly off limits to folks like me! Gago himself said that Ayvazian's men have not been to the village for months, remember? They won't know we are there. Besides, we really don't know everything. We do not know how their daughter ended up in Moscow or Greece or wherever. Clearly Ayvazian is involved in that somehow, but how? We don't know any of that."

"It's already almost five pm. If we go to Saralandj now, and then try to go back to Vardahovit, it will be early morning by the time we arrive. Is it worth it?"

"Saro, my friend, it is worth it. Please humor me. Worst case, we drive back to Yerevan and stay in a hotel for the night. My treat. We'll drive fresh in the morning back home. Look, we've come this far, learned so much, let's not stop now."

Saro could not argue with Laurian at that point. They still had a few hours of daylight, and Laurian was determined to pay a visit.

The road from Ashtarak to Aparan is straightforward and in relatively good condition. It passes by mountains that have ancient historical meaning to Armenians. *Arayi Ler*, Ara's Mountain, appears on the right. This is a small mountain that every Armenian child has heard about, and Laurian remembered the story of *Ara Geghetsik*, Ara the Beautiful, an Armenian king so handsome that the Assyrian queen Semiramis lusts after him, and when he refuses to go to Ninveh, her capital, she marches with an army on Armenia and, in spite of her orders to her troops to capture Ara alive, he is killed in battle. Semiramis believes that she can revive him by having the gods lick his wounds, but Ara is dead nevertheless. There are many different versions of what happens next, but most of them end on this mountain, where Ara and his spirit are said to remain until today.

Laurian loved these stories as a child growing up in Switzerland, so for him seeing the actual monuments of the mythology for the first time as a grown man was one of the most touching experiences in his life. He saw it as a validation of a nostalgic childhood spent in close touch with the ancestral homeland spiritually and mentally, while the homeland remained unreachable and inaccessible physically.

It was early evening when they entered Saralandj. The Galians live in the very last house, Gagik had said. There was only one road, with chickens running around and an occasional dog barking at them. Parts of the road were so narrow that the car barely made it between a fence on one side and a ditch on the other. But they climbed up, until the concentration of homes became sparser, and in the distance, some twenty to thirty meters from the rest of the homes, they saw a solitary two-room construction; it was the Galian residence.

"Let's see what this theater has to offer," said Laurian to a nervous Saro, using a term from his journalistic days.

VII

On the fifth day in the Dubai jail Madame Ano appears in person. "Girls, we're going home!" she declares jubilantly.

She is dressed conservatively, with a long skirt and buttoned up blouse, a scarf on her head and no makeup. Lara almost does not recognize her at first. The "enforcer" Ali is with her. Ali is the person the girls fear the most. He is originally from Morocco, but has been in the Emirates for many years. He is tall and thin, with long curly shoulder-length hair, which he sometimes lets hang loose, and other times ties in a pony tail, but regardless of the style, it always looks greased, curly and pitch black. He is as comfortable in Western attire as in local Arab dress, and he is the man who disciplines difficult and insubordinate girls. All a pimp or manager has to do is call Ali and tell him that he or she is having problems with a girl. Ali visits the girl and usually an hour later the poor girl falls in line, fully docile and obedient. They don't like to talk about it, but they all dread seeing him.

But this morning Ali is welcome for once. He seems to know everyone. Every police officer greets him like an old relative. The guards laugh and joke with him in flowery Arabic. Even Madame Ano, normally not one to be outdone, seems to be under his spell. Some last minute paperwork is sorted out to confirm the release orders, and the girls are on their way.

Five days in prison has made them jittery and anxious to get back to their routine. They have not had a change of clothes in that time, and the use of one common bathroom has not allowed them enough time or space to tend to themselves. Although they are relieved and happy to be out, their movements seem awkward and uncomfortable as they come out and board small minibuses, each group heading to its own living quarters. Ano has retrieved everyone's passports, which is an indication that the dispute has been resolved.

Back in their housing complex the quiet hallways come alive again with the excited chatter and giggles of the returning girls. There is a rush to shower and change, the gloom and doom of the prison cell already a memory. Lara has just emerged from the shower when Ano calls and asks her to come to her apartment. Ali the Enforcer is also there, draped over an armchair and acting like he owns the place, sporting a broad smile. His headdress is off and his shiny hair rests on his shoulders.

"We have negotiated a very good deal for you, Lara," says Ano. "You will not have to go back to your old work any longer. No more working clients from all parts of the world. You will be exclusively for one man. You will live in a private house that he owns. Sometimes you will travel with him, maybe to Europe, as his companion."

Ano and Ali wait for some reaction from Lara, but there is none. She sits upright on a small side chair across from Ano, just having showered and changed into a clean miniskirt and shirt, an outfit that she has become used to while out in clubs, but which makes her self-conscious and uncomfortable in the room with Ali.

She stares at her hands resting on her exposed thighs and, before raising her eyes to look at Ano, asks, "What about the money I owe? My debts?"

"All will be settled for now. This arrangement is for one year only. After that, you will return and work for Viktor. Probably not in Dubai, but it is too early to tell."

"After one year of this will I still have debts? Will I still have to work like this?"

"Probably, but not for very long," says Ano with a hint of irritation in her voice. "Maybe another year or two. And then you'll be free. You'll be free before you reach twenty, Lara. Do you understand how incredibly lucky that is? You have seen girls here in their thirties still paying off debts, haven't you?"

But Lara does not feel very lucky, nor does she look excited at the news as both Ano and Ali might have expected.

"How much is this man paying for me?" she asks.

"Now, now, Lara, what has gotten into you, eh?" snaps Ano, entirely changing both the tone of her voice and her facial expression. "A few days in jail and you have turned difficult already? You know we cannot discuss those matters! All you need to know is that you'll be very well taken care of, you will have only one client, you will live in one of his houses, and you will receive a monthly salary from him to spend as you wish. We can keep wiring the money home for you from Moscow, as before. Nothing will change on that front. But your life will be a hundred times more comfortable. And you never know; perhaps your new master may give you all types of additional gifts, right, Ali?"

"Absolutely," Ali says, smiling from ear to ear. "He is a great man."

"Who is he?" asks Lara, looking at Ano.

"You'll meet him soon enough," replies Ali. "But let me tell you that he loves women. He will be very kind and generous."

Lara is not sure if she is detecting sarcasm in Ali's voice, or if that is just the way he talks.

"But you have to be nice to him too, do you understand?" Now Ali sounds more serious. "You cannot sit there like that with a long face and expect him to take care of *you*! It is you who has to make *him* happy, not the other way around! Do you understand that, Lara?"

Lara had been at this long enough to know that she was getting a potential break. But she also knew that they were not telling her everything. She had learned a lot from Anastasia in Moscow and later from Susannah and the others in Dubai. Anastasia's strength was that she negotiated with the clients and handled the money herself. It probably took her a while to get to that point, but she had nonetheless managed to get there. That was the only way to control the situation. But here, Lara was in the dark. She was being sold and bought like a commodity, and had no idea how much money was flowing and where. She had to find out what her contract was worth, if she hoped to gain a measure of control.

She forces a smile and looks at Ali. "I understand that. When will the new arrangement start?"

"Immediately. I will take you to his house this evening. So get ready. There is a lady there who will take care of you and settle you in. Her name is Sumaya; she is like your Madame Ano here, but works just for him. She's a very nice lady; she'll take care of your needs and questions." Ali and his eyes are beaming through his ear-to-ear smile.

"Like Madame Ano?" asks Lara naively. "Why? Will there be others like me in the house?" This is a whole new dimension that Lara has not suspected. She will be exclusively his, but not the only one. Is this going to be more like walking into a harem?

"Of course there are others like you," says Ali, and his smile disappears so suddenly that his face looks like it is collapsing into itself. "You don't think a man like that has stayed alone and waited for you all his life, do you? But they will not be in the same house. One lady per house, Lara. So in that house, you are the lady. You belong to him, but you obey Sumaya's instructions to the letter. In everything, you understand?"

"In *everything*," Ano says, taking over and emphasizing the point. "Not just how to behave in general but also what to wear, personal hygiene, making love, pleasing him sexually, how to speak to him when you two are alone, how to act when there are others—*everything*."

Ali's smile has returned and the folds on his face have been reshaped to accommodate it. He stands up.

"I'll pick you up around ten tonight. Be ready. And take no more clients from this moment on." He waves goodbye to Ano and leaves the room.

"Listen, Lara," says Ano after Ali leaves, "you know that you can't judge Ali by his lovely smile, don't you? These people are vicious. The one thing that they will never tolerate, even to the slightest degree, is insubordination. Their whole system is based on full compliance. You understand, don't you?"

Lara nods.

"I don't want to scare you. In fact, I don't want you to feel any fear at all. You cannot do your job if you're scared. They can also be very generous and very kind. But they have zero tolerance for insubordination. And zero tolerance when someone talks out of turn or meddles in things that are none of her business. Just know your place."

"What do you know about this place?" asks Lara, as if she has not heard the last piece of advice.

Ano is exasperated with the questioning, but decides to humor her. After all, she is young and curious; maybe she wants to know more so she does not make a mistake.

"What exactly do you want to know?" she asks.

"How many others like me does he have? Will I meet any of them? Is this like a harem? The girls talk about harems here."

"I don't know how many there are, and it does not matter. He wants you. Who cares if it is a harem? You'll probably be the youngest and the most beautiful one there. Where you are now is like a harem too, except it has many masters. What does it matter?"

"I just want to know the system, that's all, and what is expected of me."

"Ali just told you what is expected of you. Please him, make him happy, no long faces, and listen to Sumaya. That is very important."

"But why can't I know what he paid for me? That will tell me something and give me some idea of what he expects in return."

"Now, Lara, stop that! And don't you dare go there asking questions like that. I am serious. They'll throw you to the dogs and even I will not be able to find your pieces, you understand?"

The ice-cold, unreadable mask returns and looks into Ano's eyes for a few seconds. Then Lara stands up. "I need to go get ready," she says.

$$\mathscr{L} \quad \mathscr{L} \quad \mathscr{L}$$

They enter into what looks like a gated private community. Huge iron gates are swung open by an Indian guard as Ali's car approaches. He drives through and nods to the guard, who looks as if he is standing on military alert. The place looks immaculate—beautiful street lights on ornate cast iron stands, perfectly manicured shrubs and flowers, palm trees, trees with bright red bell-shaped flowers that Lara does not remember ever seeing before.

"This whole place belongs to your master," explains Ali. "His mansion is this first house in front of us."

Lara stares at the well-lit façade of a palace to their right, with a beautifully maintained green lawn in front surrounding the circular driveway leading to the gigantic front door.

"Behind this are the houses of his ladies, one of which you'll occupy," continues Ali. "And behind that are the staff quarters, where all the household help and drivers live."

Lara notices that the entire property is fenced in with a two-meter high stone wall. There are lights everywhere, even on the wall. In several places there are water fountains in shallow, circular pools. Even though it is close to eleven o'clock at night, there are workers here and there and guards standing at irregular intervals. She notices huge cages on the side of the road holding colorful exotic birds that stir uncomfortably as the headlights of the car shine on them. Several cats cross the street and rush into the bushes. *So who is this guy?* She wonders if the key to her liberation could be hidden somewhere in these grounds. Ali is driving very slowly but is his upbeat, jovial self, pointing, explaining and highlighting features he probably thinks should matter to her. He has made several left and right turns already and Lara realizes that she has lost track of how they got to where they are. She tries to visualize their path from the main gate but cannot.

Ali comes to a cluster of smaller homes, more like small single story chalets, and pulls up in front of one of them.

"Here we are," he says with excitement. "Your new home."

The outdoor lights are on, and there are also lights inside. Ali rings the bell. A woman in a black *abaya*, the long, neck-to-ankle Arab ladies' dress, but with uncovered hair, answers the door. She has short, black hair and drawn eyebrows.

"Hello, Madame Sumaya," beams Ali on all cylinders, speaking Arabic, "may I present to you miss Lara?"

"Come in," says Sumaya in English, and shuts the door behind them.

Ali repeats the introductions in English, tells Lara that she's in excellent hands, repeats a few more pleasantries to Sumaya and takes his leave.

"Follow me," says Sumaya, leading the way. She looks Lara over from head to toe a couple of times without her noticing it and realizes that she has a new situation on her hands.

"This is your bedroom. It is your job to keep it clean and tidy at all times. There is no telling when Sir may visit. He likes the bedroom tidy. You will find nightgowns and lingerie in the dresser and closet. You will dress appropriately and seductively every night before going to bed, even if you are alone. Being seductive will be a permanent state of mind for you, and not something you do on special occasions. Do you understand that?"

"Yes."

"Good. You also need to understand that he can have any woman he wants. *Anyone.* I'm sure you know you're very beautiful. But don't fool yourself. He's had many beautiful women. You need to learn how to please him. Do you understand *that*?"

"Yes."

"Good. The door across the hall leads to an extra bedroom. Do not use it. It is there because they put it there when the house was built. This," she says, opening a third door, "is a small study, with a desk and small collection of books. You can use it. There are paper and writing pens if you want to write anything. But you cannot send any letters without my prior knowledge. Is that clear?"

"Yes."

"Good. You cannot use any computers or send emails or visit websites. You can watch TV as much as you want. You can receive phone calls only on this house phone," she says, pointing to a phone in the living room, "but you cannot make any calls yourself from here. If there is any need to call anyone, you tell me, and we'll see what we can do. Clear?"

"Clear."

"Good. This is the bathroom." Lara notices a large Jacuzzi and huge shower. "It has everything you need," continues Sumaya. "If anything is missing you let me know. Let's go to the kitchen. It will be stocked at all times. You can cook once in a while for yourself if you want, but I do not recommend doing it often. Eat what we bring you. You will always have freshly cooked meals, which you can warm up, and fresh fruit and other foods. Do you have any dietary problems?"

"Sorry, what?"

"Is there anything you cannot eat?"

"No, no problems, sorry."

"Good. Now come and sit down."

They walk back to the living room and sit down on two armchairs across from the sofa. Sumaya catches her breath, looks at Lara for a long minute, breathes deeply and begins:

"As I said, there is no telling when Sir may visit. You are at his disposal 24/7. He can come to call any day and any time. You will let me know regularly the days of your menstrual period, so I can keep the schedule properly. I presume you are on the pill?"

"Yes."

"Good. So your periods are pretty regular, right?"

"Yes."

"Good. You will keep your private parts very clean and thoroughly waxed at all times. No hair whatsoever, not even the slightest growth will be allowed or tolerated. Is that clear?"

"Yes."

"Good. You have everything you need for that in the bathroom. If you need help waxing you tell me. Now, can you give good massages?"

"Not sure, Madame."

"Okay. You'll learn. Sir likes sensual massages. He also likes all things oral. You will make love to him more with your mouth than anything else. We'll explain more details on that later. But be prepared to use your mouth and tongue all over his body. I mean *everywhere*. Do you understand?"

"I think so, Madame."

"Good. As I said, someone else will explain the details to you later. Now, do you have any questions?"

"No, Madame, I don't think so," says Lara, even though she has a hundred burning questions. Ano's stern warnings about not speaking out of turn have sunk in. But Sumaya senses the hesitation in her answer and sees the confusion on her face.

"Speak up," she says. "It will not be often that I'll ask you if you have any questions. This is your first night. Ask what's on your mind."

"Okay, Madame. Will I interact with anyone else? I mean, will I see only Sir, and be alone here all the other times?"

"Actually, good question," says Sumaya. "We do not encourage a lot of interaction with others. That is why you have books and a TV. Of course, you cannot see any other men, no matter what. From now on, you cannot even be with Ali alone, even though he drove you here. But sometimes we allow female companionship, to relieve some of the loneliness and boredom. I'll first have to get to know you a bit more and then decide who would be a good match for you. I see your English is very weak, but adequate. What other languages do you speak?"

"Armenian and some Russian."

"We do not have any Armenians here, but there is one Russian speaker, and one Turkish speaker. Do you know any Turkish?"

"Very little, Madame. Some Azeri Turkish, which they say is Turkish and they can understand it in Turkey as well. But very little."

"OK. Any other questions?"

"No, Madame."

"Good. There is an extension number by the phone. You can reach me there if you need anything. You will keep the front door locked at all times, even though this place is the safest place on earth. You will *not* leave this house without my knowledge and *never* without an escort. Do you understand that? You will not leave this house alone for *any* reason."

"Yes, Madame."

"Good. Now, stop calling me Madame. I hate that. You call me Ms. Sumaya from now on."

"Okay."

"Okay what?"

"Okay, Ms. Sumaya."

"Good." And Sumaya actually smiles for the first time. "Now, speaking of what to call people, Sir likes Arabic names. He does not like foreign names. So your new name is Leila, not Lara. Close to your name. You will answer to Leila, and when asked your name, you will say Leila, not Lara. Is that clear?"

"Yes."

"Good. As for you, you will address him as Sir or Your Excellency. Both are fine. You decide which, based on the mood. You can change the way you address him only if he asks you to call him something else. He has done that on occasion. Now one last thing before I go. Inside the house you will always wear an abaya just like mine, with seductive lingerie underneath it. But keep your hair uncovered and well groomed. You can never leave this place, even when accompanied, without the abaya, head cover and hejab. Never. Even on the grounds of this estate you have to be covered head to toe. All the necessary clothing items are in your bedroom. If you do not know how to put on the hejab, someone will show you tomorrow. Do you need someone to show you?"

"Yes."

"Good. They will also show you how to walk in something longer than you're used to so you do not trip all over your own clothes." A second smile.

"Yes, Ms. Sumaya."

"Good. Now I have to leave. Lock the door behind me."

With that, Sumaya walks over to the phone in the living room and dials four digits. A few minutes later the headlights of a car are visible through the front windows. She leaves. Lara locks the door and watches her get into a car and slowly drive away.

ༀ ༀ ༀ

Finally alone, Lara took her time surveying her new domain. She went through her bedroom and bathroom and checked every detail. She rummaged through the contents of the dressers and closets, all the toiletries, checking every item carefully. She even checked the location of the light switches and tried them all. She tried one of the abayas over her clothes and looked at herself in the mirror. She played with her hair, holding it up and letting it down. She turned on the TV, even though she had no intention of watching. She checked the thermostats in the living room and her bedroom, and tested them to make sure the gauges worked. She looked out of every window and then carefully closed the curtains again.

It was past one o'clock in the morning. She walked to the bathroom and drew a bath. She carefully laid some underwear and a nightgown on a chair next to the tub, and gratefully walked into the hot water. That morning she was in a jail cell. Now she was here. If there ever was a time to ask 'how did I get here?' it was now. But the question did not even occur to her. She was where she was.

Lying in the hot bath all alone and in total quiet had a hypnotic effect on her. She drifted, allowing her subconscious to take over. She had to figure out the layout here. What role did Sumaya play? Who were the others? And what was the master himself made of? Sumaya was obviously doing her job. *But was that all?* Could women manage other women in this environment just as a job, without any personal involvement, preferences or views? Did Sumaya behave exactly the same way with every woman in this modern-day harem? Lara wanted to go further, and wonder how someone like Sumaya got the job she had, but that would have taken her too far from her immediate reality, too far from the realm of what was relevant to her. She did imagine her as a former lover-turned-manager, which was not far from the truth. Sumaya had in fact been appointed to guide and educate Al Barmaka into sexual maturity by his family early on, and had stayed on as his recruiter/manager later at his own request. But as Lara's mind drifted it could not dwell for long on Sumaya, and focused instead on the present, and only on what mattered to her. Broader questions of life usually came later, once she had built a firmer sense of the immediate realities facing her.

She was as curious about the other women as about the master. She had heard all sorts of stories from the girls about jealousies and intrigues in 'harems.' Competition for the master's affections and generosity could turn vicious and ruthless. Granted, some of these stories probably were exaggerations. But she was sure some of that actually existed. Maybe that is why they did not encourage much interaction among the women. There was one Russian and one Turkish woman in the master's collection, but he liked his women to have Arabic names. Any Arabs? Perhaps someone like the Moroccan girl she had seen in jail? Or some Lebanese bombshell like the ones she had run into in the discotheques in Dubai? And how would Ms. Sumaya find her "match" companion? Was it really a matter of compatible language, or was there more to it? Ano had said that she'd probably be the youngest and most beautiful in the bunch. Was that a curse or a blessing? A threat to her safety or an opportunity for something different?

As she sank deeper into a trance, her mind shifted away from the present and wandered briefly through the streets of Moscow before cruising over Saralandj. What would her brother Avo think of this place? What would he think of what had happened to her, what she had ended up doing? She missed her home so much that finding a way to go back had become an obsession ever since the first night with Ayvazian. But then she had heard some gruesome stories from the girls about how families back home rarely accepted what they did. Some knew, of course, but many lived with the illusion that their daughters or mothers or wives had respectable jobs overseas. Susannah had told her one story where the brother of one of the girls had slit her throat when she eventually made it back home. Defending the family honor was big in the villages. Would Avo forgive her? It was Avo she missed more than any of her other siblings; him and her mother.

She resisted thinking about her father; he had such a special place in her heart that thinking about him would create more emotional problems for Lara than she was ready to handle. She did, however, wonder what he would have thought about her situation; but the truth was that she did not know her father well enough to guess. That was an incredibly painful gap that Lara suffered from. She remembered him as a kind, supportive figure, even more so than her mother sometimes, and she remembered his reading most of all. But her situation now was so removed from her old life that it was impossible to venture any guesses about what her father thought or how he judged things.

Lara Galian just ached, body and soul, for a moment in her old home.

The fog in the forests of Saralandj was descending again, engulfing everything in its path. It had even reached here, mixing with the steam still slowly rising from her bath. It was quiet in the forest, just as it was here, and she was alone. No sound, no one in sight. And then the calm, soothing voice of her father came to her: "What did you discover in the forest, Lara?" "Nothing," she whispered, "there was nothing there." But there is a lot here. "What are you doing here, Lara? What do you expect to discover here?" Was that her voice or her father's?

"Just trying to find my way home," she whispered.

And I have not even met the new "master" yet, she thought. Sir, who likes things just so and not a bit different. Sir, who can be kind and generous and yet he can throw you to the dogs. Sir, who loves women so much that he has many of them, and he probably loves watching them compete for him…

Is that your little secret, dear Sir? You like young girls to be clean of hair, love you with their mouths and tongues, call you 'Sir' and compete for your affection? Is that it? My forest is much more complex and sophisticated than that, even in its emptiness and silence. The trees can see in the dark. The trees watch you and listen to your steps. And the procession of Saralandj forest pines was marching in the steamy room, giving the white marble walls a greenish hue; she could feel them in the bathroom and see their reflection in the steamy mirror.

"What did you discover in the forest, Lara?" *Which* forest, Papa? Talk to me, Papa jan, tell me how you think. I remember one of your stories, how women were throwing themselves into the Arax River to free themselves from being abducted by the Turks, or was it the Kurds? You read it to us once. Who were those ladies, Papa? When was that? A long time ago, but they were brave ladies, you said. They drowned themselves in the river, so as not to be caught and raped. They were brave and honorable, you said. Talk to me now; is that what you want me to do? Or do you want me to fight back. You also said the real heroes of our people fought back. There is no honor in being slaughtered like sheep, you said.

The green hue became thicker and darker in the bathroom. Saralandj was here. There were no more voices, but the silence had more clarity than any voice.

And then she saw herself leaving the forest, confident, seeing their house in the distance, the fear and anxiety of having been lost melting away and rising above her with the steam.

I think I've seen a way out, just like in the forest, she wrote in her book. *I need to win this, whatever it takes.*

VIII

His Excellency Ahmed bin Abdullah bin Saif Al Barmaka is in his early thirties. He is the youngest son of an extended family of merchants with a long history of cooperation with the rulers of the country, who are members of the elite class of businessmen in the Dubai social scene. He and his brothers are on the boards of several state-owned corporations and have a thriving trading and contracting business throughout the United Arab Emirates. They also own close to a hundred prime pieces of real estate, residential and office buildings, hotels, undeveloped parcels of land and over twenty foreign offices in Asia, Europe and the Middle East. They are major shareholders in various regional airlines and own a fleet of private jets for the exclusive use of family members.

Al Barmaka is a rebel of sorts, at least on traditional social grounds, even though his business savvy is legendary within the family. His single largest act of social defiance has been his refusal to marry and provide his parents with additional grandchildren over the twenty or so with whom his other siblings have blessed them. At his age, most of his brothers already had three to four children. But young Ahmed does not see the point. The future of the bloodline is long secured and a few more Al Barmakas running around will not have the same net utility as the first few grandchildren have. Besides, he believes that marriage tends to complicate things and cramp lifestyles, even in this male-dominated society. He knows that one day he'll have to accept an official wife and start a family, but he is in no rush, even though by the customs and traditions of his society he probably is already late by almost a decade.

He had seen Lara's 'portfolio' only a few weeks earlier and decided to add her to his group of regular ladies. The so-called portfolio contained a brief and sketchy history focusing essentially on her age and ethnic origin, basic medical record (which was heavily edited to remove references to the abortion in Moscow), and current "status," meaning current owner and manager. This was summarized in one paragraph of text. The rest of the twenty-page file contained nothing but photographs. Everything in the file appealed to him greatly—age, looks, origin (the novelty of it for him), her being in Dubai already, and the owner's willingness to trade. It was just a matter of negotiating the price.

"First of all," Al Barmaka had told his recruiter, "why are they offering her for three years? Who says I want her for three years? Second, a quarter of a million dollars? Are they crazy?"

"Well, three years because they think her age is so young that it calls for a longer contract than normal. They say that price averages just over $80 grand a year, which is also acceptable in such cases. But I can counter any way you want."

"One year. It is plenty, no matter how young. Offer them seventy-five K. All costs and obligations released for a year. I will pay her a salary and all her expenses. Then they can have her back."

It took a week to conclude the negotiations and finalize the deal. Ayvazian played hard to get and raised the fee for one year to a round one-hundred thousand dollars, payable up front. He was very pleased. He would have her back in a year, to put her back in the high value market in Moscow, where, having spent a year as a private concubine of a celebrity, it was hoped that she would master the fine art of seduction and learn something about playing with the rich and famous. His initial $500 dollar investment in acquiring Lara had paid off very handsomely indeed.

ℒ ℒ ℒ

When Al Barmaka first walked into Lara's chalet, he was not sure what to expect. Although Sumaya was an experienced trainer, and she had not let him down before, they had never dealt with such a young person. He was excited, not just for coming to a new woman, but for the mystery. He felt the anticipation of a child about to open a nicely wrapped gift.

Lara was ready for him. She had been sitting in the living room in her abaya reading a book when he opened the front door and walked in.

"And you are my new Leila," he exclaimed with a smile. "So happy to see you."

"Happy to see you too, Sir," said Lara, jumping to her feet and standing in front of him with her head bowed down, looking at her feet.

"Look up, Leila. Do not hide that pretty face from me."

"Yes, Sir." And up came the magic eyes, the youthful face, the piercing look, the radiance, all wrapped in such a perfectly harmonious demeanor that Al Barmaka said a silent thank you to the gods. *This is a delicate flower*, he thought, *to be handled with care.* It was moments like this that validated his status, his wealth, his stature. Al Barmaka fancied himself as a modern day Arab nobleman of the same caliber as the nobility in Andalus, who ruled Spain for several centuries and lived surrounded by the richest material and cultural means ever enjoyed by a class of people in history, or so Al Barmaka imagined. They drank the best wines, in spite of prohibition of alcohol by Islam, had the most beautiful women in the realm, enjoyed the highest levels of art, music and poetry, and were at the forefront of science and medicine. That's how Al Barmaka liked to think of himself.

He took off his headdress and tossed it on the sofa. Lara immediately picked it up, folded it carefully and laid it on the side table. Then she carefully placed the *Iqal*, the round halo-like black top that went over the headdress, on top of it, making sure that the long tassels were neatly folded also. Al Barmaka was already sitting comfortably on the sofa and patting the space next to him for her to sit. She obliged, sitting at the very edge of the couch but close to him, with her back straight and turned toward him, almost as if at attention.

"Are you nervous, Leila?"

"A little, Sir." And the eyes looked down again.

"Look at me. No need to be nervous. We now belong together, okay? We will take our time getting to know each other."

"Yes, okay, Sir."

"We will have a lot of time to talk in the coming days and weeks. But now, I want you to go and draw a bath for me. Can you do that?"

"Of course, right away, Sir."

Lara noticed that Al Barmaka did not smoke, a welcome relief. He actually smelled good, and his breath smelled good. He was thin, fit, and surprisingly young. With all the evidence of wealth spread around, Lara had expected someone much older. How could someone so young be so rich? "All I know is that one has to be born in the right gene pool," Susannah had told her. "You and I are not that lucky."

But Al Barmaka did not fit the stories of the young and rich locals, who were portrayed as spoiled to distraction, with no sense of true appreciation for anything that was handed to them, and no regard for anyone other than themselves, rowdy, rude and painfully immature. The man sitting on the sofa did not appear to be anywhere close to that description. Granted, he was older than the characters in those stories, but this one carried himself with calculated calm and seriousness and a display of a consideration which was uncharacteristic of anything else that she had seen or heard. This must be the local nobility, Lara thought as she drew his bath.

But there also was a chilling distance in Al Barmaka. His small sharp eyes, thin and long face accentuated by a well-trimmed goatee, and high, pronounced cheekbones did not exude warmth, even when he smiled. There was a toughness hidden in there somewhere, bred over generations of desert life which, although no longer applicable today, still had its uses in the modern day business world. It was that core harshness that sometimes surfaced with a strong hint of understated cruelty that gave any onlooker a chill. It was a toughness that Lara recognized; the survival conditions in Saralandj, although entirely different from the desert, were equally difficult and had long imposed a similar toughness on the villagers as well.

There was no hesitation or any sense of bashfulness in his movements as he walked over to the bathroom and got undressed. He acted as if he was in the presence of his wife of many years. His body was muscular and tight, almost stringy. He approached Lara and expertly undid the embroidered buttons at the back of her abaya and slipped it off her shoulders. He looked at her body for a brief moment, with the sexy grey and green bra and panties, and got into the tub. Lara sensed his swelling arousal from his eyes, without looking at it or feeling it physically.

"Join me."

He watched her as she undressed and came to the tub. "Let me see you first," he said.

Lara was not sure what he meant. He gestured with his hand for her to turn around. She slowly made a three hundred and sixty degree turn and faced him again. She was blushing. He gestured to her to get in. Her hand was covering her sex as she lifted her right leg to quickly get into the tub, and that simple act of shyness aroused him even more. She noticed.

Their love-making was smooth and effortless. She remained coy and submissive throughout, both in the tub and later in bed, and followed his lead willingly, lovingly. For the first time she felt that this man really wanted her to enjoy it, and that it mattered to him that she did. He acted considerate, giving, caring. She had never before known this in any client, and obviously never in a rapist. But she did not dwell on that. "Never lose your head, Lara," she remembered, and reminded herself of that admonition once again. She closed her eyes and concentrated on the tough and cruel part of him, the more dominant and unchangeable part of the reality she was facing. She realized that her nagging need to be loved and cared for had to be resisted at all costs.

In the wee hours of the morning, he got out of bed, dressed, and left, giving her a short nod. Maybe he was too tired for a more affectionate good-bye; maybe his mind was too preoccupied with work for long pleasantries; or maybe he just didn't care. At any rate, she was thankful for that; she would never wonder or fantasize again about her real role in this house.

இ இ இ

Sumaya should be pleased, but she does not appear to be. Her job is to see to it that the girls make the master content, and he seems quite content. There has not been any complaint from him for two weeks. No little irritating lapses committed by one of the girls about which Sumaya has had to lecture the offending party. And Sumaya has not even sent anyone to teach Lara details of how she should behave, as she had initially intended. Al Barmaka has seen Sumaya only once in the past two weeks, which is unusual. He normally calls her at least once every few days to either complain about something or to give a new order. And that is not where it ends. He has seen no one except Lara in the past two weeks. Even when she had her period, he did not visit any of the other girls for four days, preferring to wait for Lara. That is a truly major departure from his common practice, a first in the seventeen years that Sumaya has worked for him.

Sumaya is mulling this over when Nadia calls. Her real name is Natalia, but she has been given an Arab name like the others. She is a twenty-six-year-old Russian girl, one of the favorites of Al Barmaka, until Lara's arrival. Blonde, thin and attractive, Natalia knows not only how to handle Al Barmaka, but also Sumaya. Once in a while, she has passed on to Sumaya part of the special monetary bonuses that Al Barmaka is in the habit of giving. She is a professional, determined to leave Dubai a rich woman before she is thirty and "retire" in Moscow. She needs to keep the affections of Al Barmaka and the loyalty and favor of Sumaya in order to achieve her goal. She tells Sumaya she needs to see her urgently. Sumaya has been expecting this call, and, if anything, is surprised it has taken Nadia this long.

"He has not seen me for two weeks," says Natalia as soon as she is seated in Sumaya's living room.

"I know."

"He has not been traveling, right? He is here in Dubai, in his house, right?"

"Right."

"Has he been sick?"

"Not that I know of."

"Ms. Sumaya, please. We've known each other for six months now, and you've known him for many years. Please talk to me. Is there someone new on the premises?"

Sumaya shifts her weight and crosses her leg. She looks Natalia over, with her perfectly pressed embroidered black abaya, golden locks resting on her shoulders, long lashes casting a sad shadow over her eyes. She sees the concern, almost like a panic, but she also sees the pure professionalism in her posture. She can work with this woman. She understands she is in business. Even the personal issues are about business. Leila, on the other hand, is just a kid. She has managed to enamor Al Barmaka more because of what she is than what she does. She is an unknown, with no apparent simple or single thing driving her, and therefore unreliable. But she can rely on Nadia's professionalism.

"Yes, there is," she says finally. The girls are not really supposed to ask such questions, as it is considered to be none of their business. But they always find out eventually. "She has been here for two weeks. She is very young, around seventeen."

"Has he been with her the whole time?"

"Except for four days, when she was not clean, yes."

"And in those four days, did he see anyone else?"

"He stayed alone." Sumaya still talks in short, matter-of-fact phrases, even though she has already decided that she needs to take Natalia into her confidence and possibly even make her part of a plan of action, if that were to be necessary.

There is a long silence as the two women ponder the situation. A maid brings mint tea in small glasses, sets it on the tray on the coffee table and leaves. Natalia stands up and serves Sumaya her glass, sits back down with her own glass, wondering whether she should say anything or let Sumaya open the conversation.

"We need to bring Farah into this," Sumaya says finally. The undefined "this" suggests to Natalia that Sumaya considers them to be involved in a situation together. She is relieved to find out that Sumaya shares her instincts about a possible threat to them all. His age, the family pressure on him to get married, and now a young woman that he cannot part with—this is a prescription for disaster that could bring their lucrative world to a sudden end.

Farah is the Turkish girl, real name Ferda, recruited in Istanbul by Sumaya personally on one of Al Barmaka's business trips. He had met her at one of the parties that his Turkish hosts organized. The place was swarming with ladies of the night, and Al Barmaka had returned to his hotel with Farah. He had asked Sumaya to stay behind and arrange for her to be brought to Dubai, with a one-year contract. "Don't come back without her," he had said.

Farah too is in her mid-twenties, discovered by one of the recruiters of a brothel in Izmir and later brought to Istanbul. She has thick dark hair, brown eyes, with a distant hint of Asian origins that sometimes is more pronounced when she smiles, medium height and heavier than Natalia and Lara. Farah is not as serious as Natalia. She likes to laugh and joke around, even get rowdy once in a while. Natalia is a bit surprised that Sumaya wants to include her in their "thing." There is also a fourth woman, a Moroccan, who is the only lady there other than Sumaya who speaks Arabic. Natalia would have thought she might be a better co-conspirator if they needed to resort to intimate pillow talk to extract something from Sir.

"Not Aisha?" she asks, referring to the Moroccan.

"No. She should know nothing. She cannot be trusted. Besides, her time is almost up and she'll be sent away."

"But what about Farah?"

"She still has four months, a little less than you. And she knows people in Turkey who could be helpful, depending on how things go."

Sumaya is always very frugal with her words. She does not like long conversations. To her, speaking, like undergoing surgery, should be done only when absolutely necessary. In moments like this it can lead her listeners to frustration. It is obvious that Sumaya has thought of a plan, but she won't just come out and say it.

"Depending on how things go?" Natalia is careful not to be pushy, but has to know what Sumaya is thinking. The girls cannot do anything without her.

"Look," Sumaya says, "we don't know what this is yet—a passing infatuation or something more serious. But clearly you're nervous, and probably so is Farah. The new girl is unusual and very desirable. Can you take a chance?"

"Ms. Sumaya, I am not sure what you are suggesting. I admit I don't like what is going on. I used to be his favorite, you said so yourself. And I have really appreciated your friendship in all this. But now I don't know what to think. I remember how he sent away that other girl—was her name Samya?—when I first got here. You told me about it and you said her contract still had five months to run, but he had gotten tired of her, and she had not acted properly—too aggressive, right? Am I now in the same situation? Of course I have not been too aggressive or done anything else wrong. But how can I fight a seventeen-year-old that he seems to be entranced by, assuming that's what we're facing?"

"We have to be ready for anything. But you are not in the same situation as Samya. He has paid for you in full; he had not done that in Samya's case. So he has less incentive to send you away before your contract runs out. Probably the worst case scenario for you is that he'll pay your salary until the end of your contract and then send you away without using you. Which means no gifts, no bonuses, no farewells. Probably the same with Farah."

"What can we do?"

"First, we don't panic. I'm not worried about you. But I am worried about Farah. She is hot blooded and can get out of control."

"Ms. Sumaya, please, can you tell me anything about the new girl?"

"Her name is Leila. She is from Armenia. She is seventeen. Very beautiful. Wild and feminine at the same time." Sumaya expresses pure fact and diagnosis, without even a pinch of emotion thrown in.

"She's from Armenia? She probably knows Russian, right?"

"She knows some Russian, even some Turkish, she says. Her English is very poor, but passable. She has learned it in the street. No schooling, as far as I know."

"Can she really be a serious threat?"

"He has asked her to call him Ahmed in bed. That is his first name, by the way. Did he ever ask you to do that?"

"No." Natalia is shocked; until now she did not even know what his first name was.

"He has not asked anyone else to do that. There was once a Ukrainian woman, before you, and he told her it was okay to call him 'my love' or 'lover' in bed. But that did not last long, and besides, that was different from a first name. It was more a part of their flirting."

"Okay, so this is more serious than anything else. But still, this girl was a prostitute, right?"

"Oh yes. She was working here in Dubai."

"Can he marry a prostitute?"

"Al Barmaka can do anything he wants," says Sumaya with a sense of abandon. "The girl is young. Maybe he thinks he can train her to be a good Arab wife. Who knows? Let me ask you again, can we take a chance to find out?"

Natalia notices the change in the question. The first time, Sumaya asked, 'Can you take a chance?' The second time she asked, 'Can *we* take a chance.' Until then, Natalia was still looking at Sumaya as the manager, a kind of Chief of Staff. But now she realizes that she has as much a stake in this as any of the girls. A 'wife' would threaten her job as much as the job of the concubines. She could be rendered obsolete overnight. This is a huge revelation that makes Natalia feel unusually equal in status to Sumaya. This time, they need each other, and the relationship is more balanced than ever.

"No," she says, and is conscious of the fact that she has begun to adopt Sumaya's style of talking in short, curt sentences. "We cannot take that chance. So what do we do?"

"Let's bring Farah in first," says Sumaya.

Clearly Farah has a role here that Natalia does not understand.

Sumaya reaches over to the phone on the side table, and dials. "Bring Farah," she says in English, and hangs up. It must be the Indian driver, thinks Natalia.

As they wait for Farah, the atmosphere is a bit tense. Sumaya is drawn into her own thoughts, and Natalia is trying to figure out how they all relate in this game. There is no question that Sumaya has to call the shots, but the lineup is confusing for Natalia. She likes to have things neat, organized, with everyone knowing where they fit in. Meanwhile Sumaya is trying to sort out a scheme to eliminate the Leila problem. There are several options worth considering, none of them safe, given Al Barmaka's apparent devotion to her.

Sumaya's cell phone vibrates in the side pocket of her abaya, sending shivers down her thigh. Her hand dives into the pocket and brings out the phone. It is Al Barmaka's private office calling, which is unusual in the early evening. She would have thought he'd call from his cell phone. She decides to take it in private and walks into her bedroom, telling Natalia to keep Farah busy when she arrives. But when she answers the phone, it is the voice of his Indian business manager that greets her.

"A very good evening to you, Ms. Sumaya, dear," says Manoj with exaggerated cheerfulness. "I trust all is well with you and your ever so pleasant complexion."

Complexion? Sumaya is now very annoyed, but keeps her cool.

"Yes, Manoj. How can I be of help?"

"Well, Ms. Sumaya, dear, His Excellency has arranged for Leila to start taking Arabic lessons regularly. Sheikh Nizam will come three times a week to teach her, starting tomorrow afternoon at four p.m. His Excellency has asked that you organize and oversee everything as usual, and, considering that Leila, hmmm, well, is a lady, that you be present at all the lessons, so as not to have any awkwardness whatsoever. Those are his instructions, Ms. Sumaya, dear."

"Sheikh Nizam?" Sumaya asks. "Is she to study Arabic language or religion?"

"Just language for now, Ms. Sumaya, dear. Sheikh Nizam is a first class instructor of both language and religion, but for now his assignment is to teach her Arabic."

"Okay, Manoj. All is clear. Good night."

"Many thanks, Ms. Sumaya, dear. And wishing you a superb evening."

If I hear you say 'Ms. Sumaya, dear' one more time, she thinks, I'll strangle you with my bare hands! Arabic lessons? Maybe religion will follow? And why did he not bother to call me himself? Am I now at Manoj's level? Sumaya has to sit down. She had taken the call standing up, looking out the window of her bedroom at the beautiful lawn and shrubs. But her knees feel weak and shaky. She sits on her bed and stares at the silent cell phone in her hand. She can still hear 'Ms. Sumaya, dear' oozing out of the phone in the totally fake, slippery voice of Manoj. *He's probably laughing right now at how he's keeping the real plan from me,* she thinks. *The women can come and go, but the almighty male business manager is untouchable. We'll see about that, Mr. Manoj, dear, we'll see about that.*

She hears the front door open and Farah greet Natalia with her usual enthusiasm. That too is unusual. These two are competitors, she tells herself. Why are they acting like sisters? The cold-blooded Russian professional and the excitable Turkish prostitute, hugging and pretending to be sisters in her own living room. How much more am I going to see at my age? she asks silently. And what about Leila, born Lara? She seems to have the subconscious instincts of Farah, excitable and unpredictable, but the outer behavior of Natalia. Could that be true? Could a creature that combines such entirely different worlds actually exist? And what happens when such a creature learns Arabic and converts to Islam? Who can fight her in this dominion? How can she then not become the queen, governing all, ruling the domain in his name?

Sumaya does her best not to show her anxieties as she enters the living room. She greets Farah as if nothing has happened and sits down in her chair. But they both notice that she is paler than usual, and she knows that they notice that something is amiss.

"I do not want to sound alarmist," she says to the two women, "and there is still a lot that we don't know, but we may have a little problem on our hands. A little seventeen-year-old problem."

Farah is not sure what this is all about.

"Summarize it for her," says Sumaya, acting too tired to do the talking herself.

Natalia says, "There is a new woman, or girl, seventeen. He is captivated by her and has seen only her in the past two weeks. She is from Armenia. Apparently beautiful, unsophisticated, uneducated, uncultured, but captivating nonetheless."

"So that's why I have not seen him for two weeks?" asks Farah lightly, still not sharing the concern of the other two about the seriousness of the situation.

"And that's why chances are you won't see him again at all," chimes in Sumaya, eyes still closed, her forehead resting awkwardly in her hand, showing no patience for those who are slow to catch up. "As long as Leila is here you don't stand a chance with him."

"Sorry, Ms. Sumaya. Sorry if I upset you. But I don't understand what a seventeen-year-old girl from Armenia has to do with me, with us…"

"You don't understand?" screams Sumaya, finally her patience shattered. "You really don't understand? He has seen no one but her for two weeks. He has not ever asked anyone but her to call him by his first name. He has hired a private tutor of the highest caliber to teach her Arabic. And you still do not understand? What is there to understand?"

"So sorry, Ms. Sumaya," whispers Farah. "I had no idea about all this. So sorry. I really did not know."

Even Natalia is taken by surprise by the news about the private tutor. She does not understand why Sumaya would hold that bit of information from her, and does not suspect that she may have learned about it during the phone call just a few minutes earlier.

"Well, now you know," says Sumaya, regaining her characteristic cold composure. "What do you think we should do about it?"

"What should we do? Isn't it obvious? Her tie with Sir has to end. Either she leaves, or he gets, so sorry, how you say, he falls out of love with her…"

"Falls out of love?" asks Sumaya.

"So sorry, yes. In Turkish, we say gets cold from her…hard to explain, but basically he not love her anymore…"

"Farah, talk freely. How can we make him 'get cold from her'?"

"Complicated," says Farah. "That too much complicated. We need hair, nails, maybe other things from both her and him. Too much complicated."

"Farah, I am not interested in voodoo here." Sumaya raises her voice. "Forget hair and nails and whatever. Focus, Farah, focus. We have a problem. What do we do?"

"OK, fine, focus, focus," exclaims Farah, protocol forgotten. "What do we do? Isn't it simple? We get rid of her, that's what we do. We get rid of her. If not that, *you* tell me what we do!"

Finally Sumaya feels she has the conversation where she wants it. She wants the girls in on the plan that she has in mind, but wants them to come up with it together. Thinking ahead, she knows that there will be very serious repercussions with Al Barmaka later, and the girls have to be fully implicated along with her so they do not point the finger only at her.

"We get rid of her," she repeats with a measure of sarcasm in her voice, indicating that she is still not sure what that means. "We just get rid of her? Nadia, what do you think?"

"There are many ways to get rid of her. If this was Moscow, she would just disappear. Simple. But here? I don't know."

"So you agree we should get rid of her," says Sumaya.

"We have no other choice. It looks like she may have the power to get rid of us soon, no?"

"We cannot make her just disappear as in Moscow. How then?" It is Sumaya again leading them on.

"I not seen her," says Farah, "but I think Mehmet in Turkey would love to have her."

Finally we are getting somewhere, thinks Sumaya. This is the only logical choice that she can see. She knows Mehmet. She negotiated Farah's contract with him, or through him, but it was never clear who the ultimate boss was. But Mehmet seemed to have the authority to make decisions on the spot.

"Why would Mehmet love to have her?" asks Sumaya, but regrets the question, worried that it will take them off track.

"Well, as I say, I not seen her, but if she really is young and beautiful and Armenian, she's for Mehmet. He loves to fuck young Armenian girls."

"How do we get her out of here and into Turkey?" asks Natalia, for the first time getting the sense that Sumaya has planned this scenario all along. She is brilliant, thinks Natalia, with newfound respect for the lady who is now staring at her with very serious and penetrating eyes.

"It can be done, if planned carefully. But there will be serious consequences. He will be furious. All the blame and suspicion has to go to her and a few security men. It has to look like she planned an escape and seduced the guards to help her. We know nothing about it."

That's going to be a very delicate operation, thinks Natalia. We'll have to make the new girl do something against her will, and still somehow pin the whole thing on her.

"How do we handle her in this?" she asks. "I mean will she know that she is escaping? Or are we going to have her think that she's taking a trip to Turkey, maybe to meet Sir there, and then she just ends up with Mehmet?"

"What do you think?" asks Sumaya.

"The first is easier, because she'll be more cooperative, assuming that she wants to escape. But the second is much safer. The less she knows the better."

"So we make her 'escape' without making her know that she's escaping?" asks Farah.

"If she knows she's escaping, then she'll know we are helping her. Why take that risk? Maybe we can make her believe that she is going on a trip to meet Sir somewhere. Then she lands in Istanbul and disappears."

"Mehmet should not keep her in Istanbul," says Farah. "Maybe Izmir, or Antalya. Too much traffic in Istanbul. And Sir goes there sometimes." Farah is thinking ahead, which is unusual for her.

Sumaya is satisfied with the meeting, even though her face does not show it. She is all business.

"I need some time to think," she tells them. "Farah, think of what message to send Mehmet. In some ways, the less he knows the better too. We should pull this off while keeping everyone involved in the dark."

"It will be easy to keep Mehmet in the dark," says Farah. "He not care about details. He get girls against their will all the time. So no surprise for him if Leila kicking and screaming and telling fantasy stories about Sir. In fact, better if she do, then it will be normal for Mehmet. And he's used to Armenian girls sold in Turkey against their will. This is good plan, Ms. Sumaya."

"Does this Mehmet know Sir?" asks Natalia.

"Of course not," answers Sumaya. "He knows me, and he knows of him, but no details. Not even a name. Farah, you understand that it should stay that way, right?"

"Of course."

"Sir should not suspect that she escaped to Turkey," says Natalia. "That will be very difficult for us to arrange. If we send her there, there'll always be some trail. And if he suspects anything, he may start asking questions and investigating."

"We have a lot to plan," says Sumaya. "If we're smart about this, all will fall into place. Farah, you understand what you need to think about, right? And the absolute need for secrecy."

"Of course."

"Good. Now I need to think. I'll contact you later. Do not show any concern. Do not speak about this in your own houses. There are ears everywhere. We talk about this only here and always in person. No phones. Off you go."

IX

Laurian was not prepared for what he saw when they entered the house. Silva Galian, Lara's mother, was lying in bed, covered toes to chin by a blanket. Her face was so pale and shriveled that for a moment Laurian thought he was staring death in the face. The oldest daughter, Martha, who had recently married, was named after her paternal grandmother. She had the manure-burning stove lit under a pot of water and was waiting for it to boil. The late afternoon sun poured into the otherwise dark room from a small high window; the glass was dirty and cluttered with cobwebs, but the beam of light was strong. It rushed into the room and hit the grey wall, highlighting the framed photograph of the late Samvel Galian that hung from a rusty nail right over his bed. One of Martha's sisters was also in the room, but the rest of the children were not in sight.

Laurian and Saro had knocked the door, but not having heard any response, had gently pushed it. The door opened and they walked in. Martha was startled at first, but when Saro explained that they were old acquaintances of her father, she greeted them and invited them to sit on the small dining chairs. Martha introduced her sister, Alisia. Saro explained that they had just met with an old friend of their father named Gagik, in Ashtarak. Martha recognized the name.

The water started to boil, and Martha put a teaspoon of tea leaves from a cubic tea-tin in a brown mug and poured the hot water over it. Then she approached her mother, sat at the edge of the bed, holding the mug with her left hand and gently rubbing her mother's covered shoulder with her right hand.

"Mama," she whispered, moving her hand from her mother's shoulders to her graying hair, "get up and have some tea. We have visitors."

Silva Galian slowly opened her eyes. She stared at her daughter for a long moment, as if searching in her memory for her resemblance. Then she started moving, and eventually sat up in bed. Martha wrapped the blanket over her shoulders and handed her the mug of tea, which she held in her lap with both hands. She finally looked up toward the two men seated awkwardly at the other end of the room.

Saro stood up and introduced himself, but was careful not to offer to shake her hand, given that both of her hands were needed to steady the mug, and then he introduced Laurian. He nodded and smiled; he didn't know what to say. He hoped that Saro would at least start a conversation, any conversation, to give him more time to recover and to think. Martha asked if they would like some tea, but they kindly declined. Alisia was seated on a low stool behind the stove where she was peeling potatoes. Behind her, against the wall, there were a couple of wooden shelves resting on cinderblocks, lined up with glass jars full of various pickles and other preserves. A few burlap sacks stood in the corner, and Laurian guessed from the round shape of the contents protruding from the burlap that they were filled with either onions or potatoes.

"We were in Ashtarak, visiting an old friend of Samvel's," repeated Saro, "and decided to drive up here to pay you a visit. I really hope that we are not inconveniencing you, *tikin*—Mrs.—Galian."

Silva Galian looked at them again and nodded, but she had nothing to say.

"I hope that everything is fine here with you," continued Saro. "*Tikin* Galian, you do not look well. Gagik in Ashtarak mentioned that you had been ill, and that you had been to the hospital there. I hope that the doctors are taking care of whatever is bothering you."

"The doctors know nothing," mumbled Silva Galian and fell silent again.

"Did they at least tell you what they think is wrong with you?" persisted Saro.

"First they suspected cancer, then they thought I had a liver problem. They took a lot of blood, but they know nothing."

"Would you like us to take you to a hospital in Yerevan?" asked Laurian, encouraged by the fact that she was at least talking. "They have better equipment and maybe even better doctors there."

"What's the point? They won't be able to cure me. I will not leave Saralandj again." Then she seemed to withdraw into herself again.

"Martha jan," said Laurian, turning to the daughter, "how long has your mother been ill like this?"

"Ever since Papa died."

"And there has been no change in her condition that whole time?"

"First we thought it was the mourning. She took it very hard. She would not eat, rarely slept, got tired quickly and would lie in bed for hours on end. But after two months we realized it could not be the mourning alone. Something else had to be wrong."

"Is that when you took her to the doctors in Ashtarak?"

"Yes. First my aunt convinced her to go. They just gave her some medicine, but I am not sure what. She took it, but things did not get any better. Then she stopped taking the medicine. Two weeks ago my husband Ruben convinced her to go again; he borrowed a car from a friend in Aparan and we took her ourselves. Exactly the same thing. Now she does not want to leave the house at all."

"Did you talk to the doctors?" asked Laurian. "Did they tell you or anyone else what she has?"

"They think she has cancer—of the female sort. They did not say much else, except for they did not sound hopeful that it could be cured."

Alisia finished peeling the potatoes and placed them in a pot of water over the stove. She then started washing and peeling cucumbers and tomatoes. She apparently was trying to set the table, and Laurian was not sure how they should respond if invited to supper.

"Where is the rest of the family?" he asked Martha. Supper preparations were a good indication that the rest of the family would appear at some point.

"The youngest two boys returned from school and are with my in-laws doing their homework," she said. Then, noticing Laurian's approving glance at the mention of schoolwork, added, "My father was adamant about the importance of education. He kept saying that we should all study, and, if we could, go beyond our local school here. His big ambition was to have at least a few of his children graduate from the University in Yerevan."

"What about the others?" asked Laurian.

"I got married and will not continue school. The eldest of the boys, Avo, is needed to tend to the sheep and cows, and cannot focus on school. My younger sisters are needed at home and in the garden, but they will try to finish the local school."

"I meant where are the others now?" asked Laurian again.

"Oh, sorry, my sisters are also at my house with my in-laws, helping them finish the preserves for winter."

"How old is Avo?" asked Laurian.

"He has turned sixteen already." Then, as if sensing either disbelief or disapproval in Laurian's glance, she added, "He is the oldest boy. Age doesn't matter. The oldest boy has his responsibilities regardless of age. That is how it is here."

The last phrase, 'that is how it is here,' was a clear indication that Martha had already placed Laurian out of what 'here' implied. He was not from these parts and needed the system explained to him.

"Of course, of course," Laurian assured her. This is the second time that Martha had read him correctly. *Maybe I'm too transparent*, he thought. *I wonder if I am.* He made a mental note to be careful about not showing his emotions so readily.

Silva Galian had taken several sips of her tea, placed the brown mug on the floor, and lay down again in bed. She pulled the blanket under her chin and shut her eyes. Alisia placed small dishes of cucumbers, tomatoes, cheese, pickles and sausages on the table. The beam of light coming through the window had faded, and the room was noticeably darker than when they first came in. Martha turned on the switch and a solitary light bulb hanging from the ceiling was illuminated. Silva stirred in bed and gave a short moan. The light was another legacy of the former Soviet Union: Every village in the realm had to be electrified. So even the most remote and backward villages, which did not have indoor plumbing, gas, running water or any of the most basic necessities, had electricity.

Saro signaled to Laurian that they should leave, but Laurian seemed intrigued with this family and ignored him. Besides, they had not even talked about the famous seventeen-year-old daughter.

Then Avo, the teenage man of the house, walked in. He was surprised to see the visitors, but was quickly briefed by Martha. He went to sit by his mother at the edge of the bed. He was much taller than Laurian had expected. He was about Saro's height--handsome, with thick curly black hair, arched Armenian nose, sun-burnt bony face, and radiant eyes. He was dirty from working outside and looked tired. Silva Galian opened her eyes briefly and smiled at the sight of her son.

"*Vonts es*, Mom jan," asked Avo.

"Lav, *balés*, du vonts es?"

"Lav, mom, *esor inch es kerel*? Fine, mom, what have you eaten today?"

"I've eaten, don't worry. Are the animals all settled?"

"Almost. A few more weeks and we'll be settled before winter descends."

Then Silva Galian shut her eyes again, with the vague hint of the smile still lingering on her otherwise lifeless face. Avo joined the visitors on one of the chairs by the dining table. Alisia offered him a cup of tea, which he accepted with a nod.

"I'll be happy to arrange to take her to Yerevan to see a specialist doctor," said Laurian to Avo. "It cannot hurt, and it may help."

"She will not go," said Avo with finality. "She will not leave the house again. I don't think she will survive the winter."

Laurian was amazed at Avo's apparent lack of emotion, but he also could sense that it was the sixteen-going-on-forty man of the house that was talking. There was something about the boy that he found intriguing. The cool, gathered composure clearly belied his age. But there was something deeper, which he could not pin down, that disturbed Laurian, but this was not the time to dwell on that.

The door opened and the other two daughters and two brothers walked in. They were introduced and quietly sat at their chairs around the table. Laurian and Saro exchanged a few more pleasantries with the group, and then Laurian decided it was time to leave. But he had to ask the burning question before leaving.

"We'll have to leave now," he said to the group at large. "But we are curious about your youngest sister. Have you heard from her lately?"

"All we know is that she is a model in Greece," said Martha, clearly indicating that she did not want to have a long conversation about Lara.

"But have you heard from her directly?" persisted Laurian. "I mean, has she called or written?"

"No," said Avo, taking over the conversation. "She called only once, the day she left, and talked to mother, but we have not heard from her since."

"I'm sorry," said Laurian, very careful not to sound offensive, "I do not mean to intrude, but don't you think that is a bit unusual? I mean, if Lara has the time to wire money, why can't she find the time to call? Or send a note?"

"I suppose you're right," said Avo, showing his discomfort with discussing the subject. "But you have to understand that we no longer have a phone here. So she could not have called even if she tried. And I am not sure about writing. Mailing a letter all the way from Greece seems too much trouble, to be honest."

"But she can still wire the money?"

"Well, the post office says that all the cash transfers are made from Moscow. So we believe that she has asked her agents to wire the money on her behalf. They probably just deduct it from her salary. Everyone says it would be easier and simpler that way."

"That makes sense," conceded Laurian, wanting to put the young man at ease. "She must have a very good agent. Do you know who her agent is?"

"I have not met him yet, but mother has. It is Viktor Ayvazian, or maybe his uncle Sergey. They found Lara her job, organized her papers, and now help her wire the money. I'm sure one day Lara will write or maybe even visit. Everyone says it is almost impossible to take time off and travel home during the first two years. It is too early to expect direct contact with her."

Laurian wanted to ask about his reference to "everyone" who was telling him these things, but thought better of it. This was not the time.

"Why don't you stay and have a bite with us?" invited Avo, pointing at the table. They were all gathered and ready to start.

"We are very grateful, Avo," said Laurian. "But we still have a few hours' journey to get back home. It is very late, and we ate in Ashtarak before coming here. Some other time. I am sure we'll meet again." Laurian stood up. "Is there anything we can do for you?" he asked, taking Avo's hand and looking him straight in the eye.

Avo smiled and shook his head politely.

"Anything at all," insisted Laurian. "For example, would you like to have a cell phone? I think it might come in handy. If nothing else, I would like to call you once in a while and check to see how your mom is doing, or if you need anything else."

"Oh, I had a cell phone but it fell in the watering pond in the garden and was ruined. I just haven't had the time to get a new one. This is a very busy season for us," he added, with a helpful tone so Laurian could understand. "We need to get ready for winter, which means the next three to four weeks we'll have to work from sunrise until late at night. But I'll get a phone soon."

Laurian and Saro bid farewell to every member of the family, but Silva Galian seemed to have fallen asleep, so they did not bother her again. They asked if Martha needed a ride to her home, but she said that her husband would arrive soon to accompany her. With that, they left.

꒓ ꒓ ꒓

Laurian called Gagik again and asked if he knew the doctor that Silva Galian had been seeing in Ashtarak. The answer was yes. "I'd like to see him briefly," said Laurian.

Gagik called back in a few minutes.

"He'll be off in half an hour and can meet us for coffee. When can you be here?"

"Half an hour is perfect. We'll see you at the same place we had lunch."

Saro had long stopped rushing. He was as involved in this now as Laurian. The intensity of Laurian's interest and attachment to the Galians, which had worried him at first, had proven to be contagious. Now he too was taken by the Galian family. The unanswered questions about the father's death, the mother's illness and Lara's whereabouts, which haunted Laurian, were haunting him as well.

They drove in silence for a while. It was early evening and the country road from Saralandj to Aparan's town center was dark and deserted. Black-billed magpies had descended on a dead rodent in the middle of the road and were having a frantic feast. They waited until the very last second to hop off the road as Saro's car approached. A light-brown dog with a puffy curled up tail was limping down the edge of the road, giving the car curious sideways looks as it hopped away, as if checking to see if it could hitch a ride. Laurian was deep in thought as Saro drove his Chevy Niva, carefully avoiding the huge potholes as they entered Aparan from the east and turned left headed toward Ashtarak. As they drove past the city limits, the condition of the road improved considerably, and Saro's car gained speed.

Dr. Hakobian was a small, thin man in his mid-fifties, with a balding head and thick-rimmed eyeglasses. Laurian thought he would make a great character in one of John Le Carré's early books as a Soviet spy. The man was very polite and composed, but answered questions sparingly. Laurian had had a long day, and wanted to come straight to the point. This suited Dr. Hakobian fine. He too came to the point after some reluctance, largely because of Gagik's nods of encouragement for him to speak up.

"Silva Galian has advanced stages of ovarian cancer," he said. "I have to admit, it took a while to diagnose, because she does not fit the risk profile. Even I did not suspect it for a long time."

"But now you are sure?" asked Laurian.

"Yes, I'm sure..." Laurian noticed that the doctor hesitated to say more, but after catching an encouraging eye from Gagik, he continued. "It is more common in women who have not had children. Silva has had eight. So we did not look for it at first. But the symptoms kept suggesting it, so we checked, just to be on the safe side."

"What type of symptoms?" asked Laurian.

Dr. Hakobian did not answer for a few minutes. He looked at Gagik, and then Laurian, and finally said, "Mr. Laurian, because of your friendship with Gago here, and my respect for him, I have already told you what I normally consider more than appropriate; considering that you are not related to her, I do not wish to get into any further details."

"Fair enough," said Laurian apologetically, impressed by the doctor's comments. Patient confidentiality had not meant much in any former Soviet republic. "Please forgive me. You're right; I am not related to them. Rest assured though that I am only trying to be helpful. I have no other interest in this matter. Is there anything that can be done?"

"I doubt it," said Hakobian, scratching his chin with his skinny fingers. "I told the family that this is very difficult to cure, given its advanced stage. Any treatment at this stage is likely to be intrusive, painful, and ultimately fruitless."

As usual, Laurian had a lot of questions, but he had to suppress them. After his early encouragement, Gagik was being uncharacteristically quiet, which did not help Dr. Hakobian open up further. Laurian had a sense that even Gagik was not comfortable discussing the medical case of a friend's widow in Saralandj. There was no point, especially if the doctor was basically saying that it was hopeless. For once, Laurian agreed with what Saro would have said. Nightfall was upon them already, and they had to head back. Laurian knew that he'd have to make this trip again soon, and perhaps find various ways to bond with Avo. And, as he had guessed, it was too late now to make it all the way back to Vardahovit.

"Saro jan," he broke the silence once they got on the main highway to Yerevan, "I am very thankful for your patience today. I know I made you waste a whole day, and I know you were not always comfortable with the meetings and conversations. But this could actually have something to do with what we're facing in our village."

"No problem, Edik jan. I know you're right. And it certainly was not a wasted day. Sometimes I think about how much you care about things, how connected you become, and I think that we all need to be more like that. So no problem."

"As we had guessed, it is too late to drive all the way to Vardahovit. We've had a very long day. Please let me treat you to a nice evening in Yerevan, and then we drive back in the morning. Okay?"

"Ha, Edik jan. As you wish. Thanks."

Laurian debated which hotel to book. He usually stayed at the Marriott on Republic Square. But that was an expensive hotel, and could make Saro uncomfortable. He decided on the Congress, a few blocks down the square. It was a Best Western, and adequate for a night's stay. And there was a good Armenian restaurant right around the corner, which he thought Saro would enjoy. He called the hotel and booked two single rooms for the night. He asked the receptionist if the hotel could provide each room with basic toiletries, as they were arriving with none; he specifically made sure that they would have toothbrushes and toothpaste, shaving kits and combs. Then he called the restaurant and asked for Hakob, the owner. They knew each other well, as Laurian had entertained many guests at his restaurant over the years. He reserved a table and pre-ordered several dishes, so they wouldn't waste time after arriving. Having completed the chores, he focused his attention on Saro.

"So, Saro jan, what do you make of it all? From *Khev Gago* in the morning, to the doctor in the evening, and everything in between."

"Hard to tell," said Saro, sounding genuinely absorbed in the story. "There is too much information to process in one day. But," he added with a laugh, "just so you know, I like your friend Gago."

"I wish he was in Vardahovit," said Laurian. "We could use him there these days, don't you think?"

"I wouldn't go that far," laughed Saro. "We still have to be very careful up there. Your *Khev Gago* would stick out there like tits on a bull!"

"Yeah, can you imagine him unleashing one of his *Khev Gago* laughs, guffaws really, in Vardahovit?"

"We'd have a mass stampede in three villages at once!" laughed Saro, glad to lighten the mood, and glad that he and Laurian were pretty much on the same wavelength.

"Seriously, though, I think we should help the family. Maybe there is nothing we can do about the mother, but I want to help Avo. I cannot tell you how my heart aches every time I think about that sixteen-year-old kid assuming the responsibility of a large family like that. Think about it, Saro. He is sixteen, he has three sisters to marry off, and you know what that's like in the villages. And we're not even counting Lara yet. He also has two younger brothers to take care of. He wants them to finish school, because that was the wish of his late father. Can you imagine that? How can we be indifferent to all that?"

"The problem with you, my dear, dear Edik, is that you focus too much on what you know, but there is a lot that you don't know. Do you know what I mean?"

"No, Saro jan, I do not know what you mean."

"I agree this Galian story is captivating, but do you know how many families like that exist today in Armenia? Unfulfilled potential, unrealized dreams, unnecessary suffering, unnecessary deaths...If you knew, you'd either go crazy or become so insensitive that none of this would matter to you, not even the Galians."

"I doubt if none of it would matter," said Laurian, moved by Saro's words. "Saro, listen, we cannot solve the world's problems, and that's certainly not what I'm saying. But here is one concrete case where we possibly can be of some help. So what do you want me to do? Ignore it because there are bigger problems? Because it's not so unique? You're right; we focus on what we know. So let's focus. What's wrong with that?"

Saro was quiet for a long time. Laurian imagined him thinking of all the sad stories in his villages, maybe even in his own family that needed attention. He imagined Saro having a moral conflict, between helping these total strangers and those much closer to home. 'Focus on what we know?' he could hear him think to himself, 'Okay, Paron Edik, here is what I know…' and he could just hear Saro listing a dozen sad cases that have been haunting him. But then, Laurian would respond, once you have seen a problem first hand and very close, how do you ignore it, even if it isn't supposed to 'concern' you? Is that what Saro was thinking now, while maneuvering around the pothole-ridden entrance into Yerevan city?

Besides, Laurian too could bring up a story or two that haunted him and made the Galian story much more personal for him than anyone could suspect. But he was not ready. He was not ready to talk about his youngest sister, Sirarpi, or about the circumstances under which she disappeared and died at twelve, when Laurian was sixteen, the same age as Avo. He kept telling himself that Sirarpi should have nothing to do with the Galian story, that she was not influencing his objectivity, that it happened thirty years ago, under entirely different circumstances.

As they pulled into the front entrance of the Congress Hotel, a young doorman approached them. After confirming that they were guests, he removed one of the 'no parking' signs blocking a parking space and let them park. They agreed to go to their rooms for a quick wash and meet in the lobby in ten minutes.

Laurian was at the lobby bar having a brandy when Saro came down a few minutes later.

"You have earned a good cognac," said Laurian, ordering him a Nayiri, the twenty-year old Ararat brandy that was famous throughout the Soviet Union in the old days.

"Thanks. No more driving tonight?"

"No more driving. The restaurant is right around the corner. And Hakob is waiting."

They downed their drinks and walked over to *"Hakob's Place."* The sign across the entrance boasted "Authentic Armenian Cuisine." Hakob, the middle aged owner and manager of the place, greeted them personally and proceeded to list the day's specials. There were ten types of authentic

Armenian and Russian soups, a dozen stews, countless appetizers and main courses, all promoted as the real thing, as opposed to the less authentic versions one finds these days in Yerevan.

Laurian ordered a rich menu. He was in the mood to indulge. He ordered more brandy also. They both needed to unwind and look at the events of the day from a distance. Food and drink would help a lot. Hakob came over often and chatted with them. The restaurant itself was small, with around ten tables, but he made most of his business by catering to state dinners and large parties. He also had two small private rooms in the back of the restaurant, which Laurian had used in the past.

As other guests started to arrive, Hakob's visits became less frequent. Laurian got back on the topic.

"The kids are incredible," he said.

"I noticed," agreed Saro.

"I felt as if Martha could read my mind. She is very, what did you say before? Yes, very '*connected*.'"

"The oldest daughter and first child," said Saro, as if that explained everything.

"Yes, but she cannot be much over twenty, has seven younger siblings, a dying mother and no father. And she's recently married, with a load of new responsibilities at her husband's home."

"But it looks like her husband's family and hers manage pretty well together, almost kind of merged. That is a huge plus, Edik jan. Imagine if the two families didn't get along."

"I agree. I wish we had met Martha's husband."

"I have a feeling that you'll make sure we do!" laughed Saro.

"Here's to survivors," said Laurian and raised his glass.

Saro toasted him. "To survivors."

"And Avo? Walking tall, owning up to his family, telling us his mother may not survive the winter with such calm composure; would you think he is sixteen?"

"Edik jan, now I feel obliged to tell you about this theory of mine." Saro was leaning forward, the effects of alcohol apparent in his speech, his voice lower than normal, indicating that what he had to say was of utmost importance. "People grow up when they have to, *not* when their age says it is time to grow up. That's the way it is. That's why some grow up at sixteen, some at sixty and some never."

Laurian was impressed with Saro's theory. He gave it due respect by thinking about it for a few minutes. A sixteen-year-old kid from a rich family in Yerevan would be better schooled, would know more about the world, but would not be able to handle any of the heavy responsibilities that Avo was now burdened with. Saro was right.

"That's like my theory about marriage," he said after a while. "People get married when they're ready, *not* when they meet the right person," he added, copying Saro's style and tone. "And if someone just happens to be lucky enough to meet the right person when he's ready, wow! That'll be a great marriage. But in most cases 'right person' means nothing if you're not ready."

"Edik jan, are you talking about yourself?" Saro raised his glass again. "To you, my friend, the most 'connected' person I have ever known."

"Thanks, Saro, but actually I was talking about everyone. Tell me, who gets married if they're not ready? Of course, being 'ready' is also relative. In Saralandj, probably the family decides when one is ready. But in my case, I met the best candidates when I was not ready, and then when I felt ready I met no one. Now that I feel as if I am past the 'ready' stage, the whole issue is increasingly irrelevant."

"But was there actually a time when you felt ready and met no one?" asked Saro with a skeptical smile. "I find that hard to believe."

"Well, you may have a point, my observant friend. But only partially; my work was not one that could accommodate a traditional marriage. I used to travel four weeks at a time in the most dangerous places on earth, return for a week or so to finalize my report, and then take off again. How can one have a family life like that?"

"So even if you had been ready, you wouldn't have known it, right?"

Laurian had known Saro for years, but had never before talked to him about his personal life. The most he had said when asked was, "I'm single." Of course in Armenia the oddest thing would be for a man in his mid-forties to be single; most had grandchildren at that age. Usually, everyone was too polite to ask further. But that night something felt different for Laurian.

"Actually, I knew it. And there was someone I would probably have married. Someone very special. But I couldn't settle down then. And she wouldn't wait. I didn't blame her. I wouldn't have waited for me either in those days."

"Sorry to ask a personal question, my friend," said Saro, sensing that Laurian felt like talking about himself, "but there must be someone special now, no? I've heard you sometimes having long telephone conversations with someone in that impossible language you call English, but even I can figure out that these conversations haven't always been with your editor!"

"Very observant again!" laughed Laurian. "Maybe you should have been an investigative reporter instead of me! But you're right, there is someone. She is special, but not in that way. You know the old Armenian saying, '*nman znman gtani?*'—likes find likes. Well, she's like me. Same profession, same crazy travel schedule and dedication to work, same inability to commit and settle down. So we're perfect for each other. We have an agreement; when we're both around and have time, we spend the time together like a couple. But it stops there. So you see, for me the whole thing about being ready or not being ready is already irrelevant."

"It's not irrelevant, Edik jan," Saro was saying, trying to make light of it. "We're going to find you a great girl right here and we're going to create a million new problems for you! And you know what? You'll deserve every one of them! And then you'll be 'connected' like never before." As he said that, Saro wanted to go for a *Khev Gago* laugh, but could not manage it alone.

Laurian had not seen Saro in this mood either. He downed his brandy and poured another for both himself and Saro. They were getting tipsy now, and they knew it, but did not mind. They toasted heartily to the new problems a man needed to face, and downed the shot. Laurian poured again. Hakob noticed the dynamics from a distance and decided to leave them alone.

"I'm way past forty," Laurian said, "and way past the 'ready' period. Besides, I am now so used to being alone, that a family seems like it would be too scary, believe it or not. It's a beautiful thing--don't misunderstand me--but not at just any phase in one's life. I'm too set in my ways now."

Saro raised his glass again. "You already have many families, my dear friend Edik," he said. "Maybe you don't realize it yet. Maybe you do." He was clearly sounding drunk. "But let me tell you this: you wouldn't be more married if you had five grandchildren! Do you know what I mean?"

"Actually, believe it or not, I do!" laughed Laurian. And in fact he did. "So you see my friend, forget hooking me up with anyone. I'm already hooked."

The two together managed to produce half a *Khev Gago* laugh; it was impossible to go the whole way without Gagik leading the chorus. But it was enough to clear the air and to turn some heads. It was also loud enough for Hakob to finally approach them, just to check if everything was okay.

"A very wise man I know once told me, 'Life's too short to drink bad wine,'" he declared. Then turning to Saro, he added, "And, my dear Honorable Mayor, that's a direct quote from your friend sitting here. So I hope all was in accordance to your taste?"

"All was great," laughed Laurian. "In fact the bit about bad wine was embroidered on the cushions of the sofa in my lawyer's office in Switzerland."

"Not the type of message I'd expect to be displayed in a lawyer's office," said Hakob. "It would fit better on a restaurant menu, don't you think?"

"Actually this lawyer was great. He asked me when I was going to learn French. So I said to him, 'Life's too short to waste it on French.' He laughed and pointed to the cushions on his sofa. 'No, no, Monsieur Laurian,' he said, 'Life's too short to drink bad wine. You learn your French!'"

"Hakob jan, everything was great," said Saro. "I just hope we did not overstay our welcome."

Laurian paid the bill and they walked into the cool night. Instead of going straight to the hotel, they walked up to Republic Square, watched the fountains and the light show, took a leisurely walk around the square and then returned to their hotel. They bid each other goodnight and went to bed.

X

There is a roadside restaurant on the way to Vardahovit, past the spectacular rock formations of Noravank, right before reaching the junction that turns toward Getap, where Laurian usually stops to break up the drive and have a cup of coffee. It is a relatively busy place, where travelers and tourists stop regularly. The owner, a young, skinny man called Nerses, with pale, honey-colored eyes and a hairless head and face due to alopecia, has become a good friend of Laurian's over the years. Nerses also knows that Laurian is working very hard to have the road from Shatin to Vardahovit repaired, which will increase the tourist traffic considerably in that region and give a boost to his business.

Laurian has extended his stay in Vardahovit from the initial planned three weeks to over two months, and wants to set up with Nerses a regular weekly catering service to his house. The restaurant has excellent *khorovadz*, the popular Armenian charcoal grilled meats of lamb, pork, beef and chicken. Laurian often takes the marinated meats home uncooked and grills the khorovadz himself. This requires pre-ordering, to make sure that Nerses has enough to meet the needs of his eat-in clients as well.

Nerses joined Laurian and Saro as they were having their coffee at one of the outdoor tables. It was a wonderful fall afternoon, under a cloudless sky, and the sun giving out a delicious variety of warmth that Laurian claims, to the skeptical amusement of the locals, is unique to this region. The huge poplar trees lining the front of the restaurant's parking lot are almost bare; only a few stubborn yellow leaves remain stuck on the top branches.

Laurian ordered three skewers each of pork and lamb *khorovadz*, marinated but uncooked, to take with him. He also told Nerses that he would need more in the coming weeks, and would call with specifics. As they were finishing their coffee and getting ready to leave, two black SUVs with darkened windows pulled into the parking lot, and the drivers got out. Two husky, muscular men with clean-shaven heads and dark sunglasses walked over and took a table at the end of the outdoor section, several tables away from where Laurian, Saro and Nerses were sitting. The waitress who served that section, a friendly young girl in her late twenties named Arusyak, gave Nerses a pleading look, clearly indicating that she wanted to be relieved from serving that table. Nerses then signaled to the male waiter to approach the new guests.

"I see your clientele has become more interesting since my last visit," said Laurian.

"We see new faces here almost every day, Edik jan, but I'm not sure what to make of that crowd over there. Not your run-of-the-mill happy tourists. They yelled at poor Arus last time for not serving their order fast enough. They're rude, but so far haven't done anything alarming."

"Do you know who they are?"

"Not really. They stop here for a meal or coffee, but we've also seen them just drive by without stopping. Local folks say they mostly turn toward Getap, but then it is less clear where they go. They've been seen past Shatin."

"Any other passengers?"

"Usually only the drivers come out, so it's hard to tell. The windows are blacked out and they are careful to sit very close to where they park, so as to keep a close eye on their cars. They never leave the cars unattended."

"Do you *think* they have passengers who stay in the car?"

"As I said, it's very hard to tell, but my sense is they have *something* they're protecting, either valuable merchandise or passengers. They get in and out of the car very quickly, and they never keep the door open for more than a minute. It's not normal."

"How often do they pass by here?"

"Actually, not very often. We've seen them only three or four times in the past few weeks—I mean three or four times going and three or four times returning. One day they came with two cars, but only one of them returned the same day; the other a day or so later."

"Nerses jan, it is important that we figure out who they are and how many different cars are passing by here, how often, and if possible which direction they come from and which direction they go once they leave. Can we start by recording their license plate numbers?"

Nerses did not need to be told why this was important. This type of visitor almost always meant trouble.

"I haven't bothered with license plate numbers until now, but if you want I'll start recording. And we haven't tried to follow them. We assume they come from Yerevan and go back there, even though my brother said he thinks he saw one of the cars passing through Yeghegnadzor, which as you know they wouldn't have to pass through if they went straight to Yerevan from here. But of course he couldn't be one hundred percent sure."

Saro, who had been quiet until that point, stirred uncomfortably in his chair. "It's a good idea to record the plate numbers, but you need to be very discreet, Nerses jan. They must not suspect anything. Act like you don't even notice they're different from anyone else who stops here. But following them is not a good idea. They are much better at noticing that than anyone here. We cannot follow their cars and stay unnoticed."

"I agree," said Laurian. "No point in following them. If we have their license plates and we have people watching for them in various locations, we can get an idea where they're going, no? We know people in both directions of the Getap crossroad, both toward Yeghegnadzor and toward Yerevan. Toward Yerevan, you have friends at the nearby gas station, right, Nerses?"

"Of course. And also past the gas station we have friends in most of the street vendors and shops for at least fifty kilometers. We have even more friends on the Yeghegnadzor side, all the way to Vayk and Martashen."

Saro was happy to notice how Laurian did not show any reaction to the mention of Martashen. In fact, Laurian's response couldn't have been better phrased as far as Saro was concerned.

"Nerses jan," he said, lowering his voice a notch and leaning toward the middle of the table, "we do not want a lot of people to know what we're doing. The fewer the better. Think of the most trustworthy people on either side, and let's agree on a plan now. We know some people too, so we can compare. No more than two observers on the Yerevan stretch, and at most three on the Yeghegnadzor stretch, say one in Yeghegnadzor, one in Martashen and one in Vayk. No need to go past Vayk, I don't think. And all that these people have to do is look for the license plates that we give them and let us know if the cars pass by there. Nothing else."

At that point, the burly drivers stood. They threw a few one-thousand dram notes on the table and started walking toward their cars. Laurian was very quick on his feet. He excused himself and went inside the restaurant as soon as the two stood up. From the corner of the window, he took some pictures of the drivers on his cell phone. He managed to get one face clearly, but only the profile of the second. He also managed to get pictures of the license plates of the two cars. The drivers had barely started the cars when Laurian was back at his seat at the table. He smiled at the others and resumed the conversation, totally ignoring the SUVs that were pulling out of the parking lot and turning toward the Getap crossroad.

When the cars were out of sight, he called Agassi in Vardahovit.

"Tell the boys in Shatin to expect two black SUVs in around fifteen minutes," he said. "Tell them to call you when they see the cars. Let me know when they call."

"Ha, Edik jan. *Eghav.* Done."

Although they had a lot organized in Vardahovit and Sevajayr already, this was the first time that Saro felt they were running a well-coordinated surveillance of what was happening in their villages. He now saw firsthand that they had assets and resources, trustworthy people who would cooperate just on the basis of friendship and camaraderie. Between the surveillance operation of the homes in Vardahovit and Sevajayr and the monitoring of car movements on either side of the Getap crossroad, they had engaged over a dozen individuals and they were not paying any of them. These were all volunteers, cooperating because of loyalty to their community, but also because they were asked by Saro and Laurian. It was gratifying for Saro to know that he enjoyed so much credibility with the people in the region, not just those in his village.

Nerses was a valuable recruit. He wondered if Laurian would have talked to him about the newcomers in the region if the cars had not appeared while they were there. Knowing Laurian, he probably would have. Saro wouldn't even put it past Laurian to suggest the stop at the restaurant just for that reason, using food as a pretext. Although the stop was not unusual for Laurian, Saro would have thought that he'd be more anxious to get back to Vardahovit and hear the latest from the surveillance team about the deserted homes than spend so much time having coffee. He must have had this in his mind all along, and the appearance of the two SUVs at that time was a lucky break.

They had discussed and agreed on the individuals who would monitor the car traffic. In Yeghegnadzor, Nerses's brother; in Martashen, a cousin of Nerses that Saro knew; and in Vayk, an in-law of Nerses. There were also two contacts on the Yerevan side of the road, one in a gas station and one in a large roadside market. It was agreed that all five would deal only with Nerses and report their findings to him. They did not need to know about the involvement of Saro and Laurian. Nerses would report what he heard to Saro, not Laurian.

It was mid-afternoon and the sun was still deliciously warm when they left the restaurant. Agassi had called back twenty minutes after Laurian had alerted him to say that the SUVs had passed Shatin as expected and were headed straight up to Vardahovit. Some forty-five minutes later he called back to say that they had crossed Hermon and had almost reached Vardahovit. Saro and Laurian left too, headed in the same direction. Saro and his Chevy Niva seemed more at ease navigating the disastrous road than Laurian and his Prado. As he drove, Saro seemed to know the location of every pothole by heart, even the ones that sometimes popped up in front of the driver immediately after a dangerous turn. He seemed to be bypassing the potholes even before seeing them. The constant zigzagging turns to avoid the countless potholes, which tired and frustrated Laurian to no end, did not seem to bother Saro at all. Potholes were a fact of life; there was no point in getting emotional about them.

At mid-afternoon, the road was almost empty. Most of the moving activity in the villages happened in the early morning or later afternoon, when the animals were either being taken to the fields to graze or returning home, and when the children, already back from school, were playing in the streets. The only things to watch for on the road at this time of day, aside from the potholes, were the occasional chickens or geese wandering around. The area seemed even more peaceful and quiet than usual.

"Well, Edik, you should be happy with all we've done in the past three days," Saro told Laurian as he maneuvered around another major pothole. "The surveillance operation is now fully underway."

"Let's see where it will lead us," said Laurian. "I hope we'll be equally ready to deal with what we find."

"It all depends on what we find. Ayvazian may get away with a lot, but even he cannot get away with *everything*. I doubt this is just a matter of illegal goat hunting. If he's doing something criminal here in our own backyard, he can and must be stopped."

Laurian was impressed with Saro's last comment. This was the first indication from Saro that he actually wanted to catch Ayvazian.

"I wonder how the boys are doing in Sevajayr and Vardahovit," said Laurian.

"We'll get a report as soon as we arrive at your place, I'm sure," said Saro. "By the way, getting Nerses involved was very smart."

"He has a stake in this as much as any of us," said Laurian. "Ayvazian can be very bad news for him too. He could decide to take over his restaurant from him for a song and use it for his other activities. Nerses is no fool."

"But does he know it is Ayvazian? He did not say anything."

"I think he knows, but is being careful. We know, right? Why shouldn't he know?"

"I don't know... We know because his men bought the houses in our villages. Nerses may suspect, but I don't think he knows for sure."

"At any rate, the presence of those thugs cannot be welcome by Nerses or any of the businessmen along the road, regardless if Ayvazian is behind it or not. If not Ayvazian, some other mafioso would be behind it, right?"

"Right."

They fell silent for a while. Laurian looked at the mountainsides and at the brook flowing in the valley at the right of the road, and his heart seemed to slide into a blanket of calmness. It was one of the streams that joins the Yeghegis river, which flows south and in turn flows into the Arax river that marks the border between Armenia and Iran. The Arax river is very much part of the Armenian psyche, and Laurian watched the happy stream in the valley right below the road, its flow bumpy because of the rocks on the riverbed, the little waves jumping and dancing, seeming anxious to get to 'Mother Arax,' the popular name that the river has acquired over the centuries. The thought that these waters, originating right here in these mountains, go to feed an eternal, legendary symbol of Armenia moved him in a way that he could not explain.

Agassi swung the iron gates open and they drove in, continuing straight to the main house. Agassi's dog, a young white pup of unknown breed but with traces of Alaskan Husky on her face, ran the distance with the car, reaching the main house before the men. Agassi closed the gate and followed them by foot.

Although it was one of those crystalline afternoons when Laurian would insist on sitting on the front terrace to wait for the miraculous Vardahovit sunsets, they sat inside. Agassi's grandson Hayk had also just arrived and was holding Laurian's Nikon D-90 camera.

Before anyone had a chance to say much, Laurian checked the photos in the camera. Most were too dark. Some had slightly visible images that were dark, grey and grainy, almost like shadows. But there were clear silhouettes of people, and not just of drivers and bodyguards.

Vartiter brought in coffee.

"We better take a look at these on a larger screen," said Laurian, walking over to his bedroom to bring his laptop. As they were sipping coffee he inserted the memory stick from the camera into his laptop and opened the file. Agassi and Saro got closer on each side of him. Hayk, who had taken the pictures, sat on the opposite sofa. Laurian took his time with each shot, all of which were taken at night.

"These are at the Sevajayr house, not Vardahovit, right?" asked Laurian.

"Ha, Paron Edik. I was in the barn across the street from the house, on the upper loft. I took all these pictures last night, from the top window. It was dark. The only light was from the car when they opened the door, and a little from the house when they opened the front door. The curtains were drawn on the front window of the house, and there was very little light."

"Hayk jan," said Laurian, "come sit next to me here. At what time were these taken?"

Hayk squeezed between his grandfather and Laurian on the leather sofa. "Around ten o'clock," he said. "We got the news that the cars were on their way when they crossed Shatin, and we were ready for them."

Laurian looked at the first three photos for a long time, but skipped each one without asking any questions. They showed two SUVs pulling in and parking perpendicular to the façade of the house, to the left of the main door. Their headlights had illuminated the front wall and door; no one had yet left the cars in these pictures. He dwelt longer on the fourth one. The headlights were turned off. The back right door of the car was open, and the inside light of the car was on. Hayk was facing the back of the cars and front of the house. One of the bodyguards was standing in front of the open back door, as if allowing someone to exit. But his body was blocking whoever was getting out. All that could be seen was the back of the bodyguard.

"Did you see someone else get out of the car?" asked Laurian to Hayk.

"I can't be one hundred percent sure," Hayk said. "You will see in the next pictures that a second man came from the other car and they all went inside. The two men were all I could see, but judging from their movements, there could have been a third hidden from view."

Laurian zoomed in on the area right next to the open door of the car. Then he zoomed in farther, not on the person, but on the ground. There were two shadows on the ground next to the car. One was clearly that of the bodyguard, but next to him was another, shorter shadow.

"You see that?" asked Laurian to no one in particular, pointing at the second shadow, which was sandwiched between the shadow of the bodyguard and that of the open car door. "Whose shadow is that? There is someone else standing in front of this guy. The person is totally blocked from the view of the camera, but his or her shadow is not."

"You think it's a woman?" asked Saro.

"Could be. He or she is shorter than the man. The bodyguard is obviously taller than the car, so his shadow is truncated above the neck; you can see here the shadow of part of his head, maybe that of his chin, but nothing above that," said Laurian as he pointed to where the bodyguard's shadow stopped. "But you can see a clear shadow of the head of another person, here, see? It's hard to tell anything else from this photo. The shadows of their bodies are overlapping and fuzzy. But there are distinct shadows of one full head and one truncated head. Let's see what else Hayk has for us."

The fifth photo showed roughly the same scene, but the second driver was standing in front of the smaller person, facing the camera. His face was too dark to make out any details. But as Laurian zoomed in again, his overall posture and the position of his right arm suggested that he was helping the person walk into the house. The front door of the house was open also, even though they could not see anyone at the door.

"Did you see who opened the front door?" asked Laurian. "I mean, was it someone from inside, or was it one of the drivers?"

"I'm sorry, Paron Edik. I did not notice. I was watching the second driver get out of his car. Also for a few seconds I did not look out because

I changed my position. You can see in this picture I have a wider view of the side of the car. That is when the front door must have opened. The whole process of them parking, turning off their headlights, getting into the house and closing the front door lasted less than a minute."

"Hayk jan, you've done a very good job," said Laurian, sensing that the fifteen-year-old kid was desperate to impress him. "Really excellent. Now we know that they brought someone into the house, and that person needed assistance walking the few steps from the car into the front door. I just want to say, for the future, you could have had ten maybe even a dozen pictures between the fourth and the fifth. Easily a dozen. You can just snap almost continuously, especially when your targets are moving. That way we can look at each frame and get something new. You understand, Hayk?"

"Ha, Paron Edik, I understand. *Eghav.*"

The sixth photo was the most informative and probably the most interesting. There were three silhouettes inside the doorway, and one person at the threshold. None of the faces could be made out clearly, as the back of the bodyguard at the threshold was blocking most of the view. But the three silhouettes were clear and distinct, two men standing inside and facing out, and a smaller, diminutive figure, already inside and facing in. Although he still could not be one-hundred percent sure, Laurian felt certain that the diminutive figure was a woman. The picture showed a slight profile, the tip of the nose barely visible as a dark spot, and a dark patch at the side of the silhouette that could easily be her hair, straight, medium-length, possibly reaching a bit below her shoulders.

The next several photos did not offer much new information. They showed a closed front door and a faint light inside showing through the curtained front window. The front of the house was dark, the street quiet, the black SUVs barely visible in the dark night. When Laurian got to the very last photo, he was a bit surprised. It was already morning and there was only one car in front of the house.

"What happened here?" he asked Hayk.

"When we woke up, one of the cars was gone. We did not notice it leave, so we don't know when it left or how many people left in it. Sorry."

"That's okay, Hayk. Did you sleep in the barn?"

"Yes, Paron Edik. It was my cousin Sago and I. We slept in the loft on the hay."

"What time do you think you fell asleep?"

"It was past two in the morning, but I'm not sure of the exact time. I remember Sago saying it was two already. We both must have fallen asleep after that."

"No problem, Hayk jan. You've done very well for your first surveillance mission. Remember what I said about taking many shots when people are moving. Now, we know that two more SUVs headed there earlier this afternoon, so it is important that you get back in there. Be very discreet. Can you get back to the barn without anyone in the house noticing you?"

"Yes, that's not difficult. The entrance to the barn is on the other side altogether. The loft window is at the back of the barn. We can sneak in without being noticed."

"Good. Be very, very careful. Never show that camera to anyone, and never let anyone see it in your hands by accident. Who will take you back there?"

"My son is here," said Agassi. "He'll drive him back now."

"So here is what we know," summarized Laurian. "Two SUVs arrived last night. Two drivers and one other passenger went into the house. There was at least one more person in the house at that time. One car left sometime after two am this morning. Two more SUVs headed toward Sevajayr a little while ago. Is that about it?"

"That's pretty much it," said Saro.

"Anything at the house in Vardahovit?"

"Not much there, I'm afraid," said Agassi. "There is no one taking pictures there. The boys are watching the house, but there has not been any new activity reported. I don't think that house is as active as this one in Sevajayr."

"That's better, since we cannot watch it as well as the Sevajayr house," said Laurian, but in his mind he had already brought the meeting to an end.

"We can't let all this spoil a good cigar and a good sunset," he told Saro as they moved to the front terrace.

"Edik jan, with your permission, I need to head home too. I've been away for two days. There are some things I need to attend to. But I'll call you if I hear anything."

"Of course," said Laurian, feeling bad for being so insensitive. Saro had a family and a home in Vardahovit, and he was the Mayor of the village after all. Laurian had already taken two days of his time. "Go, Saro jan, go. And thank you so much for all your time and trouble these past two days. I'll be here, waiting for news."

ᘉ ᘉ ᘉ

It was seven o'clock by the time Laurian settled into the teak armchair on the front terrace. It felt wonderful to finally be alone. He had chosen this remote mountaintop as a refuge for solitude, to think, read and write in peace. The closest human presence to this place was over two-and-a-half kilometers away, and that was the small village of Vardahovit. The closest city, Yeghegnadzor, was over thirty kilometers away. The Laurian estate was a solitary place indeed, and yet he always seemed to have people around. People from the village and the region, people from Yerevan, and often even from overseas. He had entertained visitors from Switzerland, the Middle East and China, who had stayed overnight as his guests.

He lit his cigar and allowed the delightful aroma of the *Romeo & Julietta Churchill* to take him away for a moment. Then he noticed Vartiter approaching from the guardhouse. He held off delving into his thoughts until she arrived, prolonging his focus on the exquisite first few puffs of the cigar. A pair of Eurasian Jays playfully flew past Laurian and perched on the poplar trees in front of the house. They were jumping from branch to branch, chasing each other, filling the peaceful air with their unique '*chuck-chuck*' chatter. The locals called these birds 'forest magpies,' even though they looked nothing like magpies. Agassi was not fond of them because they caused serious damage to the apples and walnuts. They would fall on an apple tree and peck at each apple several times, then move to the next tree. If left alone, they could destroy the harvest of an entire orchard in one afternoon. So Agassi would chase them away and had asked Laurian several times to just shoot them, but Laurian wouldn't.

"They were here before us," he'd say to a baffled Agassi. "I should shoot them for tasting your apples?"

Vartiter and her smile arrived at the terrace together as usual.

"*Vonts es*, Edik jan?" Her warmth always touched Laurian.

"*Lav, lav*, Vart jan, *du vonts es* ?"

"Normal. *Inch sarkem kez hamar*? What shall I prepare for you?"

"Something light, Vart. I've been eating too much lately. Don't go into any trouble with a meal. Just some cheese and vegetables. That's all I'll have tonight. And of course some wine."

"*Eghav.* Done."

The Eurasian Jays flew away as Vartiter went inside. Laurian couldn't hold back his thoughts any longer. He forced himself into the discipline imposed by his profession. You're not involved, he kept telling himself. This is not personal. You're just observing and documenting. You're asking questions, seeking answers, explanations. This is not personal. This is not personal. You want to solve the puzzle, and move on. Okay, maybe you want to expose something; that too is part of the job. But then you move on. This is not personal.

What, then, is the puzzle we're trying to solve, Mr. Laurian? Who is Ayvazian bringing into these homes? Are they being brought against their will? Most probably. That woman in the picture looked drugged to me. Are you sure it was a woman? No, but I will say it was for now. It makes a big difference, you know. You'd better think this through. How does it make a difference if it was a man or a woman? Well, if it was a man, it could be one of his business 'problems' that he's trying to eliminate and needs to extract some information from him first. You know his reputation of having his enemies disappear. But if it is a woman, chances are that your story will change entirely. He's not likely to have any young women as business competitors or enemies now, is he, Mr. Laurian? If he is bringing young women here, what could it be? Well, go ahead and say it, you know it happens here, in your beloved Armenia, don't you? You know what Ayvazian is capable of, don't you? So why not? Why not here?

Vartiter had not come out yet. He needed his wine. The first few glasses always cleared his head and helped him think better. He put his cigar on the ashtray and walked inside to the kitchen.

"Almost ready, Edik jan," smiled Vartiter. She was setting up a beautiful tray of snacks and appetizers.

"No problem," said Edik, returning her smile. "You finish that delicious spread you're working on, and I'll take care of the wine."

He took a bottle of white Swiss wine from the refrigerator, a superb Chasselas from Valais, opened it, and walked back out with a wine glass. He had shipped a few cases of the wine over when the house was built, and he still had a few bottles left. Considering that he could not buy this wine in Armenia, he cherished his dwindling stock.

He poured himself a glass and re-lit his cigar. Sunset was imminent, and the usual light show on the Western sky and mountains was in full swing. This, without its man-made problems, could easily be heaven, he thought, as he took a sip of the wine. The contrast between the immediate reality in front of his eyes and what was going on around him couldn't be more pronounced.

Vartiter came out with the tray and laid it on the table.

"Here you go, Edik jan. *Bari akhorjak.* Bon appétit."

"*Apres*, Vart jan."

"Can I get anything else for you?"

"Nothing, Vart. Many thanks. You go home now. Take care of Agassi before he starts complaining," he said with a chuckle.

"Never short of people to take care of," laughed Vartiter.

"Good night, Vart."

"Good night, then, Paron Edik jan. I'll check on you in the morning."

Laurian was anxious to return to his thoughts about the 'puzzle,' though his instincts were craving something else. He normally would have submerged himself into poetry at that moment. Either reading or writing or both. The volumes in his library were calling for him. The wine and cigar were reprimanding him for dwelling on Ayvazian rather than Varoujan's *Pagan Songs,* for example. But he could not shake the nagging questions.

Okay, let's say it was a woman, brought against her will, probably drugged. Why would such a woman be brought to Sevajayr? To that god forsaken house? Where there probably is nothing to give her any comfort? Probably no indoor plumbing, no water, no heat. Where is she sleeping tonight? On some foam mattress thrown on the cement floor? Is she being abused by the guards? She has been kidnapped, a victim in a plot that she does not understand. You're sitting here enjoying your excellent Chasselas and cigar, and she is there drugged on some cold mattress.

Just wait a minute, Paron Edik. Are you sure this isn't about Sirarpi? His twelve-year-old baby sister had disappeared in the streets of Madrid while the family was on vacation there one summer. One minute they were busy taking pictures of the statue of Don Quixote and Sancho Panza; the next minute they were frantically looking for Sirarpi. She was nowhere to be seen. To this day Laurian gets goose bumps thinking of the five sleepless days and nights that the family spent with the Madrid police trying to find his sister and the imponderable recurring images that haunted him about what might have happened to her.

The police had no hesitation telling them what they thought had happened: abduction by human traffickers, to be sold into an international network of child pornography and prostitution. His parents were beyond devastated, and the apparent insensitivity of the police only made matters worse. After five hellish days, they decided that his mother should take him and his other sister back to Geneva, while the father stayed behind to continue the search. Every weekend his mother would leave them with some friends and fly to Madrid. But Sirarpi was lost. It was two months later that her body was found in Casa de Campo park, at the bank of the river Manzanares. She had been dead for twenty-four hours. She bore no wounds, either from blades or firearms. Just bruises. She had died after repeated beatings and rapes and prolonged malnutrition.

His cell phone rang. He was tempted to ignore it at first, but decided to answer it when he saw it was Agassi.

"Edik, jan," he said, "two cars just left Sevajayr. One is still there. Hayk thinks that one of the newcomers stayed behind, and whoever was in the house left. A kind of changing of the guard operation; and he has new photos all taken during daylight this time. I wish we could follow the cars."

"Thanks, Agassi. Don't worry about the cars. Let Hayk stay there and keep a close eye. I'll check all the pictures in the morning."

"Ha, Edik jan. *Eghav.*"

Laurian then called Saro.

"Tell Nerses two cars are on their way down. Forty-five minutes or so. He should be on the lookout. Even if they don't stop by the restaurant let him try to take the plate numbers."

"Ha, Edik jan, *Eghav.*"

"Saro, see if he can also check the drivers and get a good description," added Laurian.

"*Eghav.*"

He's kidnapping young women and bringing them here to these abandoned houses. Then what? Obviously, they won't be staying here for long.

So this has to be some type of temporary station. Say it, Laurian! What is going on here, right under your nose?

He poured another glass of wine. The sun had already slid behind the Western mountain chain. He realized that this was the first time ever that he had missed the precise moment of the sun setting while sitting here on this terrace. *This is costing me too much*, he thought. He allowed himself to focus on the afterglow of the sunset. Everything else could wait. The colors and lights were as spectacular as usual over the Western sky. It was Medzarents all over again—grandeur, harmony, perfection, love, mystique, romance, humanity. Elation and celebration of nature, always unique, like nowhere else. *Every time it is different,* he thought, *even if it is exactly the same.*

He is trafficking people, that's what he's doing. Young girls and women, abducted, disappear from their homes, are kept here for a while until they sort out papers or let the dust settle, then are shipped somewhere, sold into brothels...You don't have enough to conclude that yet, Laurian, so go slowly now. But what else could it be? You've heard that it happens, why not here? Nothing else would make any sense. That may be, Mr. Investigative Reporter, but you still don't have evidence; and even if you want to forget about evidence for now, you yourself cannot be one-hundred percent sure yet, can you?

The phone rang again.

"Nerses got carried away a bit," Saro said.

"What happened?"

"He toppled a tree trunk onto the road. An unfortunate accident. The cars should be getting there in the next few minutes. This way, he says, he'll get to meet the drivers for sure."

"He's good," laughed Laurian, "better than I thought."

"I'm in touch with him," said Saro. "I'll keep you posted." And he hung up.

XI

It was a very long night. Tired as he was, Laurian couldn't wait until morning to pour over all the pictures that had been taken. Hayk arrived at his place around two in the morning. He had outdone himself this time, with several hundred photos taken since mid-afternoon the day before. There were also the verbal reports of Nerses to consider. Laurian downloaded Hayk's entire photo file on his laptop and started going through them. Hayk sat in the large leather armchair by his side, in case he had to answer any questions, but soon fell asleep.

The first hundred or so photos did not have what he was looking for. The regular traffic of the cars arriving and drivers rushing into the house was no longer of much interest to him. He was looking for that elusive 'third person,' who was probably being held there against her will. Almost an hour had passed viewing the first hundred pictures, and Laurian was getting tired and a bit frustrated.

It was down about another hundred photos when something finally caught his eye. It was a shot of the window of the house in Sevajayr. It was taken at dusk, with the last dying traces of daylight hitting the window, creating a glare in the upper right corner of the windowpane. The rest of the window was darker, and at first glance the curtains looked drawn as usual. Laurian wondered why Hayk had bothered taking the picture in the first place, but when he looked closely, he noticed a slight opening, no more than a few inches, at the left side of the curtain. There was a sequence of twenty-two shots of the scene, and in each photo the curtain was pulled a fraction of an inch farther. As the opening of the curtain got wider with each consecutive shot, the blurry image of a face appeared inside. First, it was no more than a faint shadow; but the twelfth photo in the sequence was the most alarming. Laurian could clearly see the horrified face of a woman; she was staring outside and holding the curtain back with her left hand. This was the proverbial picture worth not just a thousand, but several thousand words. Laurian first thought that it was something she was looking at outside that was causing the terror in her eyes. But there were many pictures of the front of the house, and he did not remember seeing anything there that would cause such horror. She must be reacting to something else, even though she was looking out.

He studied the eleven photos, from the twelfth to the twenty-second in this sequence. The twelfth was by far the most telling in terms of the expression on the woman's face. It was a successful photograph in its own right, and had it not been for the specific context, Laurian would have been tempted to submit it to a photographic magazine for publication. The woman's expression reminded him of Edvard Munch's *The Scream*. Although this woman was not screaming, the terror in her eyes was almost identical to the screamer's terror. The photograph showed the window's glare on the top right corner, the face on the bottom left corner, and the progression of light in between, which created a mysterious atmosphere.

He guessed that the eleven photos between the twelfth and the twenty-second were taken within fifteen to twenty seconds. After the twelfth photo, the curtain did not appear to be opening any farther, and the face barely changed in position or expression. But the twenty-second photo was different. The curtain was almost fully drawn again, with no more than a few inches remaining open. Judging from the shadows showing through that opening, Laurian guessed that the face had turned sharply to the left. His suspicion was that someone had just noticed her opening the curtain, and had rushed to draw it back and pull her away from the window. But he could not be sure.

That is when he decided to wake Hayk up. It was approaching four in the morning and he probably would need to get into a bed soon anyway.

"You see this?" he asked the sleepy boy, pointing to the twelfth photograph on his screen. "This, Hayk jan, is a winning picture in more ways than I can count. We'll call this one the twelfth picture."

"The twelfth?" asked Hayk, confused.

"Yes, this is the twelfth picture in a series of twenty-two photos that you took. The twelfth in this particular sequence, not in the whole deck."

"Yes, I remember now. That was an exciting moment, when she appeared. We were getting tired of staring at that curtained window for hours."

"And you did a superb job with this sequence," said Laurian. "Now watch this." And he went back to the first photo in the sequence and flipped through all twenty-two in quick succession. "You see what you've done by taking many pictures quickly? You have almost filmed the action, but we can stop and inspect each screen of the action as a still snapshot."

Hayk, who had no idea that he'd be getting such a result while taking the pictures, was impressed and fully awake.

"Now," went on Laurian. "The twelfth picture is clear, and we can talk about the details later. But the twenty-second needs your input." He opened the twenty-second and enlarged it to focus on the small opening between the curtain and the window frame. "Now watch this," he added, going back to the twenty-first photo and quickly moving back to the twenty-second. "If you took these two immediately one after the other, it is clear that the curtain was drawn very suddenly. Do you remember if this is true??"

"It definitely was very quick," said Hayk without hesitation. "I remember clearly. There couldn't have been more than a couple of seconds between the two shots, and as you can see the curtain is almost fully drawn."

"Very good. Now I want you to really think back to that moment. Did it look like the woman decided to close the curtain herself, or did you get the feeling that there was someone else in the room doing it? There is nothing here in the picture that would indicate either way. So you need to think back and try to remember what you saw *between* these two shots."

"That's harder to answer," said Hayk, struggling with his recollection. "She did look somewhat surprised, almost as if she snapped out of something, between twenty-one and twenty-two. You see her face has turned left, right? That was almost like a sudden jerk. I did not see anyone else, but it wouldn't surprise me if there was someone who came from her left and grabbed the curtain and pulled it."

Laurian didn't say anything but studied the last several pictures in the set. Then he zoomed in further on the edge of the curtain, and moved between twenty-one and twenty a few times.

"You are brilliant, Hayk jan!" he exclaimed at last. "Just brilliant! Of course there was someone else who came from her left and jerked her around. Look here and focus strictly on the edge of the curtain. We are on number twenty-one. See this? That is where she is holding the curtain ajar. That little indentation in the edge of the curtain is caused by her hand. Now look at twenty-two. There is a bigger bunching up of the curtain, about thirty centimeters above the indentation in twenty-one. Do you see this?"

"Very clearly!" Hayk almost yelled. "And Paron Edik, look, it looks like the woman is still holding the curtain too, but the upper bunch-up has moved to the left."

"Exactly, and great observation, Hayk," said Laurian almost as excited as the teenage boy. "You got it all, my friend. No more questions about what's going on in these two pictures. The horrified woman opened the curtain and looked out, and a taller person, most probably one of the body-guards, noticed and came rushing to close the curtain and pulled her back in."

Of course Laurian knew that all the real questions would start here. He was very glad to shower Hayk with praise and reward his hard work with full recognition of his achievement. The kid had done very well, staying up several nights, not getting much sleep on a pile of hay in the barn, and fol-lowing instructions to the letter. And all that he expected was recognition, especially from Laurian, and also from his grandfather.

"Hayk jan," he said, "you deserve a good bath and a very good night's sleep in a comfortable bed, not in the barn. Do you know if your father is at the guardhouse?"

"I don't know," said Hayk, "but Paron Edik, I really should return to the barn. What if they come back?"

"We've learned what we can from watching them, Hayk. In fact, we've learned a lot more than I had ever hoped for, thanks to your expert pho-tography. You can take the rest of today off, and maybe we can even call off the stakeout. I'm still worried about you missing so much school. What do you say we take a walk to the guardhouse to see who's there, and if they're all asleep, you can take the small room next to mine and sleep here today?"

The invitation to sleep in Paron Edik's house was the ultimate sign of recognition to an elated Hayk. Laurian noticed his reaction and decided to have him sleep in his house even if his father and grandfather were waiting for him at the guardhouse.

They put on their coats and hats and left the house from the back door. Laurian grabbed his twelve gauge shotgun from the cabinet, along with the belt of shells; it was his habit not to leave the house late at night without the gun. One never knew what could get in your way in these mountains. Hayk reached for the camera. "Leave that here," said Laurian, "I have a feeling you'll return here with me after the walk."

It was a cold but spectacular night. The half moon was in the middle of the sky directly over their heads, and a slight breeze was playing among the bare branches of trees. The outside light above the front door of the guardhouse was on, but there were no lights inside. Alice, the half-Alaskan puppy, was sleeping on the doormat. When she heard them she jumped to her feet and started running towards them. But she suddenly stopped half way, her hackles raised, frozen in her tracks, and popped her ears sharply upward and started barking.

"She's smelled something," said Hayk.

"Call her," said Laurian, loading the gun with two buckshot shells. "I don't want her chasing after whatever it is and getting chewed up." Wolves were known to strangle and eat younger dogs in the region. Alice didn't change the direction of her gaze as she reluctantly approached them. They met halfway, and Hayk grabbed her collar. But she was totally focused in the direction of the wild pear tree a few hundred meters down in the field.

"Don't let go of her collar," said Laurian, and started walking very slowly toward the wild pear tree. He had barely taken twenty paces when he noticed them.

"Hold on to her tight, Hayk. Come, you're going to see an amazing resident of these mountains!"

They approached another ten paces and sat down behind the cluster of poplar trees. In the moonlight, they could see the mama bear and her two cubs clearly. Alice was struggling to break free, but Hayk was restraining not only her movements, but also held her snout tightly so she wouldn't bark. The bears picked the wild pears and ate, absolutely undisturbed by anything. The cubs could easily reach the lower branches, standing upright on their hind legs and imitating the mama bear by grabbing a branch and wiping it clean with their mouths and claws, pears, leaves and all. Laurian knew that the mama bear had sensed their presence. She sniffed the air a few times, in long noisy sniffs, raising her head upward and looking in their direction, and then calmly continued to eat and watch the cubs. These were large brown bears, indigenous to the region, just a little shorter than the American grizzly, with huge heads and arms, which looked disproportionately large compared to their bodies. Hayk watched breathlessly, as the bears grew tired of the tree and calmly walked down the path to the next cluster of wild fruit trees.

"Paron Edik," he whispered, "aren't you going to shoot?"

"Shshsh…" said Laurian. "Watch. You don't get to see something like this every day."

"Then I should have brought the camera," whispered Hayk again.

"Hayk," whispered Laurian, "this was just for you and me to enjoy and to keep in our memories. This was not for shooting, either with a gun or with a camera. This is a gift for us to share for all the great work we've done today."

When the meaning of Laurian's words sunk in, Hayk's heart was about to burst with pride and joy. This was true bonding with Paron Edik. For the fifteen-year-old boy from Shatin, there could not have been a greater reward for his unstinting efforts of the past few days.

They sat under the poplars quietly for a long time after the bears had gone. Hayk let go of Alice's snout, but held on to her collar. He petted her head gently to calm her down. The moon had made headway towards the Western mountains. But there was no sign of daybreak yet. They heard the barking of a dog way off in the distance, and Alice stirred, but remained under Hayk's reassuring arm.

"Paron Edik?" said Hayk after a long silence.

"Yes?"

"Did they know we were here?"

"Who?" Laurian's mind was already way past the bears.

"The bears."

"The mother knew for sure," said Laurian. "The cubs may not have noticed."

"But they were so calm."

"She did not *sense* danger, Hayk. Here I am with a loaded gun, and she smelled us, but she did not sense danger. We have a lot to learn from the bears."

"I don't know what you mean."

"When I was young, my father used to tell me that once in a while I needed to rely on my instincts. We could not answer all the riddles of life by logic alone, he would say. Unfortunately, when we learned to rely on logic, we lost the sharpness of our instincts. That mama bear did not lose it, see. She just did not sense danger, that's all. And she was right. I would never have turned a gun on a scene like that. And you know what else?"

"What?"

"If I had any intentions of hurting them, she would have sensed it. She would have rushed out of here with her cubs. And if she had sensed more imminent danger, she would have attacked us herself, to protect her cubs."

Hayk was silent for a long time.

"Let's go see what your folks are up to," said Laurian, finally standing up.

"You know," said Hayk as they started walking back toward the guard-house, "my father once tried to hunt a bear. For one full week, he and his friends kept watch all night at the mouth of a path not too far from here where bears were known to pass. Imagine, Paron Edik, one whole week, every night keeping watch until dawn! And they did not see a single bear! Not one. And here we are, taking a casual walk, and we run into a whole family!"

"I told you this was a special gift just for us, didn't I?" chuckled Laurian. "To get something you really want, you don't have to necessarily chase it blindly. You have to know when to let it come to you instead. And that too is a matter of trusting your instincts." When he saw Hayk's somewhat cynical look, he added, "And of course a little luck never hurts."

Hayk laughed and was walking very tall indeed as he knocked on the door of the guardhouse. Agassi opened the door after the second knock.

"Hey, grandpa," yelled Hayk, "while the guard was asleep, the bears came and went, the wolves came and went, the thieves came and went…"

"Ha, ha, *balés*, sure they did," laughed Agassi, kissing Hayk on the forehead. "That was all? No tigers? No foxes, boars? So it was a quiet night all in all, no?"

"This young man and I will be heading back to the house to get some well-deserved sleep," said Laurian to Agassi. "Your watch now. Tell Saro we need a meeting, but not before noon. I will call him to arrange the time later. Also, Gabriel is coming in the early afternoon to check some of the repairs we need to finish before winter."

Gabriel was the builder of the house who took care of seasonal maintenance tasks as well.

"*Eghav*, Edik jan. You mean you two have been up all night?"

"It is a long story, but yes, we have. See you around noon."

"You want Hayk to sleep in the big house?"

"Absolutely. He'll be in the small room next to mine. I just hope he doesn't snore," laughed Laurian. "And, Agassi, when daylight comes, go check the newly planted pine saplings at the border over there, next to the wild fruit trees. I bet most of them are trampled by the thieves Hayk spoke about. Some guard you are!"

And Agassi watched with some bafflement as the two walked away toward the main house, laughing as if they were old friends of the same age, teasing an older man with an inside joke.

Laurian called Mayor Saro around noon.

"Can we meet in about an hour?" he asked.

"Ha, Edik jan, I'm in the village. I'll come over."

"Could you call Nerses and see if he can come up too?"

"I'll call, but it is not easy for him to leave the restaurant," said Saro.

"If he can find a way, it would be great. We can cover everything all at once."

"I heard you had a late night," said Saro. "Anything interesting?"

"I'd say so," said Laurian. "I believe we can now draw some solid conclusions. The big question, as you keep reminding me, is what can we do about all this."

"Okay, Edik jan, let's talk in person in an hour. I'll see if we can get Nerses up here. Maybe I can arrange to send someone from the village to relieve him for a few hours."

Vartiter set the table on the back terrace and Agassi started the fire for *khorovadz*. While Hayk helped Agassi with the fire, he told him the story of the bears with such enthusiasm that Vartiter stopped to listen as well.

"I saw their traces this morning," said Agassi. "And Paron Edik was right; they had destroyed around ten pine saplings. Some of them may survive; I've straightened them and tied them upright again. But a few are totally uprooted and broken in half under their feet."

"Paron Edik says we can always replant pine trees, but watching the bear family on its pre-dawn stroll is a rare pleasure he wouldn't change for anything," said Hayk, "and grandpa, I agree with him. It was really great. And when they were calmly walking away, the cubs looked so funny from behind, following their mother, their huge behinds moving right and left so clumsily, I could barely control my laughter."

"That is a great sight, *balés*," said Agassi. "You're lucky."

The fire was burning and while they waited for the coals to form in the bottom of the pit, Agassi and Hayk took on the job of lining the *khorovadz* over the long, wide skewers.

Laurian went over the key pictures one more time: Number twelve, twenty-one and twenty-two from the sequence last night, and the three photos taken a day earlier, showing the movement of the girl from the car into the house in Sevajayr. He copied the six photos into a separate file, and named them—fourth, fifth, sixth, twelfth, twenty-first, twenty-second. That was all they needed to focus on. *I need to print these at a decent photo shop*, he thought, and decided that would be worth a trip to Yerevan. He also had decided to go back to Saralandj, and would have to pass by Yerevan anyway. The circumstances of Samvel Galian's death, a month before his daughter's employment by Ayvazian, were still a major unresolved issue for Laurian, and the revelations of the past couple of days had added a lot of troubling dimensions to his speculation on the story.

The group was finally seated around Vartiter's superbly set table.

"Nerses jan, thanks so much for coming," said Laurian. "We all know it is not easy for you to leave the restaurant on such short notice."

"No problem," said Nerses. "My brother stops by a lot these days from Yeghegnadzor. His work is very slow; they're not getting any new orders at the carpentry shop. He'll stay as long as I'm here."

Saro and Agassi were anxious to hear the latest news. They had gathered a few bits and pieces but not the whole picture. Laurian himself had not yet heard Nerses's story, nor seen his pictures. Hayk, who according to custom kept quiet until asked a question, was happy keeping busy with what was on the table—*khorovadz*, roasted potatoes, a few types of cheese and various sausages, salads, yogurt, and pickles.

"I think we have enough to conclude that Ayvazian is up to no good," said Laurian once they had made the first toast. "What I mean is that he's involved in illegal and criminal human trafficking. That is a crime everywhere in the world, including in Armenia. I am basing this strictly on a few photos that were taken at the house in Sevajayr, mind you, but we're not here to prepare for a court case; just to figure out what he's up to."

"That's good," said Saro, "because chances are that whatever we have will not stand up in any court in this country if it is against Ayvazian."

Laurian had a separate discussion in mind about destroying Ayvazian's operations altogether, but, given Saro's comments, he did not want to stir up the deep-rooted fears of challenging authority. He turned to Nerses instead.

"Nerses, we haven't heard from you yet, and I don't know if what you have to say corroborates my conclusion. I'll show the pictures I'm talking about after lunch. Tell us what you have."

"I'm afraid what I have is a lot of details of who and where, but not much in terms of what. We have pictures of the drivers and bodyguards; we know exactly where they went after they left the restaurant; we have details on all the cars that passed by us. But we can say next to nothing as to what they are up to."

"Did any of the cars go to Martashen?" asked Saro.

"Both of them did. We delayed them by thirty minutes or so with our fallen tree, gave them some tea, took pictures, etc., and warned all three posts to watch for the cars. We had pictures of their license plates on our phones and SMSed them to our people, so they could check for sure. Both went straight to Ayvazian's house in Martashen."

"Any passengers aside from the drivers?" asked Laurian.

"None that we could see, either here or in Martashen. Around an hour ago the cars were still parked in front of Ayvazian's house."

"All the information and pictures that you've gathered will be very useful," said Laurian. "As far as I can tell, there are three drivers/bodyguards who are actively involved. Viktor may have come here in person once at the beginning to inspect the area and the houses, but I don't think he's been back since. I think the three are managing the two houses in Vardahovit and Sevajayr. There is at least one woman in the Sevajayr house, maybe two. I'll show the pictures of the one they brought in a couple of nights ago. We have no proof of a second, but I wonder why they were guarding the place before if there was no one there. Also, I think there is at least one captive in the house in Vardahovit; otherwise they wouldn't be guarding it either. But we simply cannot organize a stakeout there to take pictures. The position of the house does not allow it. There is nowhere to hide or watch from."

"Pardon, me, Edik jan," said Nerses, after listening patiently. "Maybe I've missed out on some meetings the rest of you have had. But what are we trying to do with all this? It is clear that you have watched these movements on this side of Getap, just like we have from the other side. But to what end?"

"Good question," said Laurian, very much aware that what they had done so far in terms of surveillance was entirely uncommon for these people. One simply did not take on the likes of Ayvazian. That was the incredible vicious circle of dealing with the oligarchs: they got away with murder because no one dared to question them, and no one questioned them because they always got away with murder. It was precisely this vicious circle that Laurian wanted to break. *It could so easily be turned into a virtuous circle of accountability and crime control*, he thought. We question them, they get caught, and because they get caught, more people question them and hold them accountable. It could all start with just one case. One major scandal that would shake the country and wake it up.

But Laurian knew that this was not the audience for his large-scale reform dreams. These folks were honest, hard working, but rightly scared and truly powerless. They could not share his vision on a grand scale, but they understood dangers close to home. They all understood that getting rid of Ayvazian's operation from Sevajayr was important for the security and safety of their own families. That was much easier to sell than a fancy story of vicious and virtuous circles.

"Good question," he repeated, looking at Nerses. "Look, Nerses jan, we never intended to keep you in the dark about what we're doing on this side of Getap, and that's why I'm glad you could make it today. The problem is, the local nest of this beast is right here in Vardahovit and Sevajayr. It's not in Getap. This is where they have set up a base and are keeping captives. This is what makes none of us safe here. *None* of us. Especially those of us with families."

Agassi and Saro were nodding in agreement. Hayk was busy with a large piece of pork khorovadz, but was fully tuned in as well.

"Saro and I discussed this at length," continued Laurian. "We agreed that doing nothing was not necessarily a safe option, because if Ayvazian built up a major operation here, it would end life as we know it in these villages. It could even affect your business, and many other businesses along the road."

"I can see that," said Nerses, anxious to hear what else Laurian had to say.

"So what we now want is to find a way to make Ayvazian leave the region. We're not going to pick a fight with him, which we can't win, nor confront him in any way. That would be stupid. But let's think of ways to make him believe that it would be wiser to move somewhere else."

"That's the idea," chimed in Saro. "Let him figure out that he's better off somewhere else."

"How?" Nerses's question was what everyone wanted to know.

"Why has he chosen these villages in the first place?" asked Laurian rhetorically. "Because they are secluded, and there are deserted homes that no one cares about. No one ever goes to Sevajayr or misses the deserted home, right?"

"Right," said Saro, curious to know where Laurian was going with this line of reasoning, "but don't forget another very obvious factor: he knows this area and he probably considers it his own region."

"True," conceded Laurian. "He knows the area well, especially Sevajayr. And he probably thinks that the few villagers there are ignorant idiots who are scared of him and pose no danger to him. But imagine if Sevajayr and Vardahovit had not been so secluded, and if all of a sudden there was a lot of demand for houses to accommodate workers and their families. Wouldn't that give him some concern? Wouldn't he start thinking that what he's doing cannot be done safely with that kind of traffic?"

They all agreed that it would, but they still had skeptical looks on their faces. How could Laurian change the isolation of Sevajayr and Vardahovit? But Nerses had a more immediate question.

"Edik jan," he said, "what exactly is he doing that he needs isolated homes for? We haven't answered that question yet."

"True," said Laurian, "so true. We haven't covered that yet." With that, he walked inside the house and produced his laptop. They had mostly finished eating, so he moved some dishes and placed the computer in the center of the table. Saro and Nerses sat on either side of him, and Agassi sat next to Saro, leaving only Hayk across the table.

Laurian started with the fourth picture, explaining the two shadows and the presence of the image of a smaller person, then continued with the fifth and then sixth, focusing on the profile of what he thought was a woman entering the house. These were all important photographs for him, but he knew they would not necessarily impress his guests. He was counting on the twelfth to do the job. And the twelfth did not disappoint. The face of the woman was unmistakable. The horror in her eyes was equally unmistakable. No one could argue that this woman was just having a casual look out the window. And when Laurian explained the details of the twenty-first and twenty-second photos, no one could argue that she was there of her own free will.

"Dear friends," said Laurian somberly, adopting the style and tone of the master of ceremonies at formal dinners about to propose a historic toast, "as we sit here enjoying this wonderful afternoon, enjoying our freedom, there is a woman only twenty minutes from here being held in a godforsaken house in Sevajayr against her will. Who is she? Whose sister? Whose daughter, wife, mother? How can we deserve our own freedom, knowing she's there, a captive? How can we live and enjoy this freedom with a clear conscience?"

Laurian knew that he was being a bit dramatic, but he allowed himself to get carried away anyway. That was the style that worked and he decided to take it a notch higher, talking to them directly:

"And I know that you may think this does not really concern us. It is not one of our women held captive in there. But think about it. What if it was? God forbid, what if it was someone we knew? Could we sit here toasting each other and enjoying Vartiter's superb lunch? Saro jan, a thousand pardons, please, and again, God forbid a thousand times, but what if she was one of your relatives? Do you think I could just sit here and have a lunch party? Wouldn't I be there at the door of that house with all guns blazing trying to rescue her? So what is the big difference in this case?" asked Laurian to the frozen faces staring back at him. "Please tell me, what is the big difference? That we do *not* know her? Is that what makes it acceptable? Or is that what makes it just not our business?"

As he spoke, Laurian was keenly aware that he had diverged from their stated objective of getting Ayvazian to voluntarily take his dirty operation elsewhere. Clearly his last outpour was not about that. He had somehow managed to bring moral issues into the discourse, something he had intended to steer clear of. His speech had already acquired a mind of its own and was bursting out of him; there was nothing he could have done to stop it. But he needed to get back on track.

He took a deep breath and continued, changing his tone entirely.

"At any rate, let's return to what we can do. As I was saying, what if this place was not so isolated, what if there was more traffic, more hustle-bustle. We can do something about that. I know for a fact that the government has approved the repair of the road from Shatin to Vardahovit, and the plan may even extend it to Getik Vank. Even though it is already fall, they will start now from Shatin, and put in a good two or three months of work before the first snow, and then continue in the spring. This will require a lot of new workers, right? They will need to house people, equipment, materials, right?"

"They will repair the road?" asked Nerses, as if that was more important news than Ayvazian's activities. For most villagers, it actually was.

"Oh yes," said Laurian. "It's done. The funding is allocated. They have even staged a bidding process, and one of their people has won the contract." Laurian did not specify who 'they' was and everyone knew better than to ask. "They should start in a week or so."

"But Ayvazian must already know this," said Saro, and he set up his operation here anyway.

"I don't think he appreciates how much additional traffic the road work is going to create," said Laurian. "And I know people who can make sure that it does. We'll get the word out that homes are needed to house workers and materials. He'll get the message, I assure you. The problem is, can we wait that long?"

"What choice do we have but to wait?" asked Nerses, still a bit nervous from Laurian's earlier outburst.

"Maybe no choice at all, but that horrified woman is there now. They'll probably move her soon. This place is just a temporary holding place, till they sort things out. She'll probably be sold to a pimp or a brothel somewhere outside Armenia."

Everyone at the table was quiet. Vartiter appeared, which was a welcome interruption for everyone. She came smiling as usual, asked if they wanted anything else, and started gathering the dishes as they declined. There was a lot of leftover food.

"You men haven't eaten much," she said almost as a reprimand. "What's the matter? You didn't like the food?"

"Everything was great, Vart jan," said Laurian laughing. "Everyone here except Hayk is watching his figure, for fear that you'll get on their case for being too fat!"

Vartiter laughed out loud and got busy with the cleanup.

"Okay," said Laurian at last, "we really have no choice. I'll do my best to expedite the roadwork and start getting the word out on incoming workers and housing needs. I can do the latter immediately. I'll call Yerevan later today to see when they're planning to start the actual work itself. In the meantime, what do you propose we do with the surveillance we've set up?"

"There's no harm in continuing that," said Saro. "We may learn something new about their ways, and we may be able to confirm that they have other captives."

"Fine then," said Laurian. "The road monitoring is very low key anyway and we can gather information on all their movements. But the stakeout on the Sevajayr house is more hands on. Hayk jan, can you keep it up a bit longer?"

"Of course, Paron Edik. As long as it takes."

"How about your school? Can you skip classes a few more days?" Laurian was very worried about Hayk falling behind in school. He worried about that as much as any other risk involved in the stakeout.

"Of course I can, no problem," answered Hayk cheerfully.

Laurian was not so sure, but at the same time he needed a few more days of surveillance.

"As long as your father is okay with it," he said.

"His father is okay with it," answered Agassi.

XII

Laurian knows he should wait at least a week before visiting the Galians again, but on the third day he is itching to go back. There is too much that does not make sense, least of all Samvel Galian's accident. He feels a strong need to befriend Avo and to find out more about what happened to his father and sister. He has already decided that the two are somehow related; he needs more details and facts to understand the link.

He manages to meet his instincts and his impatience halfway and waits one more day before leaving for Saralandj. He tells Agassi that he'll be gone overnight and leaves relatively early in the morning. He speeds past Nerses's restaurant; no time for chitchat or coffee. He has an important meeting in Yerevan, then plans to head off to Ashtarak to see Gagik before going to Saralandj, where he hopes to be by early afternoon.

He can't get his mind off the Galians. Samvel Galian, a resident of Saralandj, falls off a cliff and dies in Sevajayr. It all looks like an accident and no one gives it a second thought. Then, a month later, his daughter Lara gets this incredible job as a model in Greece and starts sending money to her family almost immediately, through the able offices of her agent, none other than Ayvazian. Laurian's mind is bursting with the implausibility of the story, even though everyone else in Saralandj and Martashen seems to be accepting it at face value.

He arrives at the appointed time of 11:15 at the office of the Minister of Agriculture. The Minister is an old friend and one of the few in government that Laurian trusts. In fact, he is the only reason why Laurian has staked his personal reputation to facilitate the provision of substantial development funds from more than one multilateral organization in order to build the agricultural infrastructure in Armenia. These include major irrigation projects in about a dozen villages, agricultural product processing plants, and road repairs and construction in remote and generally neglected regions, such as the Shatin-Getig Vank road repair project, which falls in the scope of this scheme. The Minister administers and manages the projects funded through international agricultural assistance programs.

"Just a few days in the mountains and you're tanned already," says the Minister, getting up from behind his desk to greet Laurian. "The sun is strong up there, you know, you should be careful." He is a tall, balding man, with a warm smile. His desk is cluttered with project maps, business plans and proposals. The shelves around the office are full of agricultural products from around the country, displaying a large variety of wines, brandies, jams, preserves and boxes of cheese.

"The sun up there is delicious," says Laurian, embracing his old friend.

"Well, you'd be happy to know that we're all set for your road," says the Minister once they're seated and he's asked his secretary for some coffee. His large ashtray is already full of cigarette butts from the few hours that he has been in his office. He puts out a half-smoked cigarette and immediately lights another one.

"I'm very happy to hear that, Sevak jan, and that's partially why I'm here. I want to see them start right away. We have at most three months before winter stops all work, and we should try to get the road at least past Yeghegis in that time."

"You worry too much," says the Minister. "I told you we would finish that section before winter, and we will. It's around seven kilometers from Shatin to Yeghegis. They'll finish it in three months."

"Sevak jan," says Laurian, "I have a personal favor to ask. I won't bother you with details now, but it is critical that they start right away and they create a lot of new activity in the upper villages; I'm talking specifically about Vardahovit and Sevajayr. They'll have to move materials there, right? Some equipment? Workers? Can they start looking for places and homes to rent as of now?"

"What are you up now, Laurian?" asks the Minister, squinting as he looks Laurian straight in the eyes.

"We just need to liven up the place a bit, that's all, and the sooner the better," says Laurian with a smile.

The secretary comes in with two cups of coffee and a fresh ashtray, and takes the full one with a grimace. She is an elderly woman, with dyed orangish hair and makeup so heavy and colorful that every inch on her face looks painted.

"I don't blame her," says Laurian when she leaves, referring to her grimace. "You're worried about me getting too much sun, but you alone are destroying the air quality of Yerevan with your smoking."

"She'll be fine," says the Minister. "She smokes too, you know, almost as much as I do. Anyway, coming back to your problem, you know I can't tell them how to do their job, or go and rent houses in Sevajayr," he says as he lights a new cigarette. "That is too specific and detailed for the Ministry to get involved in. What we can do is push them to start immediately, and to move fast. Maybe even ask them to finish a couple of kilometers more than what's planned for this year, but I can't give them such specific instructions."

"Well, the pressure would be a great help. But since the repairs are starting from the Shatin side and moving up, they may not think of setting up bases in Vardahovit and Sevajayr until next spring. I need them to do that now. How can we 'help' them plan things with a longer term view?"

"All we can do is suggest," says the Minister.

"Rents in some of those deserted homes are very cheap," says Laurian. "People can rent homes there for fifteen to twenty dollars a month. So if they complain about increasing costs, they'd be bullshitting you. You can tell them the Ministry will take care of all additional costs involved in setting up operations in the upper villages, and I'll be happy to reimburse the Ministry every penny."

"This is really important to you, Edik my friend, isn't it?" asks the Minister, increasingly more curious about Laurian's motives. But he is too polite to ask any direct questions. Laurian has been extremely helpful to his Ministry.

"Sevak jan, yes. One of these days you should drive up there. I'll show you a few things on the spot. But let's not waste time on the details now."

"Fine, *eghav*. I'll talk to them."

"Many thanks, old friend. I truly appreciate this."

"What else is on your mind?" asks the Minister with a smile. "You said this was *partially* what you were here for."

The second issue churning in Laurian's mind is broader and he doesn't want to distract the Minister with it, especially now that he is satisfied with the way the conversation on the upper villages went. But, seeing the eager smile of the Minister's face, he finds it difficult to just ask him to forget it.

"Sevak jan," he says after taking a deep breath, indicating his reluctance to bring up the subject, "the second issue is in a way related to where this country is going. It is not directly related to you or your Ministry, and if you want we can put it off until later, maybe when you visit me in Vardahovit. It is the kind of topic that we need to discuss with a good cigar, at much higher altitude than Yerevan!"

"Then we'll do just that," says the Minister. "Where are you off to now?"

"I'm going to Ashtarak to see *Khev* Gago. Do you remember him?"

"How could I forget?" laughs the Minister. "Give him my best regards. We have a few projects lined up in his region as well, mostly irrigation and one hydroelectric power plant."

"See you soon, my friend. And many thanks for the help with the upper villages issue."

𝒳 𝒳 𝒳

Laurian plans to meet Gagik briefly and then take him to Saralandj. Gagik has already agreed to this, even though he does not know any details. They meet at the usual restaurant in Ashtarak. It is already one in the afternoon, and both he and Gagik are hungry.

"Let's not turn this into a long and elaborate lunch," says Laurian. "Let's have something light and head off. I can't drink anyway since I'm driving."

"No problem. I'm in no mood to drink either. Now tell me, what's your infatuation with the Galians?"

Laurian summarizes to Gagik the story of Ayvazian's operations in Vardahovit and Sevajayr, his suspicions about his involvement in Samvel Galian's death, and his guess that there is a connection between that death and Lara's unlikely career.

"So you see, Gago," he says, "our two regions may be more connected than we thought."

Gagik has listened very quietly the whole time, and finally emits a long, low-pitched whistle.

"So what do you think?" asks Laurian.

Gagik has not said a word.

"This is big, Edik jan," he says finally. "This could even be bigger than Ayvazian. I knew there was some of this going on, but I never imagined it being so close."

"That's the problem; we always tend to think that these things happen somewhere else."

"But in Saralandj and Sevajayr?" Gagik whistles again.

"God knows where else. These girls are shipped mostly to Turkey, I hear. That's how the business initially started. Some of the better-looking or younger ones end up in Moscow. More recently, Dubai has opened up as a good market, and some go to Sharm El Shaikh in Egypt. The pattern is to take them to tourist or business hot spots."

"It looks like you've done your research, as usual."

"We've barely scratched the surface. I've been checking out a few web sites about human trafficking, and the stories are amazing. There is an establishment called The Progeny Foundation that helps children who have become victims of human trafficking. I know someone there. I ran into him a long time ago in Europe, and we kept in touch. He is watching this region for the Foundation now. He's the one who told me about the four destinations where they take the young women. He says boys are equally at risk."

Gagik's long whistle returns.

"Let's go talk to the Galians," says Laurian. "The mother is too sick and unwilling to talk. But if we could get Martha and Avo to a quiet place, we might learn a lot."

"Yes, let's go," says Gagik. "We should at least be able to learn why Samvel Galian ended up in Sevajayr, and how Ayvazian convinced the mother to let Lara go."

As they leave the restaurant, Agassi calls.

"A second woman has been seen," he says. "They took her out."

"You're sure it was a different woman?"

"Yes, absolutely. This one has much shorter hair, and a narrower, thinner face. We have one picture showing her face, not a very good one but enough to show that it is a different woman."

"What do you mean when you say they took her out?"

"They took her away an hour ago. Edik jan, they had to carry her from the house to the car."

"Hayk has these pictures?"

"Yes, we just saw them on your camera. We didn't see them bring this woman in, so she must have been there. And they were very careful when they took her out. One guard got out of the house first, checking to make sure no one was watching. Then he opened the back door of the car. The second guard got out of the house carrying the woman and threw her into the back seat. One of Hayk's shots shows her face as he is tossing her into the car. The whole thing took a few seconds, Hayk says."

"What was the woman wearing?" asks Laurian on an impulse. He is not sure if his question has any significance.

"Jeans and a heavy brown sweater," says Agassi. "And, Edik, she had socks on but no shoes. That is clear form one of the pictures."

"Okay. Well done, Agassi. I'll check the pictures when I get back. Let me know which direction the car takes after Getap."

"Oh, sorry, I forgot. We already got word just a minute ago. It is headed towards Yerevan."

"Thanks. I'll call later." Laurian hangs up. They leave the restaurant and get into Laurian's car, leaving Gagik's in the parking lot.

"They're shipping her out of the country," mutters Laurian aloud when they are on the main road to Aparan.

"What did you say?" asks Gagik. "They're shipping who, where?"

"Either by train to Georgia and then Turkey, or maybe on a flight to Moscow." Laurian is still talking to himself, even though he is aware of Gagik's question.

"Edik jan, what in the hell are you talking about?"

"It would be more difficult to fly a drugged woman; and she probably will not cooperate if awake. So chances are they're taking the train to Tbilisi."

"Edik! Wake up! Talk to me! What is this all about?"

"They just took a woman out of one of the houses in Sevajayr. She was carried to the car by one of the guards. She could not walk on her own; do you understand? Why do you think that was? She was obviously drugged, because they did not know how she'd behave, which leads me to believe that they're transporting her against her will. Now, tell me, if you were transporting a woman against her will out of the country, what would be safer, by commercial flight or by train?"

"Edik, you're way ahead of me here. But I'll play along. Okay, fine, if I were to transport a person out of the country against his or her will, then the train would be safer than a commercial flight. So what? Where are you going with this?"

"I have no idea where this leads," says Laurian desperately. "Maybe nowhere. I'm just trying to make logical deductions at this stage. They may or may not lead to anything."

"Edik jan, don't overanalyze everything. At the most basic level, they are moving a woman against her will out of the country, right? Didn't you know this already? Why is this shocking news to you? Where is the great revelation here? Which part of this is news?"

"So you're saying it is okay?"

"Edik, listen to me! You're not listening, my friend. Who said anything about any of it being okay? I just ask, is this *news*?"

"When I confirm it, it is."

"No, when you confirm it, you just confirm it. It is news before that. In fact, when you confirm it, it is *no longer* news. Do you see? Confirmation of news does not make news, it ends it. Confirmation of something you already know is just for your idle and vain gratification, my dear old friend."

Laurian, the veteran investigative reporter and journalist, never imagined that he could be challenged to this extent by *Khev Gago*, on purely professional grounds. Gagik had a point, and an incredibly important one. Confirmation of what I already *know* is not new knowledge. Of course it would be different if I had doubts; then confirmation would be very important new knowledge. But do I have doubts? Is that what this is about? Do I *want* to have doubts, perhaps because deep inside I do not *want* to believe any of this? Is that what's bothering you, Laurian? You don't want to accept that in your beautiful, idealized, romanticized country such crimes can be committed? Wake up, Laurian. Listen to *Khev Gago*. Listen to *Khev Gago*...

He maneuvers around the potholes of downtown Aparan. Do not react, do not judge, understand reality, deal with it. Accept it as reality, even if you do not accept it in principle. You cannot deal with anything if you do not accept it as fact first. Things are the way they are. Just, fair, good, are not factual standards. They have nothing to do with what *is*. They are concepts that blur your sense of reality; they distract you and weaken your understanding of what you're dealing with. Learn from Saro and *Khev Gago*, Laurian. Don't let *anything* come between you and the reality you're facing. Strip your mind of the ridiculous emotions; don't feel sorrow, or anger, or joy. Just think of what you are facing. Then think of what you can do about it. That's how these people are; and just because they do not display your moral indignation, it doesn't mean that they don't have moral standards. Has it occurred to you that they have learned long before you that moral indignation solves nothing?

Gagik is deep in thought too. The crazy revolutionary has lived through his share of disillusionment with what independence would bring. Is this a new battle cry calling him to war? A post-independence challenge that he had never imagined would haunt him? So all that you really achieve after winning one battle is the chance to fight the next one? Is that it, *Khev Gago*? Is there really such a thing as victory or defeat? We're too stubborn to acknowledge defeat even when it hits us in the face. Defeat is not and has never been an option. Victory, on the other hand, is always an option, but *always inconclusive*. As soon as you win one battle, you realize that all you've really won is the right to fight another. Victory is inconclusive… illusive and unreal in many ways; all that victory has been for us so far is the absence of absolute defeat; but the absence of defeat and true victory are different things, aren't they?

They can see the houses of Saralandj in the distance, nestled at the foot of a mountain, with the patchy forests clearly visible beyond the cluster of small stone homes. It looks like an enclave where things just end; there is nothing else that one expects to see, as the road enters the village but does not continue past it, as if decapitated by a sudden truncation caused either by geography or by some inexplicable fate.

"We may have to park the car a bit before we reach the house and walk the distance," says Laurian. "Let's see if the puddles have dried up."

"Now you can understand why the Soviets did not allow any tourists here," says Gagik. "Frankly, I don't blame them. What business would tourists have up here during the Cold War?"

"And now? You don't question the business that I have here?" asks Laurian with a chuckle. "Frankly, the authorities today might have a more justifiable reason to stop my visit than the Soviets did in their day."

"First of all, Paron Edik, you're not a tourist. I don't think anyone in Armenia sees you as a tourist, even though most remain baffled by your foreign ways. Second, what you're doing here isn't necessarily opposing what you call the authorities. You need to be more nuanced when you talk about the authorities in this country, my friend. There are layers of them, and many shades, some visible and some not, some honest and some not, so don't go lumping them all in one category like that."

"Fine, but at the end of the day, they all support and feed off each other, right? Who protects the likes of Ayvazian? Who lets them get away with all the crimes they commit? Certainly not you and me! The Ayvazians of this world are protected by those highly nuanced 'authorities,' and I don't care how many layers you may see there. At the end of the day, the system not only protects them, but also purges those who question and challenge them."

"I know this will sound terrible, but it is much more complicated than that," says Gagik. "What you've told me about what Ayvazian is doing is not only much bigger than him, but it is bigger than the 'authorities' in this country. This is huge, and gets into the regional human trafficking trade. I bet if you ask your friend at that foundation you were talking about earlier, he'll corroborate what I'm telling you. I've started to doubt that our authority figures here have a lot of real power. They are pawns in a bigger game. They have their masters."

"Gago, maybe they have their masters. But they know precisely what they're doing. They also know the cost in terms of human suffering of their actions and the actions of those they protect. And still they do it. But listen, we'll tackle this issue again some other time. Let's focus on the Galians right now."

There is a young boy walking toward the village on the road. As they approach, Laurian stops to offer him a ride. He is barely ten or eleven, and is carrying a bag that looks heavy.

"*Barev*," says Laurian through the rolled down window of the Prado, "can we give you a lift?"

"*Barev*," says the boy, staring Laurian in the face. "Paron Edik, *duk ek?* Mr. Edik, is that you?"

Laurian is surprised; he does not recognize the boy.

"We haven't met," says the boy, as if answering Laurian's unspoken question. "I am Aram Galian. My brother has told me about you."

"Aram! Barev, *ari*, get in," says Laurian. "We're headed toward your house anyway. Are you going home?"

"Yes," says Aram. He gets in the back seat of the car.

"Out of school already?" asks Gagik. It seems too early for the kids to be out of school.

"Yes," says Aram. "Today one of our teachers was sick so they let my class go early."

"Aram jan, are you the youngest or the second youngest?" asks Laurian.

"I'm the youngest. I am almost eleven years old."

Laurian knows that the youngest son is supposed to be the most promising at school.

"How is school?" asks Laurian.

"Very good, I have all fives. But sometimes it gets boring."

"Boring?"

"Yes; the teachers repeat everything. Too easy."

"How is your mother?" asks Gagik.

"The same. She stays in bed most of the time."

Laurian slows down as they enter the village. An old sheep dog is sleeping against the wall of a house, forcing Laurian to bear so far left that he almost scrapes the car on the fence of the house across the street. The dog opens one lazy eye, gives them a bored look, and goes back to sleep. These mountain sheep dogs, called *Gampr* in Armenian, can be vicious and serve as a shepherd's best protection against wolves. This one would have chased them barking all the way out of the village in its younger days.

"Whose dog was that?" asks Laurian to Aram, trying to make lighter conversation.

"He has been with the village for a long time; right now the Dalians take care of it. He cannot go to *Yayla* any longer. Can't keep up with the animals, and can't fight wolves anymore. His name is Zrah. Uncle Dalian says Zrah has killed over a dozen wolves." Aram is doing his best to sound like an adult.

"Zrah is a great name for a dog like that," says Laurian. The word means 'armor' in Armenian. "I can imagine the fights between these dogs and a pack of hungry wolves. Must be pretty fierce."

"There are always more wolves than dogs," says Aram, assuming the confident tone of an expert. "There would be at most three or four dogs at the *Yayla*, guarding the whole herd of the village. But wolves come in bigger packs. Five or six, sometimes even more. So the dogs need to be very good. Zrah could probably handle more than three wolves by himself."

"Have you seen a wolf attack?"

"No," says Aram. "I went to the *yayla* only once, when we took food to the shepherds with my mother. Avo was sleeping there that summer. He had a small tent in one side of the camp. We stayed one night with Avo and returned the next day. He had seen a wolf attack and he told us about it. But I never saw one."

The road winds out of the cluster of homes that define the village, and they see the Galian house in the distance.

"How deep are these holes that always seem to be full of muddy water?" asks Laurian. "Can we take a chance driving over them?"

"Maybe it is safer to walk the last stretch," says Gagik. "I don't trust these next few potholes. What do you think, Aram?"

"Only the old tractor has passed over these potholes," says Aram. "Its back wheels are much larger that your car's and they don't get buried too deep."

"Why don't they just fill these in?" asks Laurian.

"Oh, they do. They filled them with rocks and pebbles at the beginning of the summer. But it gets like this within a few months. The holes are right at the curve, and people say that is what causes the damage; my father used to say that there could be an underground water stream that keeps moving the rocks from the bottom. But no one knows. They just fill it in every few months."

They walk up the several steps to the front door of the Galians, and Aram leads them in. There is no one in the house other than Silva Galian, who is asleep in her bed. Aram checks on his mother. She seems sound asleep.

"Where are your brothers and sisters now?" asks Laurian in a low voice.

"Avo is at the stables. The rest are at school. The stables are not far, so we can walk there if you want."

"And your oldest sister, Martha?" asks Laurian.

"She's probably home. She comes here later in the afternoon every day for several hours to take care of Mama."

Laurian wants to talk both to Martha and to Avo. He decides it would be best to wait until Martha arrives to talk to her, so the best thing to do for now is go to the stables to see Avo.

The stables aren't far. They walk out of the house and before reaching the village turn right on a narrow dirt trail, which is covered by overgrowth of vegetation. But it leads up to open fields and they see two long, single story buildings in the distance. The earth is moist and soft, though it has not rained for several days. Even though the Galians keep their sheep in the 'basement' of their home all winter, they also own these barns where they house the villagers' cattle and horses for a nominal fee. The barns also serve as the main veterinary center of the village. It is an important communal responsibility that the Galians take very seriously, dating back to the days of the grandfather.

They find Avo stacking the bound bales of hay in one huge pile in a corner of one of the buildings. Next to the pile is an even larger pile of bound grass bales, harvested in July and August, to be used as feed all winter. The place looks well organized and clean, with half of the long rectangular hall used for storing feed, and the second half for housing cattle. He is surprised to see them approach. He comes out and waits for them to reach the barn. They sit on a pile of haystacks at the entrance of the building, and Avo lights a cigarette. Laurian doesn't remember seeing him smoke, but he realizes that they met in his mother's room, and maybe Avo didn't want to smoke near her.

"I hope we're not interrupting your work," says Gagik. "I'm Gagik Grigorian. I was a close friend of your father. We actually met a long time ago, when you were a baby. You might not remember."

"Barev," says Avo. "We're just getting ready for winter."

"It looks like a lot of hard work," says Laurian, shaking his hand.

"Once I have all the hay and grass stored safely, we'll be fine. We're lucky this year, since we have more than enough to last all winter. It hasn't always been like this."

"I'm glad to hear that, Avo," says Laurian. "Any news about your mother?"

"Nothing new. She sleeps most of the day."

"That's what I told them," says Aram.

Avo smiles at him and ruffles his hair. "What are you doing out of school so early?"

"*Tikin* Fermanian was ill. They let us go."

"Avo, since we've interrupted your work already and you're taking a break, I want to ask you a few questions. I hope you don't mind," says Laurian. "Something has been troubling me about how your sister Lara found her job. Do you mind if we talk about that a bit?"

"What would you like to know?"

"How did the Ayvazians find her? How did your parents agree to let her go?"

"I have no idea how they found her," says Avo, lighting up another cigarette. "The first time they came I was not at home."

"They came more than once?" Gagik asks, curious about the circumstances as well.

"My mother says that they came once, told them that Lara had this incredible potential, and they offered to become her managers. My father refused. Then they came back after he died, and this time my mother accepted. They convinced her, I guess. I was home when they came the second time, but was outside in the garden, and my mother did not call me in. I wish I had talked to them before Lara went. I only remember saying goodbye to her the night before, and I had already left the house when they came for her later the next day. We never thought that we wouldn't hear from her for so long after she left. Had I known, I would have tried to find out where they were taking her."

"So your father refused to let her go the first time they asked. Do you know anything about that first meeting?"

"Not more than what I already told you. They came, they made their offer, he said no, then they left. Those are the details."

"But then your father went to Martashen to see Ayvazian, right?" asks Gagik. "Avo jan, this is very important. Do you know anything about that?"

"Actually, *that* was the second time they came," says Avo, correcting his earlier story. "The second time they came to ask for Lara was the *third* time they were in Saralandj. All I know is that they invited my father to pay a visit to Ayvazian, and he agreed. I now wish I knew more about what was going on. But at the time none of it seemed important. Nobody imagined that they'd send his body back."

This was news to Laurian, and, judging from his facial expressions, to Gagik as well. For the first time they saw the events in three distinct phases:

the first proposal and rejection; Galian's death; the second proposal and acceptance. It was unreasonable to assume that the three weren't related.

"Avo," Laurian asks after a long silence, "who was in those meetings with them? Who knows firsthand what was discussed?"

"Only my mother. I know she was there at the first meeting, and at the third meeting when she agreed to let Lara go. But I'm not sure who was there at the second meeting, when they convinced my father to go to Martashen. As I said, I saw them briefly but had to leave. Maybe he talked to them alone that time. We'll have to ask my mother."

Laurian and Gagik offer to help Avo finish up at the stable. Aram chips in as well. It is heavy work. The bales of hay are heavy, and they need to be stacked high. Avo simply throws one on his right shoulder and climbs up the stacked bales to place it on top of the stack. Aram climbs up and helps arrange the bales neatly. Laurian and Gagik cannot do what Avo is doing, so they awkwardly roll some of the bales closer to the barn. In less than thirty minutes Laurian is already out of breath and perspiring.

When all the bales are arranged and stored to Avo's satisfaction, he makes sure that the cows have enough feed and then locks the door of the stable. He walks over to the second building, which houses more cows and several horses, throws some feed in front of the animals and locks the gates. They start to walk back to the house.

"Is it safe to leave the stables like that?" asks Laurian.

"Oh yes," says Avo. "Most of the villagers have animals in there. No one would steal them."

"No, I meant from wolves," says Laurian. The stories of Zrah the Gampr are still fresh in his mind.

"Wolves won't come so close to the village, at least not in the fall. They might in January or February, when they're more desperate to find food, but by then we'll have some of the dogs inside. Besides, they rarely attack cows and horses. They go after the sheep, and we don't keep the sheep here."

"Well, you basically seem ready for winter; what else is there to do?"

"Not much. There are some repairs to be done at the stables, and we need to agree with the villagers what animals they want to keep there during the winter months. They pay us a small amount to take care of the stables and feed their animals. I will be done in a week or two."

"Then what?" asks Laurian.

"Just maintenance work," says Avo, "but no heavy lifting. During winters we don't have much to do except wait for spring. We're talking about four lazy months. Everyone puts on some weight." He laughs. Avo does not laugh often, and Laurian is happy to hear it.

As they make the left turn onto the main road toward the house, they run into Martha. She looks very tired but greets them warmly, hugs Aram and kisses his cheek, but is a bit more formal with Avo. Laurian and Gagik let them walk ahead, and Martha and Avo manage to chat a bit before reaching the house. They probably need to catch up on family matters, Laurian thinks. He is happy to walk behind them with Gagik and Aram. At that moment, perhaps because he has worked a little at the stables, Laurian feels particularly close to the Galians. He never met Samvel Galian, but he senses his influence and presence everywhere around the family. Laurian feels a strong connection with Avo, Martha and their youngest sibling, Aram. He wants to get to know the mother better, and learn more about Lara, the mystery beauty who is at the center of the puzzle he is struggling to solve. *So what's your true story, Lara*, he wonders as they walk past the last mud puddle and turn into the steps leading to the front entrance, which is also the door of the parents' bedroom. *If you were recruited by Ayvazian*, I wonder…

The questions that Laurian and Gagik have been asking have aroused Avo's interest. Now he too wants to know about the three meetings with Ayvazian's men. He wants to know why his father went to visit him, and why he refused to let Lara go the first time they asked. For some reason, all that had not seemed important until now. Just hearing the questions out loud made them more relevant and important to him. And indeed, what was Papa thinking when he said no? And why did mama say yes only a month later? And why did Papa go to Martashen? It was all a set of givens until now; it was just the way things were, the simple facts. But now it didn't seem so simple; the supposed facts had turned into nagging questions in his mind.

Why indeed. It seemed amazing to him that he never asked the question before. And why did his sister Lara have to go, never to be heard from again? Just asking the question in his mind was a revelation to him. It was a novelty simply questioning the why of facts. If you can ask why, you do not just accept; you rule a little, you control a little. You *can* ask why, even if everything seemed 'normal' to you before. And then Avo suddenly had a chilling question push its way into his mind: Why on earth is this Laurian fellow so interested in us? Why does it matter to him?

As soon as they enter the house, Martha gets busy making tea for her mother. She offers some to them as well, and this time they accept. She puts a small jar of honey on the table; "from our own bees," she says with pride. Then Avo awakens his mother. She opens her eyes slowly, like last time, and attempts a brave smile at the sight of her son. The whole scene is a repeat for Laurian, but in the grander scheme of things, it seems insignificant compared to the sense that not much has changed in this village for hundreds of years.

"Mom jan," says Avo, gently stroking her arm. "Get up; we have our friends visiting again."

"Avo, *balés*," smiles Silva Galian. "*Inch aretsir? Amen inch normal a?* What did you get done? Is everything normal?"

"Ha, Mom, normal. Listen, I need to ask you a few questions. Sit up. Martha will bring your tea in a minute. Now listen, Mom. I need to know about the times when Ayvazian's men came over. The first time they came, they asked for Lara, right? But papa refused. Why?"

"We both refused," says Silva Galian, struggling to sit up. "We said she was too young to go to Greece."

"But then you let her go. Why did you change your mind?"

"When they came again your father was already dead. I don't really know why I said yes the second time. But they sounded genuine and they were sure Lara would do well. 'What kind of future could she have in Saralandj,' they asked. They were so sure, they made me believe it too. She's done well, hasn't she? They were right. How would she send all that money otherwise?"

"Yes, Mama, of course she's done well. But why did they ask Papa to go to Martashen?"

"Oh, Ayvazian wanted to do some business with Papa; they were going to start a dairy farm or something. Your father was not interested but he went to be polite. He told me that when he left. He said he shouldn't refuse Ayvazian twice in one week."

"But then they sent his body the next day." Avo remembers, talking more to himself than to his mother. "What happened to him?"

"They all said it was an accident, *balés*, but why are you asking these questions now? He tripped on a fallen log and fell off the cliff. All the wounds confirmed that. The police report confirmed that. Eyewitnesses confirmed that."

"Silva jan," says Gagik, approaching her bed. "Samvel and I were good friends. He used to tell me great stories about his family. So I am also curious, like Avo. Did you meet any of the eyewitnesses? Did anyone in Saralandj actually talk to them? Do you know who they are or how many of them saw the accident?"

"The people who brought his body told us everything," says Silva Galian, noticeably tired of both speaking and of the topic. "They had papers, signatures, everything. I did not look at everything, but the local police did."

Gagik looks at Laurian with a hint of frustration in his eyes, as if trying to say that they won't get much more information from Silva Galian. People weren't in the habit of questioning authority, and any story became fact when repeated a few times.

Laurian sips his tea as he approaches Martha, who has already served her mother and started preparing a meal.

"Martha, what do you remember about how Lara left?"

"What I know is what mother has told me," says Martha as she washes the vegetables and puts them in a bowl. "Papa didn't like Ayvazian very much and did not want to deal with him. 'They're not like us,' he would say. Papa used to say that it is important to know the people one deals with; and he said one could never know Ayvazian well. Too many secrets, rumors and stories."

"But then he agreed to see him again, right? To even go to him. How come?"

"He was afraid. Papa thought that they'd harm one of us if he did not go."

"Did they threaten him?" asks Gagik.

"Not that I know of. But he thought he should go; otherwise it would look like he was being disrespectful to Ayvazian. They didn't have to threaten directly. He somehow got the message that it would be better if he went."

"Did you talk to Lara right before she left with them?"

"Yes, we talked the night before. First Mama talked to her, advised her, and then she and I talked in our bedroom."

"How did she feel about leaving?"

"Lara was always a bit crazy," says Martha, still not interrupting her work. "She acted like a boy. She is so beautiful, but that had not yet started to matter to her. So she thought she was just going on another adventure, as if going hunting with the men, or chasing and rounding up the sheep like the sheepdogs."

"Did she know that your father had refused to let her go the first time they came for her?"

"No, none of us did. My parents did not talk about their first visit to us at the time. And we didn't ask. It was parents' business, not ours."

"When did you find out?"

"Very recently, actually. Mother mentioned it one day, but I'm not even sure why. It doesn't matter much to us now."

"But you're sure that the day Lara left she didn't know about the purpose of their first visit and about your father's refusal, right?"

"Yes, I'm pretty sure. Mama wouldn't have told her that; why would she? Lara left here excited; she was probably looking forward to a new adventure, even though none of us understood exactly where she was going or what she would be doing. There were the same explanations, Greece, modeling, good money, but we could not picture what any of that really meant."

Laurian has already decided that sooner or later he will have to take Avo into his confidence and explain his concerns about Ayvazian. But this is not the time or place. He signals to Gagik and they stand up. Avo and Aram walk them out and accompany them to his car.

He pulls Avo aside and says, "I'd like to invite you to come and spend a week with me in Vardahovit, when you're finished here, that is. I think you'll find it interesting."

Avo is surprised and intrigued by the invitation.

"I'm not sure I can leave for a week, even when I'm done here," he says politely, "but thanks. I could come to visit for a day." He is now as curious about Laurian as Laurian is about him.

"You said yourself that there isn't much to do once you close up for winter," says Laurian with a smile. "It will be a good break, I promise. The rest of the family can take care of things once you're done with the heavy stuff."

"We'll see how Mama feels," says Avo. "But I'll definitely come. I'm just not sure how long I can stay."

Laurian hands him a piece of paper with his cell phone number.

"Call me," he says. "And please get a phone. As I offered last time, I'll be happy to send you one myself."

"Thanks, but no need for that, really," Avo says. "I'll get it soon, I promise. I'll call you within the week. And maybe visit a week after that."

They are largely silent during the thirty-minute ride back to the restaurant in Ashtarak. Laurian thinks about asking Gagik to check a lot of details about what was known about human trafficking in Armenia and about Ayvazian, but he dismisses the idea. It wouldn't be right to involve an old friend in his personal obsessions, especially potentially dangerous ones. So the two say goodbye without any further discussion or a clear plan, and Laurian heads back to Vardahovit.

He has decided to tell Avo everything he knows, including showing him some of the pictures. Unlike *Khev Gago*, Avo has a reason to know and to be involved. He now has to wait for his visit.

XIII

I saw Avo in my dream last night. He looked like a grown man; tall and handsome. He did not look happy, though. Kurig jan, he said, Mama is very ill... and then he left.

Kurig jan...dear little sister. It has been a long time since Lara has heard those words. What does the dream mean? Has she missed Avo so much that her mind is forcing the dream on her? Has she missed being called *kurig*? Mama must be really ill. Sumaya told her once that dreams have a lot of meaning in the Middle East. They do in Armenia too. People believe in dreams and in their predictive power. Mama did not look well at all when she left the house such a long time ago; she had spent a whole month crying. So maybe she has fallen ill. Are they really receiving the money that she sends them? Viktor had reassured her that every penny that she gave him to send was received by her mother. He had shown her small pieces of paper, which were transfer and receipt confirmations; they were in Russian, but she could read enough to understand the content. They were sealed and signed and looked official.

"I want to talk to her again," she had told Viktor a long time ago, when she was still in Moscow.

"No," he had answered. "Not yet. When you start feeling truly comfortable in your new self, then we'll arrange it." That was a good strategy, as far as Viktor was concerned. It would not only avoid any risk of alarming her mother, but would also give her an added incentive to accept her new situation as a prostitute.

She had even appealed to Anastasia to help her get in touch with her family, but Anastasia tried to talk her out of it.

"Why, Lara, why? There's no point. They will never accept what has happened to you, and you can never go back. So what's the point? Just focus on doing well, and keep sending them money. That way everyone will be happy. The less they know the better, believe me."

She gave up the thought of contacting home while in Moscow. Then she tried to get permission a few more times after reaching Dubai, but Madame Ano would not hear of it. She was given a cell phone that operated only locally in Dubai. She could not make or receive calls from overseas, not that she had any phone numbers to call home even if permitted to. She would have tried to reach the main post office in Aparan, and send word that she'd call again at a specified time, and ask her mother or Avo to be at the post office at the time. She could manage that much, if allowed. But the girls were watched closely, and they were not allowed to get their own phone services. Ali the enforcer made that very clear to them.

Kurig jan, Mama is very ill... That's all he said, and then he left. It was a scary dream, which was very disturbing considering that it was Avo. Why did Avo appear to her in a scary dream? Why not in one that was sad, or happy or full of tears of nostalgia? Why scary? The old women in her village would have had many interpretations about this. He showed up like a ghost, said Mama was ill, and disappeared like a ghost. He was there just for a minute to give her the message. But this was Avo, after all, her closest brother and friend, and not a single word from him about her, about how much he missed her, about how she was doing. Nothing personal. That was scarier than the message. What did that mean? Was he out to harm her to defend the family honor like in some of the stories that she'd heard? Would Avo be capable of killing her?

How she ached for her father's reassuring embrace, his strong arms and calm gaze. It was his calming presence that she needed the most, not an interpreter of dreams. He'd be able to give her peace with his all-knowing silence, his understanding warmth. *What did you discover in the forest, Lara?* She reached for Araxi Dadik's ring, rubbed it, kissed it and pressed it first to her cheek and then to her heart. Both Al Barmaka and Sumaya had noticed the dynamic with the ring and had asked her about it. It was such a thin, simple ring, barely a few grams of gold in it. It was virtually worthless in Dubai. But she seemed to treasure it more than anything else that she had.

"Is it from a lover?" Al Barmaka had asked, attempting to sound jealous.

"No, nothing like that, Sir," she had answered.

"What then? Someone you secretly loved or, god forbid, still do?"

"No, Sir, really. It was my great-aunt's ring. It has only sentimental value to me."

That's when Al Barmaka had asked her to call him by his first name. "My name is Ahmed," he had said. "When we're alone, you call me Ahmed." She had found it difficult to do at first, but he had insisted. Her voice, her accent, her inability to pronounce the heavy Arabic 'h' in Ahmed, her faint blush and soft smile, all had moved Al Barmaka deeply. And that was also when he gave her a beautiful ring, with a shiny emerald stone.

"I hope this too will have sentimental value to you, my dear Leila," he said. "Because it is from me. Because you give me so much happiness."

ᘒ ᘒ ᘒ

Sumaya has been very friendly to Lara lately. She invites her over to her apartment and spends hours talking to her. Woman to woman, personal stuff. Often she stays at Lara's apartment long after her Arabic lessons are over and goes over some of the lessons again, explaining details that Lara has missed, and practicing conversational Arabic with her. Her characteristic curt style of speech disappears during these sessions and is replaced by a more patient and personal tone.

"Sir really likes you, Leila," she says, looking at her warmly. "I'm very happy for you."

"But I'm here just for one year, right? What usually happens after the year is up?"

"Leila, *habibty*, there is no 'usually' with Sir. He has even sent some away before their term was up. And he may keep you long after your term ends. Everything is negotiable. Would you like to stay longer than your term?" asks Sumaya warmly, sounding as if she would like that herself.

"Sir is very kind," says Lara carefully. "But sometimes I miss my home." Lara does not fully trust Sumaya yet, but she also realizes that there will not be a better opportunity to find out the possibilities of finding a way out. There is no doubt in her mind now that she needs to get home. Sumaya likes what she hears. This could be an interesting 'plan B' if the plan for Turkey falls through. But she decides not to follow up on that just yet.

"You sound exactly like I did a long time ago," she tells Lara, "and I am still here. There are always solutions to everything, you know, but I also believe that we end up living for our priorities, and our priorities change. Trust me, Lara, your priorities will also change as you grow up."

"What happened a long time ago?" asks Lara. "Why did you say I sounded like you?"

"Well, it was around seventeen years ago," says Sumaya. "Sir was only seventeen then. Hold on, that's exactly your age now!" she exclaims, suddenly realizing the coincidence. "Seventeen years ago, he was seventeen, as you are now, and I was about ten years older than him, and they hired me to be his, um, teacher."

"Teacher?"

"Yes, of sorts. I did not teach him Arabic, though. I taught him love, sex, sensuality. I was his introduction into the sensual world."

"So *you* were Sir's first lover?" asks Lara with a huge smile. "You taught him everything?"

"Well, I'm not sure about everything; he's had many lovers since. But yes, I introduced him to sex."

"Well, Ms. Sumaya, I congratulate you!" laughs Lara, which was unusual for her. "You can be proud of your student. He is very kind and considerate. Men do not turn out that way naturally, especially if they learn about sex from each other, and I know that for a fact."

"Thank you, *habibty*," smiles Sumaya. "As I said, that was a long time ago. You were just born, he was seventeen, and now, when *you're* seventeen, here we are sitting together talking about this. Life is a mystery, *habibty*, which we'll never understand. Who would have guessed? Who *could* have guessed? Does everything really happen for a reason? You know, here everything is attributed to God's will. *Everything*. Good, bad, fair, unfair, doesn't matter. There is one and only one source for everything that comes your way in life, and everything that comes in everyone else's way. It's hard to understand, really, but once you accept it, it answers a lot of questions that you cannot answer otherwise."

Lara is quiet for a while, looking past Sumaya, and it is obvious that her mind is somewhere else.

"Do you think there is one source for everything?" asks Sumaya after a while.

"Religion is not as big in my country as it appears to be here," says Lara. "It used to be, a long time ago, but not anymore. My father used to read the bible to us, the stories about how God created everything, the heavens and the earth, the oceans and the land, the mountains and the valleys, the night and day…and how He worked all types of miracles. I guess it is the same thing, right? If He created everything, then he is the source of everything."

Did He create Ayvazian too? Lara wonders. *Did He make Ayvazian do to me what he did? Will the same God now help me do to Ayvazian what I must? No, my dear Ms. Sumaya, accepting God as the source of everything does not answer all the questions, not all of my questions.*

"I guess so," says Sumaya, and decides to change the subject. "You said you miss your home; do you ever think of going back there one day?"

"Of course," says Lara matter-of-factly. "Doesn't everyone? Don't you?"

"Not anymore, Leila. Many years ago, I missed home. Today I miss the days when I used to miss home. There is something very sweet about missing home; it gives one hope. I've lost that now. Now when I look back, I no longer want to *go* home, but I yearn for the days when I was like you, still able to picture home, to feel its warmth, to need to see family members. And you help me remember, Leila, *habibty*, you really do."

I don't want to ever reach that point, thinks Lara, realizing that what Sumaya is saying is even a greater loss than what she has endured.

"Can the girls take some time off, like a short vacation?"

"That would be impossible," says Sumaya. "There can be no contact with the outside world. You know that. It just doesn't work."

"Ms. Sumaya, you said there are always solutions to things. Then what's the solution to my need to go home, at least for a visit?"

"My dear Leila," says Sumaya, assuming her motherly tone of voice, "I also said that we live our priorities. What is your priority now? To stay, please Sir, and build a substantial financial future for yourself, or to go home? Once you answer that, the solution will come to you." And, as if reading Lara's mind, she quickly adds, "And no, you cannot do both. Priority means you have to choose one."

But Lara is not thinking of doing both. Her 'priority' is one thing that is still clear in her mind. But she cannot yet bring herself to trust Sumaya enough to tell her that all she wants is to get home, that her break from home was far too abrupt, that she was not prepared for any of this. Sumaya senses her hesitation to answer her question and decides not to push things. She is making good progress in building trust and a real bond. Rushing could ruin it.

At last she says, "Sir will probably call on you tonight. Go get ready for him. And when you're ready to talk about my question, let me know."

♃ ♃ ♃

Al Barmaka did call on her that night.

"I have a little surprise for you, Leila," he said, handing her a CD. "Play it."

Lara noticed that the CD had no jacket and no writing anywhere. It was clearly a home-burnt CD.

"There are only two songs on it," said Al Barmaka with a smile. "And then I have a good story for you to go with the songs."

Lara put the CD in and walked over to him.

"Bring the remote," he said.

She took the remote and sat next to him. He placed his hand on her thigh and closed his eyes. The CD had started playing what seemed to be the prelude of a song, with the typical Arabic slow rhythm of drums accompanied by the oud filling the room. Al Barmaka seemed to be carried away by the music. Then the song came on. A beautiful, velvety female voice chanted one of the most alluring melodies Lara had ever heard. The song had a mysterious, calming effect on her. *Lamma bada yatasanna...Aman, aman, aman, aman...Lamma bada yatasanna...*She could not understand the Arabic lyrics, but the music alone had an ability to transport the listener.

Al Barmaka was waving his free hand in the air to the tune of the melody, while still holding her thigh with the other hand, as if he was trying to link the two in one reality, one world.

The song went on for a few minutes. Without understanding the words, Lara could easily guess that it was a love theme; the voice of the singer, the melody itself, Al Barmaka's reactions, all spoke of love and deep emotion.

When the song came to an end, Al Barmaka picked up the remote and stopped the CD. Then he looked at Lara for a long minute.

"That was beautiful," said Lara in a soft voice, clearly moved by the music. "Really beautiful. What is it about?"

"It is about you, my sweet Leila," said Al Barmaka.

"About me?"

"This is a very old song, Leila. Its genre is called *Muwashaha Andalusiya*. Muwashaha is a genre of Arabic music that became popular in Andalus, Spain, where we ruled for several centuries. It speaks to me."

"But you say it is about me?"

"It is about a lovely woman, who moves and sways so seductively that her beauty simply captivates her onlooker. Whoever looks into her eyes becomes a prisoner of those eyes forever. Yes, my dear Leila, it *is* about you."

Lara was moved, not so much by his words, but by the honesty of his emotions and the truthfulness of what he claimed he was feeling.

"Thank you, Ahmed," she said so softly that he felt his heart miss a beat. "Thank you for telling me this, for sharing this music with me. I did not understand the words, but it moved me beyond description." And Lara realized that she too was being very truthful.

"Wait, we're not done yet. My real surprise is yet to come, my sweet Leila. Now we have to listen to the next song."

With that, Al Barmaka pressed the play button on the remote, closed his eyes, and began to caress her thigh again. "Now listen to this," he said gently, as if preparing himself for a profound spiritual experience.

The next song had no long musical preludes with drums and oud. The song started almost immediately, and it was sung by the same woman as the first song. But Lara froze in her seat, unable to suppress her tears no matter how hard she tried. She had goose bumps all over her body and was thankful for her long-sleeved abaya, because she didn't want Al Barmaka to notice the standing hairs on her arms. The same lady was now singing *Sareri hovin mernem*, a song Lara knew well. Throughout her childhood she had heard her mother humming this tune while doing her endless chores. *Sareri hovin mernem, im yari boyin mernem, mi dari yar chem desel, desnoghi jukht achin mernem....*She could sing along, and had the strong urge to do so, but she controlled herself. But she could not control the tears that had filled her eyes and were flowing down her cheeks. She did not care. Let Sir see the tears. Let him know that he had finally hit home, touched her soul, knowingly or not.

"It is my turn to say that I did not understand the words, but the song moved me beyond description, *ya habibty* Leila," said Al Barmaka softly, his eyes still shut, his hand gripping her thigh so tightly that it almost hurt her. "Now tell me, what's this song all about?"

"It is about love, Ahmed. About a woman who has not seen her lover for a year, and in her deep sorrow, she says she is up on her feet but cannot walk; she's overflowing with emotion but cannot cry; and she says she'd die to be the two eyes of the person who saw him last...Crazy, stupid love."

"If it's so crazy and stupid, why are you crying, my sweet Leila?"

"Because my mama used to sing this song," she said, as she got up from the sofa to remove the CD from the player.

"Come back," he said, "and we'll play it again. I want you to explain the words. How can such a beautiful voice fit so perfectly both with a *Muwashaha Andalusiya* and with your mama's song? But first, let's listen again."

Lara returned to the sofa, rested her head on his shoulder, and put her hand on his chest. "Let's listen again," she whispered. "I'll do my best to explain what it's all about."

As the song went on, and as Lara whispered short translations into Al Barmaka's ear, he was not listening to what she was saying; he was listening to *her*. He did not care about the translation. He cared about her and what she was transferring to him. What did the song really mean to her? Who was this little girl that he was falling in love with? Half his age, but sometimes with twice his depth, twice his sorrow, twice his grief, and half his joy of life.

They sat there for a long time after the song ended. He held her tight and would not let her get up.

"Her name is Lena," he said at last. "She is an Armenian singer from Syria. She can sing Arabic songs that would make me cry, and Armenian songs that would make you cry. Now isn't that something?"

"That is something," said Lara, impressed. "Do you know her?"

"Not yet. But a friend does. And he recorded the two songs for me. He knew the first was one of my favorites, but we were both taking a chance with the second. I had no idea if it would be a good song for you. All we knew is that it sounded beautiful."

Come back to earth, Lara. This isn't real. Don't fall for this. Remember who you are and who he is. Remember the toughness in his desert-hardened eyes. Stop it. Why are you kissing his cheek now? Why is your hand soothing his chest? Get up, Lara. Go wash your face. No, don't kiss him, not now!

Their kiss was long and deep; it engulfed and overwhelmed them both, and they surrendered to its force in total abandon. This was the first time that Lara had initiated an intimate gesture toward him, and the first time ever that she had led a seduction. They stayed on the sofa; he did not want either of them to get up. Afterwards, he got up, got dressed and left, while Lara lay there covered by her abaya.

Tonight he won me over with a song and I loved him. Then he left. Nothing has changed. I wish Avo would return.

ℒ ℒ ℒ

"Any news from Mehmet?"

"Not yet," answered Farah, letting the frustration show in her voice. "But it would be much easier if I could just call him directly."

"You know that's not wise," retorted Sumaya with her typical dismissive tone. "Do you want a link between you and Mehmet?

"I understand," said Farah with a sigh, "but we're being so careful that we cannot move!"

They had decided to draft a written message to Mehmet and send it inside an envelope containing a letter that Sumaya had arranged for Farah to send to one of her relatives in Istanbul. She was a distant cousin but also a prostitute, working in Istanbul under Mehmet's patronage. In her letter to her cousin, Farah had asked her to deliver the enclosed sealed envelope to Mehmet. The note to Mehmet was short. *"A seventeen year old beauty from*

Armenia is yours for next to nothing. She'll probably come to Istanbul from Oman. Do not keep her in Istanbul. Better in Antalia or Izmir. Respond via Kuchuk. We need to mobilize soon, so respond ASAP."

The risk of Farah calling Kuchuk, which was the nickname of her distant cousin, was considered acceptable. Farah had called her and confirmed that she had received and delivered the message, not personally hand-to-hand as instructed, but through one of Mehmet's most trusted associates. Mehmet had not yet responded.

"We're not even a hundred percent sure that Mehmet has received the message," said Natalia. "And we cannot be unless we either hear a response or Farah calls him directly."

"Let's not go over the obvious again," snapped Sumaya. "Farah cannot call him directly. Nor can anyone else from here. Now tell me again, Farah, what is the problem with Kuchuk calling him and following up?"

"She tried. They keep saying he is not available."

"Not available?"

"Not available. Maybe not in Istanbul. Maybe not at home. It is not clear."

"You have to do better than that, Farah. What makes you think you can reach him directly, then? If Kuchuk cannot reach him from Istanbul, neither can you. Who else do we know in Istanbul who can check directly?"

"Maybe this is no longer such a good idea," said Natalia, possibly echoing what was going on in Sumaya's mind. "Just chasing and pinning down this Mehmet guy seems to be full of its own risks. I wonder what new risks will arise once we actually locate him and manage to get a response. This whole operation needs to be more solid and predictable. There must be no surprises."

"What are you saying?" asked Farah. "Do you have another suggestion?"

"Not yet, but we should think of an alternative plan. I don't think going after Mehmet is going to do it for us."

"I still would like to know what's going on with Mehmet. He would have been our best bet; this Leila girl would have disappeared in his network like you said people just disappeared in Moscow. No traces, no leads. All we need to do is locate him. Ms. Sumaya, coming to your question about who else we know in Istanbul, let me work on that. I'll give you a couple of names tomorrow."

Sumaya had the impression that Farah did not want to speak her mind in front of Natalia. The jealousy and mistrust between the competitors was surfacing. But she did not dwell on it; there were far more important things to sort out.

ℒ ℒ ℒ

Avo came back. It was a grey, wintery day, and he was walking toward her in the dark fields. She could not tell exactly where she was standing, but it was somewhere in their fields in Saralandj. The trees in the distance were lost in a gray blur. He approached with fast, determined steps, and first walked right past her without looking at her; he then turned around, faced her, and said, *"Mama is very ill."* No *"kurig jan"* this time. *"Avo, wait, are you angry with me?"* she asked, as he was turning away to leave. He turned back and looked at her for a long moment. His face looked old and tired. There was a dark shadow over his eyes, and his forehead was glistening from perspiration. *"I'm not angry, kurig jan,"* he said, and the very faint trace of a smile appeared on his face. He then turned around and left.

Lara woke up in a cold sweat. The look on Avo's face gave her a chill, even after she was awake. He was looking at her, but he did not seem to be looking into her eyes. He was looking past them, beyond them. He had lost weight; his face was bonier than what she remembered. What did it all mean? The old questions kept popping up in her mind. Why was Avo coming to her in terrifying dreams? Both times he had looked like a ghost, not really alive, not entirely real, but clearly there, and clearly Avo. Both times he had looked rushed and angry, and even though he had attempted a smile, she could tell it was forced, almost as if he wanted to appease her.

I have to find a way to get back home, she wrote. *Will Ahmed just let me go if I ask him to? Can I trust Sumaya?*

It was past nine o'clock in the morning and Lara had barely managed to get a couple of hours of sleep. After Al Barmaka had left, she had taken a quick bath and gone to bed, but could not shake the uneasy feeling about what had happened on the sofa. Her seventeenth birthday had already passed, and, after having had hundreds of sexual encounters, she had made love to a man for the very first time. She had never imagined that she'd be able to do that. Was this the sign that she was finally accepting her fate, or was it just Al Barmaka? Was this the dreaded capitulation that she had fought, finally imposing itself on her in a sweet disguise? *Remember that this man has bought you,* she kept telling herself. *What are you doing, Lara? A song? Is that what it took in the end, after all the other ways to drag you in had failed?* She could hear her friend Susannah make fun of her. *'You sweet homey thing, a song that your mama used to sing, eh? So now you're finally one of us, then?'*

She desperately needed someone to talk to. Someone whom she could just ask if Avo was angry or not. That mattered. And it mattered to know how ill her mother was. Lara had felt this type of loneliness ever since she left Saralandj, and it had not eased; nor had she become used to it as Anastasia had once told her that she would. First Anastasia, then Susannah, and now Sumaya were the only women who had opened up to her, or pretended to, but these were not questions she could raise with any of them.

And Ahmed? *He sometimes acts like he's in love with me, and other times treats me no differently than any of the clients that I've had. I can't yet figure him out,* she thought, and the thought surprised her. This man was the most important reality in her life. He owned her. But she could not understand the hot-cold treatment from him. Perhaps he was fighting it too. He who could have any woman on earth, as they had kept reminding her, was fighting his feelings towards her. Does he sit there wondering what he's doing loving me, as I do? Does he say to himself 'remember who you are and who she is?' He doesn't have to say anything like that. He's at home, and he knows exactly who he is. He's not fighting to remain the man he is. I am the one fighting.

Come down to earth, Lara. You are all alone and you'll stay that way until you get back home. And when you do get back home, then what? Do you really think that you will no longer be alone? Your papa is dead, your mama is ill, your brother Avo may or may not accept you, your sisters will never understand where you've been and what you've done. Do you really think that there will be a single person in Saralandj who will understand you?

Lara suddenly began to understand what Sumaya was talking about when she said she no longer wanted to go home. But she swore she would never allow herself to get to that point.

She was in her bathrobe sitting on a chair at the kitchen counter looking out the window to the garden, having her first cup of coffee of the day. She stared at the perfectly manicured lawn, two date trees in the distance and the bright red bougainvillea flowers flowing down like a cascade between the date trees. What a contrast this was to their garden in Saralandj, where they would not waste even the smallest piece of fertile soil with a lawn. This was nothing like the fields where Avo appeared to her. This was a fairy tale land, where one could dream. But she could never be sure how far beyond the fences those dreams could travel.

So it is all about context, she thought; what I do depends on where I am; and my worth depends on where I am. Does *who* I am depend on where I am? This compound is like a chessboard, and I'm now a queen on this board. I'm worth nothing *off* the board, just like the queen would turn into a worthless piece of wood off the chessboard. No one can define herself in absolute terms. Remember who you are, Mama said. But who am I *where*? Here or in Saralandj? Can they be the same? Need they be the same? What *am* I worth off the board?

𝄞 𝄞 𝄞

She was not expecting a call from Sumaya so early. She normally called in the afternoons, and it was not even noon yet. Sumaya sounded friendly but firm.

"We need to talk," she said. "How quickly can you get here?"

"Is an hour okay?" asked Lara, resenting the intrusion.

"Okay. I'll send the car."

And Sumaya hung up.

As she started getting ready, Lara felt the pressure to make a decision about whether or not she could take Sumaya into her confidence. The question had weighed heavy in her mind in the past two days; there were only two ways for her to try to find a way back home: trust Sumaya or trust Al Barmaka. The two may or may not be mutually exclusive, but at that moment she could not imagine how she could orchestrate both together. Both had risks. The thought that Sumaya herself might be eager for her to leave had not yet crossed her mind.

XIV

L ara was surprised to see another lady in Sumaya's living room. Until then, Sumaya had always met with her alone. The visitor was a pretty woman with dark brown hair and brown eyes, and her embroidered abaya suited her very much. Lara thought she must be an Arab lady.

"Leila, meet Farah," said Sumaya. "She's your neighbor, both here and more far away."

"Hello," said Lara, extending her hand; then, turning back to Sumaya, "neighbor?" she asked.

"Yes, here, she lives in the chalet next to you. But she comes from Turkey, so she's also a neighbor to you in Armenia, no?"

"I understand, yes," said Lara, surprised by the introduction, as such meetings were not commonplace. This must be the Turkish woman that Sumaya had mentioned earlier.

Farah seemed to be surprised too, not by Lara's presence, which she was obviously expecting, but by her youth and beauty. Even though Sumaya had mentioned it to her more than once, she was not prepared for what she saw. Farah was sitting on the sofa next to Sumaya, and Lara took the side armchair closer to her. Even as she looked at Sumaya, she could feel Farah's gaze on her face.

"I thought it was about time that the two of you met," continued Sumaya. "After all, you are neighbors, and, if I recall correctly, Leila, you had once asked me if you could have some interaction with other women here, hadn't you?"

"Yes, I had," said Lara, shifting her eyes from Sumaya to Farah. "It is good to finally meet you."

"It is good to meet you too," said Farah, who smiled warmly.

"Well, we have a few things to talk about," said Sumaya, "but first, Leila, *habibty*, I know I called you at an early hour. Shall we have some breakfast together? I haven't had breakfast yet, and I'm sure Farah hasn't either."

Without waiting for an answer from either of them Sumaya lifted the phone, pushed one digit, said "set the table" into the receiver and hung up.

It was an awkward silence as the two women didn't quite know how to start a conversation. Farah sat there smiling absently, and Lara looked at Sumaya, waiting for her to break the ice. Farah seemed absorbed in trying to unlock Lara's secret, to imagine her with Sir, and understand his attraction to her. Was it about sex or was there something else? She wished she could get close enough to Lara to be able to compare notes with her about Al Barmaka in bed.

"Leila," said Sumaya at last, "Farah knows someone in Istanbul who may be able to get news from your family. I thought you'd be interested in that, given our last conversation. That's why I decided to introduce you two."

"Someone in Istanbul?" Lara didn't understand how someone in Istanbul could have news from her family.

"Yes, and it's not a short story. So why don't we move to the table and continue there?"

The two guests were surprised at how quickly such an elaborate table could be set. Sumaya must have arranged everything well in advance. It was a large round glass dining table that could seat a dozen guests, set by a bay window overlooking a fountain and garden outside. It was set for three, facing the window. Beautifully arranged trays of every imaginable Middle Eastern breakfast delicacy had been set out, ranging from fried Halloumi cheese, to labni, various types of olives, za'atar, tomatoes and cucumbers, fresh fruits, boiled eggs, beef and chicken sausages. A young maid from the Philippines was there to help them fill their plates. On the side table was a large assortment of fresh juices, coffee and various teas. The maid offered to serve them beverages, but soon Sumaya signaled her to leave.

"The Halloumi and the za'atar are divine," said Sumaya. "Please dig in."

After she arrived in Dubai, Lara had actually acquired a taste for za'atar, a thyme-based spice that is served as a dip, mixed with olive oil. It was a Lebanese delicacy common all over the Gulf and best enjoyed with freshly baked pita bread. Even though she was anxious to get to the topic of the news of her family, she could not resist partaking in what the table had to offer. She usually did not have the patience to eat properly when alone at her apartment. She could order everything at Sumaya's table at her own place, but it rarely occurred to her to do so.

Sumaya had a few bird feeders outside the window, and as they started eating, the garden was suddenly swarming with finches and humming-birds. That was one of Al Barmaka's many attempts to give his estate the look and feel of the old Arab palaces; he had created ideal conditions for the birds to thrive in his compound, so none would fly out into the dry and inhospitable desert. The women couldn't avoid being distracted by the scene, which reinforced the fairy tale sense of their surroundings.

Sumaya stood up, taking the large oval serving plate full of beef and chicken sausages, came around the table and started serving Farah and Lara.

"Farah," she said as she placed the sausages on her plate, "why don't you tell Lara about your friend?"

Lara was anxious to hear about the 'friend' as well, but was outwardly admiring the china. They were beautiful Limoges pieces, perfectly matched sets of plates of various sizes with exotic floral designs. As was her habit, she tried to picture all that in her home in Saralandj, and such attempts usually either brought tears to her eyes or made her laugh. At that moment, she had to suppress a loud burst of laughter.

"Do you know someone named Apo Arslan?" asked Farah, taking a bite of the beef sausage.

"No," answered Lara. "Is he someone I should know?"

"Well," said Farah looking her straight in the eyes, "he knows the people who brought you to Dubai very well, and probably hates them as much as you do."

Lara was not prepared for this. Apo was an Armenian nickname, short for Abraham. It would be pronounced Abo in Eastern Armenian. But more importantly, the references 'the people who brought you to Dubai' and 'he hates them as much as you do' worried her. Are they talking about Ayvazian? Viktor or Sergey? Ano? How do they know I hate the Ayvazians? Do they also know why? What exactly do they know?

"I have never heard of him," said Lara quietly. Then, looking at Sumaya, she added, "And I do not understand why this is important for me."

Sumaya was composed and calm, with a gentle smile on her face, which was not characteristic of her, but somehow looked like it suited the moment very well. She could tell that Lara was deeply disturbed by Farah's revelations.

"Apo hates Ayvazian," said Farah without any emotion, as if it were the most natural thing to say. "They are competitors in the Turkish market. They have had major clashes over the years. The Turks of course play both sides, as they should. So they both have friends in Turkey, and sometimes their friends are the same people. But they cannot stand each other."

Lara said nothing. So they knew about Ayvazian, which probably was not a difficult discovery considering the connection with Ano. But how much did they know about the details of her personal story? She was not about to volunteer any information.

"Apo also has his resources in Armenia," continued Farah. "He knows about your village and your family."

Lara calmly dipped a piece of pita bread in the za'atar, turned it around to make sure that the olive oil would not drip, and brought it to her mouth. It was actually very good. Dried thyme, sumac, white sesame seeds and olive oil made a brilliant concoction, which for some reason had never reached Armenia. She deliberately focused on the za'atar because she did not want her interest in Farah's story to be obvious.

"Oh, so he knows my village and my family?" she said, trying not to speak with her mouth full, apparently paying more attention to her table manners than to the subject matter.

"No," said Farah gently, "I said he knows *about* your village and your family. He does not know your family yet, but he can easily visit them if you want."

A chill went through Lara's body and she wished she could talk to Sumaya alone. Her family did not know where she was or what she was doing. Having one of Farah's friends contact them would be the worst risk to take, even though she was dying to hear from them. She could not trust Farah with any of her personal family issues. The thought of her last night with Al Barmaka popped into her mind, and a very uneasy sense of betrayal started to take shape in her thoughts. He would not approve of this conversation. This whole conversation could very well be a violation of Al Barmaka's trust. It all boiled down to the original question when she came to Sumaya's house: Who could she trust? Sumaya or Al Barmaka? And now she was concerned with a more dangerous thought: Who could she afford to betray? Because it had just dawned on her that trusting one meant betraying the other.

"I would not want a stranger to go to that kind of trouble," Lara said calmly, "going from Istanbul to Armenia, let alone traveling to my village, which is no small matter. Besides, what would be the point? There's no point in that at all. But Farah, many thanks for the offer anyway. I truly appreciate it."

"We just thought perhaps you'd like to hear some news from home," said Farah, still smiling gently and looking back and forth between Lara and Sumaya. "If you don't see any point in it, then of course there is no point."

"Leila, I understand your position perfectly," said Sumaya, who had just realized that the meeting was a big mistake and should not have involved Farah. She was kicking herself for her error in judgment. She had assumed that the prospect of contacting home would so overwhelm Lara that she would put all other considerations aside, but she had not factored in the risks that such a decision could pose for Lara. "But no harm done. It is always good to know the options that one has, no? And this Mr. Apo is an interesting option, which one day you may want to use, that's all. We can forget about him for now."

The rest of the breakfast passed with barely disguised tension and apparent pleasantries. All three were very polite and cultured with one another. Lara had already made up her mind about how much she wanted to reveal to Sumaya. She had also decided that there wasn't much that she could possibly tell Farah, at least not at this stage in their relationship. Farah had long sensed that Lara would not trust her and that Sumaya would have to smooth things over if they wanted to pursue the Turkish connection.

≈ ≈ ≈

A few days earlier, about an hour after the meeting in which they had tried to plan Lara's fate, Farah had called Sumaya.

"You asked who else we know in Istanbul," she had said. "I know someone who would give us an entirely new angle. We might not have to bother with Mehmet."

"Come back over," Sumaya had said.

Farah had told her about Apo, the Istanbul Armenian. He was very active in the Turkish market and handled a lot of traffic from Armenia.

"Could he have been involved at all with Leila?" Farah had asked.

"I doubt it. The people who brought Leila here have a different name. I cannot think of it now, but I have it written somewhere."

Sumaya went to the desk in her bedroom and produced a thin file.

"Here it is," she said. "Ayvazian. Is this Apo of yours Ayvazian?"

"No," said Farah excitedly. "But I have heard the name. From Apo, in fact. They are competitors in Turkey and they don't like each other. So actually this may be good. Apo may be happy to embarrass Ayvazian by having Leila disappear somewhere in Turkey. Unlike Mehmet, he may also be able to ship her back to Moscow. The farther the better, don't you think?"

Sumaya had agreed. In Apo's case, she had no objection to Farah calling him directly; this was different from calling Mehmet, as Al Barmaka had had no dealings with Apo, so the risk associated with establishing a link was much lower. Farah had called Apo and talked to him about a young Armenian girl who may need his "help" in relocating out of Dubai. Apo had not asked a lot of questions over the phone but had agreed in principle. He knew Farah. Based on the information provided by Sumaya, Farah had given him some details about the involvement of Ayvazian and the region in Armenia that she came from. Apo said he knew the region; and he was intrigued by the prospect of snatching the girl from Ayvazian.

Sumaya suspected that Lara would call her as soon as she got back to her house, just as Farah had done a few days earlier. And sure enough, Lara did.

"Thank you for a delightful breakfast," she said.

"You're welcome, *habibty*," said Sumaya. "I'm glad you enjoyed it. I only hope the mention of this Apo guy did not upset you."

"No, it did not upset me. But frankly, I'm still wondering what that was all about."

"I understand," said Sumaya. "Leila, I need to run a few errands now, but I could stop at your place later this afternoon. We can talk then."

"Okay," said Lara, "see you soon." And then to show her progress in her Arabic studies, she added, "*Ma fi mushkele.* There's no problem."

Sumaya chuckled and hung up.

Actually, thought Lara, *there is nothing but problems*. She had far too much to sort out, ranging from Saralandj to Al Barmaka and every complication in between. These included Sumaya, Farah, and the new piece on the chesboard called Apo, whom she mistrusted with a passion.

Finally, a link to home, which was the missing factor in her life. But such enormous risks were involved that it would be crazy to use that link without first figuring out what was behind it. And why was the very guardian of the system, Sumaya herself, who had been so careful to explain to her all the rules, acting as facilitator to what could easily lead to an unforgivable breach of those rules?

She sank into the side armchair in her living room, put her feet up on the ottoman, and drifted into her favorite escape, memories of her father, Saralandj, and Avo. That world had all the answers, if one had the patience to probe. And if some answers were not forthcoming, it only meant that the questions weren't worth asking in the first place. Her father had taught her that a long time ago. "You don't have to answer every question that you face in life, Lara," he had said. "But you do have to choose your questions very carefully. Half the trick is in not dwelling on the stupid questions that have no answers. People can waste a very frustrating lifetime on those. Choose your questions carefully, just as you choose your fights. Don't lose sight of your ultimate objective. Ask yourself, what are you trying to achieve? That's what the questions you ask should help you with. If they don't, they're not worth asking in the first place." Right now Lara was just plain confused.

What surprised her was that she was now remembering all this. These were the random conversations she had had with her father while she helped him graft the trees or water the vegetable garden. They did not seem to be important at the time, as they were just passing the time while doing chores. One day her father had told her about the virtues of living within one's means. "My father taught me this, Lara, and now I hope I can pass it on to you. He used to say that the greatest dignity and greatest freedom came from living within one's means. Do you understand that? That means you are never beholden or indebted to anyone. You are your own master. Think about it, Lara. One day you'll understand it better."

He lived by those words, thought Lara. *He actually practiced that all his life.*

How she wished she could have a conversation with her father now. Why couldn't he just appear in her living room, and tell her what to do? She had some good questions for him, the kind he'd agree are worth asking.

It was close to four in the afternoon when Sumaya knocked on her door. She came in bothered, complaining about all the chores that she had to do on any given day, and how incompetent some of the employees in their compound were. She especially had complaints about Manoj, Al Barmaka's business manager, whose responsibilities in certain areas overlapped with hers, creating a source of tension between the two. Everyone knew that there were no clear job descriptions for household employees in the Gulf region. One did everything the master asked. Period. This was not like a local bank where some British or American consultant had drawn up a detailed human resources manual, outlining the duties, responsibilities and rights of every employee. This was the private jungle, and depending on his whims or, more frequently, on his instincts, Al Barmaka would ask Manoj to do something that was in Sumaya's realm of responsibilities, or vice versa. That would create tension, which was ultimately useful to Al Barmaka. It was never helpful if all key employees in the palace liked and trusted each other. Competition and mistrust were actually helpful in the long run, even if they led to various dysfunctionalities in the short term.

Sumaya perched on the sofa and accepted the glass of water offered by Lara, fanning herself with the flat of her hand. *Akh ya ana, akh ya ana…* she kept saying as she fanned. Oh me, oh me…

"Ms. Sumaya, what's wrong? Are you okay? Can I help with anything?"

"That's sweet of you, *habibty*, thank you, but unfortunately this is something I have to handle myself. Just normal everyday problems, but they have to be attended to nonetheless."

"But what's the matter?" asked Lara, sounding genuinely concerned.

"Oh, it's that stupid Manoj. He is impossible. And his way of talking annoys me. I have to admit that part of this is just a personal dislike of the guy. But he is the one who is supposed to arrange all travel plans for everyone, from Sir on down to the gardener, but he likes passing half those details off to me. So now I have to arrange not only for Sir's return from his trip to the UK, but also two of the maids have to go on home leave, and I have to sort that out too. This is his job, not mine."

That was a mouthful and Lara had to absorb the significance of it all. First, she was arranging for Al Barmaka's return, which would be valuable information for her, because she usually was in the dark as far as his comings and goings were concerned. He would disappear for a few days, and sometimes for a whole week, and only when he returned would he tell her about his trip or at least the fact that he had been out of town. Second, she mentioned two maids going on 'home leave'. What was that all about? Was Sumaya dropping a hint? Was it fine for the maids to go on home leave, but not for the queen on the chessboard?

"Maybe I can get you some chamomile tea, Ms. Sumaya?" asked Lara. "It helps you relax."

"Okay, *habibty*, yes, thank you."

Lara went to the kitchen and plugged in the electric teapot. The water started boiling in just a minute. She put two tea bags of chamomile, a small dish of honey, a teaspoon, and a teacup on a tray and brought them out to Sumaya.

"Here," she said, "it will be better with some honey. This honey isn't bad. We used to have our own hives in my village; that honey was very pure, but this comes pretty close."

If you can drop hints, she thought, *so can I. Let's see where you go with this one.*

Sumaya sipped the tea gratefully.

"So what was the story with Farah and Apo?" asked Lara when she was satisfied that Sumaya had calmed down a bit.

"Oh, nothing important, really," said Sumaya, trying to make light of it. "She got all excited because Apo is an old friend, and she thought there might be a connection there for you. That's all."

"Ms. Sumaya, I'm going to trust you with some information, but I do not want this to go past the two of us, okay?"

"Of course, *habibty*, you can tell me anything."

"My family does not know where I am. They probably still think that I am a model in Greece. That's what Ayvazian told my mother, and that's what my mother told me. That's what we all believed when I left home. I have had no contact with them, or them with me." Lara's voice was beginning to shake a bit, and she could not stop her eyes from getting moist. Sumaya seemed genuinely moved; she took Lara's hands in hers and held them tightly, then gave her a warm hug.

"Leila, *habibty*, I understand; I understand fully. You don't have to say anything more. I know these situations, and it is not very different from my own. It is a classic dilemma. You want to keep in touch with home, but how do you keep up the lie?"

"Thank you, Ms. Sumaya," was all that Lara could say.

"That's why I was telling you that after awhile you stop wanting to go back. Every day that you live a secret life apart from your family takes you a step further away from them. You are a stranger to them already, and they are strangers to you."

Lara was not ready to accept that fate. She felt it was time to probe further.

"Ms. Sumaya, when you introduced me to Farah and allowed her to tell me about Apo, what were you expecting me to do? Did you want me to talk to Apo myself?"

"I did not expect you to do anything that you were not comfortable with, Leila. As I said, it never hurts to have options."

"Options? Options to do what? Will you allow me to contact home, just like Farah contacts her friends?"

"Would you like to contact home?"

"Yes," said Lara gently. "I've wanted to ever since I left, but they wouldn't let me. Everyone has either advised against it or downright forbade it. So I assumed you'd oppose it also. But then you let Farah tell me about Apo, so I'm wondering if it is possible to for me to try."

"Leila, listen," said Sumaya choosing her words carefully. "This is a private home, so there is no absolute yes or no. It depends on your intentions, on what you plan to tell them, on what type of follow up conversations will then be required once you make your first contact, and all kinds of things. Everything here is very private, and that is better for you as well. Sir does not like it at all when the setup here is discussed outside. And he believes in prevention, rather than having to sort out problems later on. And prevention often means not starting things that seem harmless but which can lead to complications later. Do you understand, Leila?"

"Some of it, yes. The privacy, I understand. But what do you mean by complications and prevention?"

"We had a girl here a few years ago, and I let her call home. Her case was actually simpler than yours. She was from Morocco and her parents knew exactly where she was and what she was doing. In fact, they had made the arrangements for her to come here, so I did not think any harm could come from her calling home. Well, it turned out that when she called she found out that her father had been arrested and was in jail in Morocco, for smuggling or something like that, and her mother was crying her heart out, begging her daughter to do something to help. Now in this place that turned into a major *complication*. The girl first pleaded with me, and of course I could do nothing. And then, against my strongest advice and warnings, she brought it up with Sir one night, begging him to use his influence to free her father. That was it."

"What happened?" asked Lara.

"He just left her place without saying anything. The next morning we packed her things and sent her back home to Morocco. She was crying so hard that my heart bled for her. She did not want to leave. This place was perfect for her. She had lost everything. But it was over. Sir absolutely refuses to be involved in any family matters. And he was furious with me for letting her call home. He ordered me never to let anyone do it again. That's the prevention part. Now do you understand?"

"Yes," said Lara, wondering if that was her way out. What if someone didn't want to stay? Would they send her back home, or back to Ayvazian? She was almost sure that the answer was Ayvazian. They'd send her back to whomever they had bought her from. The Moroccan girl was lucky, she thought, as she had been sent here by her own family. And then the irony of that thought hit her so hard that she started crying. Sumaya could not even guess what the real reason for her sudden outburst was; she just assumed that Lara missed home.

"Sorry," said Lara wiping her tears. "Yes, I do understand about the complications now. I promise you I would never mention anything to Sir about my family. And I will not abuse your kindness, by asking to call often. My family is a simple peasant family; I don't think anyone is in jail, and my father is dead. The worst thing that I fear is that my mother may be very ill. She did not look good at all when I left home. She had not slept properly for over a month. That's the worst thing I may find out, and there would be nothing that either I or anybody else could do about that. So no complications, Ms. Sumaya. I promise."

Sumaya was touched. She genuinely liked Lara and she wished that she did not pose such a threat to the established status quo. She also felt a strong instinct to try and protect her. Sumaya, tough and business-like as she was, still had an old fashioned sense of guild-like loyalty to the girls that she managed. Of course it would be entirely different if one of the girls broke the rules or, even worse, betrayed her. Then she'd show no mercy.

"Okay," said Sumaya at last, "do you have a number you'd like to call?"

Lara did not. She had to explain to Sumaya her scheme of calling the post office of Aparan, leaving a message for her brother, and then calling back at a pre-specified time. No one in her family had a phone, she explained, and there was no landline at their house. If any of her family members had acquired a phone, she said, she did not have the number. So this was the only way.

Sumaya pondered the situation. This really was quite unusual. No phones. This was unheard of anywhere in the Middle East, no matter how poor or backward. Calling the post office of the largest town next to the village sounded complicated and seemed like it would leave a trail. But she was determined to let Lara give it a try.

"We'll use my cell phone," she said. "The landlines can all be monitored more easily. Now Leila, you understand that I will hold you to your promise of no complications, right? I hope you also understand the personal risk that I am taking in allowing this."

"I understand, Ms. Sumaya. And I really appreciate this. I will keep my promise."

Sumaya called the international operator, reached Armenia and handed the phone to Lara. It was not difficult to get connected to the post office in Aparan. The person answering the phone knew of Lara and the Galians, even though Lara did not know him. To be on the safe side, he said they should allow at least an hour for him to send someone up to the village and have someone from her family come down to the post office.

Sumaya asked Lara to go to her place and wait for an hour before they tried again. She left Lara in her living room with some magazines and went into her bedroom office to make a couple of phone calls. She returned after a while, looking more relaxed.

"Finally," she said, "it's all set. Sir's jet will pick him up the day after tomorrow from Heathrow. He'll be home by evening. And the maids' home leave is arranged. Sometimes the only way to be sure that something is arranged properly is to do it yourself."

She sat next to Lara on the sofa.

"Is it time to call back?" she asked.

"We can wait ten more minutes, if you don't mind," said Lara. "I'm really sorry I am imposing on your time like this. I know how busy you are."

"No problem, *habibty*. I want you to get this out of your system."

The maid brought tea and pastries, served them both and left.

Sumaya picked up her cell phone and called again, this time directly to the number of the post office in Aparan, then handed the phone to Lara. Lara introduced herself again.

"Oh yes," said the voice, "one minute."

"Alo ?"

"Lara jan, *du es* ? Dear Lara, it is you?"

"Ha, *yes em*, yes, it's me," said Lara, somewhat surprised by the female voice on the phone. She had expected Avo. But this was neither Avo nor her mother. At first she did not recognize the voice.

"Lara jan, *vonts es? Jan, tsavd tanem, shat em karotel.* How are you? I've missed you so much."

"Martha?" said Lara.

"Ha jan, *Marthan a*. Yes, it's Martha."

"Martha jan, I've missed you all so much too. I cannot even begin to tell you. How is everything? How is everyone? I can't talk long."

"We're fine," said Martha, but Lara could already tell that she had started crying. "All is very well now, thanks to you, Lara jan. Thanks to you. I got married, and we've paid all the debts. And everyone is fine, except Mama."

"You got married?" asked Lara, preferring to speak about the good news first. "Congratulations, Kurig jan. That is great news! How is Ruben?"

"He's great, really great. He's been a great help to us."

"Now tell me about Mama. What is the problem?"

"She's very ill, Lara. Very ill. The doctors have given us no hope. We don't know how much longer she has, to tell the truth."

"What's wrong with her?"

"She has cancer. It just got worse after you left. We've tried everything. They all say it's hopeless."

"And where is Avo? Why didn't he come with you?"

Lara had dreaded asking that question the moment she heard Martha's voice on the phone. *So he is angry at me. My dreams were right*, she thought. *Why wouldn't he come to speak to me otherwise?*

"Oh, Avo is not here right now. He left for Vayots Dzor for a few days."

Vayots Dzor? She knew that's where Ayvazian was from. That's where her father had gone never to return alive. Lara felt her heart sink to her stomach. This couldn't possibly be good. Even though she had not yet made the connection between her father's death and Ayvazian, something about Avo being in Vayots Dzor sent shivers down her spine. She took a deep breath to calm herself, then asked, "What is Avo doing in Vayots Dzor?"

"Oh, you won't remember this, but there is this old friend of Papa's by the name of Gagik. He came here recently with a guy from overseas, some Armenian from Switzerland. Anyway, that guy had been here before, and he was asking a lot of questions about Papa, you and Mama. He is a very nice man, Lara. Anyway, he invited Avo to visit him in Vayots Dzor. Apparently he has a fancy dacha there. He should be back in a few days."

"He was asking questions about us?"

"Yes," said Martha, very much aware that there were people in the post office who were openly listening to the conversation. She did not want to tell Lara that the man was also asking questions about Ayvazian. That would be an entirely unnecessary disclosure, which could lead to more questions in the village. The villagers knew better than to bring those names up in phone conversations. Martha had no idea about Laurian's obsession with Ayvazian, nor any idea of how he had wronged her sister, and yet instinct told her not to say his name aloud in public.

"What kind of questions? What does he know about me?"

"He only knows what we told him," said Martha carefully, lowering her voice. "Nothing important. He is a very good man. As I said, Avo is spending a few days with him. And he now has a cell phone. Maybe you can call him directly. Do you want the number?"

"Of course!" Lara almost yelled, scrambling to find a pen in her purse. Sumaya, without understanding a word of the conversation, had already sensed what was going on and quickly produced a piece of paper and a pen for her.

Lara scribbled a number. That is all that she needed for now.

XV

"She's not as naïve as we've been assuming," Sumaya told Natalia and Farah. "I'm not sure we'll be able to keep her in the dark and simply send her away to someone in Turkey."

Farah understood what she was talking about, even though she did not know all the details. Natalia understood much less. She waited in expectation of a more complete explanation. They were in Sumaya's living room. Sumaya had perched on the side armchair and taken the unusual liberty of putting her bare feet up on the ottoman. The other two were seated on the sofa, all three in their usual black abayas, ornate with beads and crystals around the collars and the cuffs. The living room was bursting with the colors of several large bouquets of flowers, a gesture of gratitude from Manoj, no doubt paid for by Al Barmaka's general budget for flowers in his own house, for her help with the various travel arrangements.

"She's smart," continued Sumaya. "Her family is a conservative peasant family in some primitive village and knows nothing about where she is and what she does. She is very attached to them and does not want them to know what has become of her. I let her contact her village and she had a chat with her oldest sister and her brother. The whole thing was quite dramatic, especially the chat with her brother."

Farah was not aware of this but was not surprised.

"Does she want to go back home?" she asked.

"She did not tell me as much, but, crazy as it may sound to us, yes, I think she'd welcome a chance to go back."

Natalia was noticeably uncomfortable with the conversation, in part because she did not know what had happened.

"Ms. Sumaya," she said at last, certain that unless she started asking some questions, no one would volunteer the facts to her. "I personally wouldn't count on her wanting to leave this behind and just go home to some primitive village. Sorry to be so skeptical, but it just doesn't make sense. Aside from that, don't you think it would be unsafe to let her go back home?"

"What do you mean, unsafe?" asked Farah.

"She can be easily found if she goes back home," said Natalia. "She was recruited here in Dubai, if I recall correctly, right?" Both Sumaya and Farah nodded. "Sir bought her from her manager, who is from Armenia. Obviously, the manager runs an operation in Armenia. Do you think he wouldn't find out that Leila had returned home to her village? Especially since Sir would launch a search for her, contact her manager and demand that he return Leila to him?"

Sumaya had thought about that, but Farah had not. She had assumed that their mission was to get Lara out of Dubai, without being implicated themselves. And she still argued that point.

"Look," she said, "I think we're complicating this. If Lara escapes to her village, her future here is finished, regardless of whether she is found or lost. Do you think Sir will trust her again after that? Or that he'll decide to marry a girl that ran away from him?"

Sumaya had to admit that Farah had a point. Letting Lara return home might in fact be simpler than arranging for her to disappear. Knowing Lara, she did not believe that anyone could make her disappear for long anyway, unless they killed her. She'd find a way to contact home, now that she had the experience. But would she escape? And how could they help her escape without inviting any suspicion on them?

Natalia was not convinced. Having Lara escape to her village was not the safest strategy.

"Farah, maybe you're right, but do we want to take that chance? Let me describe a different scenario for you. She escapes and returns to her village. Her former master finds her and brings her back. He has to, because if he does not he's all but finished in Dubai. Okay so far?" Farah nodded. "Okay, now imagine our seventeen-year-old beauty, who has won his heart, and imagine her whispering all types of sweet nothings in his ear, blaming everyone for her disappearance, and crying her beautiful eyes out and apologizing, telling him how much she missed him while she was away, how she'd never, never try anything like that again, how she has fallen in love with him, and so on. Can you be sure that he won't forgive her? Can you honestly tell me that her future would be really finished here? In fact, if I know anything about men and relationships, their bond might grow stronger after an episode like that."

Sumaya and Farah were quiet. They actually had envisioned the scenario Natalia was talking about. Could it happen? Sure. But Farah was still very skeptical.

"Natalia, this is the Middle East," she said. "Remember that Sir has bought her from the market here in Dubai. Let's not forget that she's a prostitute, like us. She may not be as professional, but she is one nonetheless. Granted, she may be young, pretty and unassuming, but let's not forget the basics. I see your scenario, but I just don't think it's very likely. I could live with that risk. The risk we couldn't live with is getting implicated in any of this."

"Why live with the risk if we don't have to? I understand taking calculated risks when we have to, but why do we have to in this case? I think that we'll all be safer if once Leila leaves Dubai, she never returns and never sees Sir again. And arranging that might not be any more difficult than arranging her escape and return home."

"Maybe, but I still say that it would be much easier to get her out of here if she believes she's going home," said Farah.

"You're both right," said Sumaya, who had been listening to the exchange between Farah and Natalia with fascination.

"What do you mean, Ms. Sumaya?" asked Natalia.

"She should leave thinking she's going home, but she should never make it home and never return to Dubai. She should disappear. Until now we've been going about this all wrong."

The girls were impressed. Sumaya had not only skillfully resolved their dispute, but what she was saying made a lot of sense. *No wonder she is the boss*, thought Farah. They saw Sumaya thinking, and did not want to interrupt by asking questions, even though they both were curious to know why she thought they had been going about it all wrong.

"As I said," went on Sumaya, "she's not naïve. We can't take her for a fool and just send her away. She has to be the main mover of the process, not us. She has a lot of personal baggage, which only she can maneuver around." Sumaya shifted her weight in the armchair, re-crossed her feet on the Ottoman, and looked like she was staring at one of the vases of long-stemmed red roses sent by Manoj. She was rubbing her forehead with her index finger.

"She does not fully trust anyone," continued Sumaya. "She definitely does not want Farah involved in any of this, and she has not met Natalia yet, so that's not an issue, at least not so far."

Natalia controlled her burning desire to ask how and when she had met Farah; this was not the time to interrupt Sumaya.

"So we need to keep the two of you out of the picture. She'll feel safer that way. She's beginning to open up to me. If what she wants is something that breaks the rules, then she obviously will assume that she cannot trust me."

Sumaya shifted again and re-crossed her feet, scratching the sole of one foot with the big toe of the other. Her abaya had moved up a bit, and the girls could see the heavy varicose veins above her right ankle.

"You two, on the other hand, are in this together and have to work together. I want to see you as one, as a team, and no more mistrust between you when it comes to this mission. Is that clear?"

They both nodded, even though they still did not understand exactly what the mission was.

"Here's what we should try to do," continued Sumaya. "Leila should go to Turkey first, with the expectation of continuing to Armenia via Georgia. But from Istanbul she should be diverted to Moscow. Staying in Turkey is too dangerous. She will eventually find a way to contact her family. So now you understand why the two of you have to cooperate?"

They both nodded again.

"Farah, your friend Apo has a critical role to play. He should take over in Istanbul and put her on a plane to Moscow almost immediately. Natalia, your folks have to meet her at the airport in Moscow and take her away. Apo may have to send someone with her on the plane, just to be safe. She is a minor after all, even though her Russian passport says she is twenty-two. All this will cost a lot of money, which I will cover. But the two of you have to handle almost all of the logistics outside of Dubai. So, to be very clear, here is how the tasks are divided: I cover all costs and am responsible for putting Leila on a plane from Dubai to Istanbul; Farah is fully responsible for her from the minute the plane lands in Istanbul to when she lands in Moscow. Then Natalia's folks are in charge, to make sure that she 'disappears' in Russia. We'll discuss and agree on details, but I want you to understand and accept these responsibilities, subject to sorting out of the details."

Natalia was impressed. "I agree," she said, "subject to all of us agreeing on the details. It is important that we all know all the segments, even if they fall outside of our responsibility. And I also want to be clear on what 'disappear' means."

Farah was less enthusiastic. "Is all this really necessary?" she asked. "I mean all the phases, all the trips and the 'disappearing'? Are we exaggerating the threat in the first place?"

"We're not exaggerating the threat," said Sumaya. "Sir has now started bringing Armenian music to her. Has he ever brought you Turkish music? And he even listens to the music with her. Every day the risks increase. I've seen no signs of 'growing cold' yet; on the contrary, every day they grow warmer. And knowing Sir, and how he likes to be different, he may decide to marry this seventeen-year-old Armenian girl to make a statement. It's been done before. And then there won't be any room here for either of you, I promise you that."

"Okay," said Farah, still showing some skepticism. "But isn't he going to marry someone sooner or later? Aren't we better off with this inexperienced kid than someone else?"

"Not really," said Sumaya, a bit tired of Farah's questions. "If he does not marry soon, his family will arrange something for him and force him into it. Probably a cousin, whom he does not care for, nor she for him. There will be no passion there. None of this will be at risk then," said Sumaya as she swept her arm widely, covering Farah, Natalia and the living room at large.

"Okay," said Farah again. "How do we sort out the details?"

"We don't have everything yet, but here is what I am thinking. There are a few trips coming up for Sir. One of them is for a week in Asia, which may even get extended. During that week, I'll offer Leila a five or six day home-leave, but it will be strictly our secret. She will leave Dubai with her face covered. I'll arrange for a driver from outside the compound. No one here will know anything about it. She will go to the airport and check in alone. That is a risk we'll have to take. The driver can help her through to passport control, and then she'll be fine. If she believes she's going home, she won't create any problems. She'll do exactly as instructed. Another option is to drive her to Oman and have her fly from there, to add an extra layer of precaution. That way passport control and customs officials here won't be involved. Also, I know an Omani driver here in Dubai whom I trust. So that could be a safe option. I'll check the flights and Sir's schedule, and decide. But this will happen in the coming two weeks. So we need to be ready with the other parts of the plan."

"Okay, so she lands in Istanbul," said Farah. "Then either Apo or someone he sends meets her at the airport, I presume with a sign, and takes her to one of Apo's safe houses. She'll believe that her next destination is in Georgia, probably Tbilisi. I'll check the flight details. I suggest that they also promise her a cell phone, so she can contact her family. So far it's easy. But now they need to put her on the next flight to Moscow, right? How? The only way is to have her drugged, which may arouse a lot of suspicion at the airport. So Apo has to use his contacts at customs and passport control. It can be done, but it will take a lot of bribes. That increases the cost. Ideally, she should be drugged *and* have an escort caretaker, *plus* have the airport officials alerted and bribed. Then we can get her on the plane and off the ground. Then God help the escort if she wakes up before they land!"

"How long is the direct flight to Moscow?" asked Sumaya.

"Around three hours," said Farah.

"That's manageable," said Sumaya. "There are other risks in your plan, but we'll discuss those later."

Then she turned to Natalia. "So what happens when they land in Moscow?" she asked.

"We have many options," answered Natalia, "but probably the best bet is for me to contact my old manager, Anton. He can take her over, and move her out of Moscow, if necessary, even though if this Leila is as beautiful as you say, he'll try to work her into the Moscow market."

"That wouldn't constitute 'disappearing'," said Farah.

"That won't do at all," said Sumaya. "Leila probably knows her way around Moscow much better than Istanbul. The reason we're sending her to Moscow is to take her out of circulation."

"Out of circulation?" asked Natalia.

"You said it is easy to make people disappear in Moscow."

"Are you saying that we want her *dead*?" Natalia's question was deliberate, but cold. She wanted to be very clear about what her instructions were. She would not be shocked or surprised at all if they decided to have her killed.

"We want her out of circulation," repeated Sumaya. "Out of *our* circulation. Maybe she could end up as a maid in some remote village in Russia. Or the wife of a peasant in Siberia. I don't care. If all else fails, maybe she could be the victim of an accident. But that wouldn't be my first choice."

"The wife of a peasant in Siberia," repeated Natalia. "Now there's a thought."

"Well, I've read that that's where people generally disappeared during Soviet times. I don't know these things. What is the safe thing to do? But I do know that we can't have her go to work in Moscow."

"Then Anton won't do," said Natalia. "I better contact my uncle Arkadiy in Krasnodar. He runs a different operation than Anton. He is a recruiter; Anton is a manager. We need Arkadiy in this case."

"Where is Kras..what?" asked Farah.

"Krasnodar. It is a town in Southern Russia, on the Kuban river. Picturesque and attractive to tourists. A two-hour flight from Moscow. My uncle runs his operation from there. I grew up there. He can take care of Leila just like we want."

"Are there direct flights from Istanbul to Krasnodar?" asked Sumaya. "Connecting flights in Moscow may not be the most convenient, under the circumstances."

"I'm not sure, but that's easy to check. And even if there aren't, my uncle has a lot of contacts both at Moscow airport and in Krasnodar. He can handle the situation easily once she lands in Moscow."

"Okay," said Sumaya. She sounded tired. "That's all we can agree on right now. We have made the overall plan, and we'll have to regroup for the details. There are still a lot of risks involved. The key ones are related to these people: Apo and the uncle in Russia. Why should they do as we ask? That is a huge risk. Even if we pay them what they want, we have no guarantee that they'll deliver. So we need to plan this very carefully.

"We need to talk to them," said Farah. "How can we arrange that?"

"You both must come back here this evening," said Sumaya. "I will have a safe cell phone. Farah will call Apo and Natalia will call her uncle from here, on that cell phone. There can be no other communication overseas whatsoever. We'll do everything from this house, is that clear? No conversations in your houses are safe, as you may have guessed by now."

Natalia knew that her place was bugged, but Farah did not. They both agreed to return later and left.

$$\mathcal{L} \quad \mathcal{L} \quad \mathcal{L}$$

Avo was with Laurian at the westernmost tip of his property, at the edge of the spectacular ravine where his property ended. Boundless valleys, rivers, lesser plateaus and meadows spread before them as far as the eye could see.

This was only his second day in Vardahovit, and he was already overwhelmed with the new information about Ayvazian and his operation in the region. Until now, he had not given any of this much thought; he had assumed that his parents knew what they were doing, and that they would never have agreed to anything that put Lara in harm's way. Even his father's initial rejection of the Ayvazian proposal had not rung any alarm bells until Laurian had brought it up. Then his accidental death, right there in Sevajayr and subsequently Lara's departure. And now the breathtaking view, which reminded him of one of his father's readings from the Bible, where the devil took Jesus to the mountaintop to tempt him. *It must have looked something like this*, he thought. *Imagine being offered dominion over everything your eye can see. That's what that story Papa used to read must have been all about.*

Avo could not decide whether to focus on the awesome scenery or what Laurian had just shown him in Sevajayr, after showing him some of Hayk's most telling photos. That's when the phone call came. He did not hear it at first, and when he did, he was tempted not to even bother answering, thinking he could always return a missed call, which could only have been from home. But then he thought of his sick mother, and wondered if this could be the dreaded call summoning him home, and reached in his pocket in a panic and answered.

"Avo jan, *kyank, du es?* Avo, my life, is it you?" It was unmistakably Lara's voice. He froze for a moment. He felt the perspiration in his palms and forehead. He looked at Laurian, who could tell that this was no ordinary call, but could not be sure yet whether it was good news or bad. Avo had not said a word, other than his initial 'alo.' He waited for a few seconds, then mouthed the question '*ov e?*' who is it? without saying anything out loud.

Meanwhile, Lara came on again. "Avo, *du es? Mi ban asa.* Avo, is it you? Say something."

"Kurig jan," said Avo. His voice was composed, deep and in control. "Where are you? How did you find me?"

"I'm fine," said Lara, deliberately not answering the 'where are you' part of the question. "I cannot talk for long. Tell me, how are you, how is Mama, how is everything at home?"

"Mama's not fine," said Avo, again using a mature matter-of-fact tone. "Everything else is fine. We are receiving what you send. Thanks. But I am very worried about you, Lara. Where are you? In Greece?"

"No," said Lara quickly. "It is a long story. Don't ask any more. Tell me more about home."

"I think I know some of the story," said Avo, sensing the caution in Lara's voice. "I am very worried that you may be in trouble. I have seen things here, about the people who took you away."

"Avo, as I said it is a long story. Please don't dwell on it now. I will try to come see you soon. Would that be okay with you?"

"Kurig jan, why do you have to ask that? Of course it would be okay. We are all dying to see you again. We want to make sure that you're safe. I don't trust these people. Not at all. Have the people who took you been treating you well?"

"Avo, listen, forget that now. The important thing is that I am fine and I now I have a way to contact you. Keep this phone next to you all the time. All the time, Avo, you understand? You can never tell when I'll need to call you next. Do you understand, my little brother?"

"I understand *kurig*. But can't you tell me where you are?"

"No. Don't ask again. Tell me about Mama."

"She won't make it through the winter. She has cancer. There is no cure."

"Have you tried everything? I can send more money if that's what you need."

"We don't need more money. There is no cure. Lara, I want to ask you something else. Did you know that Papa rejected Ayvazian when he asked to take you the first time?"

"No. Don't say that name on the phone again. But no, I did not know. Are you sure?"

"Yes. They came with a proposal when Papa was alive. He said no. Then he went to see the man in his hometown, I am not giving any names anymore. And that is where he had the accident. Then they came back after a month and Mama said yes. And then they took you."

"I did not know," said Lara and Avo could tell from her voice that she was crying. "Papa was wise, Avo jan," she said sobbing, "wise and decent. Maybe too decent."

That was the most revealing thing that she told Avo in that conversation. The man who rejected Ayvazian's proposal was wise. If it was a bad decision to reject them, would she say that? Avo's worst fears about what may have befallen Lara seemed to be coming true.

"Lara," he said, "can you really come home?"

"I'll try," she said. "I promise to try. Now I must go. I'll try to call again when I get a chance. Kiss Mama for me. Take care of her. I don't want her to die before I make it back home."

"I'll take care of her," said Avo, doing his best to suppress his tears. "But hurry up, Lara. There isn't much time."

"Goodbye, Avo."

And the phone went silent.

In two different worlds, there had been two different witnesses to the phone conversation between Lara and Avo. Sumaya in Dubai and Laurian in Vardahovit. And they both had sat there mesmerized. Sumaya, without understanding a word, had felt the power of Lara's outpouring of emotion. She had seen her tears and witnessed her heroic effort to suppress them and keep calm while she talked. This was no ordinary nostalgic call home, she had thought, and wondered what else was involved. Laurian, who heard and understood the other end of the conversation, felt so much at the center of the unfolding drama that he could not hold back his own emotions. He stood up from the bench and gave Avo a long hug.

"Don't worry about the details now," he said. "She is alive and well, and that's all that matters right now. We'll find a way to rescue her, I promise. Don't think about the dark possibilities now."

XVI

"Kiz şimdi nerdedir?" asked Apo Arslan. "Where is the girl now?"

"The same place I am," answered Farah. "We are, well, what you would call colleagues, I guess."

"Ve Müdür bu konuda biliyor? And does the director know about this?"

Farah was not sure how to answer that, because she was not sure who he meant by 'the director,' Al Barmaka or Sumaya. Of course the logical thing would have been to assume that he meant Sumaya, because Al Barmaka couldn't possibly be helping one of his women escape. But Farah was very careful not to appear as if they had misled Apo in any way.

"Büyük olani bilmez," she said. "The big one doesn't know. *Ikinci bilir.* The second knows."

Apo Arslan was clearly intrigued with the second phone call from Farah. Her request had changed considerably. Farah was no longer offering him the girl, but was now asking him to meet her at the airport in Istanbul and send her off on a flight to Moscow, with an escort. Apo was generally against saying much over the telephone, so he could not ask many of the questions that he wanted to ask. Even what they already had said was beginning to make him nervous.

"When is all this expected to happen?" he asked.

"Within the next two weeks. We don't know the exact day yet. When we know, we will have a window of only a few days to make all the arrangements."

"We cannot plan this over the phone," said Apo. "Either you or someone else has to come here so I can discuss everything properly. Something like this will cost a lot of money. Who will pay all the costs?"

"That's all arranged," said Farah confidently. "The second director will take care of everything."

"Someone still has to come in advance to discuss this, and make a down payment. This won't happen without a down payment."

"I'll have to get back to you about the advance visit," said Farah. "How much is necessary for the down payment?"

"Twenty thousand US."

"That's just the down payment or the total cost?"

"The total cost depends on how complicated this is. I can say only after I find out the details. But it would be at least double that, and probably more."

"I'll have to get back to you," said Farah, giving Sumaya a concerned look and waving her hand back and forth rapidly, as if to say she could not believe what she had just heard.

"Call back in an hour." Apo hung up.

Apo Arslan sank in his armchair and lit a cigarette. He was in his mid-fifties, but looked younger. A thin and wiry man, with a wide forehead and a full head of dark wavy hair, he had an eagle nose, large dark eyes, and an enormous mustache, which had turned yellow from years of smoking. His business manager and associate of many years, a younger man who knew most but not all of his secrets, was in the room as well. Apo had a very large operation in Turkey. He started by exporting all types of Turkish products to Armenia, from textiles and electronic goods to fresh produce and chocolates, and then expanded his trade into Georgia, where he stumbled almost accidentally on the human trade and trafficking. He started bringing young girls from the Ukraine, Georgia and later Armenia into the Turkish market. His biggest competitor in the latter was Ayvazian; their competition turned so intense that it led to personal animosity between the two men.

The most vicious clash between them was over control of the Dubai traffic, where Ayvazian was by far the most powerful Armenian operator. He had on numerous occasions successfully undermined Apo's efforts to penetrate the Dubai market, not only with traffic from Armenia, but also and to Apo's great dismay, from Turkey.

It was a spectacular afternoon, and from his wide front window Apo counted more than fifteen ships sailing on the Bosporus. Some were large container ships, an oil tanker or two, several smaller ships, and a few leisure vessels. In the distance he could see the full display of the minarets and crowded buildings of the eastern part of the city.

"Let me ask you this, Timur," he said to his associate, keeping his eyes on the ships. "What would you think if I told you I can make an easy twenty grand US and open up the Dubai market for us at the same time?"

Timur was all too familiar with Apo's obsession with Dubai, so at first he took the comment with a grain of salt.

"One of Ayvazian's top prizes is ready to be snatched from him," said Apo, taking a deep drag on his cigarette. "What makes it even more interesting is that she is already sold to a Dubai big shot, and probably for a lot of money. We can end up having 'custody' of the snatched beauty."

"I'm not sure I follow you," Timur said, but his interest was heightened. This did not sound like another of the many futile attempts that Apo had engaged in in the past to bribe an officer in Dubai who was already in Ayvazian's pocket.

"He has this seventeen-year-old beauty from Armenia," continued Apo, "and he has sold her with a year's contract to someone very influential. I am not sure of all the details, but there seems to be a palace coup of sorts against her, and they want to ship her here to me. They're asking that I then ship her to Moscow. It sounds to me like someone is trying to get rid of her. Crazy as this may sound, it smells like she is threatening the balance in the harem. It's the only way I can explain it right now."

"A threat to the harem?"

"There could be only a few possibilities," said Apo, as if speaking to the ships in the distance. "First, Ayvazian himself may be behind this, in which case my plan will blow up. But what is the probability of that? Why would he steal his own girl after selling her to this hot shot? It makes no sense to me. Second, the big boss himself is trying to secretly smuggle her out of Dubai. Again, why? She is now living in a house on his estate, is his property, and he can take her anywhere he wants. Why smuggle her? Third, the young girl herself wants out, and has convinced the manager and the others inside to help her. Once again, why would they help her and take such a huge risk, and pay for the cost on top of that? So we agree that none of these three options are very likely?"

"We agree," said Timur. This was far more analysis than he had ever expected from Apo.

"That leaves us with the fourth possibility, namely, that the manager and others in the harem want her gone. What I don't understand though is why they at first offered her to me, but then came back after just one day and said I had to ship her to Moscow. That is a mystery which we cannot solve unless we talk to them face to face."

"Let me see if I am getting this right, Apo *agha*," said Timur, giving Apo the traditional title of respect. "If I'm not mistaken, the only way you can use this to open up the Dubai market for us is to get the girl here, and then instead of shipping her to Moscow, trade her back to Ayvazian for an entry visa into Dubai, right?"

"You've been with me too long, Timur," said Apo affectionately. "Now you're reading my mind. You see, if what my gut is telling me is correct, Ayvazian will be in a whole lot of trouble when his little canary flies away from the new master. The guy has probably paid a fortune for her and will be understandably furious. He will go after Ayvazian with a vengeance. He will even suspect foul play by Ayvazian himself. He will threaten to destroy his entire operation in Dubai, and Ayvazian will know that he can make good on the threat. So now you tell me. In that state of mind, he gets a call from his old friend Apo, offering him the girl as a peace offering, in return for a piece of the Dubai market. What do you think he'll do?"

Apo was now smiling ear to ear and the ships look particularly beautiful that afternoon.

"Apo *agha*," said Timur thoughtfully, "you mentioned something about meeting these people face to face. Given this plan, do you think that's wise?"

"You're right, Timur," said Apo, again impressed by his associate. "When I asked them to come and see me, I was actually still thinking of doing the job they were asking. The thought of trading her hit me after I hung up. Obviously, a face-to-face meeting will not be necessary anymore. She will call back soon, and I'll sort that out. I had asked for a twenty-thousand dollar down payment, but I'll raise that now to thirty; we won't get more money from them once we hand the girl back to Ayvazian.

Sumaya had checked the flights from both Dubai and Muscat to Istanbul. There were more options from Dubai, but she was leaning increasingly toward the Omani route, as it provided an added measure of security to the operation. She wondered at first about Apo's quick change of heart about a face-to-face meeting, but was also relieved that the requirement had been waived. Sending Farah over to negotiate details in advance would have increased her risks significantly; so she did not dwell on the reasons for the change. She was also suspicious about the demand for a larger down payment, but did not dwell on that either. She agreed to wire the thirty thousand dollars and, based on Al Barmaka's likely travel schedule, she even sent Apo three different possible flights on which Leila could arrive in Istanbul.

In the meantime, Apo went through the motions of planning the operation as prescribed by Farah in great detail. He in turn sent them flight details to Moscow based on Leila's three different arrival times, and demanded that he be told in advance who would be meeting them in Moscow. He gave Timur's name as the companion, and told Farah that the person meeting them in Moscow should have a sign with Timur's name on it. Farah said that there could be more than one Timur on the plane, and asked for a last name. Apo refused. He said the sign would just read 'Timur K.'. They even discussed where exactly at Moscow airport they would meet in case they missed each other upon exit from customs. Apo did not want to give Farah any reason to doubt that he'd follow the script.

There wasn't a lot more they could do other than wait for the finalization of Al Barmaka's travel plans. This was the time of year that he made a tour of their Asian offices and operations. It usually was his longest business trip of the year and could last as long as ten days. The tour took him to India, Singapore, Malaysia, and sometimes Hong Kong. The Al Barmaka Group had not yet started operations in China, even though there was talk of it in the family. If they decided to open a base in China, Al Barmaka could be gone even longer than ten days, as opening new operations and bases would require several extra days, possibly in both Beijing and Shanghai.

Every day that Al Barmaka was in Dubai, Sumaya's determination to send Lara away increased. He spent more and more time with her. He had started going there earlier in the evenings, and had even had dinner with her on a couple of occasions, which also was a first. One night, he had taken Leila a bottle of champagne, which was another first. Everyone knew that Al Barmaka liked to drink wine, and was even known to get pretty drunk once in a while in his youth, but he had never taken alcohol with him when visiting one of his ladies. The rapid blossoming of the relationship with Lara simply reconfirmed to Sumaya that she was doing the right thing.

There was another piece of information that she did not share with Farah and Natalia. The wife of Al Barmaka's older brother, with whom Sumaya had been close for many years, had told her that the family was putting a lot of pressure on the young renegade to get married and settle down. They even had a couple of candidates, both first cousins and a few years younger than him, and both from rich families. In the traditional system, either would make a perfect wife. Spouses for each of his brothers had been selected in this manner. That was the accepted custom, largely because it kept the wealth and the power relationships within the extended family. Sumaya was convinced that sooner or later Al Barmaka would have to succumb to that pressure and marry one of the two cousins, which would secure the future of her job as manager of his other relationships. Secure it, that is, as long as he did not spring a surprise on the family and marry the seventeen-year-old Leila first.

Lara, on the other hand, was finding it more and more difficult to keep her mind on Ahmed Al Barmaka. Her first conversation with Avo had changed everything. She had asked Sumaya the next day to make one more call. Avo was still in Vardahovit, which had disappointed Lara, because she had hoped that she could talk with her mother as well. She had explained this to Sumaya, and Sumaya had agreed to let her call back when Avo returned home. The second conversation was less rushed and less emotional, but also more informative.

"What are you doing in Vardahovit?" she had asked, with a hint of disapproval in her voice. "Is everything in order back home?"

"Ha, Lara jan, don't worry about that. This visit is very important. I wish I could explain more."

"When will you go back home?"

"In just a few days. I'll return before the week is over. Any news about when you're coming home?"

"I'll let you know when I know, Avo. How is Mama?"

"The same. There is nothing we can do. Martha is there every day."

"Avo, stay away from the people we talked about last time. I don't want you to get involved with them."

"But you're involved with them, right?"

"That's different. Promise me you won't get involved with them."

"*Lav, kurig jan*, I promise. But are you still with them?"

"Yes and no," said Lara curtly. "Don't ask more. Stay away from them, whatever it is you're doing up there."

"*Eghav, kurig jan*," said Avo, knowing that he wouldn't be able to keep that promise. Lara did not know what he had learned in Vardahovit.

"And under no circumstances can you tell anyone that I'm planning to come home, Avo. No one. Not even the family. We cannot have the word get out."

"I understand," said Avo, and realized that his sister was planning something dangerous. How he wished he could just go to her and rescue her. "I'll wait for your next call."

𝔏 𝔏 𝔏

Al Barmaka was being extremely charming. He had started talking to her in Arabic to check her progress, and was very complementary and encouraging. That week there were signs of uncharacteristic intimacy from him: he had asked her what her real name was. Lara had told him, even though she knew that he must have known all along.

"Did you mind being given a different name," he asked.

"No, of course not," she assured him. "Leila is a beautiful name."

"It means night," he said. "Dark and mysterious like your eyes. You see, here in the desert, the night is the best part of the day, when the scorching heat of the sun recedes, temperatures cool, and people focus on love and poetry and forget everything else. It suits you very much, my lovely Leila."

Lara didn't know how to deal with Al Barmaka's kindness. After two conversations with Avo, her mind was now entirely focused on home and her desire to escape. She had no idea how she could pull it off. Getting to call Avo was a huge step, but leaving the premises was an entirely different matter. She could never pull it off without Sumaya's agreement and help.

As her thoughts focused on the prospects of returning home, another fear entered Lara's mind. How could she return without being noticed by Ayvazian? He would never leave her alone if he found out that she was back in Saralandj. She had to keep her presence in Saralandj a secret, which was next to impossible. The whole village would know a few minutes after she got there. There was only one way to avoid Ayvazian's wrath, thought Lara, and a chill passed through her body. He and his nephew had to be silenced, to be put out of commission. Only then could they have some peace again. She realized then that dealing with Ayvazian was a matter of survival, not just sweet revenge.

Lara was keenly aware of the fact that everything she was thinking about was way, way over her head. She couldn't even take the most preliminary steps on her own. In her heart, she had her forest, her father's memory and Araxi Dadik's ring; in real life she had Avo. The value of all else, including Sumaya and Ahmed Al Barmaka, depended on her wits. It was her turn to manipulate others, rather than be manipulated; it was her turn to chart a course and trigger a chain of events where others would have to react to the conditions created by her. The thought scared her; she had not had to deal with so much planning and so many different risks before. She remembered the days when she viewed her life as a series of reactions to conditions created by others and imposed on her. Reacting to a given situation, even when unbearably unpleasant, was relatively simple compared with the need to create the situation herself.

Lara also realized that in order to succeed she had to mislead people and betray their trust; this too was new to her. She was going to deliberately lie to Sumaya and Al Barmaka; she was going to put Sumaya at great risk, and cause a lot of pain and anxiety to Ahmed. Not that she felt any loyalty to either, but she also knew that these were not the people who were most responsible for her suffering. They had not done anything against her per se, nor had they been unfair or unjust in any way. And yet, she had to betray them. Withholding her inner thoughts and withdrawing into herself was one thing; outright lying and taking actions against them was another.

Throughout her experience of the past year, her various friends and captors had exhorted her to 'grow up,' by which they meant for her to accept her fate and get on with the program set in front of her. But now she felt that growing up in her case meant betraying trust and hurting those who had been kind to her.

ℒ ℒ ℒ

Ayvazian was furious. His men had called to tell him that the tiny, desolate village of Sevajayr was suddenly swarming with several visitors looking for places to house equipment, materials and workers. The two homes that they had rented were visited by one of the managers of the road construction company, who was accompanied by a couple of supply and logistics staff. His men were not happy. They had rudely asked the manager to leave and never return. They had put their hands on the handguns at their waists while they talked. Even though the workers left, the guards had the uneasy feeling that they had been discovered. Their quiet, anonymous stay in Sevajayr had been exposed. Surely the manager would recount the story to his bosses, and very soon all neighboring villagers would know that there were armed men guarding seemingly deserted homes in Sevajayr.

Ayvazian had managed to get the president of the construction company on the phone. He was an experienced infrastructure engineer named Ararat, who, along with two competitors, handled most of the roadwork in the region. All public works had to go through competitive bidding, but every bid and award was arranged in advance, and the awards were given more or less in order to one of the three competitors. Ayvazian had a lot of influence on the process, even though he was not the final decision maker.

"What kind of stupid operation are you running now?" yelled Ayvazian in the rudest gangster tone he could muster, which was characteristic of bosses in the region.

"Why, what's the problem?" asked Ararat. He knew the caller was Ayvazian; no one else would talk to him like that. He also recognized the voice.

"When do you think you will reach Sevajayr? You haven't even started construction at Shatin yet! A year from now? *Two* years from now?" Ayvazian had worked himself up in a fury; his face was red and he was yelling.

"We should be there by next fall, why?" Ararat was getting very angry too from such a rude interrogation, but he kept calm.

"So now you want to rent places in Sevajayr a whole year before you arrive, is that it? As I asked before, what type of stupid operation are you running?"

"There are a lot of reasons for …"

"You listen to me and listen very well!" interrupted Ayvazian. "You have *no* reason to rent anything in Sevajayr right now. I want your men out of the upper villages immediately! Out! Is that clear?! Rent in Shatin, where you're starting work! And don't go up there again till I say it's okay!"

Ayvazian hung up the phone. He knew Ararat would comply. But he also knew that he might have to vacate his operations in the two villages, not immediately, but earlier than he had planned. His screaming and threatening was not smart. It would simply raise more questions and suspicions. He bet that Ararat would go around asking people why Ayvazian was so mad. But he could not control his rage; nor could he tolerate unexpected and inexplicable complications.

Ջ Ջ Ջ

Lara requested a meeting with Sumaya and was asked to head over right away. It was early afternoon, and very hot outside. The early afternoon heat imposes a type of tranquility and quiet in the desert that is not possible to find anywhere else. It is as if everything stops breathing—no birds, no animals prowling on the lawn or in the bushes, no breeze, no movement of any kind. Just oppressive heat, descending in waves from the sky and rising from the earth at the same time, the two currents clashing in mid air and suffocating every living thing that happens to stumble in their midst. In the few seconds that it took from her front door to the waiting car, Lara was drenched in perspiration.

Sumaya looked pale to Lara. There were dark bags under her eyes, which did not have their normal intensity or shine. Her hair did not look as clean and tidy as usual either.

"Come in, come in," she said, quickly closing the door behind her. "It is too early for this type of heat. I don't know what's happening with our environment. The whole world seems to be suffering from unusual weather. Hot where it should be cold, cold where it should be hot, raining where it should be dry, like those rainstorms in Saudi Arabia yesterday. Did you see the news on that?"

"Yes I did," said Lara. "And there were floods in the deserts of Oman as well. Several cars were swept away in the gushing currents. Some villages had severe floods."

"Unbelievable. Floods in the desert, followed by premature heat waves and early snow on some mountains west of here."

They sat down and Sumaya asked her maid to bring tea.

"I need to talk to you," said Lara. "Please don't get angry for what I am going to say. You always have the option to refuse anything I ask, so you don't need to get angry."

"Leila, *habibty*, what kind of opening is that? Why should I get angry with you? Tell me what's on your mind."

"I want to go on home leave," said Leila without hesitation. "Just for a few days. Maybe a week, if Sir is away for that long. I don't want him to know that I have left. Can I go and return without anyone noticing?"

Sumaya stared at her for a long moment. Was this the perfect opportunity that she had been waiting for?

"Leila, *habibty*, you know I have broken some rules and taken some serious risks for you already by allowing the phone calls. And you promised me no complications, remember? This could turn into a major complication."

"It doesn't have to, Ms. Sumaya," said Lara. "I can go and return, with your blessing, and no one needs to know. I can do this without raising any suspicion anywhere. Of course I'll take care of all the expenses. But I cannot make any arrangements without your help."

Lara had kept a major part of her monthly salary in cash. Manoj paid the rest to Madame Ano by prior arrangement, who saw to it that it got to her family via the Ayvazian office in Moscow.

"Oh, *habibty*, you are so young and naïve," said Sumaya, with such honest tenderness that for a minute Lara felt guilty for misleading her. "So many things could go wrong that would create huge complications for me here. God forbid, you should get into an accident, or get sick, and not be able to return on time. Sir could return early from his trip and catch me by surprise. Your former boss could find out that you're back home and would raise hell. And maybe ten other complications, which I cannot even think of right now. Then what would I do? How could I explain this?"

Lara was happy that Sumaya was talking about the risks of getting caught, rather than outright refusing her request. That was a major step. The risks could always be mitigated.

"If anything like that happens, I'll take all the blame myself," said Lara. "I'll say I escaped and you did not know. I'll say I had to go see my sick mother before she died, which is the truth. I promise that even if complications arise, they won't affect you directly."

Lara did not realize how important her words were and how intently Sumaya was listening to her. Having to explain Lara's disappearance was a major challenge. She had Lara's passport, for example, which Lara would need before she could leave the country. The scheme that Lara was now proposing made it easier to plan these details.

"How would you go from here to Armenia?" asked Sumaya.

"Isn't there a direct flight from Dubai?" asked Lara. She knew there was. The girls at Madame Ano's had talked about it often.

"Yes, but that won't do," said Sumaya. "You'll have to leave here covered head to toe. You'll have to leave at night, so you can sneak into a waiting car with less chance of being seen. The flights to Yerevan are in the early afternoon. Besides, I don't think it's safe to leave from Dubai."

"Then how would I leave?" asked Lara, barely able to control her excitement. Sumaya was actually plotting her escape with her.

"It would be safer to leave from Muscat. It is a quieter airport, and you wouldn't be taking the chance of the customs officials here in Dubai remembering you."

"Are there flights to Armenia from Oman?"

"No, I don't think so. This will prolong the trip, but it is a worthwhile precaution, believe me. Sir knows every official at Dubai airport."

"Maybe I could fly to Moscow," said Lara enthusiastically. "There are many flights from Moscow to Yerevan."

Sumaya thought about this option, to send her directly to Moscow and bypass Istanbul. Natalia's uncle could then meet her and take her away. This would simplify the plan considerably, but something was bothering her about it. She knew Lara had been in Moscow and spoke some Russian. Having her arrive alert and unescorted would not be wise. If they went that route, Lara would want her Moscow Yerevan ticket arranged in advance, and would not expect to be met in Moscow, so Natalia's uncle would have a very hard time convincing her to leave with him. No, Sumaya decided, the direct flight to Moscow wouldn't work.

"That would raise too much suspicion," she said at last. "Think about the scene, Lara. A young Muslim woman, fully covered, leaving for Moscow alone from Oman. That just doesn't happen. When you leave the Gulf you're leaving as a single young woman. So you need to go somewhere more logical, like another Muslim country. It could be Beirut, for example, or Amman, or Damascus. But getting from those places to Armenia is not easy. There might be a flight from Beirut—I'll check--but I don't think it will be frequent enough to give you the flex-ibility you need.

"I think your best bet would be to fly to Turkey. It is a Muslim country, and there is a lot of traffic lately going between the Gulf and Istanbul, so you wouldn't raise suspicion; you could be going to join family members who are vacationing there. From there, you have many options. You could go to Georgia and catch a passenger train to Yerevan. You'll have much more control over your schedule that way."

It occurred to Lara that it was odd for Sumaya to know so much about transport options from Turkey to Armenia, but she did not want to dwell on that; the plan was taking shape and that's all that mattered. She would have preferred a simple direct flight to Yerevan. The new plan was much more complicated and it would probably take her a couple of days just to get home. Of course this did not matter to her because she had no inten-tion of coming back. But she had to plan a return anyway, to put Sumaya's mind at ease. She was convinced that Sumaya believed she would come back.

Sumaya, for her part, was convinced that Lara had every intention of coming back, but if Sumay'a plan worked she knew that she would not.

"We can help you once you land in Istanbul," continued Sumaya. "We have friends who can meet you and help you reach Tbilisi, from where you can catch a train to Yerevan. Depending on the schedules, you may be able to do this whole thing in the same day; it will be a long day, but at least you won't have to spend the night anywhere."

As complicated as this scheme sounded, Lara was beginning to see a concrete plan and was becoming excited and restless.

"Ms. Sumaya," she said, "I cannot tell you how much this means to me. My mother is very sick. I just want to see her one more time, and there is almost no time left. I truly thank you for agreeing to this."

"We still have to talk about a good story, in case, God forbid, something goes wrong," said Sumaya. *Things could go wrong*, she thought. *Apo could screw up, or Al Barmaka could return early. I have to come out looking clean in all this.* "What will be your story?"

"I'll say I had friends in Dubai who helped me make the arrangements. I know a girl, Susannah, and I can say she helped me."

"How did you manage to get hold of your passport?" asked Sumaya.

"Oh, that. Sorry, I had not thought of that. Where is my passport now?"

"Inside. In my drawer."

"I stole it," said Lara without any hesitation. "I asked to see you, you invited me over, and when you were in the other room taking a call, I snuck in and stole it from your drawer. The whole thing took a few seconds. I arranged for my friend to send me a car, the driver somehow managed to pass through the gate, and I disappeared that same night. Can you explain how the car got through?"

"Well, the driver could tell the guard that he was here to deliver a package for me," said Sumaya. "They won't question that, because it happens several times a week. It would be better if I arrange the driver. That way he will be someone they recognize. I know one who is actually from Oman and will drive you straight to Muscat airport. He's been here a few times, so the guards know him."

They fell quiet for a while, each lost in her thoughts. Lara was envisioning a period of hiding near her village and visiting home secretly until they figured out how they'd eliminate the Ayvazian threat. Sumaya was envisioning Lara landing in Istanbul and being captured by Apo, then being drugged and put on the next flight to Moscow, possibly after being raped a few times by Apo and his men.

XVII

It was a brilliant morning in Vardahovit. Laurian and Avo had awoken early, and were sitting on the front terrace with their coffees. The air was chilly and they breathed in a million faint scents of the freshness of the meadows and mountains; the first dusting of snow appeared on the highest peaks to the Southwest. The sun barely peeked from behind the Eastern mountains.

Avo was planning to return home that afternoon. Laurian had arranged for someone from the village to drive him to Saralandj. Vartiter arrived as usual and started setting the table for their breakfast.

"Let's go for a walk while she sets the table," said Laurian.

Avo, who was barefoot, went in and put his shoes on. They walked eastward, toward the old wheat fields, which had not been cultivated since the collapse of the Soviet Union. There was a small graveyard lost in the rising grass in the fields, and Laurian showed Avo one of the tombstones with carvings in Arabic letters. The inscription was of a lady Mariam, in Farsi, with the date 1317 carved at the bottom. Laurian knew enough Arabic from his travels in the Middle East to make that much out.

"One day I'll study the history of this place," he told Avo. "This, for example, is a Persian lady's grave. Most other graves don't have headstones, and the few that do have no inscription on them. They're just decorative pieces of stone. So this one must have been someone special, someone of rank. Don't you wonder why a Persian lady was buried here? Did Persians live here in the fourteenth century? Or maybe she was just part of a group of merchants passing through?"

Actually, Avo did not. He had seen this type of historical remnant all over Saralandj and Aparan too. Deserted tombs and prehistoric artifacts, such as thousand-year-old stone instruments, could be found everywhere in the fields. No one paid much attention to such relics. Laurian, on the other hand, seemed to be interested in everything.

"Avo," said Laurian, focusing on what he really wanted to talk to him about, "I cannot stress enough how important it is to keep everything I've shown you confidential. The only reason I showed you these things is because I don't want you to remain in the dark as to what may have happened to Lara."

"We still don't know what has happened to her," said Avo.

"We don't," conceded Laurian, "but at least we now know that we should not just assume she's a happy and successful model living in Greece."

"What do you plan to do here?" asked Avo, "I mean about Ayvazian's operations?"

"Right now, there isn't much we can do, unfortunately. Let's see how long he stays around. The word out there is that he is really furious that his cover in Sevajayr is possibly blown."

"But the road company backed down, right?"

"Yes, it backed down. They won't show up in Sevajayr again until the road repairs reach Vardahovit. That may be a year from now. But still, would Ayvazian feel safe there knowing that all the villagers now know he has armed men guarding deserted homes in the most desolate part of this region?"

"The Ayvazians of this world don't give a shit about villagers or what they know," said Avo with such absolute resignation that it annoyed Laurian.

"Still, he thought no one was the wiser about his presence in the upper villages, and now everyone seems to know, mostly due to his own temper tantrum."

"He doesn't give a shit," repeated Avo with finality.

"We'll see," said Laurian. "The point is there isn't much we can do right now. I will talk discreetly to some of my friends in the government. If anything new develops here, I'll let you know. Don't forget my offer to lend you what monry you need to buy a tractor with the full set of implements. You can pay me back whenever you can; no rush."

"Thanks," said Avo, "but winter is already upon us and there will be no cultivation or harvesting for several months. We can reconsider that in the spring, right?" He was reluctant to accept Laurian's offers of help, partly because of pride, and partly because of his resistance against building permanent ties with a foreigner. His visit and stay with Laurian had done a lot to melt the ice between them, but the visit would end when he returned home. Borrowing money would keep him morally tied to Laurian much, much longer.

"Sure we can wait until spring," said Laurian. "In the meantime, we'll keep in touch. I'll come visit you with my friend Gagik. He is much closer to you than I am. He can get to Saralandj in half an hour in an emergency. And Avo, he really was a good friend of your father's. He always speaks with great affection about him. Promise me you'll call him if you need anything."

"I like him too," said Avo. "He's a good man. I'll call him. Even if I don't need anything."

"When do you think Lara will call back?"

"I don't know. I got the feeling that they won't let her have her own phone. So she is calling when she can borrow one."

"It's interesting that both times she called her number was blocked. Whoever is letting her use their phone does not want anyone to know the number."

"I hope she calls back soon," said Avo, "I'm not sure how much longer Mama will be around and Mama really wants to talk to her."

"Let's go have some breakfast," said Laurian, turning back toward the house.

"I'm going to populate that entire mountainside with pine trees," said Laurian, pointing to the northern slopes. "In a few years, when you come here, you'll see thick forests on these barren slopes."

Avo stared at him for a long moment. Why did all this matter to this man? That's what some romantic Soviet official had done in Saralandj many years ago. Why did Laurian want to see the slopes covered with forests? Why not just leave things the way they were and concentrate on securing a living for his family? Avo didn't think he'd ever find out the answer.

Vartiter's table was inviting as usual, set with cheese, yogurt, tomatoes, cucumbers, olives, honey, heavy cream, and fresh bread. Everything except the olives was home grown and fresh from their house. There was black tea for Laurian, and coffee for Avo. They had not realized that they had worked up quite an appetite during their walk.

Avo's phone rang, and he jumped. He was kind of hoping that it was not Lara; he wanted her next call to come when he was already home and could pass the phone to his mother. But it was not Lara. It was Martha calling from the post office in Aparan.

"You better hurry back home, Avo," she said. "Mama has been asking for you."

"Is she worse?"

"Avo, she is dying. Hurry back!" Martha broke into sobs and Avo could barely understand a word she said after that.

"I'm leaving right now. Sorry, Edik jan," he said. "I cannot wait until this afternoon. I have to leave right now. I think this may be the end for Mama."

"I'll drive you myself," said Laurian and got up too.

"No, Edik jan, please," said Avo. "No offense, but this is a very charged and emotional time for my family. We cannot fit you into this, if you know what I mean. Sorry. Nothing personal, but I better go alone."

"Someone has to drive you," said Laurian. "I had arranged for someone to take you this afternoon. Let me see if he can come now. He is here in Vardahovit."

Avo went inside and hurriedly gathered his things while Laurian made the call. The driver's brother was available. He made it to the house in less than five minutes in his old Russian car. Laurian gave him his car keys and saw them off.

"Call me," he told Avo. "No matter how bad it is at home, remember to call me."

"I will," promised Avo. "*Dsdesutyun*. Until we meet again."

Laurian watched his Prado leave the main gate and then called Gagik.

"Avo is on his way back," he said. "They called for him. I think it is his mother. It may be the end. Keep an eye on Saralandj."

"Ha, Edik jan. *Eghav.*" And Gagik hung up.

ℒ ℒ ℒ

It was a quiet and peaceful Friday in Dubai, Friday being the Islamic day of rest. Al Barmaka was in town, but he was not expected to visit Lara. Fridays were for family; he usually visited his ailing father, who was in his eighties, and then spent some time with his favorite nieces and nephews. Sometimes he went to the Mosque to pray with his brothers. Although Al Barmaka was not religious, adherence to some of the old traditions was a matter of principle for him. This was unusual coming from the social renegade, but history and culture, in their broadest sense, appealed to Al Barmaka, even as he rebelled against the inescapable everyday implications of those same traditions.

It was around noon when Sumaya called Lara.

"Come over," she said.

Two minutes after Lara hung up she heard the car pull up in front of her house. She straightened her hair and ran out.

"You leave next Tuesday," said Sumaya seriously, with no excitement or emotion in her voice. "Sir is also leaving on Tuesday, in the morning. Your flight to Istanbul is very early the following morning, around three a.m. So the car will take you late at night and drive you straight to the Seef International Airport in Muscat. The driver's name is Omar. He is Omani. He will have the Omani dress, with the Omani turban. I don't know if you've seen them before, but their headdress is different from the rest of the Gulf. At any rate, he will make sure you get on that flight without any problems."

Lara was stunned. Her departure was only a few days away. Even though she had been getting mentally prepared for this day, Sumaya took her by surprise when she laid out all the details.

"You'll have two separate round-trip tickets," continued Sumaya. "Muscat-Istanbul and back, and Istanbul-Tbilisi and back. And although both tickets are on Turkish Airlines, you still have to come out through security in Istanbul and then re-check in for the Tbilisi flight." This was entirely unnecessary, of course, as Lara could have checked in all the way to Tbilisi from Muscat, and simply connected to the onward flight in Istanbul. But that would clearly not serve Sumaya's plan. She needed Lara in Istanbul. And as she had suspected, Lara did not even question this; she simply did not have enough travel experience to know.

"In Istanbul," continued Sumaya, "our contacts will meet you at the airport. The name of the main contact meeting you is Timur. He'll take care of everything. You'll arrive in Istanbul around eight-thirty in the morning, and you'll be in Yerevan around nine in the morning the next day. So you'll be home on Thursday. Now listen carefully, Leila. You will have to leave again on Tuesday. No delays. Is that clear?"

Lara nodded, still trying to absorb all the details.

"So you'll have four full days at home. That's all we can arrange right now. You cannot miss a single detail on the way back. I'll be in very deep trouble if you do. Do you understand?"

"Yes," said Lara, looking and sounding confused.

"Don't worry, I'll give all this to you in writing," said Sumaya with an encouraging nod. "The point is that you'll catch a flight to Tbilisi from Istanbul. There is no faster way. But as I said, first you need to clear customs in Istanbul. Timur will help you. The flight to Tbilisi is not until early afternoon, so you have plenty of time. You will have five hours in Istanbul, to be exact. Then you arrive in Tbilisi at around 5:30 in the afternoon, and you catch the train to Yerevan at 7:00 p.m. It is an overnight train. You'll have a well-deserved sleep. You'll open your eyes when the train pulls into Yerevan at 9:00 a.m. the next morning. You can call your brother and let him know the plan from Tbilisi so he can pick you up at the train station."

"Can't I just fly from Dubai to Yerevan?" asked Lara, exhausted by just listening to the details of the trip ahead of her.

"Leila, we discussed this. That would involve a huge and unnecessary risk. I have gone into a lot of trouble organizing this for you. I know it is a difficult course, but that's exactly why it is safer. Leaving from Dubai is not safe."

ॐ ॐ ॐ

It was early afternoon when Avo reached Saralandj. The car had to stop as usual around twenty meters short of the house. He thanked the driver warmly, grabbed his bag from the back seat, and walked toward home. He could tell something was wrong even before he reached the front steps of the house. There were too many people by the window of his parents' bedroom, and the few children playing outside seemed unusually quiet.

As he entered the room he knew that his mother had passed away. Martha was sitting on a stool next to her bed, his sisters were gathered around her, and some neighbors and relatives were standing quietly around the room. Everyone was somber and quiet. He walked over to Martha, and saw that a blanket had been drawn over his mother's face.

"She just passed away a few minutes ago," said Martha. Her eyes were red and wet, but she was not weeping. She looked angry in her grief.

Avo gently pulled the blanket down, kissed his mother's forehead, and covered her face again.

"She was very peaceful," said Martha. "Right before she died, she said, 'Lara will be home soon,' and smiled. Then she shut her eyes. That was it."

Avo contained the avalanche of emotions rising inside him. He first had to give his mother a proper burial next to his father in the family section of the village cemetery. Then he had to deal with the anger that was rising in him like a volcano. He had not made it in time to see his mother one last time, and Lara would not be able to even hear her voice as she had been so anxious to do. The fact that they had been expecting her death did not help much. Avo's anger at first was directed at fate, at some unreachable, invisible and uncontrollable force that seemed to be causing all this from a distance. But slowly it moved toward Ayvazian, like a storm changing its direction as it gathers speed. Or maybe Ayvazian's image simply replaced the invisible fate. Laurian's stories and pictures hit home in a way that they had not done while he was still in Vardahovit. His anger arose from the circumstances of his father's death, as he pictured the cliff that Laurian had shown him in Sevajayr as the likely spot where Samvel Galian had accidentally fallen.

Avo collected himself. He had to remain calm. His family needed him more than ever now. There would be plenty of time to deal with the anger later on. As he calmed down, he realized what Martha had said about her mother's last words. 'Lara will be home soon.' A chill passed through his spine. What did she know? No one knew about his conversations with Lara except Laurian. Did she feel something? Women were scary in that way; Avo had heard of some women in the village who could foretell things; they sensed things or saw events in their dreams before they happened. Of course he had never believed the stories, because men were not supposed to believe that type of stuff. And none of it had meant anything to him anyway, until now.

That same afternoon the medical examiner and Dr. Hakobian arrived from Ashtarak, along with Gagik. The next afternoon was the funeral. Silva Galian was laid to rest in the family cemetery, next to her husband and to the right of the small head stone placed in the upper left corner of the section in memory of Araxi Dadik.

ӌ ӌ ӌ

Laurian heard the news from Gagik. Avo had not called as promised. One couldn't blame him. He had three sisters and three brothers at home who were now his responsibility.

The day after the funeral, the post office in Aparan called Avo.

"The money from your sister arrived yesterday while you were at the funeral," he said. "I did not want to bother you. You can come and collect it anytime."

Avo needed to clear his head anyway and decided to walk to Aparan. It was a forty-minute walk. Autumn was in full swing; he could feel nature brace for the coming winter. For Avo, the feeling had always been unmistakable; he loved this season. The heaviest work was already done, the animals were back from *yayla,* and enough food for the winter was already stored for both the animals and the family. And they had enough cow and sheep manure to burn all winter as well. It felt good to be prepared. He realized for the first time that this feeling had been instilled in him by his father. He had walked on this deserted road to Aparan a few times with his father, and his father had the habit of making small talk whenever he was with the children; at least it felt like small talk even if it wasn't, because he never made a big deal of anything as he went on talking to them about life.

When he arrived at the post office, the director asked him to come to the interior room, which served as his private office. He normally would hand the cash to him at the main office, even if there were other people around. The amounts varied between one-hundred-and-fifty to two-hundred dollars, sent every three to four weeks.

"First," he said once they were in the interior office and he had shut the door, "I want to express my condolences to you. Both your mother and your father were honorable people, Avo. I liked them a lot. Your father worked here, as you know. What you may not know is that your mother and my wife were good friends, going back to their childhood. But after they both had children, it became impossible to spend time socializing. You know how it is."

"I know," said Avo, moved by the postman's warmth. "And thank you very much, Paron Artiom."

"Now, for the main business at hand. Your sister has sent a lot of money this time. Much, much more than usual. The transfer service could not bring that much cash here." He reached into the top drawer of the desk and took out a small slip of paper. It was a light blue piece of paper about a quarter of the size of a regular sheet. "You need to take this to the bank, Avo," continued the postman. "This small piece of paper is worth eight thousand dollars."

"Eight thousand dollars?" Avo could not conceive of the significance of that amount.

"Eight thousand. You need to take your identity card with you. I don't think you have a passport yet, do you?"

"No."

"It's okay. They'll need some identification, even though they know you. This is a bank formality."

"How did she manage this?" murmured Avo more to himself than to the postman.

"Listen," continued the postman, ignoring Avo's last question. "I strongly advise you to open an account at the bank and keep the money there. You can go and withdraw any amount anytime you want. But it would not be safe to carry that much cash with you. Besides, they will give you some interest on your deposit."

"Interest?"

"Yes, if you transfer everything into Armenian drams, it will total more than four million drams. They'll give you five to ten percent on dram deposits, depending on how long you commit the funds. That's a lot of money, Avo."

As Avo was getting ready to leave, the postman added: "This transfer was made to your name, unlike all the others, which came in your mother's name. Do you think she knows Mama passed away?"

"I don't know how she could," said Avo, genuinely bewildered. He then put the slip in his shirt pocket and left.

Avo had been looking forward to Lara's next call and dreading it at the same time. He couldn't wait to talk to her again, but how could he explain that she wouldn't be able to hear Mama's voice? 'Take care of Mama,' she had said. What could he have done?

He was already out of Aparan when his phone rang. His heart jumped, thinking it could be Lara. But it was Laurian.

"I'm very sorry, Avo," he said.

"Thank you. Sorry I didn't call."

"I understand. How is everything at home?"

"It will be okay," said Avo, truly meaning it. "I think everything will turn out fine. I think Lara will be home soon."

"When do you think it will be okay for me to visit?"

"Edik jan, you can come anytime you want. But I just don't want you to go to so much trouble. It is not a short distance."

"I'd like to come see you and the family," said Laurian. "Unless you think it is too early. I really appreciate your honesty when you told me the family couldn't fit me in last time. So please tell me."

"You're really welcome anytime you want. I mean it."

"Okay," said Laurian. "Probably next week. Let things settle a bit. I have some ideas I'd like to discuss."

"Very good, Edik jan. I'll wait for your news."

"But you'll let me know if Lara contacts you again, right?"

"Right. And this time I'll keep my promise."

XVIII

Lara was not used to wearing the veil. She could see hardly anything through it. In broad daylight it would have been easier, almost like wearing dark sunglasses. But at night, it was different. She had only a small carry-on bag and her purse, and was wearing flat, comfortable shoes. When she saw the headlights of the approaching car, she unlatched the door and waited for it to reach her front door.

Omar the driver got out of the black Mercedes sedan and opened the back door. Lara rushed out of her house and got into the car without bothering to lock the front door. The car moved; her heart was beating so fast that she became lightheaded. She wondered if Omar could hear her heartbeat echoing in her own ears. She wiped her sweaty hands on her handkerchief, and lifted her veil off her face even though they were not out of the compound yet. Just for a minute, she thought. She had to breathe.

The guards at the main gate were inside the air-conditioned guardhouse even at night; it was far too hot and humid to stand outside. As Omar's car approached the gate, he lowered his window and Lara instinctively laid down flat on the back seat.

"Thank you, my brother," said Omar to the guard who peeked from the guardhouse window, "and good night."

"*Ma'a al salame*," answered the guard with a smile. "Go in peace." And the large iron gates swung open.

The three-hour drive was uneventful. Omar was very quiet, which was a relief to Lara. She did not want to engage in small talk. They arrived at Seef International Airport a little past one in the morning. The airport was very crowded when they arrived. "Too many flights to Mumbai and Karachi," explained Omar. He decided they would wait in the car for a while, as they had plenty of time. Thirty minutes later the same airport was very quiet and looked almost deserted. He took Lara's carry-on and led her to the Turkish Airlines check-in counter. He checked her in while she waited behind him with her veil drawn. Then Omar walked to passport control with Lara's passport and boarding pass. He greeted the officer warmly and handed over the two documents. The officer looked at Lara's Russian passport carefully and then looked over Omar's shoulder at Lara, who was standing quietly with her face covered.

"Lara Galianova," he read. "Is she Muslim?"

"She converted recently," said Omar confidently, as instructed by Sumaya. "She's going to join some relatives in Istanbul."

The officer gestured Lara to go to a small room behind his post. Omar signaled to Lara to go to the indicated room. There, a woman officer, who had been given Lara's passport, asked her to lift her veil, and she looked back and forth a few times at her face and her photo. She handed Lara the passport and waved her to go. Her passport was stamped, and Omar handed her the carry-on and directed her to go through the security check. He could not go past that point. Lara placed her carry-on and purse on the conveyor belt, and then she passed through the metal detector, tripping it. Again, she was escorted to a private room where a woman officer lightly searched her, and, seeing her bracelets and rings, just waved her through. The rest was very simple. She found her gate and waited. The plane was not full. The seats next to Lara were both empty. Eventually, when the plane finally took off, she lifted her veil. She was crying.

An hour into the flight, all the passengers were sound asleep and the lights in the plane were dimmed. Lara reclined her seat but could not sleep; she could not even close her eyes. Every time she did, an immense, overwhelming fear engulfed her. This was different from all the other fears that she had endured, even the one at Ayvazian's house. She was responsible for this. She had orchestrated a daring scheme and implemented it. She was in a cold sweat and her hands were shaking so hard that she sat on them. She had never felt fear of such intensity before. She tried to force her mind to calm down, to feel excitement instead of fear, but she realized that this was the first time in her life that she had been alone, with no one else around who was responsible for her. Until the plane landed in Istanbul, she would be all alone.

She fetched her little green book from her purse and turned on the reading light. It was almost half full of notes and doodles. She started reading through it, to get her mind off her fear. On one page she had outlined Araxi Dadik's ring, tracing the ring both from within the band and from outside, and then shaded the thin area in between the concentric circles. The page was filled with seven images of the ring. She couldn't remember exactly when she had drawn them; maybe while they were in jail, or maybe before the arrest. She had wanted to make the most of the ring; to have it everywhere. Once she left Dubai, she put it on her ring finger, with a determination to wear it for the rest of her life.

On another page she had written the names of everyone in her family. *Martha, Sona, Arpi, Alisia, Lara, Avo, Sago, Aram.* She had drawn a rectangular frame around each name. Below them, in one frame, were the names *Silva* and *Samvel.* Then she had printed *Araxi Dadik*, in large capital letters. There was nothing else on the page except floral doodles, with vine-like designs creeping through the different rectangles. Another page was full of *"Avo is angry, Avo isn't angry"* written at least twenty times, in small script.

Going through her book began to calm her down, but the intense fear kept creeping back in waves, bringing back the cold shivers and the shaking hands. Each time, she fought back by delving into her book. She spent a long time on the drawings and doodles, and read most of her notes. Towards the end, she even had a few words in Arabic. *"Ahmed,"* she had written several times in Arabic, as if practicing writing the word. *Full of contradictions,* she added next to the name. *Kind, tough; warm, cold; close, distant; generous, generous, generous...* Then she saw the note she had written the evening he had brought the music. *Tonight he won me over with a song and I loved him. Then he left. Nothing has changed. I wish Avo would return.* She laid the open book on her chest and stared into the dark cabin, reliving the dreams in which Avo had appeared, going over her conversations with him, trying to imagine their house, her mother, the garden and the animals.

The cabin crew passed by a couple of times during the flight, but did not bother checking on anyone, as everyone either was asleep or was trying to sleep. Lara didn't want anyone to notice her. She pretended to be asleep every time someone passed by her seat. The uncertainty of what would happen once the plane landed haunted her. She had to walk to passport control and pass through in her abaya and headdress, but certainly without the veil. What if they asked her questions she could not answer? She could imagine dreadful imponderables with Turkish border police, and remembered Anastasia's stories back in Moscow. What scared her even more than these visions was the very fact that she was scared. Collect yourself, Lara, she kept telling herself. Keep your head together; the die is cast, the plane is in the air, and it will land in Istanbul. It's done. You can't turn back; you're going home, you're doing what you've wanted to do for a long time.

The four-and-a-half hour flight was an intermittent nightmare that Lara lived through wide awake. But as the plane was getting ready for its descent into Istanbul, she suddenly began to regain her composure. She left her seat for the first time and went to the restroom. She took a long look at herself in the mirror. She and Sumaya had discussed whether she should change into Western clothes on the plane, or wait until she boarded the plane to Tbilisi. In the end, Sumaya had advised her to stay in her abaya while in Istanbul. "Chances are less that they'll bother you as a Muslim woman," she had said.

Lara stared into her own eyes for a long time, thinking that these same eyes had stirred so much awe, love, lust and violence in others. It was finally time for them to inspire something in her. What she needed most was confidence, confidence to overcome all hurdles and complete the mission that she was on. And then she realized that her eyes were actually very beautiful; penetrating, dark and deep, as if they could see through things, through facades and veils, through darkness and obstacles. Her eyebrows were plucked only slightly, accentuating her youthful look. Her face was well proportioned, with high cheekbones and a pretty forehead. In the bathroom of that plane, emerging from four excruciating hours, Lara finally woke up to what everyone had been saying for years; this was not like any other face after all; this was a powerful face, one that could move people, could do a lot more than just turn heads, this was a face that could inspire and attract. This was a face that should not feel any fear.

The cabin crew was knocking on the door. The plane was about to land and she had to return to her seat. Lara quickly straightened her headdress, wiped around her eyes, lightly touched up her makeup and returned to her seat. She was ready for Istanbul.

ℒ ℒ ℒ

As Lara's plane was landing, Laurian got into his car and started his drive to Saralandj. The weather had changed very suddenly; a severe cold front had gripped Vardahovit and the upper villages overnight. Temperatures had plummeted to below freezing, although it was still dry. Freezing rain or hail could follow soon, with disastrous effects on the roads. Laurian was prepared; he had already put his winter tires on and packed his winter coat and an extra pair of heavy boots. After spending some time in Saralandj with the Galians, he was planning to spend the night with Gagik in Ashtarak.

He picked up Gagik and arrived in Saralandj just before noon. Fortunately, the cold front had not affected Yerevan and Ashtarak. Avo was in the back garden pruning the grape vine. It was an old vine, with a thick trunk creeping up onto an arbor that seemed too small to contain all the overgrown shoots from the last season. Avo had pruned more than half of the growth.

"Make sure you don't kill that vine," joked Laurian, embracing him. Gagik embraced him also, admiring his work.

"This is how my father used to do it," said Avo. "You take each shoot, you leave around three buds on it and cut the rest. Sometimes you take out the entire shoot if it is too close to another or if it has grown vertical, either straight upwards or downwards."

"You learned that just by watching him?" asked Laurian.

"My father had a way of talking to us when he worked," said Avo nostalgically. "If we were around, he was always talking about something, either about what he was doing, or about something, some story in general. I remember him telling me about keeping just three buds when I was watching him prune once. It has stuck in my mind."

In about half an hour the thick, overgrown arbor looked trim and almost naked.

"Now it's ready to start all over again in the spring," said Avo, satisfied. To Laurian, that sounded like a quote from his father.

They went inside; Alisia made coffee and left them alone. The two younger brothers were at school.

"Any news from Lara?" asked Gagik.

"Not yet, Gago jan," said Avo. "I'm very worried. I expected her to call by now. She was so anxious to call back and talk to Mama."

Avo told them about the money that Lara had sent. He also told them how he had opened an account at the bank, at the postman's suggestion, and deposited the money. He had withdrawn a few hundred dollars just to make sure that he could, as promised. The rest of the money was in the bank.

"That's very good," said Laurian. "The postman gave you good advice."

"But all that money? And wired to me, instead of Mama, the day after Mama died?"

"She told you that she was trying to come home, right?" said Laurian, pretending the whole thing was nothing out of the ordinary, even though he was as intrigued by it as Avo. "I think that explains the amount. She probably sent everything she has saved this past year. And why to you, instead of your mother as usual? Well, I think since she knew your mother was very ill, she did not want to put her through the trouble of going to the bank. I bet that's all there is to it, Avo. I wouldn't worry about that now. Let's just hope she calls soon."

Avo was quiet for a while. He lit a cigarette, which he had never done inside the house when his mother was alive. His parents' bed was made, covered with a blanket, and looked untouched. They still had to cook and bathe in the room, but it didn't look like anyone had moved in to occupy it as a bedroom yet.

"Lara slept here the night before she left," said Avo. "We want her to have this as her room when she returns."

"Avo, you know that we'll probably have to deal with Ayvazian when Lara returns, right?" asked Gagik.

"Do you know that I asked her not to go that night?" asked Avo, as if he had not heard Gagik. "I asked her twice not to go. '*Kurig*, don't go,' I said. She just held me and told me that all would be well."

"And maybe all is in fact well," said Laurian. "You don't know that it isn't."

"All is not well," said Avo somberly, in the same dispassionate tone that he had used when he told Laurian that his mother wouldn't make it through the winter. "I know all is not well." Then, turning to Gagik, he said, "Gago, I know we need to deal with Ayvazian. I know from the phone calls with Lara that she is very careful when speaking about him. Something is definitely wrong. If she does make it home, we'll have an Ayvazian problem to deal with, that's for sure."

"Avo, listen," said Laurian, "we'll take each step in turn. Let's see when Lara calls. In the meantime, focus on your family. Both Gago and I are here to help in any way we can. There is nothing we can do until you hear from Lara. And remember what I told you in Vardahovit. Everything you saw there is strictly between us. Even Gago here doesn't know all the details."

"You two have been here a few times but we've never honored you properly," said Avo, changing both the subject and the mood of the conversation. "We shall have a bite to eat together. And we will not speak of this subject until we have something concrete. Even though it's barely been a week since we buried Mama, everyone in this house needs a break from mourning. We'll have a bite and raise a glass and forget all the sorrow for a few hours."

Laurian and Gagik looked on with surprise and some admiration as Avo called his three sisters from the other room, all older than him, and instructed them to prepare a meal to honor their guests. "Have everything ready by the time the boys return from school," he instructed. "And see if Martha and her husband can join us."

ᒍ ᒍ ᒍ

"Your next flight has been delayed," said Apo Arslan to Lara. "They don't know how long of a delay yet; I have arranged for a place for you to rest and freshen up."

What made Lara most uncomfortable was not so much the news of the delay, but Timur's staring at her. The man hadn't been able to take his eyes off her since he met her at the airport and drove her to Apo's place on the Bosporus. He spoke only Turkish, so there was no verbal communication between them other than the most basic pleasantries. Apo, on the other hand, was civil and exceedingly polite. He personally offered her a cup of Turkish coffee, and asked if she needed anything from Istanbul while they were waiting. He spoke with a heavy Western Armenian accent, which made it difficult for Lara to understand everything, but they managed to communicate.

"Thank you very much, Paron Abo," said Lara. "You've been very kind. But I don't need anything. I am only worried about my flight to Tbilisi; I have only a couple of hours in Tbilisi to catch the evening train to Yerevan. This delay could cost me a whole day if I miss the train tonight."

Lara was seated on the sofa facing the large windows overlooking the Bosporus; the light poured over her face, highlighting both her features and her tiredness. Timur was on a chair facing her in the far end of the room, and Apo was seated closer to her, also facing her. Her Eastern Armenian pronunciation of his name as 'Abo' instead of Apo, appealed to him.

"I understand, Lara *Khanum*," said Apo, "but there really is nothing that we can do but wait. Timur is constantly in touch with the airport. I suggest you go to the room I've arranged for you and rest. I'll personally follow up with the airline and let you know as soon as they are ready to depart."

Apo's manners were so polite and refined that Lara became both suspicious and disarmed at the same time. There was nothing she could do but follow Apo's suggestion. She quietly nodded in agreement.

"Are you sure there is nothing you need from Istanbul?" asked Apo again. "Anything at all, please don't hesitate to ask."

Lara was about to refuse again when she remembered something.

"Are there any toy stores nearby?" she asked.

"You need some toys?" asked Apo, surprised.

"Well, I promised to bring back a slingshot for my younger brother," said Lara, feeling a bit embarrassed.

"Oh, I see. No problem at all," said Apo. "Timur will have a few of the best slingshots in Istanbul in your room in an hour."

"Thank you," said Lara.

"Your room is in the apartment one floor below. You'll find everything you need there. Are you sure you're not hungry?"

"No," said Lara, "not now. But I'd appreciate some drinking water."

"There are several bottles of water for you there. Also you can make tea or coffee in your room. But let me know if you need to eat something. I will take you there now." Apo stood up and reached for her carry-on bag.

"There's one more thing," said Lara, with some hesitation.

"Anything, Lara *Khanum*," smiled Apo.

"Can I make a phone call?"

Apo should have expected that, but, for some reason, had not. Lara noticed that he was taken by surprise. Apo was weighing the risks of letting her make a phone call, and needed time to think.

"Where would you like to call?" he asked. "Is it someone here in Istanbul?"

"No," answered Lara, aware of Apo's hesitation, "I'd like to call home."

"Is it a house phone or a mobile?" asked Apo, still trying to think about how to handle the request.

"Does it matter?" asked Lara, keenly aware that Apo's super polished, polite manners had disappeared.

"It does," he replied dryly. "The telephone reception from here to Armenia is very poor and often entirely dysfunctional. A lot depends on the area code. Yerevan sometimes works, but cell phones and the rural regions can be very problematic. We can spend hours dialing a number repeatedly until we get through."

"I see," said Lara, not convinced by this story. For the first time since she landed in Istanbul she had the eerie feeling that her plans for the second leg of her trip to Armenia were in jeopardy.

"Come," said Apo, "and give me the number you want to reach. We will try, and as soon as we get through, I'll transfer the call to your room." Then, as if preempting a temptation that Lara might have been facing, he added, "The phone in your room is internal, which means you cannot get an outside line. But if I make the connection from this office, I can transfer it to you. Is that fine with you?"

"We can forget it, then," said Lara. "I do not want to put you through the trouble of spending hours on the phone for me. You've been very kind already. Thanks anyway." It was obvious to Apo that Lara did not want to give him the phone number.

"As you wish, Lara *Khanum*," he said politely, and held the door open for her.

They took the elevator down one floor, and Apo led her through the hallway to an apartment, opened the door, and let her in. Inside, he took her to a suite within the apartment. It had a large bedroom, bathroom and a small sitting area, where there was a refrigerator stocked with soft drinks and juices and a coffee and tea set.

"I believe you'll be comfortable here," he told her. "We use this suite for our most important guests. You can lock the door of the suite for privacy. No one will disturb you. If you need anything, just dial 11 on the phone next to the bed, and I'll respond. I will let you know as soon as we hear about your flight."

♌ ♌ ♌

As Lara sat in a chair pondering what had gone wrong with her plan, Apo managed to track down Ayvazian. He was in Martashen.

"Sergey *effendi*," he said, using his most cordial Istanbul style, "this is Apo Arslan disturbing you from Istanbul."

"What a nice surprise, Abo jan," said Ayvazian. "I hope all is well with you; how can I be of help?"

"Sergey jan," said Apo, dropping the title *effendi*, "I am calling to see if I can be of help to you in a very delicate matter."

"Is that so?" said Ayvazian. "I'm afraid I don't know what you're referring to."

"I believe one of your ladies in Dubai has made an unauthorized excursion, and is currently in my custody."

"I still don't know what you're talking about," said Ayvazian, beginning to lose his patience. "Come to the point, Abo jan, so we don't waste time."

"Her name is Lara Galian. Also known as Leila, and also as Lara Galianova. She ran away from Dubai, fell into my hands, and believes that she is heading back home."

Ayvazian's hands were shaking with anger. Apo's calm and composed tone simply added to his mounting fury. A million scenarios flashed before his eyes as to what could have happened.

"I believe the big *effendi* in Dubai will be very upset when he returns home and finds that his little love has flown the coop," continued Apo in his exaggerated calm and polite style, "so I thought I'd save you the trouble and the embarrassment of having to go looking for her."

"How did she end up in your custody, Abo?" asked Ayvazian, making an enormous effort to control his urge to yell and curse.

"That is a very long story and not one to be told over the telephone," said Apo. "But as you may remember, I have always believed that you and I should cooperate, not compete. We can both do better by cooperating. So I offer you this assistance in that spirit, hoping that you will appreciate my gesture."

Ayvazian could barely control his anger. Hearing Apo start negotiations so soon, with such a haughty attitude, infuriated him.

"Abo, all I can say is that you better not be involved in this," he said rudely, but keeping his voice calm.

"Now why would you say that, Sergey?" asked Apo. "I am already involved since I have custody of the girl, right? But if you are asking whether I was involved in her escape from Dubai, I can assure you most absolutely that I was not. I have no idea whatsoever how she managed that. But you should be happy, not angry, that she is now in my care and I am willing to return her to you. Imagine how bad it would have been if you had no idea where she was. So, I am offering you a helping hand in this difficult and embarrassing situation. Please do not respond to me with threats."

"Very good," said Ayvazian. "I need to find out what happened. Give me an hour and I'll call you back. In the meantime, I'll send my nephew Viktor to Istanbul on the next available flight. Where can I reach you?"

Apo gave him a phone number and hung up, smiling ear to ear.

XIX

Sumaya was in a panic, and with good reason. Natalia's uncle's man had waited at the Moscow airport with a sign announcing "Mr. Timur K." but no one had approached him. All the passengers had disembarked and left. They had checked the passenger list, and had found neither the name Timur nor Lara Galianova. Sumaya had then asked Farah to contact Apo, but Apo was not answering the phone. This was clearly the nightmare scenario that Sumaya had feared. Lara had disappeared in Istanbul.

They tried calling Apo all night with no success. Then Sumaya decided she'd have to let Al Barmaka know that Leila had escaped. There was no point in postponing telling him. It was already midnight in Dubai, which meant around 3:00 in the morning in Beijing. She had to wait until morning. And she had to have a plausible story, not only of the escape, but also of how she came to discover that Lara was missing.

Earlier that afternoon, while they were still trying to get in touch with Apo, Sumaya received a call that shocked and dismayed her. It was from Madame Ano.

"Where is Lara?" Ano asked, skipping all the traditional pleasantries.

"I was about to call you to ask the same question," said Sumaya, doing her best to act much calmer than she actually was. How could Ano know anything was amiss so early?

"Why should I know more than you, Sumaya?" asked Ano rudely. "Lara has been your responsibility since she moved there. Then suddenly we find out that she is in Istanbul. Does His Excellency know about this? Do you know where she is? And I'd like to remind you that her safety is his responsibility while she is under contract with him. We will hold him personally responsible."

"And I'd like to remind you that you are in Dubai," said Sumaya, allowing her utter distaste for the woman to show in her voice. "So you better stop making threats. Your girl, for whom we paid so dearly, has escaped. You and your boss will be held responsible and can very easily be thrown in jail! Do you understand *that*?"

Madame Ano realized that her offensive strategy had backfired. It was time to back off.

"Sumaya, we cannot be responsible for her escape from your premises. We have not been in contact with her since she joined you. But let's put that aside for now; we're in this together. We face a problem. We know she is in Istanbul, but we don't how she could have reached there."

"How do you know she's in Istanbul?" asked Sumaya, trying to extract as much information as she could while Ano was in retreat.

"Mr. Ayvazian received a call from someone in Istanbul, saying he had Lara. That is all I know, I swear."

"You don't know who called Ayvazian?" asked Sumaya even though she had already started putting the puzzle together.

"I really don't know. He wouldn't tell me. He was so furious when he called that he did not make much sense. Your boss may do the same, Sumaya, when he finds out, and I won't blame him. Now you and I are stuck with the mess. Ayvazian wants to confirm that Lara is missing. That was his first concern, and I assume that we have the answer."

"She is missing," said Sumaya dispassionately. "I just discovered it myself. So now I am thinking about how to break the news to His Excellency, who is on a business trip to Asia."

"But how could she have escaped from there?" asked Ano, genuinely bewildered. "Don't you have the most elaborate security measures?"

"She must have had some help from outside," said Sumaya, remembering Lara's own story about her friend who could have helped her. "She had to have a driver pick her up with some alibi, and she had to have help arranging her ticket. But what I don't understand is how all of a sudden your boss got a call from Istanbul. Her plans must have gone wrong somewhere along the way."

"And thank God for that," said Ano. "The only good news in this whole story is that we have a good chance of getting hold of her and returning her to His Excellency. So when you talk to him, please mention that."

"I will," said Sumaya, feeling entirely defeated and stupid for having started the operation.

$$\mathcal{L} \quad \mathcal{L} \quad \mathcal{L}$$

Lara left her suite and surveyed the rest of the apartment and discovered, as she had suspected, that the front door was locked and she could not open it from the inside. She knew that her plan had been ruined, but did not know how. Sumaya couldn't possibly have an interest in causing this. Why help her escape only to trap her in Istanbul? Apo was a contact of Farah's, but what was her role in all this? For that matter, what was Apo's role? Clearly, Apo was not following the plan that Sumaya had told her he would, namely, to put her on a plane to Tbilisi. So he was betraying Sumaya, but to what end? Once again, Lara felt that her life was at the mercy of others. This was no longer her plan and her doing, as she had thought it was. She felt trapped and helpless, just as she had felt since the first night in Ayvazian's house.

She dialed 11. "No news yet, Lara *khanum*," said Apo. "They have not fixed whatever problem they're having. I think you'll end up spending the night here. I am very sorry for your delay."

Apo offered her food again, and this time she accepted. She ate, showered, and changed into a pair of jeans and a black turtleneck sweater. She put on a light brown jacket, which she had brought in her carry-on bag, and packed her Abaya.

After a night of terror and a taste of freedom, I am back to living the fear of captivity, she wrote in her book. *I'll never get used to the latter. My next escape will be final.*

"Catch the next flight to Dubai," Ayvazian told Viktor. "Try to go see this Sumaya woman. Find out as much as you can about what happened; try to get some details, like who helped her manage something like this, how she left the compound, how she booked her tickets. From there, catch a flight straight to Istanbul. By then I'll have things sorted out with Abo."

"You think Sumaya's hiding something?" asked Viktor.

"We can't rule out anything at this stage. Lara couldn't have managed this alone. Someone helped her, either from outside, as Sumaya claims, or from inside."

"Does Al Barmaka know?"

"Not yet, but he'll know soon enough. Maybe Sumaya has called him already, I'm not sure. It is very important that you reassure them that we know where the girl is and we'll return her immediately."

"Understood," said Viktor, but he did not like this mission. Cleaning up after someone else's mess was not something he liked to do.

"You need to be very careful, Viktor," advised Ayvazian, knowing the impulsiveness of his nephew. "We are in their territory. They are claiming Lara escaped with outside help. The most likely outside help, they'll assume, is someone from our organization. That makes no sense to us, but it may make sense to them. We have to dispel all such suspicions. But not by yelling and threats."

"I understand," said Viktor, and when he saw the worried look on Ayvazian's face, "really, I do," he added.

"Okay. There is a flight to Dubai tomorrow. Try to finish everything there tomorrow and fly to Istanbul either the same night or the next day. Let me know the schedules. Call as soon as you know something."

𝒬 𝒬 𝒬

Sumaya couldn't wait until mid morning as she had planned. It was a little before nine a.m. when she called Manoj.

"I need to get in touch with Al Barmaka urgently," she said, "and his cell phone is turned off. Is he staying at the usual hotel in Beijing?"

"Yes, he's at the Ritz Carlton," said Manoj. "But Ms. Sumaya, dear, it is around noon in Beijing now. He could be in a meeting. That's probably why his cell phone is turned off."

"This cannot wait," said Sumaya. "I need to find him. Please give me the number."

"Is there any way I can help?" asked Manoj, as he read off the hotel phone number and his suite number. "Please don't hesitate to tell me."

"Thanks, Manoj, but I need to handle this myself."

On the third ring Al Barmaka answered the phone. He sounded like he was still asleep.

"I'm sorry to bother you," said Sumaya. "But it is important."

Al Barmaka sat up in bed and rubbed his eyes. The Chinese woman next to him was sound asleep, with her back to him, her naked shoulders looking very inviting outside of the covers.

"What is it?" he asked.

"Leila has escaped."

"What do you mean 'escaped'?" asked Al Barmaka, with nothing but sleep coming through in his voice.

"It must have happened last night. I called her to invite her for breakfast this morning, but there was no answer. Then I sent the maid to check. She said the bed was not slept in. She's not here."

"Where is she?" asked Al Barmaka, sounding like the full impact of the news had not hit him yet.

Could it be that he doesn't care? thought Sumaya. *More likely, he is still sleepy.*

"Ayvazian's pimp here in Dubai called to say that she was in Istanbul, and that Ayvazian had found out where she was, and that he could return her to you within twenty-four hours." Sumaya knew that what Al Barmaka said next would be critical for her future at the estate.

But Al Barmaka was quiet for a long time. He looked again at the Chinese lady lying next to him, with her smooth, waist-long hair covering half the pillow and part of her shoulders, and gently ran his index finger down her back. She stirred, turned around, smiled sweetly, and rolled closer to him and cuddled under his arm.

"How did they find her so easily?" asked Al Barmaka at last.

"I have no idea," said Sumaya. "I am so sorry about this. I have no idea how she could escape without some help from outside. She was in my place yesterday afternoon for tea, and when I went to the kitchen to take a call she must have gone to my office and taken her passport from the drawer." Sumaya started crying. "I'm really sorry," she repeated between sobs.

Al Barmaka yawned. He felt the warmth of the Chinese woman's breath on his side and looked at her again.

"Here's what I want you to do," he said after another long pause. "First, tell them I don't want her back. My house is not a prison and we don't keep people against their will. Second, tell them I want the balance of my money back. She was with me for three months, right? So they owe me seventy-five thousand dollars. If they don't transfer it to Manoj within twenty-four hours, they'll be finished in Dubai. Third, I want you to find out exactly what happened. I want to know how she left the compound, how she flew out, everything. They have to fully cooperate on this also, since they already know where she is."

"I understand," said Sumaya quietly. "Again, I am very sorry."

"That's all," said Al Barmaka, yawning again. He had done a good job hiding his true emotions about Leila's escape from Sumaya. She did not need to know what a hurtful blow this was to him. "Tell Manoj everything and let him report to me on the progress." Then the phone went dead.

Sumaya was in a cold sweat. The fact that Leila wouldn't return was welcome news; in a way, she had achieved her objective. But her nightmare scenario was unfolding in front of her eyes. Al Barmaka wouldn't rest until he understood what had happened; Sumaya started making plans for her own departure from the compound.

♌ ♌ ♌

Ayvazian called Apo to say that he needed more time to decide what to do with the girl. Finally, the long expected call from Ano came.

"He doesn't want her back," said Ano. "He says his house is not a prison. But he wants seventy-five thousand dollars back. By tomorrow at the latest, or we're finished here in Dubai. And he wants you to find out exactly what happened, since you already have found the girl."

"Viktor will be in Dubai tomorrow," said Ayvazian, holding back his anger. "He'll   sort things out. Tell them that."

If Lara had been standing there in front of him, Ayvazian would have slit her throat right then and there. And although normally Ayvazian could not usually control his angry tantrums, when the rage exceeded a certain level, he became uncharacteristically calm. He stopped yelling and shaking, but that was when he was the most dangerous.

He called Viktor.

"Go to Dubai and check the situation on the ground first hand," he said. "Transfer seventy-five thousand dollars to Al Barmaka and reassure them. Ano can give you the details. Then fly straight to Istanbul. Thank Abo on my behalf. Tell him we'll cooperate in Dubai. He can send up to twenty girls initially, and build a force of up to forty in three years. He will have our protection."

"Are we really going to let him bring forty girls?" asked Viktor, surprised.

"Well, we'll have to see about that later, won't we?" snapped Ayvazian. "A lot can happen in three years. But I have another key demand from Abo. Aside from returning Lara, I want to know everything he knows about how she escaped and how she ended up in his possession. Everything. Tell him unless I know exactly how he got his hands on her, there is no deal. Then bring Lara and take her straight to Sevajayr. We either break her or kill her."

Then he called Apo.

"Viktor will be there the day after tomorrow," he said. "Everything is arranged. He will make you an offer that will meet with your agreement, I'm sure. Let me know if it doesn't after you hear it. Then you hand the girl to him."

"Very well, Sergey *effendi*," said Apo. "I'll wait for the safe arrival of your nephew."

Apo had stopped the pretense with Lara. She had spent her second night in the suite in his apartment, and he didn't even bother explaining it as a flight delay any longer. He was firm but unusually civil with her.

"I cannot let you go," he said. "I will have to hand you over to Ayvazian. After that, I don't know what will happen to you. He may take you back to Dubai, or back to Armenia, or to Moscow. I have no idea. But I have to hand you over to him."

There was no point in arguing or fighting. Things could be much worse. She was being treated very politely, even as a captive. They had not raised a hand against her, nor had anyone tried to rape her or physically hurt her in any way. Only once had Timur come to the apartment to bring three different kinds of slingshots, compliments of Apo *agha*. He had knocked on the door of her suite and handed her the package, but he had not attempted to enter. His intense stares had persisted, but nothing else.

"So you've been in touch with them," said Lara. "When do you expect this handover to take place?"

"Very soon, in a day or two. His nephew will come to pick you up."

"Do you know what type of people the Ayvazians are?" asked Lara, looking him in the eyes.

"Lara *khanum*," said Apo politely but firmly, "please do not go there; I know them, and you know them, and we may know the same things about them. I have to hand you over to them, and that is not open for discussion. What I can promise you is that no harm of any kind will come to you while you are in my care."

"I appreciate that," said Lara. "But can I ask you a question?"

"Sure, go ahead."

"What went wrong in the plan? I have a ticket to Tbilisi and was expecting to be home by now. Where did the plan go wrong?"

"That is an interesting question," said Apo almost sympathetically, "but it does not have a simple answer. Your plan to go to Tbilisi and then home was spoiled before it was even conceived. It was just a way to fool you. I was asked to send you off to Moscow to be handed over to someone else. So I spoiled *that* plan by keeping you here. I did not spoil your plan."

It was unusual for Apo to be so kind to a woman he held captive and even more unusual to tell her so much. He never treated his own recruits like that. His own girls would have been beaten and raped a few times by now, and not just by him, but also by Timur and sometimes others in his employ. But he had taken a liking to Lara. Besides, it was not his responsibility to break her. He had no reason to beat her or rape her, and decided to treat her like a *khanum*, a lady. Timur had requested permission several times to have Lara, but Apo had refused.

"You keep your hands off her, Timur," he had said. "You treat her with respect and you behave very politely with her, do you understand?"

"Yes, Apo *agha*, but why?"

"She's not our property. That's all."

In his convoluted way, Apo considered himself a professional, and believed that the beatings and rapes served an important business purpose by bringing the difficult girls into line. He had no such need in Lara's case.

Lara was now staring at him, more confused than defiant.

"They wanted you to send me to Moscow?" she asked, stunned.

"That's what your colleague asked me to arrange, yes."

"My colleague?" It had never occurred to Lara to think of Farah as a colleague.

"Yes, the Turkish woman who works there, Farah."

"But I have a ticket to Tbilisi. I paid for the whole trip in advance."

"Lara, listen. I told you already that your ticket to Tbilisi was just a way to mislead you. They paid me to put you on a flight to Moscow." Apo was beginning to get uncomfortable with the conversation. He had said enough and wanted to leave her alone.

"Just one more question, Paron Abo, please," said Lara as Apo stood up to leave. "Who was going to meet me in Moscow?"

"I have no idea. Someone was going to be at the airport with Timur's name on a sign, and Timur was supposed to hand you to him. I really do not know the details after that. Now I have to go."

"Thank you for the information," said Lara quietly.

Lara was very confused by Apo's behavior. He was kind, responsive, but dead-firm on keeping her captive and handing her over to Ayvazian. She did not want to scare him away by abusing his willingness to be helpful, but wanted to use it at least one more time before the handover. She had to make that phone call to Avo. But noticing his impatience to leave, she decided to give it a rest for now. She would surely have another chance before Ayvazian sent someone to collect her.

It is full circle back to the beast. I only hope he takes me back to Armenia, and not Dubai.

The panic at Al Barmaka's compound had spread beyond Sumaya. Farah, Natalia, the guard at the gate, and even Manoj were shocked and had started expecting the worst when he returned. Some of the maids and workers in the gardens were questioned, which did more to frighten them than lead to any new information. There would be no mercy for betrayal. The mildest punishment would entail losing their jobs and being deported from Dubai. The harshest could easily be long jail terms.

Viktor arrived and after a brief meeting with Ano, called Sumaya and drove to the compound. Manoj and Sumaya met him at the front entrance office. All three looked tired and dead serious; no pleasantries were exchanged, no coffee or tea offered.

"The money will be transferred today," said Viktor. "Just give me the wiring instructions. And we'll get the story soon. But first, tell me what you know."

Sumaya was noticeably the most uncomfortable.

"She just escaped," she said. "She stole her passport from my office, arranged for a driver who had been here before, which put the guards at the gate at ease, and just left. Someone from outside must have helped her."

"She has not contacted anyone in our organization," said Viktor so dryly and confidently that it sent a chill down Sumaya's spine. It would not be easy to make that story hold. "Besides, how did she manage to call outside from the compound? Ano tells me that this is neither allowed nor possible."

"I wish we knew," said Manoj. "There is no record of phone calls from the compound. I've checked everything. There is also no record of her being on any flight to Istanbul from either Dubai or Abu Dhabi. We checked all the records."

"Well, record or no record, she got there. Even more so than His Excellency, we want to know what happened. So we'll get to the bottom of this soon. Are you sure there is nothing more you can tell me?"

"There is one thing," said Sumaya. "You know how we have an arrangement whereby she wires money to her family through your office in Moscow?"

"Yes," said Viktor impatiently.

"Well, several days before she disappeared, she asked me to send instructions to wire a larger sum than usual. She said her mother had looked very ill when she left home and was worried about her health, and then she dreamt that she was ill and felt that they might need the money. I didn't think much of it. She gave me the cash, and I sent it through Western Union to your offices, and from there I believe it was transferred like all the other transfers."

"How much money was it?" asked Viktor.

"Not much, just a lot more than usual. Usually she'd send a hundred or two. This time it was eight-thousand dollars."

"Eight thousand?" asked Viktor. "How did she get hold of that kind of money? She's barely been here for three months."

"I don't know," said Sumaya, even though for her the amount did not seem so unreasonable. "His Excellency can be very generous at times, but we don't know how much money she had when she arrived here. She may have had some savings."

XX

Viktor caught a late morning Emirates Airlines flight from Dubai to Istanbul. He needed the five hours of quiet on the plane to think things through; their most lucrative recruit had just caused the single most costly incident, and they may not have seen all of the fallout yet.

Everyone agreed on one thing. Lara couldn't possibly have pulled off the escape without some help, either from inside the compound, the possibility of which Sumaya and Manoj were categorically refuting, or from outside the compound, which both he and Ano found extremely unlikely. And if she indeed had managed to build some relationships outside of their organization in Dubai, then he would have to admit that they had entirely underestimated the naïve, unworldly seventeen year old.

Viktor had seen his uncle's calm anger only twice before, and both times things had ended in bloodshed. He shuddered to think what would happen in this case, especially since sending Lara to Dubai had been his idea. But clearly, the problem was not Dubai; it was Lara. She could have done even worse things in Moscow.

Madame Ano was worried as well; she was afraid the incident would have a permanent impact on their Dubai operations, regardless of how it was resolved. For starters, they probably wouldn't be able to sell anyone else's contract for a while. And the security bureaucracy wouldn't look kindly at all on such an extreme breech of the rules. Ultimately, they would be blamed, whether they had anything to do with the incident or not; after all, Lara was a product of their organization.

Viktor shared these concerns. He decided to focus on the most immediate tasks. He had to reach an agreement with Apo about access to the Dubai market, even though he knew that Ayvazian would sooner or later find an excuse to renege on the deal. Had Al Barmaka wanted Lara back, Apo's contribution would have had a lot more value; they'd keep their money and get back in the good graces of Al Barmaka. But under the circumstances, it made very little sense to let Apo onto their turf when they already had suffered a major blow both financially and in terms of their credibility. But regardless, he had to make the deal and take Lara away. His plan was to fly with her to Tbilisi and connect to a flight to Yerevan, then drive straight to the safe house in Sevajayr. His bodyguards would be at the airport with two cars. The guards at Sevajayr had been alerted. It would be easy once they landed in Yerevan; the trick was to get Lara to behave on the two flights. If Viktor didn't feel that fear would be an adequate deterrent for Lara not to misbehave, he was prepared to drug her heavily.

The money was another mystery haunting Viktor. If she sent eight thousand dollars after covering the cost of her escape, which, Viktor assumed, must have included bribes in addition to the cost of tickets, how much money must she have had? She couldn't possibly have 'saved' much, as Sumaya had suggested. Viktor knew exactly how much she was paid before being handed over to Al Barmaka, and how much of that she sent home. Her so-called savings couldn't possibly have added up to more than a thousand dollars. How generous was Al Barmaka? Had Lara been stealing from them or not declaring everything she made? Viktor then remembered that he used to suspect that with Anastasia, when Lara was still in Moscow. They were generating a lot of money in those days. Could they have stashed away a few thousand each? Very likely. And now Lara's family had the money that she and Anastasia had stolen from them. There were many scores to settle, he thought.

No one yet knew what to do with Lara once they got her to Sevajayr. Even Ayvazian wasn't sure. Breaking her seemed to be his first choice, but he had not ruled out killing her. Even factoring in the huge setback with Al Barmaka, Lara was still one of the best earners they had ever had. So she was worth keeping, if they could manage her. But this time they had to be absolutely sure.

Lara decided enough time had passed since her last meeting with Apo, so she called him again the next day.

"Paron Abo, can we please have another short conversation?"

"Ha, Lara *khanum*," responded Apo cordially, "I have news for you anyway. I'll be down soon."

When he entered the apartment, Apo was surprised to see Lara so relaxed. She was in her jeans and sweater, hair down, lying down on the sofa in the living room of the apartment, watching television. For a moment he imagined her as his lover, living there at his beck and call. What a prize that would be. But he put the thought out of his mind as quickly as it had arisen. Lara sat up straight, turned off the television and put on her slippers.

"You have news for me, Paron Abo?" she asked sweetly.

"Yes, someone's coming for you. He'll be here this afternoon. You will most probably leave with him today."

"Do you know who it is?" asked Lara. "Is it his nephew as you mentioned last time?" Her calm, composed manner was distracting for Apo.

"Yes, Viktor. Ayvazian's nephew."

"Oh yes, I know him," said Lara dismissively. Then she turned her attention on him. "Paron Abo," she said, "you've been very kind to me considering, well, the circumstances under which we met. I have had captors before, but none as kind as you, and none as gentlemanly as you. First, before I take my leave, I want to thank you for that."

"You are very welcome, Lara *khanum*," said Apo. The irony of the situation had not escaped him.

"So even at the risk of appearing like I am abusing your kindness," continued Lara, "I have one last request; like the last request they grant prisoners on death row."

"Oh, Lara *khanum*, you exaggerate," said Apo with a chuckle. "You most certainly are not on death row. Just being returned to the barn, so to speak."

"Maybe so," laughed Lara. "The barn, eh? Interesting way of putting it. Anyway, maybe so, but one never knows for sure in this business. So I still have one last request, if you'd be kind enough to hear it."

"I'll hear it," said Apo, "but I cannot promise anything until I know what it is."

"Very well. Before I am taken away, I would like to make that one phone call that I requested earlier. And," added Lara with a little hesitation, "ideally, I'd like to make the call after I know where they intend to take me."

Apo was impressed with her persuasiveness. He had thought about letting her make the call anyway, as a final departing good will gesture. But now Lara had added a new dimension to the request, and Apo saw through it immediately.

"First of all, that is two requests, not one," he said, maintaining a warm smile. "You want me to first find out where they plan to take you and then let you make a call before handing you over to them, is that it?"

"That's it," said Lara.

"Second of all," continued Apo, "you hope to alert someone about their plan by your call, which could get me into a lot of trouble. Is that what you want?"

"Paron Abo," said Lara so seriously and softly that it almost broke his heart, "*nothing* I do can ever get you into a whole lot of trouble. You are the boss here; I'm a prisoner. Please consider my request."

"I'll let you make the call," said Apo. "But I cannot promise that I'll be able to find out your next destination."

"Thank you," said Lara. She stood up to shake his hand, as if sealing a deal.

Do not be surprised—

    from the beginning I have searched for you

in foreign places

    in every teardrop and every laughter

my restless soul

    scrambling in the dark like a specter

has yearned for your traces...

When Laurian wrote that verse, he was not sure whom he was searching for. His thoughts were on a lost and rediscovered homeland, but could it have been about an old love? Or maybe a future love, one that he was still seeking? Or an idea? A nostalgic memory?

Ever since they had eased the surveillance, his evenings had quieted down and he had spent more time on his poetry. He was considering publishing a collection of his poems, but, unlike the confidence he had in his professional reports, he had recurring doubts about his poems. A poem that inspired him one moment could seem lame and lifeless the next. Literature, and especially poetry, depended a lot on moods; one's mood while writing a verse set the tone, and if the mood was different when reading the verse later, it could sound so different it might even be difficult for the author to recognize it as his own work.

In spite of the partial reprieve, the Ayvazian phenomenon still haunted him. The men had not abandoned the houses in Sevajayr, and their SUVs were still sighted up and down the road. Saro was relieved that the stakeout had gone unnoticed by Ayvazian's men, and even more so that it had been suspended, albeit temporarily. There was no point in risking being discovered, especially when they didn't know what to do with the evidence they had managed to gather so far.

There was no news from Lara. Avo, who had managed to suppress his fury right after his mother's death, had become increasingly belligerent every time Ayvazian was discussed. And now that he didn't have much to do until next spring, he had a lot of time to nurture his anger. Both Laurian and Gagik became very concerned when, during a meal at Saralandj, Avo, after a few glasses of vodka, started talking about taking revenge and 'erasing Ayvazian's shadow from Saralandj.'

"He is angry, he has time, he now has money, and he's sixteen," Laurian said to Gagik on the drive back. "If that is not a recipe for disaster, I don't know what is."

"And he has identified the enemy," Gagik added. "If this was the old days, I'd say you're describing one of our revolutionary comrades."

"I hope he doesn't make a habit of drinking like that," said Laurian. "There should be an adult watching him. He has no one with any authority to advise him. None of his sisters, even though older, can tell him what to do."

"I'll talk to his brother-in-law," Gagik had said. "He seems like the reasonable type."

"Yes, he could be a stabilizing influence, if he spends the time," agreed Laurian.

Laurian used his free time to do more soul-searching about his attachment to the Galian family.

"Their struggle is not much different than the struggle of this nation," he had once told Gagik. "I could draw a hundred parallels."

"Ha, Edik jan, I understand," Gagik had answered, "but that still doesn't make it our business to get too involved. We'll help where we can, but you need to keep a little distance."

But of course Gagik did not know about Sirarpi. Was her story and her fate being repeated here, in the newly liberated homeland, thirty years later? Laurian's personal recurring nightmare was hearing one day that Lara's bruised and mutilated body was discovered somewhere. For him, saving Lara, a girl he had never met, had become tantamount to avenging Sirarpi; as if, if the same fate befell Lara, Sirarpi's death would be in vain.

He called Avo every day, asked Gagik to drop in once in a while and invited both of them to Vardahovit, where he thought he could keep an eye on Avo. Avo promised to revisit, but had not managed to.

So Laurian buried himself in his books and writing. He still sat on the front terrace during sunny days, even though the evenings now were too cold to sit outside even to watch the sunsets. The mountains still talked to him in ways that he had never been able to express; they stared back at him in expectation, almost as if they meant to hold him accountable for something.

Do not be surprised, he said aloud looking at them in the distance, *from the beginning I have searched for you...*

"So good to finally meet you," said Apo, shaking Viktor's hand with gusto. "I trust your flight was comfortable?"

"Yes, thank you," replied Viktor, but he was unable to return Apo's polite enthusiasm.

"Is everything settling down in Dubai?" asked Apo, and offered him a seat facing the window with the view of the Bosporus.

"It will be sorted out, thanks," said Viktor, anxious to finish his business and head out. He was tired, irritable and didn't care for Apo's highly refined and totally false Istanbul manners. "My uncle has a good proposal for you."

"First, can I offer you anything? Do you need to freshen up, rest a bit, have something to eat?"

"Thank you, Abo jan. But I'd like to catch the next flight this evening. I think it leaves for Tbilisi around eleven-thirty."

"Oh," said Apo, surprised, "you're taking her to Tbilisi?"

"Yes, then on to Yerevan."

That was far too easy, thought Apo. In the first few minutes the information that he thought he'd have to coax out of Viktor was volunteered. Either he's so tired that he has become careless or he just doesn't care that I know.

"I understand," said Apo, wondering why they were not taking Lara back to Dubai as he had assumed, but deciding not to ask further. It was not his business. "In that case, I'll let you run the meeting," he added with a chuckle.

"We would be happy to help you set up an operation in Dubai," said Viktor. "We will also provide advice and network support until you get organized."

"Thank you," said Apo, somewhat on guard, as he expected caveats and conditions.

"You can start with up to twenty girls," continued Viktor, "and you can use our organization to receive the necessary facilitation with visas, security and police. Over time, in say three years or so, you can build up to forty women, and if in that period you need to establish your own network of local support, you can, or if you want to continue using ours, you can also do that."

"And what happens after I have forty girls and my own setup?" asked Apo, even though he was happy with the offer so far, assuming of course that it could be enforced.

"After that, God is great, as they say," smiled Viktor reluctantly. "You'll eventually have the means to break the forty women limit, but we hope that you stick to it, so as not to overcrowd the market."

"Understood, Viktor jan. We'll have to trust each other, just like I have to trust that you'll keep your word once I hand the girl over to you."

"You have my uncle's word. If you're not sure, you can call him and he'll confirm."

"Oh, no need for that. I know you speak for him. But your own word matters to me as much as his."

"You have my word as well as his."

"How do you propose we proceed?" asked Apo.

"I suggest that you come to Dubai for a visit first, preferably sometime when I can be there as well; I'll show you around, you know, our apartments, the hotels that we have arrangements with, the main nightclubs, and so on. It is important that you form a firsthand feel for the place before you start." Viktor hoped that the more specific he became the more confidence he'd inspire in Apo. "One more thing," he added, as if he had forgotten a very important point. "It is best to appoint a manager there early on, to get used to the system. Dubai is very different from Istanbul in almost everything, customs, traditions, rules, ways around the rules, the competition, security, you name it. The manager should speak good English, and a little Arabic wouldn't hurt. Let me also say that we've been happier with female managers."

"Interesting," said Apo. "In that respect at least Dubai sounds similar to Istanbul; I have been happier with woman managers here also."

"They understand the girls and have a way with the police," agreed Viktor. "And most importantly, they don't try to take over."

"Thank you for the advice," said Apo. "This is a very interesting proposal indeed. But what do you say we stop the conversation now, and continue sorting out the details over a light dinner? It is only six o'clock. You have five hours before your flight, and I cannot just send you on your way without some hospitality."

"We still have a lot to talk about," said Viktor. "One of my uncle's conditions is that we find out exactly what happened; I mean how she escaped and how she ended up with you. I'm afraid that part is not negotiable."

"And I won't make it part of any negotiation," smiled Apo. "I'll tell you everything I know over dinner. Everything."

Viktor was anxious to confront Lara; he imagined that she'd squirm when she saw him. He was looking forward to reprimanding and abusing her before their flight. But he did not want to show that side of his personality to Apo. He accepted the dinner invitation.

"Great," said Apo. "Timur will take you to one of our special guestrooms to freshen up. I'll pick you up in thirty minutes. I promise to have you back and ready to leave for the airport in plenty of time."

Apo watched as Viktor reluctantly followed Timur and then left to visit Lara.

The atmosphere at the Al Barmaka estate had become much tenser. Regardless of who had helped Lara escape, the staff was responsible. The guard at the gate was supposed to record the license plate number of every car entering and leaving the compound, along with the exact time of entry and exit. He had not done so for weeks with any car that he recognized. There was only one entry in his registry, which happened to be a new delivery vehicle from a catering company. There was no excuse for this lapse, and the guard knew it. He had tried to remember all the cars that came in on the night Lara disappeared, but could generate neither license plate information nor drivers' names. The several security personnel posted around the property claimed that they had not noticed anything unusual. The fact is, with Al Barmaka traveling, they had all taken the evening off.

Sumaya's explanation of how Lara got hold of her passport was lame at best. Farah was nervous because she would clearly be at center stage of the whole drama as soon as Al Barmaka found out about Apo; she had been the only one in touch with him. She was convinced he'd have no problem telling anyone that. Only Natalia seemed to be out of the limelight for now, assuming that the others didn't drag her down along with them.

To everyone's relief, Al Barmaka had not cut his trip short as they had feared. He had trusted the investigation to Manoj, and was following it from China through daily phone calls. He had discovered the sensual traditions of oriental aristocracy and their concubines, and was already planning significant changes in his own domain. Even though he had been going to the Far East for many years, this was the first time that he had encountered the unfailing Asian discipline in all things. Their engrained sense of duty transcended normal everyday concerns. He saw many Middle Eastern values in Asia, but he also saw a dedication and devotion to perfection, which had not yet appeared in the Middle East.

Lara's escape and the exposure of how pathetic his staff was had revealed an ominous weakness in his setup in Dubai. It was time for a complete overhaul; he was going through with the investigation simply to know the truth; but he did not need the truth to make decisions; he had already made up his mind to replace much of his staff with new faces from China.

But Al Barmaka knew that while the investigation might reveal what had happened, it would not reveal why. The affection that he felt toward Leila was genuine. Why had she opted to escape? He felt a sense of loss much more strongly than he admitted on the phone to Sumaya. He knew

Leila's absence would trouble him even more once he returned home. He vowed to figure out the why later, when he had more time to focus on the situation after he returned to Dubai. He also knew deep in his heart that he would seek her out.

The phone call came around 8:15 in the evening in Saralandj, which was two hours ahead of Istanbul. Avo was at home in the kitchen, repairing a crack in the old, rusty stovepipe. His siblings were in their bedroom, the boys busy with homework and the girls mending clothes and embroidering.

"Avo, listen well," she said quietly as soon as she heard his voice. "I cannot talk long. I'll be in Armenia tomorrow morning. But I am not free."

"*Kurig*, what do you mean you're not free? Where will you be in Armenia?" Avo almost screamed in a panic.

"Listen," said Lara in the same low voice, without repeating his name; she had already regretted saying his name out loud the first time. "I'm not alone, and I'm not free. And I can't talk. Be very careful of the people we talked about before. Now I have to go."

"Wait!" shouted Avo. "When will you call back?"

"I don't know. Just be very careful." The connection was abruptly lost.

"Sorry," said Apo as he snatched the cell phone from her hand. "That is all I can allow. I believe I have now granted both of your last requests, Lara *khanum*. They will bring you some food soon, and in a few hours you will leave. I wish we had met under different circumstances; and I wish you well."

"Thank you, Paron Abo," said Lara.

But somehow Apo felt so small at that moment that he wished he had never called Ayvazian.

While Lara was calling Avo, Viktor was on the phone with Ayvazian.

"So far so good," he said. "I'll get the details of the escape story over supper. But we need to check something back home."

"Are you sure it's safe to talk?" asked Ayvazian.

"What I have to say is fine," said Viktor. "Check the brother. She wired him a lot of money recently. I'm guessing our money. I'm not sure what he knows."

"Understood, and enough said. I'll take care of that. And how is our friend in Istanbul?" Ayvazian changed the tone of his voice, giving it a friendly ring, just in case Apo had a way to listen in on the conversation. Viktor understood what Ayvazian was doing.

"Oh, he's very well," he said, taking on the same happy tone as his uncle. "I think we'll enjoy working with him in Dubai."

Avo sat down on the stool in front of the stove, deep in thought. He had the strongest feeling yet that something was about to unfold that would bring together all the risks and dangers he had been worrying about; and yet he was unusually calm. *She'll be back in the country tomorrow, she's not free, and there is a danger from the Ayvazians*, he thought, as if pondering a math problem from his school days.

He was about to call Laurian to tell him about Lara's call when he heard footsteps on the front stairs. It was Ruben, Martha's husband.

"Avo jan, good evening," he said as he walked into the kitchen. "Come sit, we need to talk."

Avo was surprised by the visit. It was approaching nine o'clock in the evening, and Ruben usually didn't pay visits at this hour.

"Rubo, is everything okay at home?" he asked. "Is Martha doing well?"

"All is fine at home. Listen, I was at the post office in Aparan earlier. They got a phone call that scared Paron Artiom. I could tell he was not happy with the call, or with the caller. You know the old telephone in the post office; sometimes the voice of the caller kind of echoes and you can hear it if you're standing close. All I could hear was a very rude voice, like a thug threatening Artiom."

Avo was intrigued by the story, even though he didn't quite understand what this had to do with them.

"At first Artiom said that he could not disclose that type of information because it would be against the rules of the post office. But I could hear the heavy echo of what sounded like yelling from the other end. Anyway, this went on for a while, and then I heard Artiom say your name."

"My name?"

"Your name. He told the man on the phone your name."

"What do you mean? He just said 'Avo'?"

"No, he gave them your full name. He said, 'It was sent to Avetis Galian.' No, sorry, he said 'Avetis Samveli Galian'."

The only place where Avo had seen his full name recently was on the blue slip of paper of the wire transfer from Lara.

"I think I know what this is," he told Ruben. "Ayvazian was asking the postman about the wire transfer. I received some money from Lara the day Mama died. It was a large amount. They're asking about that."

"How did they know?" asked Ruben.

"It was wired from their office."

"Then why question poor Artiom?"

"They're probably confirming it, that's all. The office gets instructions and just makes the transfers; Ayvazian doesn't always know every detail when these things happen. But sooner or later he finds out, and the amount was much larger this time. So he got curious, or angry, I guess. Did they ask him anything else?"

"I'm not sure what all the questions were, but at the end Artiom was answering 'yes' and 'no' to many different questions. It was not a short call. They may have asked what you did with the money, because Artiom said something about a bank. Did you put the money in the bank?"

"Yes. It was too much to carry around."

"Just how much money was it?" asked Ruben, now curious.

"Eight thousand American dollars."

"Wow, that is a lot."

"I'm surprised he took the call in your presence," said Avo.

"He was very scared; he was shaking, and his voice was shaking. I think he wanted me to hear as much as possible, so I could warn you. Whoever called didn't know I was there, and didn't even bother asking Artiom if he was alone. He started with the interrogation the minute Artiom answered. But when I left, Artiom gave me this look, it is hard to explain, it was almost as if he wanted me to warn you. He was probably warned by the caller not to talk to anyone. But I got this very strong feeling that he wanted you to know; it was the way he looked at me and gently nodded, almost like saying, 'Go tell Avo'."

"He is a good man," said Avo. "Papa used to work for him, and he told me his wife and Mama were childhood friends."

"Avo, listen. Artiom had good reason to be scared. Ayvazian is very dangerous. You cannot be careless with him. We all have to be careful, because he goes after entire families. What is the problem between you and Ayvazian?"

"I have not even met him," said Avo. "There is no problem with me that I know of. Mainly, I think he fooled Mama, and Lara did not end up where he had promised. I know she's not in Greece, so God knows what else he has lied about. And on this money transfer business, I bet it is the amount that's pissing him off."

"We just cannot sit here and wait, especially if he's upset about something," said Ruben. "Maybe we should talk to him, or maybe we should talk to the police."

Ruben was ten years older than Avo, but Avo still felt a huge responsibility not only to guide him through this thought process, but also to protect him. His sister was pregnant, and with both of his parents now diseased, Avo had already started thinking of his sister's family as an extension of his own.

"Rubo, listen. Ayvazian cannot be handled either by talking to the police or by talking to him directly. We have no high level connections anywhere, and he has them everywhere. He has connections with politicians, government Ministers, judges and especially the police. He also has Lara, and I think Lara has been caught trying to escape. She'll be in Armenia tomorrow."

Ruben was surprised not only by Avo's calm and calculating style, but also by his wealth of information. For the first time he saw him differently than the kid brother of his wife. Physically, Avo was slightly taller than Ruben, muscular, handsome, with high cheekbones accentuated by a genetically stubborn eagle nose and thick curly hair. For someone who did not know his age, it wouldn't be easy to guess that he had just turned sixteen. He could easily pass for eighteen or nineteen. And now his physical features were being further enhanced by his demeanor and mature calm.

"So what do we do?" asked Ruben, feeling uncomfortable about asking direction from his kid brother-in-law, but also curious to hear the rest of what Avo was thinking.

"First," said Avo, "I agree with you that the whole family could be in danger. So we need to treat this situation as a family threat, and not just something that happened to Lara or that may happen to me. Second, we need to assemble a small group of people that we fully trust who can help us. Rubo jan, whether we like it or not, you and I are now the core of this small group of people. Are you with me so far?"

"I'm with you. Go on."

"There are two others that I trust. One is Gago from Ashtarak. He was a close friend of Papa, and he's been here a few times recently. He's a good guy, and he's not scared like Artiom. He can help us."

"Okay," said Ruben, feeling the need to give his approval, even though Avo had not asked for it.

"The second is Paron Edik. You may have met him also. In fact, it was Edik who first came here, and later brought Gago with him. He lives in Vayots Dzor. Ayvazian is from the same region. Paron Edik probably knows more about Ayvazian than any of us."

"But he's a *drsetsi*," said Ruben, literally meaning an outsider. "How involved can he get?"

"In some ways he's more involved than any of us," said Avo, "but you're right to ask, how involved *should* he be? I'll talk to Gago about that."

They were quiet for a while, each drawn into his own thoughts.

"Rubo, who else can we trust here, in Saralandj or Aparan?"

"Avo, for what purpose? We can trust some people, but what is it that we're forming this group for?"

"We're getting ready to fight Ayvazian," said Avo with his characteristic way of announcing absolutes with finality. "I don't know yet exactly how. We won't do anything stupid, but it will be risky nonetheless. We won't create new dangers, Rubo, as the danger is already here. We just have to fight it."

"Many people can help if we don't put them in danger," said Ruben. "The key is to keep their anonymity. People are scared, and we should be too. But we're already in this. The others aren't."

"We shouldn't approach anyone who is scared," said Avo, "like Artiom, for example. No need to complicate things more than they already are. Things could get messy. Let's leave it here for now and think some more. When we know more, we can decide if we need anyone else. I was thinking of your cousin Serge, the policeman. But no need to talk to him yet. Let me talk to Gagik and Paron Edik first."

Avo saw Ruben out and then called Gagik.

"Sorry to bother you so late, Gago" he said, "but we need to talk."

"Is it urgent?" asked Gagik.

"Yes."

"I can be there in thirty minutes," said Gagik.

"I'll be very grateful," said Avo, but Gagik had hung up already.

Avo went to their bedroom and saw his siblings each engrossed in his or her task. The room was very quiet. Sona, the second oldest sister, was absorbed in a thick novel by Raffi, one of the most prolific Armenian novelists. The boys were still busy with schoolwork. The other girls, Arpi and Alisia, were doing needlework.

"I'm going to have a guest soon," said Avo, approaching Alisia. "It is Gagik from Ashtarak. Come prepare a few snacks for us."

"He's coming so late?" asked Alisia.

"I like Gagik," said Aram. "Can I join you?"

Everyone was now paying attention. It was not often that someone visited at that hour for no specific reason.

"He and I have to talk," said Avo. "There is no need for anyone else to be there. Sorry, Aram."

"Is there a problem?" asked Sona, putting her book aside. She was the oldest one in the house now, and her tone suggested that she had a right to know.

"No problem, *kurig* jan," said Avo warmly. "We just need to talk about work. I'll be back soon."

XXI

vo and Gagik sat by the stove for several hours. They had not touched any of the food set on the table. Avo was chain smoking, the glow from the burning stove flickering and casting mysterious shadows on his face and on the smoke coming out of his mouth and nostrils.

It was midnight when they were ready to call Laurian. Avo had briefed Gagik on all the details, and they had agreed that events might force them to take extreme measures, even possibly violence against the Ayvazians. They had also agreed that they needed to use Laurian's resources in Vardahovit, while keeping his personal involvement to a minimum. After Avo described to Gagik what he had seen in Sevajayr and Vardahovit, including the damning evidence in Hayk's photos, Gagik agreed that any possible encounter with Ayvazian would probably take place in the upper villages, and not in Saralandj or Aparan. Ayvazian had many connections in Aparan, but no real base of operations. They would keep Ruben in Saralandj to keep an eye on the family, and they would go to Vardahovit.

"Edik jan, good evening," said Gagik when they placed the call. "I hope I didn't wake you up."

"No, I'm up," said Laurian. "This is the best time of the night."

"Edik jan, I'm here in Saralandj with Avo. We need to come up and see you."

"Now?" asked Laurian. All his senses went on full alert.

"It would be best if we meet early in the morning," said Gagik. "So we're thinking of leaving here around five, to get there around eight. We'll have a few hours of sleep and come over."

"That's fine," said Laurian. "How much can you tell me now?"

"We'll go over everything when we get there," said Gagik. "But you had better reactivate full surveillance in the upper villages. Do you have anyone in Martashen?"

"Yes, but not as strong as here. We can watch from a distance down there."

"Activate anyway," said Gagik. "See you by eight. Get some rest, my friend, I have a feeling you're going to need it."

When Avo finally went back to their bedroom, everyone was sound asleep. Only the small light near his bed was on. He took off his shoes and went to bed with his clothes on. He'd have to get up in just a few hours, wake the family to say goodbye, go to Martha's house to alert Ruben of the plan, and leave with Gagik for Vardahovit.

"Let me get this straight," said Ayvazian, staring at Viktor's exhausted and sleepy face. "Everyone was plotting something in Al Barmaka's palace, no one knew the full intentions of anyone else, but they were cooperating at some level or another. Then the whole operation ended up with none other than Abo *effendi*, who spoiled everyone's plans and handed Lara to us, thinking that we would return her to Dubai and save face, and in return we'd let him into the Dubai market. Am I right so far?"

"Spot on," said Viktor.

"Is there a single plan in this whole story that hasn't blown up in someone's face?"

"I don't think so," said Viktor and started laughing. Ayvazian was not amused, but Viktor could not control his laughter. The entire web of failed schemes and counter-schemes hit him, in his extremely tired state, as superbly comical. Ayvazian would have rudely reprimanded him had he been his normal self, but he was in no mood for outbursts. He watched his nephew hold his sides and bend over roaring with laughter, and with a stern look waited for him to calm down. When Viktor finally came to his senses, Ayvazian stared at him for a few more minutes to make sure the bouts of laughter were gone for good, and then asked: "Who's in Sevajayr now?"

"Lara, the other girl from Yerevan and two bodyguards; we dropped Lara off over an hour ago."

"Now listen carefully," said Ayvazian. "I don't care how tired you are. What we need to do cannot wait. I don't think we can break Lara the normal way, by just beatings and stuff. For her, the stakes have to be higher than that. What do you know about this brother of hers, Avo, to whom she sent the money?"

"Nothing," said Viktor, "but we can find out. I think he's younger than her."

"We need him here," said Ayvazian. "Maybe our little beauty queen will come to her senses when she sees how she's hurting her loved ones."

"I'll send someone," said Viktor, now beginning to imagine what his uncle had in mind, and dreading the tasks he'd have to perform in his tired physical state. He wished he could have a few hours to rest before it all began.

"By the way," asked Ayvazian, "how did she behave on the flights?"

"She was fine on the flights," said Viktor. "I made a deal with her. Drugs or good behavior. She understood and was surprisingly well behaved, even though I could tell she was scared out of her mind. She was perspiring and shaking most of the time."

"Good," said Ayvazian. "I'm glad she's scared."

"But when we landed in Yerevan and I got her into the car, she started acting up. She kicked Hamo so hard in the leg that he was limping.

Then she screamed and tried to run away in the airport parking lot. That's when we held her down and gave her a shot. She's still asleep."

"Good. We'll deal with her soon. The second thing I want to tell you," continued Ayvazian, "is that we need to talk to Al Barmaka directly. I don't trust any of his staff to tell him the full story. Find out how we can talk to him."

"He's in China," complained Viktor.

"So?" snapped Ayvazian. "Find a way to contact him."

"Uncle, I see your point, I really do, but Al Barmaka will not agree to talk to us directly. I know this for a fact. Remember, we need to go through the same staff that you don't trust to get to him. That alone is a big problem."

"Try," ordered Ayvazian. "Then find out who is conducting the investigation from his end."

Viktor spent the rest of that morning on the phone. He first placed a call to Ano in Dubai, who in turn spoke with Manoj and then got back to Viktor. Then he called some of the men on his payroll in Aparan, asking about Avo. They proved to be useless, driving Viktor to new levels of frustration and fury, because no one knew where Avo was. He had left early in the morning without telling anyone anything, or so went the story in Saralandj. His sisters told the armed men who came to their house that they were about to go and alert the police, because they were worried about their brother. Ruben had gone to the police station in Aparan and filed a report with his cousin, who was on duty at the station. Avo was missing.

Then, just when Viktor thought he'd had his share of setbacks for the day, one of the guards in Sevajayr called with some unusual news.

"We caught a kid taking pictures," he said. "He has a fancy camera that I'm sure does not belong to him. He was taking pictures of the house. What do you want us to do with him?"

"Who the hell is he?" asked Viktor.

"He says he's from Shatin and is visiting friends in Sevajayr. He says the camera was a gift from a rich uncle in America, but he sounded like he was making fun of us."

"The kid was making fun of you?" screamed Viktor at the top of his lungs. "So now you've all turned into clowns up there? You better get the truth from him before Ayvazian gets there!"

"Viktor, listen, he's barely fifteen, and he doesn't seem scared. So maybe he's telling the truth, you know. Everyone in Armenia has a rich relative in America these days. Why not? Maybe someone sent him the camera and he was here showing it off. No need to overreact; his family will be looking for him. I don't think we should give the villagers any reason to wonder about us. Grabbing one of their own is totally different than bringing strangers here."

"You listen to me and listen well," said Viktor. "Fuck the villagers! You have thirty minutes to break that kid, find out the truth, and call me. And if what you tell me turns out not to be the truth, you're finished, do you understand? We'll bury you with him right there!" With that, Viktor hung up.

Twenty minutes earlier, Hayk's cousin Sago, who had been keeping him company at the stakeout, frantically called Agassi to tell him that the thugs got Hayk.

"Talk slowly, *balés*," said Agassi. "What exactly happened?"

"I was in the loft watching," said Sago, trying to stay as calm as possible. "Hayk was coming into the barn. One of the guards saw him and yelled, 'Boy, come here!' When Hayk ignored him, the guard came after him and grabbed him at the entrance of the barn. He saw the camera and started yelling, calling Hayk a thief, then dragged him into the house."

"Just stay in the loft and watch," said Agassi, "and stay out of sight. Keep your phone close and on silent. I'll call you back soon."

Agassi ran to the main house, where Laurian was meeting with Gagik, Avo and Saro. They had word that two cars had arrived earlier that morning, dropped someone at the Sevajayr house and driven away. There was still one car parked in front of the house and they guessed there were at least two guards and possibly two captives inside, the presumption being that there must have been at least one captive inside before the new arrival; otherwise, the place wouldn't have been guarded in the first place.

Hayk's capture had changed the nature of the challenge entirely. Laurian seemed to be the most upset, partly because he felt personally responsible for Hayk's fate.

"They won't dare hurt him," said Gagik, trying to comfort Laurian. "They may slap him around a bit to find out if someone's put him up to taking pictures; but if he holds to his story, they'll let him go."

"He's seen the inside of the house," said Laurian with an intensity of concentration that caused concern in Saro. "He may have seen more than enough for them to decide it is not safe to let him go."

"Sago is watching," said Agassi. "He'll tell us if there is any movement. I don't think anything will happen soon; they'll have to call Ayvazian to get orders. He will want to know details, which will take time. So we have some time to think. In the meantime, I have to tell Hayk's father."

"Yes, by all means," said Laurian, "tell Varujan; let him join us."

Then Laurian's phone rang. It was Nerses from the roadside restaurant.

"I just got word that two SUVs left Martashen," he said. "Ayvazian is in one of them, and Viktor is in the other. Each has an armed driver, but no other passengers. Ayvazian is sitting in the front passenger seat. Viktor is asleep in the back seat."

"Thanks," said Laurian. "Let us know when they pass by you."

Laurian turned back to his visitors, his face serious and his gaze intense and focused. "Events may force our next actions," he said calmly. "We probably need to put aside all the conventional wisdom that we have lived by until now."

"You sound like you're giving a war speech," said Gagik with a chuckle, deliberately trying to lighten up the mood. "What's the story?"

"I don't mean to sound dramatic," said Laurian, "but in fact a war speech is what may be called for. Ayvazian and his nephew are headed this way as we speak. Hayk is being held. There are two other captives in there, one of whom could be Lara, but we're not sure. She told Avo she'd be in Armenia this morning and that she was not free; she also specifically warned him about Ayvazian. So she could be the new arrival. The question is, what do we now do?"

"Edik jan," said Gagik, "I understand that the moment for decisive action is here, but it is essential that you keep a low profile. I think the local villagers should handle this. The only exception is Avo, given his family's stake in this. Even I cannot have a high profile. You have to trust us on this."

Everyone was nodding in silence. Laurian thought about Gagik's words, and realized that the old revolutionary was right. Whatever needed to be done should be done by the local villagers, and then covered up by them. External involvement would unnecessarily complicate future investigations. Once a plan was clearly set in front of them, the villagers would also act in a more coordinated way if they were left alone to implement it.

"I agree," he said, "but only partially. Gago, you and I are already deep into this. We can pretend to be in the sidelines, but let's face it, we're not. The local villagers and Avo will do what needs to be done, and they'll be the ones giving testimony later, but we'll plan this together. You and I will watch closely and stand ready to participate if need be. We cannot just sit here. Now, let's plan in detail what needs to be done."

They did not have much time to plan every detail, nor to pretend that what they had to do could be done without bloodshed. Sergey and Viktor Ayvazian had to die. Nothing short of that could solve the problems that the Galians were facing. But two bodyguards were coming with them, and there were other guards in Sevajayr as well. What about them?

As they started planning the operation, a cloud of hesitation crept into Laurian's thoughts. It was not about the risks that they were about to take, even though these were considerable. It was not about fear of failure, or about all that could go wrong. With Gagik's help, the planning of the details of the operation were on solid ground. He looked carefully at the faces of the men in his living room. Avo, Gagik and Varujan were absorbed in planning the operation. Agassi was listening intently. Saro was listening too, but seemed to be absorbed in thoughts far beyond the moment.

"Saro," said Laurian, "are you okay?"

Saro looked at Laurian for a long moment, as if trying to read his mind, and slightly shook his head. Noticing the distraction, the others stopped talking and were waiting for Saro to answer. What Saro said next shocked Laurian; he couldn't have voiced his own hesitations and doubts more succinctly.

"If we do this, are we better than them?" asked Saro. There was total silence in the room. Gagik gave Laurian a confused look, but Laurian was focused on Saro.

"What do you mean?" asked Laurian, even though he knew exactly what Saro meant.

"We're planning to kill several people today, because some of them have harmed Avo's family. That's exactly what Ayvazian would have done. Are we better than him?"

Each in his own way, the others had resolved or bypassed that question by the sheer inevitability of what they needed to do. There was no other option, which, for them, meant there was no good reason to question it.

"Are we?" Laurian echoed Saro's question, turning to everyone in the room. "We need to consider Saro's question seriously before we go any further."

If Gagik was as frustrated as Avo with this interruption, he did not show it. He understood the importance of having everyone sign off on the entire mission, and not just on the specific operational details. They should have done that before delving into the details of the plan, and Laurian himself would probably have insisted on it had they not been so pressed for time, given the fact that Ayvazian and Viktor were on their way. But it wasn't too late.

"None of us has killed anyone before," continued Laurian, "let alone murdered anyone in cold blood. And yet, here we are planning to kill several people—five? Six? It depends on how many guards are in Sevajayr. Why? Have we turned into murderers like Ayvazian? Are we after revenge? What do we want?"

"We want to live in peace," said Avo, "and we cannot do that as long as Ayvazian is around. I have to protect my family, whatever it takes."

"We all agree with you there, Avo," said Gagik, even though he was not one-hundred percent sure where Laurian stood on this issue. "But there's more to it than that; otherwise, not everyone who is here today would have been involved. Ayvazian isn't a direct threat to my family or to Edik's. So why are *we* here?"

The room fell silent again. Saro appeared caught in some inner conflict and was visibly uncomfortable. Agassi, not being prepared for so much serious soul searching, was caught by surprise and did not have much to contribute. Laurian was glad that the issue was on the table, but understood the need to get past it quickly.

"Let me put it differently," continued Gagik, when no one else said anything. "Whose enemy is Ayvazian? Avo's, for all that he's done to the Galians? Agassi's, because he kidnapped Hayk? Saro's, because he set up shop in the upper villages?" Gagik looked at everyone for a minute and added: "I wouldn't even think of killing him if it was just those things, and even if he was my sworn personal enemy on top of all that. I wouldn't think of killing him for a pure personal vendetta either."

Avo and Varujan looked at Gagik, confused. Gagik was the most active in planning the killings with them, and had not even batted an eyelash at the thought that the guards would have to be eliminated too, even if they were innocent of the big crimes committed by Ayvazian. He was the one who insisted that the operation should leave no loose ends.

"We are dealing with something much bigger than any of us," weighed in Laurian at last. "I agree with Gago. I wouldn't think of killing anyone because they have harmed one of us. The problem with Ayvazian is not that he is our enemy or that he's wronged one of us. The problem with Ayvazian is that he is the enemy of this nation, of its freedom, of its independence, and it just so happens that we've stumbled into him here and in Saralandj. Unfortunately, neither law enforcement nor the courts here can deal with him yet, as Saro keeps reminding us. One day they will. Until that day, I see this as a necessary mission of retribution *because* it is bigger than all of us."

By hearing Saro's questions out loud and thinking about his own hesitation, Laurian had already overcome his doubts. But Saro did not look convinced. He had agreed with Laurian all along that the point of their involvement would not be to solve the country's problems, that they would not launch a crusade against Ayvazian, and that they would not start something that they could not win. Laurian and Gagik were now broadening the agenda in ways that made their involvement way past their legitimate realm of responsibilities.

"What gives us the right to assign that mission to ourselves?" he asked.

"Remember, Saro, we did not choose Ayvazian," said Laurian. "He chose us. He chose Lara, then Samvel, then Sevajayr."

"Saro," said Gagik, "I too am worried about killing innocent people today. But how many innocent people have been killed by him, and how many more will die if we don't act? You all have seen the pictures in Sevajayr. If we act today, we will kill Ayvazian and his men. If we don't act, we will cause the deaths of many more innocent victims that fall into his hands. The way I see it, we have no other choice. What do you think?"

"Can everyone in this room honestly tell me they are willing to have the deaths of these people on their conscience without a problem?" asked Saro.

Gagik checked his watch. Ayvazian and Viktor probably were in Yeghegnadzor by now, giving them at most an hour to finalize the plan and take their positions. He noticed Laurian was getting ready to say something, and raised his hand to stop him.

"Have you heard of 'Project Nemesis?'" he asked, looking straight at Saro. The intensity in Gagik's gaze disarmed Saro, and reminded Laurian of the old *Khev Gago* of fifteen years ago.

Saro shook his head.

"How about Soghomon Tehlirian?" asked, Gagik, not moving his eyes off Saro. "Have you heard of him?"

Saro looked confused. He had heard of Tehlirian, but did not understand why Gagik was bringing him up now. Laurian worried about Gagik going off on one his long story-telling jags, thus losing a lot of time. But Gagik had a different strategy in mind.

"We don't have much time," he said, "so I'll summarize it for you. He was the young man who, in broad daylight, in front of many witnesses, shot and killed Talaat Pasha, the Grand Vizir of the Ottoman Turks, and one of the main architects of the genocide, in Berlin, Germany. He did not deny what he had done. A German court tried him and acquitted him. He was found 'not guilty,' Saro jan. By a German court! I will not go into the details of the defense, but let me tell you this: Tehlirian was not only 'not guilty,' but he lived with the clearest conscience of all for the rest of his life. He had eliminated a mass murderer, an atrocious war criminal, a man who had the blood of over a million innocent women and children on his hands, and an enemy of his nation. Yes, he shot him in cold blood in broad daylight, but that was a mission of 'necessary retribution' too, like Edik said earlier."

"That was some eighty-five years ago," mumbled Saro, "and he killed an Ottoman Turk, not one of his own."

"That may be, but sometimes our most dangerous enemies are right here among us, my friend. And Talaat's assassination was part of a broader operation that targeted Armenian traitors as well. The enemies who are 'one of us' are much worse; make no mistake about that. They are much more dangerous than foreign enemies. Just to be clear," continued Gagik, tapping his hand on the coffee table for emphasis, "I am *not* comparing what we're about to do with that operation. We're nowhere near that. But the *moral justification* for what we're about to do is equally strong. A lot of good came from the Berlin shooting. You really should study that one day. And a lot of good will come from what we're planning to do. So, to answer your two questions: Yes, I can live with these deaths on my conscience, and yes, we *are* better than Ayvazian."

Ջ Ջ Ջ

The road to Sevajayr was in serious disrepair. There were sections that had practically disappeared, with all traces of asphalt wiped out over the years. In some parts even the foundation pavement had been destroyed, with large pieces of stone broken loose and scattered around. The villagers rightly assumed that the drivers bringing Ayvazian and Viktor knew the road pretty well by now, including which sections to avoid. Maneuvering around the potholes and the rocky obstacles forced a driver to follow a very specific course, often getting dangerously close to the edge overlooking a drop of several hundred meters.

They had word that the car with the unoccupied front passenger seat was in the lead, and the one with a passenger in the front seat was following closely. So Viktor, who was reported to be asleep in the back seat, was in the first car.

Saro went back to Vardahovit village, and held a meeting with some of the villagers in the municipality office; he had no specific agenda. He just needed to establish a strong alibi that he had been in his office that afternoon.

Agassi went down to check the beehives in the valley. Varujan and Avo were waiting behind the huge boulders on the side of the road, right across from where they expected the accident to occur.

They heard the cars before seeing them; a few minutes later the first car appeared around the curve, with the second one following a few meters behind. The driver did in fact seem to know the road well. There were occasional landslides and rock slides from the slopes above, and it was not unusual to run into large rocks newly fallen into the middle of the road. Once he had had to move a few heavy rocks to the side in order to pass. So he was not surprised when he came upon two new rocks on the right side of the road. He swung to the left, coming to about a foot from the edge of the road, without slowing down much. The passage looked clear once he bypassed the rocks; but he did not notice the sharp wedge of an old rusty pipe stuck into the ground, protruding at an angle directly in front of his left wheel. The tire blew with a loud thud and the car swung to the left; the driver pushed hard on the brakes but the car had already started its headfirst plunge into the ravine below.

The second car came to a screeching halt inches from the edge. Ayvazian and the driver, who had rolled up their windows to avoid the dust left by the first car, rolled them down again, and were about to get out when out of nowhere two faces appeared on Ayvazian's side of the car. They looked like villagers but each of them was holding a revolver. Varujan's gun was pointed at the driver.

"Do not make a move," said Varujan looking past Ayvazian and straight at the driver.

"Paron Ayvazian," said Avo, holding his revolver an inch away from Ayvazian's eye, "I am Avetis Samveli Galian. I heard you were looking for me in Aparan, and I decided to pay you a visit."

Both were speechless, frozen in their seats. The crashing noise of the car rolling down the ravine stopped. Varujan climbed into the back seat and, moving behind the driver, reached over and took his handgun from his waist.

"Give me your cell phone," he told the driver, who turned and looked over at Ayvazian.

"Give me your cell phone," repeated Varujan, pushing the nozzle of his gun hard against the driver's neck.

The driver handed over his cell phone.

"Ayvazian," ordered Varujan, "give me your gun and cell phone, now!" Avo, still standing by the window, dug his gun into Ayvazian's cheek. Ayvazian slowly handed over his gun and cell phone, and Avo quickly climbed into the back seat.

"Wait for a moment," said Varujan.

Fifty meters up the slope on the right side of the road, Laurian was watching from the scope of his rifle; its crosshairs were centered on the driver. Gagik was lying next to him and watching with his binoculars.

A few minutes later Agassi called him. "The two that went over the cliff are both dead," he said.

"Touch nothing," said Varujan. "See you later." He turned to Avo, nodded, then sent Laurian a text message—*done here, on to the next task.*

"Drive," Varujan told the driver. "Back up a little first, then make a sharp right, and a sharp left to bypass those rocks. After that the road is clear all the way to the house."

Laurian and Gagik left their post and went to Gagik's car, which they had parked on a dirt side road behind a huge boulder. They had taken his car because Laurian's car could be more easily recognized. They waited in the car for further news from Varujan.

As they drove, Ayvazian seemed to come out of his stupor.

"Do you kids know what you're doing?" he asked in the driest tone he could muster.

"I suggest you stay quiet," said Avo calmly, "it is too early to discover your tongue. I'll tell you when it's time."

The element of surprise was effective in so many ways that Ayvazian fell quiet again. The fate of the first car, with his nephew most probably dead, hadn't been fully processed by him yet; the confidence and arrogance of these poor villagers was unbelievable and yet very real at the same time; this type of challenge to him and his authority, in his own region, was inconceivable and unprecedented, even from other oligarchs, let alone from these peasants.

"Who's in the house?" Varujan asked the driver, who turned and looked at Ayvazian again. This time Varujan did not push his gun against his neck; he just cocked it and pushed it into Ayvazian's cheek.

"Any one of these potholes could force my finger to accidentally squeeze the trigger," he told Ayvazian.

"Tell him," Ayvazian said.

"I don't know exactly myself. Edgard, who was driving the other car, was here earlier this morning. He knows who's in the house."

"Well, I'm afraid Edgard cannot talk any longer," said Varujan with such cold-hearted indifference that it sent a chill down the driver's spine. "What's your name, by the way?"

"Hamo," said the driver.

"So *you're* Hamo," said Varujan, without giving any explanation of what he meant. "Talk, Hamo. Who's in the house?"

"We have Abkar and Serge," said Hamo, "and a few guests."

"Abkar and Serge. Are they armed drivers like you?"

Hamo looked at Ayvazian again. He nodded.

"Yes," said Hamo.

"And these guests," said Varujan, "they don't happen to be two lovely ladies and a kid, do they?"

If they hadn't already, both men now realized beyond any doubt that none of what was happening was an accident or a coincidence. These peasants knew too much. Ayvazian thought that they would have only one chance to stop them, and that would be when they arrived at the house and the others noticed that something was amiss. He knew that alerting them was impossible, which meant that he had to count on the wits of Abkar and Serge. For the first time since the accident, Ayvazian began to perspire heavily.

They saw the house behind a row of poplars. It was early afternoon, and the sun hit the windows facing the road, while the front door was in the shade.

"Park next to the Lexus, away from the door," said Varujan, and then he called Sago.

"Are you still there?" he asked.

"Ha. Nothing has happened. Hayk is still inside."

"We'll be there in a minute. Stay hidden."

The Lexus SUV was parked perpendicular to the façade of house, next to the front door. They parked to the left of it, so that the Lexus was between them and the main door. Varujan told them not to move or Avo would not hesitate to shoot; then he got out quickly and knocked on the door. He had Hamo's pistol in his hand.

The door opened and Abkar appeared at the threshold. He had recognized the approaching Mercedes SUV as Ayvazian's; he had expected to greet the boss when Varujan pointed Hamo's pistol at his chest and shot without a moment's hesitation. The man collapsed. Varujan ran in and saw the second guard scrambling to get up from his chair.

"Don't move!" he ordered. He went up to him, took his gun and phone, and walked backwards to the front door, where Abkar lay dead in a pool of blood. Standing at the doorway, he shot Serge with Serge's pistol in the left shoulder. Serge screamed with pain and sank into his chair. Then Varujan shot him again in the chest. Serge was dead too.

He quickly surveyed the main room. There were two heavy armchairs, with Serge's bleeding body slumped in one of them. There were three side chairs in the corner by the window placed around a small round table, and an old and extremely dirty sofa against one of the walls. There were two closed doors off the main room but he did not hear anyone stirring. Although he was impatient to go check the rooms, he did not want to leave Avo alone with Ayvazian and Hamo.

He peeked outside and saw that everyone was still in the car. "Bring them in slowly," he shouted. They marched in with their hands over their heads; Avo held his gun on them from behind.

When Ayvazian saw the two bodies he jerked back only to find Varujan's gun pointed straight at his face. "You don't know what you're dealing with," he said.

"You have the wire?" Varujan asked Avo, ignoring Ayvazian.

"Right here," said Avo, pulling a roll of heavy nylon fishing wire from his pocket.

"Good. Tie their hands behind them. Move to those chairs," he ordered the men, pointing to the three side chairs. They put them at opposite ends of the room, with their backs to each other. Avo bound their hands together and then tied their torsos to the back of the chair. When both men were secure, Avo took a small roll of duct tape from his pocket and taped their mouths. Varujan went to check the other rooms.

"You watch them," he told Avo. "If anyone moves, shoot."

The fact was that the lack of any sound was bothering him, and he didn't want Avo to go into any of the rooms before he checked what was in them. He opened the door to one of the rooms and saw Hayk gagged and tied to a chair. On a twin bed a woman lay on her side, hands tied behind her back and feet tied together. She appeared to be unconscious.

Varujan went to his son, untied him and removed the gag.

"Papa," whispered Hayk, "did you get them all?" He sounded tired and groggy, but seemed fine.

"We got them, *balés*. Are you okay?"

"I'm fine. They just hit me and tried to make me tell them how I got the camera, but I didn't say anything, Pap, really, no matter how hard they hit me, I said nothing."

"Shhhh," said Varujan, worried that Hayk may mention Laurian's name. But his eyes were wet. He held his son tight for a moment, so proud of him that his chest hurt. "You did well, Hayk. No need to give any details now. Are you hurt?"

"No, I don't think so. My head was bleeding a little earlier, but it stopped." Varujan checked where he was pointing on his head, and felt the clotted blood. Whatever it was, it had to wait.

"I saw them give her an injection," he said, pointing at the woman on the bed. Varujan untied her, felt her pulse, and then came out with Hayk. There was no telling how long it would take for the woman to wake up, but at least she was alive. He went straight to the other room.

"What's going on?" asked Avo when he saw him, impatient to find out if Lara was somewhere in the house.

"Just one more minute, Avo jan, I beg you. Give me one more minute." And Varujan opened the second door.

Lara was lying on the bed, hands tied behind her, not fully unconscious but very groggy, and gagged. Varujan recognized the resemblance with Avo instantly.

"Avo, I believe this one's yours," he said from the door. "You come here and free her."

Avo was already at the door by the time Varujan had finished his sentence. He ran to his sister, undid the gag and held her his chest. "Untie her," said Varujan. Avo untied her and made her sit up in bed. She was limp, eyes bloodshot, her hair damp with perspiration, her face bruised and makeup smeared around her eyes. She was wearing jeans and a sweater; her bare feet were blue from the tight rope around her ankles.

"Kurig jan," whispered Avo in her ear, holding her tightly and running his hand through her hair. "Kurig jan…"

"Papa, two more down, two to go. Hayk is fine. The girls are drugged but seem otherwise unharmed. Lara is safe. Meet us up there as planned; we'll leave in ten minutes. Send Saro to take the others."

Agassi hung up and called Saro, who called Gagik. Then he got into Varujan's old Russian car and drove up a steep hill just outside of Sevajayr village.

The plan was for Saro to come to the house and take Lara, Hayk, Sago and the other girl back to the village first, and then to Laurian's house. But when Saro called Gagik, Gagik told him to wait in the village instead. "We're right here," he said. "It would be easier if we go to them. We'll bring the kids home."

"Is that a good idea?" asked Saro. "Ayvazian will see you."

Laurian took the phone from Gagik. "Saro jan," he said, "I cannot just go home and wait. We are headed to the house. We can be there before you. You can come too, if you want, but there's no need. I'll take the kids straight to my place and call you."

Lara came to gradually, but when she saw Avo she returned to full consciousness so fast that she felt her heart jump out of her chest. She accepted some water and clung to Avo for dear life.

"Kurig jan, you're safe," said Avo, holding her close.

He introduced Varujan, who gave her a warm smile and said, "Welcome home."

"You've grown," said Lara softly, eyes glued to Avo. "You look just like I saw you in my dream." Then Lara suddenly realized where she was and jumped from the edge of the bed, giving out a scream. "Where are they?" she yelled. "Be careful, Avo, they'll be back."

Avo took her hand, drew her down beside him and stroked her hair.

"No, Lara, they won't be back." He spoke quietly hoping to calm her. "We'll have plenty of time to talk later, but now we need to move. There is an ugly scene in the room outside that I don't want you to see, but I'm afraid it is the only way out."

Lara was still absorbing his first sentence.

"They won't be back?" she whispered. "They're gone?"

"They're gone so far away that they cannot come back. You're safe, and now you're free; but the scene in the front room is very messy, Lara. We need to walk out of here and out of the next room, and we need to walk fast. I want you to cover your face and eyes. I will guide your steps. Just hold on to me and walk fast. Can you do that?"

"We're free and we're safe," she repeated, stupefied. "What is it that you don't want me to see?"

Avo was painfully aware that they needed to move quickly. He found her shoes and helped her put them on. Her knees were shaking, but she could keep her balance and looked alert.

"There is blood and unfinished business, Lara. There are dead bodies. You don't need to see that. Someone will take you to safety and I'll follow soon. I promise. I will not lose you again."

"I will never cover my eyes again," said Lara standing up. "I will walk with you; I want to see what's out there."

Avo knew there was no point in arguing with her. He led her into the living room, but he had a good grip around her waist. Lara looked wide-eyed at the sight of the two men tied to the chairs and the two bloody bodies. She recognized Serge, but Abkar's face was not visible to her. She stared at Hamo, who was facing the room where they had kept her. Then her eyes came to rest on the other man. His back was to her, and he was sitting motionless in the chair facing the wall. She recognized him. There was no mistaking the round bald head and the heavy torso.

"Avo, *kyank*, what have you done?" she whispered. To Avo's surprise, the blood and dead bodies did not upset her. But she was aghast at the enormity of what Avo and his friends had undertaken.

"We are free and we are safe," whispered Avo in her ear. "All scores will be settled today, yours and Papa's."

"Papa's?" she whispered.

"Yes, I'll explain later. Now we have to move. A friend will be here soon to take you somewhere safe."

Lara walked across the room to face Ayvazian. She stood there staring at his face for a long time, as if unable to decide what to do. Spit in his face? Kick him? Grab the gun from Avo and shoot him? But Avo came over and held her, as if reading her mind.

"We have a better plan," he said. "Now you need to get out of here."

The woman in the first room was beginning to wake up. Lara went into the room and gave her some water, talked to her, told her all was well, and that she was safe. Gradually, she sat up also, and started gaining consciousness, but Varujan was very anxious to leave.

"We have to go," he told Avo, peeking into the room. "We can't have too much time go by between the two accidents. We need to leave now. The Mayor will be here any moment."

"Hayk, go get Sago," said Varujan. "He'll return with you to the village."

Hayk ran over to the barn and returned with Sago.

"Saro, the Mayor of this village will take you, the girl, Hayk and Sago to the village," Avo told Lara. "Then you'll be moved to another friend's house. All is very safe. Every person you see from here on will be a trusted friend. You have nothing to worry about."

"No," said Lara firmly. "They can go to the village with Saro; I will come with you. You cannot keep me away from this now."

The other girl was now on her feet, with her shoes on. She'd be ready to leave when Saro arrived. Avo left Lara with her and stepped back into the living room. Just then, Laurian and Gagik walked in.

"Small change in plans," said Laurian, surveying the room in awe. "I couldn't bring myself to go back home. We'll take the kids home from here." Neither Varujan nor Avo was surprised; they were happy to have the two around. Gagik went around the room and studied every detail carefully. The position of the two bodies was right. All they had to do was remove the evidence that anyone else had been in the house.

While Gagik was busy inspecting the murder scene, Laurian went to Hayk and gave him a long hug and kissed him on the forehead. Then he walked over to Ayvazian. The plan had been that Ayvazian should not see him or know of his involvement. But Laurian stood in front of him and looked long and hard into his shocked and terrified eyes. He saw his fear, his confusion, his lack of understanding of what was happening and his total surprise at seeing him. Then he turned his back and walked away.

As Laurian walked back to the center of the living room, Lara emerged from the first bedroom. They almost walked into each other. The surprise on her face was no match for the complex currents of emotions that ran through Laurian's mind and heart. She simply hadn't expected the Mayor to look like that, and was surprised. But he saw so much in that wide-eyed, surprised face in one instant that it would take him weeks to process and decipher. Even though he had heard that Lara was supposed to be beautiful, he was not prepared for the face that was staring at him. But the silent exchange between them was much more than that; this was the moment he had always imagined as the vindication of Sirarpi, to see Lara alive, free, safe, to see Ayvazian defeated. This was the culmination of months of anguish. *Do not be surprised,* he said in his mind to the baffled beauty staring at him, *from the beginning I have searched for you...*

They led Ayvazian back to the car, with his hands still tied behind his back, and put him in the passenger seat as before. Then they took Hamo and made him sit in the driver's seat, with his hands still tied. Varujan had already wiped his fingerprints from the guns and put Hamo's pistol in Serge's hand and Serge's pistol in Abkar's hand. He had also changed Abkar's position slightly and returned their cell phones to their pockets.

They climbed into the back seat, Lara in the middle, Varujan behind Hamo and Avo behind Ayvazian. Then Varujan cut the fishing wire from Hamo's hands and removed the tape from his mouth.

"Drive," he said, pointing with his gun to the road bearing right toward the dirt road. "I believe you've already been to the place we're going."

Varujan was not sure of the exact location where Samvel Galian had fallen to his death. Agassi had a better idea, because he had visited the general area a few times with Laurian. Avo had also been there once with Laurian. They had established that Hamo, who was Ayvazian's personal driver and the most experienced in driving around the upper villages and over the slopes where Ayvazian did his goat hunting, had been present when the accident happened. His testimony, signed by him, was in the police records, which Saro had managed to see.

Varujan was directing Hamo, but had not yet told him their intended destination. There was no point in alerting him or Ayvazian about what they meant to do. The road, if one could call a pair of tire tracks on the rocky slopes a road, was treacherous, but Hamo was managing the drive very well.

Lara was resting her head on Avo's shoulder. She suddenly looked up with a jerk. "How is Mama?" she asked. Avo just held her tighter, kissed her head, but did not say anything. Lara tried to look up at him again, but he held her close, as if to keep her still. Lara knew then that her mother was dead. She closed her eyes and surrendered to Avo's embrace.

At the end of one of the steeper climbs they came to an open field, where they saw Agassi standing next to his car at the far end. Hamo parked next to him.

"Let's have a look around," said Varujan. "You stay in the car," he added, pointing his gun at Ayvazian.

They got out of the car, Lara holding on to Avo, Varujan keeping a close eye on Hamo. Agassi was standing right at the edge of a cliff.

"Is this where Samvel Galian had his accident?" asked Agassi, looking at Hamo. Both Lara and Avo were on full alert now, looking down the steep drop and then back at Hamo. Lara shuddered at the thought of her father making that fall. The drop was very sharp, almost perpendicular, with virtually no slope or incline. There were only tall, angular boulders, lined up densely at irregular intervals stretching several hundred meters down, looking almost like human statues standing in silence down the cliff. Lara imagined her father taking the fall, crashing and breaking bones against those boulders on the way down, and tears began to well up in her eyes. The fury that Avo had managed to suppress so well began to rise again, just like the storm that had gathered in his chest when his mother died. He let go of Lara and walked close to Hamo.

"Is this where it happened?" he asked, still appearing calm. "We know that you were with him at the time."

"It was here," said Hamo, now trembling. "He had his back to the cliff and was surveying the field, and then he took a step backwards, stepped on a log and slipped, and …"

With incredible speed Avo launched himself at him and pushed him over. They watched as Hamo rolled down the cliff, banging against pointed rocks, and finally came to rest several hundred meters below. His torso was broken and his limbs spread over the human-shaped boulders, which looked from above as if they were carrying him over their shoulders.

Ayvazian was struggling in the car. He had somehow managed to open the car door and was about to roll out, with his hands still tied behind him. Avo walked over and pulled him to the ground. He was kicking violently, his face red with anger and fear. No one in Armenia would believe the events of today, even if presented with evidence. No one would believe that someone as powerful and ruthless as Ayvazian could be taken and destroyed with apparent ease by a handful of powerless peasants. The shock of the absolute implausibility of what was happening left Ayvazian totally speechless, overwhelmed by the terror and impotence of an animal being led to slaughter.

They removed the duct tape and forced him to walk to the edge of the cliff, where they sat him down, legs dangling into the void below, holding his shoulders to make sure that his struggle to set his hands free didn't send him into the abyss prematurely. Agassi and Varujan were holding his arms on either side. Avo approached him from behind; Ayvazian had his eyes shut tight, shaking with fear.

"You have only one chance to save your life," said Avo calmly. "Tell me why you killed my father. Tell me the truth, and tell it to me right now, if you want to avoid his fate."

This glimmer of hope helped Ayvazian take a breath. He wanted to turn back to look at Avo, but Agassi and Varujan held him down firmly. He opened his eyes, saw the rocks below, and shut them again. He was still shaking.

"The truth, now!" said Avo again, placing his hand on his back.

"He wouldn't let us have Lara," mumbled Ayvazian. "We made him a very good offer, but he refused."

Lara moved next to Avo, who took out his knife and cut Ayvazian's hands free. Varujan slipped Ayvazian's cell phone into his coat pocket, and just as Agassi loosened his grip on him, Lara and Avo pushed him. Ayvazian went down screaming and kicking, his heavy torso caroming off the rocks with loud thuds. He landed a few meters from Hamo, face down, as still as the silent and unseeing rocks around him.

Epilogue

The villagers' testimonies were all regarded as plausible beyond any reasonable doubt. Agassi, who was visiting his friend the beekeeper in Sevajayr, had heard the sound of an automobile crashing on the other side of the valley. He and Arakel, the bee keeper, had dropped everything and run to investigate; it was a good ten minute run from the beehives to the crash site. They had approached carefully, afraid that the car might blow up. The car was totally demolished. They had seen two bodies, one in the driver's seat and one in the back. Carefully, they had checked their pulses from the open windows, and, having determined that they were both dead, had touched nothing else, and called Mayor Saro to report the incident.

Mayor Saro had received the call and immediately called the police in Yeghegnadzor, reporting an accident with two fatalities in Sevajayr.

Approximately at the same time, the two teenage boys, Sago and Hayk, who were playing by the deserted barn in Sevajayr, had heard gun shots from the house across the street. The second and third shots were within a second or two of each other. There was a car parked outside the house, but the boys had not paid much attention to it until they heard the shots. Since neither had a watch, they could not tell exactly what time it was, but they figured it was early afternoon. They had gone over and seen the front door partially open. They had pushed the door and seen the two dead bodies, one on the floor and one in the chair. Too scared to look further, they had left the place in a hurry and called Sago's father, who had told them not to touch anything, and then called the police department in Yeghegnadzor to report a possible double murder in Sevajayr.

It was much later that afternoon that two shepherds had seen two bodies over the rocks at the foot of the steep cliffs in Sevajayr and had gone to investigate. Even from a distance, they could tell from the contorted shapes of the torsos and limbs that both men were dead. They too had called the police department in Yeghegnadzor to report two deaths.

No one could establish a connection between the three incidents, other than the fact that all of those involved were somehow related to Ayvazian. The first looked very much like a car accident. Both bodies were confirmed dead from the car crash. They both had their guns, wallets, money and identification cards still on them. Nothing seemed to be moved or taken, and there was nothing to challenge Agassi's story.

The second incident looked like two men had shot each other. The analysis indicated that Abkar had shot Serge first in the shoulder, and then just as he shot the second time, aiming at Serge's chest, Serge had shot back. The boys did not recall anyone else coming to the house or leaving. They said they had been playing around the barn and in the fields all afternoon, and did not notice any car traffic. No one else had been in that area, as both the house and the barn were deserted and none of the villagers had any business being there. Checking inside the house, the police had found no sign of anyone else having been in the house. The place looked dirty and deserted, and other than some bottles of water and pieces of leftover bread, there was no evidence that anyone had actually lived there. Sago and Hayk did not remember when the car parked outside had arrived. They said that when they got there in the early afternoon, the car was already there.

There were no witnesses to the Ayvazian and Hamo incident. Only Nerses remembered seeing both the Mercedes and the Lexus SUVs drive by his restaurant a few minutes past noon, but he had no idea who the passengers were. As far as anyone could make out, there was no one else near the field where the fall had taken place. Ayvazian's car was still there, and the keys were found in Hamo's pocket. Hamo's cell phone and gun were in the car. Ayvazian's gun was not found, and everyone assumed that if he did carry a gun that day, it must have slipped from him during his fall, and it probably was lost somewhere among the rocks. There was no evidence of any other tracks to suggest that the two men may have had company. Either they had fallen together by accident, or Ayvazian had slipped and Hamo had tried to help him but they had both tumbled. It was even possible that they had had an argument leading to a fight, resulting in both of them rolling down the cliffs.

Six deaths in one afternoon in Sevajayr was totally unheard of, especially when someone like Ayvazian was involved. But just as Ayvazian himself had feared, no one even gave the villagers a second thought. This was way over the heads of the peasants and looked like a carefully planned and executed plot by a competing oligarch. Ayvazian had many enemies, any one of whom would have the motive and the means to execute something like this. Whoever did it had done a superb job of covering their tracks. Several weeks later, the police closed the case as two accidents and one double murder.

It was an emotionally overcharged night for all of them. Saro and Agassi were there for a while recounting the events of the afternoon, but took their leave early with Hayk and Sago, after enjoying one of Vartiter's feasts. Gagik, Avo and Lara spent the night and sat with Laurian a long time talking, recounting and catching up. Lara had bathed, changed her clothes, retouched her light makeup, and sat leaning against Avo on the sofa wrapped in one of Laurian's light blankets. The previous evening she had been a prisoner in Istanbul, and now she was sitting with Avo, in this strange house, with two strangers who had proven to be the best friends she and her brother had ever known. In order to fight back the wave of emotions building up in his chest, Laurian wanted to talk of future plans, and as usual had many ideas and questions, but had to suppress them all. This wasn't the right time; there'd be enough time for that when he returned to Saralandj as soon as things had settled down.

They left the next morning after breakfast. Gagik drove them home and returned to Ashtarak. He couldn't help thinking that what had happened in the upper villages was no less of a revolution than anything he had been involved in in the early days leading to Armenia's Independence. As he pulled into his driveway, the sound of a roaring *Crazy Gago* laugh filled his entire neighborhood.

Acknowledgements

This book is dedicated to the thousands of young women who have fallen victim to international human trafficking and suffer silently trapped in an unbearable reality from which they cannot escape. First and foremost, it is their plight, and especially the plight of underage Armenian orphaned girls subjected to the same fate, that inspired me to undertake the writing of this book.

This is a work of fiction. All characters, events and places have no connection whatsoever with actual ones. However, I have tried to tell this story in a way that allows a sense of the true nature of that plight to seep through the fiction. I am indebted to many individuals and documentaries in creating that link. Edik Baghdassarian, of Hetq Investigative Journalists in Armenia, was an invaluable source, both through his excellent documentary series entitled *Desert Nights* and through personal interviews. Ric Esther Bienstock's six-part documentary entitled *Sex Slaves* was another helpful source. My most important sources were, and by far the most valuable insights came from, the many women that I had the privilege of meeting and interviewing in Dubai, all victims of human trafficking and all there against their will, whose names I unfortunately cannot disclose.

I am indebted to many individuals who read and commented on the manuscript, including some early drafts: Armine Hovannisian, who read, edited and made countless excellent suggestions about the plot; Dr. Jane Hall, who read the entire manuscript twice and made invaluable editorial suggestions. Beth Bruno, who edited the manuscript; Dr. Vahram Shemmassian. Dr. Ziad Deeb, Hera Deeb, Silva Merjanian, Nora Salibian, as well as my wife Charlotte and two sons, Shahan and Varant, who patiently read the manuscript.

21180103R00176

Made in the USA
Lexington, KY
02 March 2013